D1570749

THE COMPLETE WILD BODY

W. Lewis

WYNDHAM LEWIS

THE COMPLETE WILD BODY

EDITED BY BERNARD LAFOURCADE

ILLUSTRATIONS BY WYNDHAM LEWIS

Black Sparrow Press • Santa Barbara • 1982

The Editor and Publisher would like to give special thanks to Dr. Seamus Cooney of Black Sparrow Press for his careful erudition and tireless assistance while preparing the manuscript of this volume for publication.

LIBRARY OF CONGRESS CATALOGING IN PUBLICATION DATA

Lewis, Wyndham, 1882-1957.
The complete wild body.

Bibliography: p.
I. Lafourcade, Bernard. II. Title.
PR6023.E97W5 1982 823'.912 82-4498
ISBN 0-87685-552-4 AACR2
ISBN 0-87685-551-6 (pbk.)
ISBN 0-87685-553-2 (deluxe)

A NOTE ON THE TEXTS AND ILLUSTRATIONS

This book is in two parts. The first presents a reprinting in full of Wyndham Lewis's 1927 book, *The Wild Body*, a selection he made of his stories and related material, most of which had appeared in various reviews from 1909 to 1917. To these Lewis added a newly written essay of commentary and two unrelated stories dating from the 1920s.

The second part of this book, under the heading "The Archaeology of The Wild Body," offers the interested reader significant materials for the study of the emergence of Lewis's finished stories. Lewis rewrote his stories for the 1927 book (in many cases this was not the first rewriting they had undergone). We reprint here the first published version of each piece, with notes calling attention to significant variants in versions intermediate between this earliest text and the final 1927 publication. Included also are early texts of associated material that did not finally get included in the book, and also a story and diary which, though unpublished during the author's lifetime, are clearly connected with the Wild Body material. Further, all the "Tyronic" writings have been included because of their close and revealing association with the second version of "Bestre," published in *The Tyro*. Last of all, two post-1927 extracts discussing the inception of the Wild Body conclude this archaeology.

In his autobiography, *Rude Assignment*, Lewis wrote, "What I started to do in Brittany I have been developing ever since"; in a loose sense, then, all his writings might be related to the Wild Body stories. But a narrower and more useful delineation of the material can be made and supported by several points. First, after 1927 Lewis never considered adding to or transforming the selection he made for his book. Second, as his "Author's Foreword" to *The Wild Body* shows, he drew a distinction between the Wild Body[1] materials and a different grouping of his writings consisting of "Enemy of the Stars" and "a group of war-stories" (i.e., "The Crowd-Master," "A Young Soldier," "The French Poodle," "Cantleman's Spring-Mate," and "The War Baby"); to these must be added *Tarr* (first version 1918). And further, early corroboration of his seeing the Wild Body material as a coherent grouping is found in a list of his "Writings" that Lewis drew up in 1916 (reprinted in the Appendix to the present volume).

All the texts have been carefully reproduced, following their original publication even to typographical style. Only obvious misprints have been silently corrected. Mistakes or ambiguities attributable to the author are discussed in notes. Textual variants in the American edition of *The Wild Body* (1928), in the Lewis archives at the University of Cornell and SUNY, Buffalo libraries, as well as proofs, have been examined and are discussed in notes whenever significant. Notes are signalled by *superscript* numerals and follow at the end of each piece. Glosses of foreign words and phrases—except where the meaning is sufficiently clear from the context—are supplied on their first occurrence in the book and are marked by *subscript* numerals.

None of the illustrations included in this volume accompanied the original publications. Lewis stuck to the principle of not illustrating his own works beyond decorative motifs or dustjackets (and not even this much with *The Wild Body* which remained totally unadorned). Therefore only thematic analogies justify the presence of these illustrations, apart from their excellence. The only guiding principle of selection has been that of a rough chronological correspondence with the dates of the stories and essays.

---

[1] Throughout this volume a distinction is made between *The Wild Body* (the book published in 1927) and The Wild Body (the whole corpus as it began to take shape in 1909).

ACKNOWLEDGEMENTS

It is a pleasure to recognize here the generous assistance received from a number of persons and institutions.

For years—with Dr. Donald D. Eddy, Mrs. Mary F. Daniels, Mrs. Joan Winterkorn and Mrs. Susan Lovenburg—the Department of Rare Books at Cornell University Library has proved friendly, diligent and invaluably helpful. Robert J. Bertholf of the Poetry Room of the Lockwood Memorial Library, State University of New York at Buffalo, also deserves many thanks. To a lesser extent necessarily, but with the same cooperative efficiency, The British Library, The Bodleian Library, the University of Texas Libraries at Austin (Mrs. Ellen S. Dunlap), the University Libraries at Chambéry and Grenoble, as well as the Libraries of the Tate Gallery and the Victoria and Albert Museum, were of assistance.

The Lewisian squad was militantly active. Paul Edwards, C. J. Fox, Walter Michel, Alan Munton and Omar Pound all helped with selecting the illustrations, providing vital information, seminal suggestions, and all sorts of encouragement. Lewis bless them! I am particularly indebted to C. J. Fox, who lent me an important set of author-revised proofs of the original edition of *The Wild Body* (1927) and assisted me considerably in correcting the manuscript. As to John Martin I am convinced this book would not have been what it is but for his enthusiasm.

Among my colleagues in the Universities of Chambéry, Grenoble and Toulouse, I wish to thank Judith Bates, Monika Ponsard and Jean-Louis Magniont, who helped me with difficult passages and bibliographical references, as well as Mylène Grand who located the statue of the Ankou.

Last of all, the family circle—Odette Bornand and my wife Pierrette—must be lauded for their patience, all the pains they took and the quality of their contributions.

Bernard Lafourcade
Grenoble 1982

CONTENTS

THE WILD BODY

THE ARCHAEOLOGY OF THE WILD BODY

+

+

APPENDICES

THE WILD BODY

A Soldier of Humour
and other stories

The organization of The Wild Body *calls for a few remarks. As made clear in the author's "Foreword," the stories were chronologically presented so as to follow the development of Ker-Orr's humorous militancy—with the exception of the first story which in fact describes his last encounter and presents a full-length portrait of the now mature soldier. The other stories can then be said to constitute a flashback, and their order strictly corresponds to the chronology of the publication of the early texts between 1909 and 1911—which is rather surprising with an author so uncertain about dates and circumstances of publication of his works.*

But is chronology enough to explain the impression that a pattern informs the whole sequence, as noted by John Gawsworth? Instead of a loose assemblage, does The Wild Body *not present a sort of demonstration conditioned by the precise order in which its stories are presented? If the two concluding essays are left out,* The Wild Body *proper is found to be made up of seven stories, which strictly corresponds to the septenary structure of both* Tarr *and* The Revenge for Love. *Structurally the two novels are strikingly parallel and reminiscent of a nest of Russian dolls: 1) the author's alter-ego (Tarr or Percy) occupies the periphery of each novel (Parts I and VII); 2) in the core (Part IV) all the actors collide in the vortex of a party; 3) an artistic failure (Otto or Victor) stands as a second doll between the periphery and the core (Parts II and VI); and 4) a harsh sexuality (Otto or Gillian) embraces the central vortex (Parts III and V). Such septenary structures are known generally to symbolize the genesis of a world, but with Lewis they clearly express a sterile parody of such global visions—*un monde pour rien. *Turning to the disconnected stories of* The Wild Body, *one cannot expect such a strict parallelism, yet the central, densely populated story ("The Cornac and His Wife") may be seen to provide a similar vortex, with its clash between a family and a public, and the final apocalyptic emergence of a child—all this somehow dramatizing, on a large scale, the family romance hinted at in the initial story ("A Soldier of Humour") and obscurely repeated in the marital encounters of the concluding story ("Brotcotnaz"). The intervening stories might then be read as further steps taken by the child in his exploration of the parental split: "Beau Séjour" illustrates the defeat of grotesque sex and the triumph of a usurper, and "The Death of the Ankou" suggests the physical elimination of the father by the son. Nearer to the core, "Bestre" and "Franciscan Adventures" certainly present degenerate pseudo-artists. Thus the formal arrangement of these stories offers a very real analogy with the progression of the novels.*

Surely all this remains inevitably problematic, but it sheds some light on the inner coherence of these stories, all concerned in one way or another with expulsion and threatened thresholds. And here a deep thematic similarity with Tarr *and* The Revenge for Love *is revealed. Anyway, such complexity goes a long way to explain Lewis's fascination with a body of intuitions he only gradually penetrated. To be wild, the body must stand on the ruins of domesticity—and this, Lewis's own life in many ways illustrated.*

AUTHOR'S FOREWORD

This collection is composed either (1) of stories now entirely rewritten within the last few months, or (2) of new stories written upon a theme already sketched and in an earlier form already published, or (3) of stories written within the last few months and now published for the first time. Titles have in most cases been changed.

The last two stories (*Sigismund,* which appeared in *Art and Letters,* 1922,[1] and *You Broke My Dream*) are of more recent date. The others now form a series all belonging to an imaginary story-teller, whom I have named Ker-Orr. They represent my entire literary output prior to the war, with the exception of *The Enemy of the Stars,* a play which appeared in the 1914 *Blast,* and a group of war-stories.

What I have done in this book is to take the original matter rather as a theme for a new story. My reason for doing this was that the material, when I took it up again with a view to republishing, seemed to me to deserve the hand of a better artist than I was when I made those few hasty notes of very early travel.

The first story of the series, *The Soldier of Humour,* appeared in its original form in *The Little Review* (an american publication) of 1917-18. In it the showman, Ker-Orr, is, we are to suppose, at a later stage of his comic technique than in the accounts of his adventures in Brittany.[2] *Beau Séjour* is the first hotel at which he stops. (This, except for the note at the end, is a new story.)[3] *Inferior Religions,* which also was first printed in *The Little Review* during the war, and the notes attached to it,[4] which are new material, will serve as a commentary on the system of feeling developed in these tales, and as an explanation, if that is needed, of the title I have chosen for the collection, *The Wild Body.*

WYNDHAM LEWIS.

July 6, 1927.

NOTES

[1] A characteristic misdating: "Sigismund" was published in 1920.

[2] This sentence shows Lewis's awareness of the complex growth of "The Wild Body."

[3] This is inaccurate. "Beau Séjour" is substantially derived from "The 'Pole.' "

[4] Presumably "The Meaning of the Wild Body."

A SOLDIER OF HUMOUR

Though "A Soldier of Humour" is the opening story of the collection, its initial version was completed later than the other Breton texts, and its nature—as well as its setting—was already different from that of the earlier texts, as it was much more of a story than a sketch. It was mentioned quite early in a letter from Lewis to the poet Sturge Moore (a letter which can be dated March or April 1911, thanks to Alan Munton's research):

> *Your remarks about the title of my book, "A Soldier of Humour," were quite just. Only no doubt you thought that it was a more general title, referring to the militant humour pervading the sketches in question. As a matter of fact it is the title of a story, in which the hero engages in an elaborate campaign, on a "quarrel of humour," as I put it: a Peninsular Campaign, Spain being the scene of operations.—But of course—it serves for a title for the whole book—if I can find something to substitute, I will. I don't like* Soldier *either.*[1]

This sheds light on the uncertainties which, from the start, affected the title of the future collection. As in the same letter Lewis adds that he is just finishing "The Bourgeois Comedians" (clearly Tarr*), which he was only to complete four years later, one may suspect that "A Soldier of Humour" was not published earlier because its elaboration was inseparable from the gropings of an observer turning into a novelist. Presumably this is why it eventually found its way into Ezra Pound's hands on the eve of Lewis's departure for the Front (see "Writings" in the Appendix below). Pound had it published in* The Little Review *issues of December 1917 and January 1918, and that first version is reprinted in part two of the present volume.*

---

[1] See "The Sturge Moore Letters" (edited by Victor M. Cassidy), *Lewisletter*, no. 7 (October 1977), 8-23, letter no. 4 (letter no. 3 suggests the story may have been rejected by *The English Review*).

Part I

Spain is an overflow of sombreness. 'Africa commences at the Pyrenees.' Spain is a checkboard of Black and Goth, on which primitive gallic chivalry played its most brilliant games. At the gates of Spain the landscape gradually becomes historic with Roland. His fame dies as difficultly as the flourish of the cor de chasse.[1] It lives like a superfine antelope in the gorges of the Pyrenees, becoming more and more ethereal and gentle. Charlemagne moves Knights and Queens beneath that tree; there is something eternal and rembrandtesque about his proceedings. A stormy and threatening tide of history meets you at the frontier.

Several summers ago I was cast by fate for a fierce and prolonged little comedy—an essentially spanish comedy. It appropriately began at Bayonne, where Spain, not Africa, begins.

I am a large blond clown, ever so vaguely reminiscent (in person) of William Blake, and some great american boxer whose name I forget. I have large strong teeth which I gnash and flash when I laugh. But usually a look of settled and aggressive naïveté rests on my face. I know much more about myself than people generally do. For instance I am aware that I am a barbarian. By rights I should be paddling about in a coracle. My body is large, white and savage. But all the fierceness has become transformed into *laughter*. It still looks like a visi-gothic fighting-machine, but it is in reality a *laughing* machine. As I have remarked, when I laugh I gnash my teeth, which is another brutal survival and a thing laughter has taken over from war. Everywhere where formerly I would fly at throats, I now howl with laugher. That is me.

So I have never forgotten that I am really a barbarian. I have clung coldly to this consciousness. I realize, similarly, the uncivilized nature of my laughter. It does not easily climb into the neat japanese box, which is the cosa salada[2] of the Spaniard, or become french esprit. It sprawls into everything. It has become my life. The result is that I am *never* serious about anything. I simply cannot help converting everything into burlesque patterns. And I admit that I am disposed to forget that people are real—that they are, that is, not subjective patterns belonging specifically to me, in the course of this joke-life, which indeed has for its very principle a denial of the accepted actual.

---

[1] Hunting horn.

[2] Witticism.

My father is a family doctor on the Clyde. The Ker-Orrs have been doctors usually. I have not seen him for some time: my mother, who is separated from him, lives with a noted hungarian physician. She gives me money that she gets from the physician, and it is she that I recognize as my principal parent. It is owing to this conjunction of circumstances that I am able to move about so much, and to feed the beast of humour that is within me with such a variety of dishes.

My mother is short and dark: it is from my father that I have my stature, and this strange northern appearance.

Vom Vater hab' ich die Statur . . .[1]

It must be from my mother that I get the *Lust zu fabulieren.*[2] I experience no embarrassment in following the promptings of my fine physique. My sense of humour in its mature phase has arisen in this very acute consciousness of what is *me.* In playing that off against another hostile *me,* that does not like the smell of mine, probably finds my large teeth, height and so forth abominable, I am in a sense working off my alarm at myself. So I move on a more primitive level than most men, I expose my essential *me* quite coolly, and all men shy a little. This forked, strange-scented, blond-skinned gut-bag, with its two bright rolling marbles with which it sees, bull's eyes full of mockery and madness, is my stalking-horse. I hang somewhere in its midst operating it with detachment.

I snatch this great body out of their reach when they grow dangerously enraged at the sight of it, and laugh at them. And what I would insist upon is that at the bottom of the chemistry of my sense of humour is some philosopher's stone. A primitive unity is there, to which, with my laughter, I am appealing. Freud explains everything by *sex:* I explain everything by *laughter.*[1] So in these accounts of my adventures there is no sex interest at all: only over and over again what is perhaps the natural enemy of sex: so I must apologize. 'Sex' makes me yawn my head off; but my eye sparkles at once if I catch sight of some stylistic anomaly that will provide me with a new pattern for my grotesque realism. The sex-specialist or the sex-snob hates what I like, and calls his occupation the only *real* one. No compromise, I fear, is possible between him and me, and people will continue to call 'real' what interests them most. I boldly pit my major interests against the sex-appeal, which will restrict me to a masculine audience, but I shall not complain whatever happens.

I am quite sure that many of the soldiers and adventurers of the Middle Ages were really *Soldiers of Humour,* unrecognized and unclassified. I know

---

[1] I get my stature from my father . . . (Goethe, *Zahme Xenien,* VI).

[2] Taste for telling stories. (*Ibid.*)

that many a duel has been fought in this solemn cause. A man of this temper and category will, perhaps, carefully cherish a wide circle of accessible enemies, that his sword may not rust. Any other quarrel may be patched up. But what can be described as a *quarrel of humour* divides men for ever. That is my english creed.

I could fill pages with descriptions of myself and my ways. But such abstractions from the life lived are apt to be misleading, because most men do not easily detach the principle from the living thing in that manner, and so when handed the abstraction alone do not know what to do with it, or they apply it wrongly. I exist with an equal ease in the abstract world of principle and in the concrete world of fact. As I can express myself equally well in either, I will stick to the latter here, as then I am more likely to be understood. So I will show you myself in action, manœuvring in the heart of the reality. But before proceeding, this qualification of the above account of myself is necessary: owing to protracted foreign travel at an early age, following my mother's change of husbands, I have known french very well since boyhood. Most other Western languages I am fairly familiar with. This has considerable bearing on the reception accorded to me by the general run of people in the countries where these scenes are laid.

There is some local genius or god of adventure haunting the soil of Spain, of an especially active and resourceful type. I have seen people that have personified him. In Spain it is safer to seek adventures than to avoid them. That is at least the sensation you will have if you are sensitive to this national principle, which is impregnated with *burla*, or burlesque excitants. It certainly requires *horseplay*, and it is even safer not to attempt to evade it. Should you refrain from charging the windmills, they are capable of charging you, you come to understand: in short, you will in the end wonder less at Don Quixote's behaviour. But the deity of this volcanic soil has become civilized. My analysis of myself would serve equally well for him in this respect. Your life is no longer one of the materials he asks for to supply you with constant entertainment, as the conjurer asks for the gentleman's silk hat. Not your life,—but a rib or two, your comfort, or a five-pound note, are all he politely begs or rudely snatches. With these he juggles and conjures from morning till night, keeping you perpetually amused and on the qui vive.

It might have been a friend, but as it happened it was the most implacable enemy I have ever had that Providence provided me with, as her agent and representative for this journey. The comedy I took part in was a spanish one, then, at once piquant and elemental. But a Frenchman filled the principal rôle. When I add that this Frenchman was convinced the greater part of the time that he was taking part in a tragedy, and was perpetually on the point of transplanting my adventure bodily into that other category, and that although his actions drew their vehemence from the virgin source of a racial hatred, yet it was not as a Frenchman or a Spaniard that he acted, then you will conceive what extremely complex and unmanageable forces were about to be set in motion for my edification.

What I have said about my barbarism and my laughter is a key to the militant figure chosen at the head of this account. In those modifications of the primitive such another extravagant warrior as Don Quixote is produced, existing in a vortex of strenuous and burlesque encounters. Mystical and humorous, astonished at everything at bottom (the settled naïveté I have noted) he inclines to worship and deride, to pursue like a riotous moth the comic and unconscious luminary he discovers; to make war on it and to cherish it like a lover, at once.

Part II

It was about eleven o'clock at night when I reached Bayonne. I had started from Paris the evening before. In the market square adjoining the station the traveller is immediately solicited by a row of rather obscene little hotels, crudely painted. Each frail structure shines and sparkles with a hard, livid and disreputable electricity, every floor illuminated. The blazonry of cheap ice-cream wells, under a striped umbrella, is what they suggest: and as I stepped into this place all that was not a small, sparkling, competitive universe, inviting the stranger to pass into it, was spangled with the vivid spanish stars. 'Fonda del Universo,' 'Fonda del Mundo': Universal Inn and World Inn, two of these places were called, I noticed. I was tired and not particular as to which universe I entered. They all looked the same. To keep up a show of discrimination I chose the second, not the first. I advanced along a narrow passage-way and found myself suddenly in the heart of the Fonda del Mundo. On the left lay the dining-room in which sat two travellers. I was standing in the kitchen: this was a large courtyard, the rest of the hotel and several houses at the back were built round it. It had a glass roof on a level with the house proper, which was of two storeys only.

A half-dozen stoves with sinks, each managed by a separate crew of grim, oily workers, formed a semi-circle. Hands were as cheap, and every bit as dirty, as dirt; you felt that the lowest scullery-maid could afford a servant to do the roughest of her work, and that girl in turn another. The abundance of cheap beings was of the same meridional order as the wine and food. Instead of buying a wheelbarrow, would not you attach a man to your business; instead of hiring a removing van, engage a gang of carriers? In every way that man could replace the implement that here would be done. An air of leisurely but continual activity pervaded this precinct. Cooking on the grand scale was going forward. Later on I learnt that this was a preparation for the market on the following day. But to enter at eleven in the evening this large and apparently empty building, as far as customers went, and find a methodically busy population in its midst, cooking a nameless feast, was impressive. A broad staircase was the only avenue in this building to the sleeping apartments; a shining cut-glass door beneath it seemed the direction I ought to take when I should have made up my mind to advance. This door, the stairs, the bread given you at the table d'hôte, all had the same unsubstantial pretentiously new appearance.

So I stood unnoticed in an indifferent enigmatical universe, to which yet I had no clue, my rug on my arm. I certainly had reached immediately the most intimate centre of it, without ceremony. Perhaps there were other entrances, which I had not observed? I was turning back when the hostess appeared through the glass door—a very stout woman in a garment like a dressing-gown. She had that air of sinking into herself as if into a hot, enervating bath, with the sleepy, leaden intensity of expression belonging to many Spaniards. Her face was so still and impassible, that the ready and apt answers coming to your questions were startling, her *si señors* and *como nons.*[2] However, I knew this kind of patronne; and the air of dull resentment would mean nothing except that I was indifferent to her. I was one of those troublesome people she only had to see twice—when they arrived, and when they came to pay at the end of their stay.

She turned to the busy scene at our right and poured out a few guttural remarks (it was a spanish staff), all having some bearing on my fate, some connected with my supper, the others with my sleeping accommodations or luggage. They fell on the crowd of leisurely workers without ruffling the surface. Gradually they reached their destination, however. First, I noticed a significant stir and a dull flare rose in the murky atmosphere, a stove lid had been slid back; great copper pans were disturbed, their covers wrenched up: some morsel was to be fished out for me, swimming in oil.[3] Elsewhere a slim, handsome young witch left her cauldron and passed me, going into the dining-room. I followed her, and the hostess went back through the cut-glass door. It was behind that that she lived.

The dining-room was compact with hard light. Nothing in its glare could escape detection, so it symbolized *honesty* on the one hand, and *newness* on the other. There was nothing at all you could not *see*, and scrutinize, only too well. Everything within sight was totally unconscious of its cheapness or of any limitation at all. Inspect me! Inspect me!—exclaimed the coarse white linen upon the table, the Condy's fluid in the decanter, the paper-bread, the hideous mouldings on the wall.—I am the goods!

I took my seat at the long table. Of the two diners, only one was left. I poured myself out a glass of the wine *rosé* of Nowhere, set it to my lips, drank and shuddered. Two spoonfuls of a nameless soup, and the edge of my appetite was, it seemed, for ever blunted. Bacalao, or cod, that nightmare of the Spaniard of the Atlantic seaboard, followed. Its white and tasteless leather remained on my plate, with the markings of my white teeth all over it, like a cast of a dentist. I was really hungry and the stew that came next found its way inside me in glutinous draughts. The preserved fruit in syrup was eaten too. Heladas[1] came next, no doubt frozen up from stinking water. Then I fell back in my chair, my coffee in front of me, and stared round at the other occupant of the dining-room. He stared blankly at me. When I had turned my head away, as though the words had been mechanically released in response to my wish, he exclaimed:

'Il fait beau ce soir!'[2]

I took no notice: but after a few moments I turned in his direction again. He was staring at me without anything more than a little surprise. Immediately his lips opened again, and he exclaimed dogmatically, loudly (was I deaf, he had no doubt thought):

'Il fait beau ce soir!'

'Not at all. It's by no means a fine night. It's cold, and what's more it's going to rain.'

I cannot say why I contradicted him in this fashion. Perhaps the insolent and mystical gage of drollery his appearance generally flung down was the cause. I had no reason for supposing that the weather at Bayonne was anything but fine and settled.

I had made my rejoinder as though I were a Frenchman, and I concluded my neighbour would take me for that.

He accepted my response quite stolidly. This initial rudeness of mine would probably have had no effect whatever on him, had not a revelation made shortly afterwards at once changed our relative positions, and caused him to regard me with changed eyes. He then went back, remembered this first incivility of mine, and took it, retrospectively, in a different spirit to that shown contemporaneously. He now merely enquired:

'You have come far?'

'From Paris,' I answered, my eyes fixed on a piece of cheese which the high voltage of the electricity revealed in all its instability. I reflected how bad the food was here compared to its spanish counterpart, and wondered if I should have time to go into the town before my train left. I then looked at my neighbour, and wondered what sort of stomach he could have. He showed every sign of the extremest hardiness. He lay back in his chair, his hat on the back of his head, finishing a bottle of wine with bravado. His waistcoat was open, and this was the only thing about him that did not denote the most

[1] Ice-creams.

[2] "A fine evening!"

facile of victories. This, equivalent to rolling up the sleeves, might be accepted as showing that he respected his enemy.

His straw hat served rather as a heavy coffee-coloured nimbus—such as some browningesque florentine painter, the worse for drink, might have placed behind the head of his saint. Above his veined and redly surnburnt forehead gushed a ragged volute of dry black hair. His face had the vexed wolfish look of the grimy commercial Midi. It was full of character, certainly, but it had been niggled at and worked over, at once minutely and loosely, by a hundred little blows and chisellings of fretful passion. His beard did not sprout with any shape or symmetry. Yet in an odd and baffling way there was a breadth, a look of possible largeness somewhere. You were forced at length to attribute it to just that *blankness* of expression I mentioned. This sort of blank intensity spoke of a possibility of real passion, of the sublime. (It was this sublime quality that I was about to waken, and was going to have an excellent opportunity of studying.)

He was dressed with sombre floridity. In his dark purple-slate suit with thin crimson lines, in his dark red hat-band, in his rose-buff tie, swarming with cerulean fire-flies, in his stormily flowered waistcoat, you felt that his taste for the violent and sumptuous had everywhere struggled to assert itself, and everywhere been overcome. But by what? That was the important secret of this man's entire machine, a secret unfolded by his subsequent conduct. Had I been of a superior penetration the cut of his clothes in their awkward amplitude, with their unorthodox shoulders and bellying hams, might have given me the key. He was not a commercial traveller. I was sure of that. For me, he issued from a void. I rejected in turn his claim, on the strength of his appearance, to be a small vineyard owner, a man in the automobile business and a *rentier*. He was part of the mystery of this hotel; his loneliness, his aplomb, his hardy appetite.

In the meantime his small sunken eyes were fixed on me imperturbably, with the blankness of two metal discs.

'I was in Paris last week,' he suddenly announced. 'I don't like Paris. Why should I?' I thought he was working up for something now. He had had a good think. He took me for a Parisian, I supposed. 'They think they are up-to-date. Go and get a parcel sent you from abroad, then go and try and get it at the Station Depôt. Only see how many hours you will pass there trotting from one bureau clerk to another before they give it to you! Then go to a café and ask for a drink!—Are you Parisian?' He asked this in the same tone, the blankness slightly deepening.

'No, I'm English,' I answered.

He looked at me steadfastly. This evidently at first seemed to him untrue. Then he suddenly appeared to accept it implicitly. His incredulity and belief appeared to be one block of the same material, or two sides of the same absolute coin. There was not room for a hair between these two states. They were not two, but one.

Several minutes of dead silence elapsed. His eyes had never winked. His changes had occurred within one block of concrete undifferentiated blankness. At this period you became aware of a change: but when you looked at him he was completely uniform from moment to moment.

He now addressed me, to my surprise, in my own language. There was every evidence that it had crossed the Atlantic at least once since it had been in his possession; he had not inherited it, but acquired it with the sweat of his brow, it was clear.

'Oh! you're English? It's fine day!'

Now, we are going to begin all over again! And we are going to start, as before, with the weather. But I did not contradict him this time. My opinion of the weather had in no way changed. But for some reason I withdrew from my former perverse attitude.

'Yes,' I agreed.

Our eyes met, doubtfully. He had not forgotten my late incivility, and I remembered it at the same time. He was silent again. Evidently he was turning over dully in his mind the signification of this change on my part. My changes I expect presented themselves as occurring in as unruffled uniform a medium as his.

But there was a change now in him. I could both feel and see it. My weak withdrawal, I thought, had been unfortunate. Remembering my wounding obstinacy of five minutes before, a strong resentment took possession of him, swelling his person as it entered. I watched it enter him. It was as though the two sides of his sprawling portmanteau-body had tightened up, and his eyes drew in till he squinted.

Almost threateningly, then, he continued,—heavily, pointedly, steadily, as though to see if there were a spark of resistance anywhere left in me, that would spit up, under his trampling words.

'I guess eet's darn fi' weather, and goin' to laast. A friend of mine, who ees skeeper, sailing for Bilbao this afternoon, said that mighty little sea was out zere, and all fine weather for his run. A skipper ought' know, I guess, ought'n he? Zey know sight more about zee weader than most. I guess zat's deir trade,—an't I right?'

Speaking the tongue of New York evidently injected him with a personal emotion that would not have been suspected, even, in the Frenchman. The strange blankness and impersonality had gone, or rather it had *woken up*, if one may so describe this phenomenon. He now looked at me with awakened eyes, coldly, judicially, fixedly. They were facetted eyes—the eyes of the forty-eight States of the Union.[4] Considering he had crushed me enough, no doubt, he began talking about Paris, just as he had done in french. The one thing linguistically he had brought away from the United States intact was an american accent of almost alarming perfection. Whatever word or phrase he knew, in however mutilated a form, had this stamp of colloquialism and air of being the real thing. He spoke english with a careless impudence at which I was not surprised; but the powerful consciousness of the authentic nature of his *accent* made him still more insolently heedless of the faults of his speech, it seemed, and rendered him immune from all care as to the correctness of the mere english. His was evidently to the full the american, or anglo-saxon american, state of mind: a colossal disdain for everything that does not possess in one way or another an american accent. My english, grammatically regular though it was, lacking the american accent was but a poor vehicle for thought compared with his most blundering sentence.

Before going further I must make quite clear that I have no dislike of the american way of accenting english. American possesses an indolent vigour and dryness which is a most cunning arm when it snarls out its ironies. That accent is the language of Mark Twain, and is the tongue, at once naïve and cynical, of a thousand inimitable humourists. To my mind it is a better accent than the sentimental whimsicality of the Irish.

An illusion of superiority, at the expense of citizens of other states, the American shares with the Englishman. So the 'God's Own Country' attitude of some Americans is more anglo-saxon than their blood. I have met many outlandish Americans, from such unamerican cities as Odessa, Trieste and Barcelona. America had done them little good, they tended to become dreamers, drunken with geographical immensities and opportunities they had never had. This man at once resembled and was different from them. The reason for this difference, I concluded, was explained when he informed me that he was a United States citizen. I believed him on the spot, unreservedly. Some air of security in him that only such a ratification can give convinced me.

He did not tell me at once. Between his commencing to speak in english and his announcing his citizenship, came an indetermined phase in our relations. During this phase he knew what he possessed, but he knew I was not yet aware of it. This caused him to make some allowance; since, undivulged, this fact was, for me at least, not yet a full fact. He was constrained, but the situation had not yet, he felt, fully matured.

In the same order as in our conversation in french, we progressed then, from the weather topic (a delicate subject with us) to Paris. Our acquaintance was by this time—scarcely ten minutes had elapsed—painfully ripe. I already felt instinctively that certain subjects of conversation were to be avoided. I knew already what shade of expression would cause suspicion, what hatred, and what snorting disdain. He, for his part, evidently with the intention of eschewing a subject fraught with dangers, did not once speak of

England. It was as though England were a subject that no one could expect him to keep his temper about. Should any one, as I did, come from England, he would naturally resent being reminded of it. The other, obviously, would be seeking to take an unfair advantage of him. In fact for the moment the assumption was—that was the only issue from this difficulty—that I was an American.

'Guess you' goin' to Spain?' he said. 'Waal, Americans are not like' very much in that country. That country, sir, is barb'rous; you *kant* believe how behind in everything that country is! All you have to do is to *look* smart there to make money. No need to worry there. No, by gosh! Just sit round and ye'll do bett' dan zee durn dagos!'

The american citizenship wiped out the repulsive fact of his southern birth, otherwise, being a Gascon, he would have been almost a dago himself.

'In Guadalquiveer—waal—kind of state-cap'tle, some manzanas,[1] a bunch shacks, get me?—waal——'

I make these sentences of my neighbour's much more lucid than they in reality were. But he now plunged into this obscure and whirling idiom with a story to tell. The story was drowned; but I gathered it told of how, travelling in a motor car, he could find no petrol anywhere in a town of some importance. He was so interested in the telling of this story that I was thrown a little off my guard, and once or twice showed that I did not quite follow him. I did not understand his english, that is what unguardedly I showed. He finished his story rather abruptly. There was a deep silence.—It was after this silence that he divulged the fact of his american citizenship.

And now things began to wear at once an exceedingly gloomy and unpromising look.

With the revelation of this staggering fact I lost at one blow all the benefit of that convenient fiction in which we had temporarily indulged—namely, that I was American. It was now incumbent upon him to adopt an air of increased arrogance. The representative of the United States—there was no evading it, that was the dignity that the evulgation of his legal nationality imposed on him. All compromise, all courteous resolve to ignore painful facts, was past. Things must stand out in their true colours, and men too.

As a result of this heightened attitude, he appeared to doubt the sincerity or exactitude of everything I said. His beard bristled round his drawling mouth, his thumbs sought his arm-pits, his varnished patterned shoes stood up erect and aggressive upon his heels. An insidious attempt on my part to induct the conversation back into french, unhappily detected, caused in him an alarming indignation. I was curious to see the change that would occur in my companion if I could trap him into using again his native speech. The

1 Blocks of houses.

sensation of the humbler tongue upon his lips would have, I was sure, an immediate effect. The perfidy of my intention only gradually dawned upon him. He seemed taken aback. For a few minutes he was silent as though stunned. The subtleties, the *ironies* to which the American is exposed!

'Oui, c'est vrai,' I went on, taking a frowning, business-like air, affecting a great absorption in the subject we were discussing, and to have overlooked the fact that I had changed to french 'les Espagnols ont du chic à se chausser. D'ailleurs, c'est tout ce qui'ils savent, en fait de toilette. C'est les Américains surtout qui savent s'habiller!'[1]

His eyes at this became terrible. He had seen through the *manège*,[2]had he not: and now *par surcroît de perfidie*,[3] was I not *flattering* him—flattering Americans; and above all, praising their way of dressing! His cigar protruded from the right-hand corner of his mouth. He now with a gnashing and rolling movement conveyed it, in a series of revolutions, to the left-hand corner. He eyed me with a most unorthodox fierceness. In the language of his adopted land, but with an imported wildness in the dry figure that he must affect, he ground out, spitting with it the moist débris of the cigar:

'Yes, *sirr*, and that's more'n zee durn English do!'

No doubt, in his perfect americanism—and at this ticklish moment, his impeccable accent threatened by an unscrupulous foe, who was attempting to stifle it temporarily—a definite analogy arose in his mind. The Redskin and his wiles, the hereditary and cunning foe of the american citizen, came vividly perhaps to his mind. Yes, wiles of that familiar sort were being used against him, Sioux-like, Blackfeet-like manœuvres. He must meet them as the american citizen had always met them. He had at length overcome the Sioux and Cherokee. He turned on me a look as though I had been unmasked, and his accent became more raucous and formidable. The elemental that he contained and that often woke in him, I expect, manifested itself in his american accent, the capital vessel of his vitality.

After another significant pause he brusquely chose a new subject of conversation. It was a subject upon which, it was evident, he was persuaded that it would be quite impossible for us to agree. He took a long draught of the powerful fluid served to each diner. I disagreed with him at first out of politeness. But as he seemed resolved to work himself up slowly into a national passion, I changed round, and agreed with him. For a moment he glared at me. He felt at bay before this dreadful subtlety to which his americanism exposed him: then he warily changed his position in the argument, taking up the point of view he had begun by attacking.

---

1 "The Spaniards are very stylish when it comes to shoes. Actually that's all they are good at. It's the Americans who have a dress sense!" (Uncolloquial French.)

2 My little game.

3 With increased perfidy.

We changed about alternately for a while. It was a most diverting game. At one time in taking my new stand, and asserting something, either I had changed too quickly, or he had not done so quite quickly enough. At all events, when he began speaking he found himself *agreeing* with me. This was a breathless moment. It was very close quarters indeed. I felt as one does at a show, standing on the same chair with an uncertain-tempered person. With an anxious swiftness I threw myself into the opposite opinion. The situation, for that time at least, was saved. A moment more, and we should have fallen on each other, or rather, he on me.

He buried his face again in the sinister potion in front of him, and consumed the last vestiges of the fearful food at his elbow. During these happenings we had not been interrupted. A dark figure, that of a Spaniard, I thought, had passed into the kitchen along the passage. From within the muffled uproar of the machinery of the kitchen reached us uninterruptedly.

He now with a snarling drawl engaged in a new discussion on another and still more delicate subject. I renewed my tactics, he his. Subject after subject was chosen. His volte-face, his change of attitude in the argument, became less and less leisurely. But my skill in reversing remained more than a match for his methods. At length, whatever I said he said the opposite, brutally and at once. At last, pushing his chair back violently with a frightful grating sound, and thrusting both his hands in his pockets—at this supreme moment the sort of blank look came back to his face again—he said slowly:

'Waal, zat may be so—you say so—waal! But what say you to England, hein?[1] England! England! England!'

At last it had come! He repeated 'England' as though that word in itself were a question—an unanswerable question. 'England' was a form of question that a man could only ask when every device of normal courtesy had been exhausted. But it was a thing hanging over every Englishman, at any moment he might be silenced with it.

'England! ha! England! England!' he repeated, as though hypnotized by this word; as though pressing me harder and harder, and finally 'chawing me up' with the mere utterance of it.

'Why, mon vieux!' I said suddenly, getting up, 'how about the South of France, for that matter— the south of France! the South of France! The bloody Midi, your home-land, you poor bum!' I gnashed my teeth as I said this.[5]

If I had said 'America,' he would have responded at once, no doubt. But 'the South of France!' A look of unspeakable vagueness came into his face. The South of France! This was at once without meaning, a stab in the back, an unfair blow, the sort of thing that was not said, some sort of paralysing nonsense, that robbed a man of the power of speech. I seemed to have drawn

1 "Eh?"

a chilly pall with glove-like tightness suddenly over the whole of his mind.

I fully expected to be forced to fight my way out of the salle à manger, and was wondering whether his pugilistic methods would be those of Chicago or Toulouse—whether he would skip round me, his fists working like piston rods, or whether he would plunge his head into the pit of my stomach, kick me on the chin and follow up with the 'coup de la fourchette,' which consists in doubling up one's fist, but allowing the index and little finger to protrude, so that they may enter the eyes on either side of the bridge of the nose.

But I had laid him out quite flat. The situation was totally outside his compass. And the word 'bum' lay like a load of dough upon his spirit. My last word had been *american*. As I made for the door, he sat first quite still. Then, slightly writhing on his chair, with a painful slowness, his face passed through a few degrees of the compass in an attempt to reach me in spite of the spell I had laid upon him. The fact of my leaving the room seemed to find him still more unprepared. My answer to his final apostrophe was a blow below the belt: I was following it up by vanishing from the ring altogether, as though the contest were over, while he lay paralysed in the centre of the picture. It had never occurred to him, apparently, that I might perhaps get up and leave the dining-room.—Sounds came from him, words too—hybrid syllables lost on the borderland between french and english, which appeared to signify protest, pure astonishment, alarmed question. But I had disappeared. I got safely into the kitchen. I sank into that deep hum of internal life, my eye glittering with the battle light of humour.

In the act of taking my candle from the hand of a chambermaid, I heard a nasal roar behind me. I mounted the stairs three steps at a time, the hotel boy at my heels, and the chambermaid breathlessly rushing up in his rear. Swiftly ushered into my room, I thrust outside the panting servants and locked and bolted the door.

Flinging myself on the bed, my blond poll rolling about in ecstasy upon the pillow, I howled like an exultant wolf. This penetrating howl of my kind—the humorous kind—shook the cardboard walls of the room, rattled the stucco frames; but the tumult beneath of the hotel staff must have prevented this sound from getting farther than the area of the bedrooms. My orgasm[6] left me weak, and I lay conventionally mopping my brow, and affectedly gasping. Then, as usually happened with me, I began sentimentally pitying my victim. Poor little chap! My conduct had been unpardonable! I had brutalized this tender flower of the prairies of the West! Why had I dragged in the 'bloody Midi' after all? It was too bad altogether. I had certainly behaved very badly. I had a movement to go down immediately and apologize to him, a tear of laughter still hanging from a mournful lash.

My room was at the back. The window looked on to the kitchen; it was just over the stairs leading to the bedrooms. I now got up, for I imagined I heard some intemperate sound thrusting into the general mêlée of mechanical noise. From the naturally unsavoury and depressing porthole of my room, immediately above the main cauldrons, I was able, I found, to observe my opponent in the murky half-court, half-kitchen, beneath. There he was: by pointing my ear down I could catch sometimes what he was saying. But I found that the noise I had attributed to him had been my fancy only.

Inspected from this height he looked very different. I had not till then seen him on his feet. His yankee clothes, evidently cut beneath his direction by a gascon tailor, made him look as broad as he was long. His violently animated leanness imparted a precarious and toppling appearance to his architecture. He was performing a war-dance in this soft national armour just at present, beneath the sodden eyes of the proprietress. It had shuffling, vehement, jazz elements, aided by the gesticulation of the Gaul. This did not seem the same man I had been talking to before. He evidently, in this enchanted hotel, possessed a variety of personalities. It was *not* the same man. Somebody else had leapt into his clothes—which hardly fitted the newcomer—and was carrying on his quarrel. The original and more imposing man had disappeared. I had slain him. This little fellow had taken up his disorganized and overwrought life at that precise moment and place where I had left him knocked out in the dining-room, at identically the same pitch of passion, only with fresher nerves, and with the same racial sentiments as the man he had succeeded.

He was talking in spanish—much more correctly than he did in english. She listened with her leaden eyes crawling swiftly and sullenly over his person, with an air of angrily and lazily making an inventory. In his fiery attack on the depths of languor behind which her spirit lived, he would occasionally turn and appeal to one of the nearest of the servants, as though seeking corroboration of something. Of what crime was I being accused? I muttered rapid prayers to the effect that that sultry reserve of the proprietress might prove impregnable. Otherwise I might be cast bodily out of the Fonda del Mundo, and, in my present worn-out state, have to seek another and distant roof. I knew that I was the object of his discourse. What effectively could be said about me on so short an acquaintance? He would, though, certainly affirm that I was a designing ruffian of some sort; such a person as no respectable hotel would consent to harbour, or if it did, would do so at its peril. Probably he might be saying it was my intention to hold up the hotel later on, or he might have influence with the proprietress, be a regular customer and old friend. He might only be saying, 'I object to that person; I cannot express to you how I object to that person! I have never objected to any one to the same fearful degree. All my organs boil at the thought of him. I cannot explain to you how that island organism tears my members this way and that. Out with this abomination! Oh! out with it before I die at your feet from the fever of my *mauvais sang*!'[1]

That personal appeal might prove effective. I went to bed with a feeling of extreme insecurity. I thought that, if nothing else happened, he might set fire to the hotel. But in spite of the dangers by which I was, manifestly, beset in this ill-starred establishment, I slept soundly enough. In the morning an overwhelming din shook me, and I rose with the stink of southern food in my nose.

Breakfast passed off without incident. I concluded that the Complete American was part of the night-time aspect of the Fonda del Mundo and had no part in its more normal day-life.

The square was full of peasants, the men wearing dark blouses and the béret basque. Several groups were sitting near me in the salle à manger. An intricate arrangement of chairs and tables, like an extensive man-trap, lay outside the hotel, extending a little distance into the square. From time to time one or more clumsy peasant would appear to become stuck or somehow involved in these iron contrivances. They would then, with becoming fatalism, sit down and call for a drink. Such was the impression conveyed, at least, by their embarrassed and reluctant movements in choosing a seat. I watched several parties come into this dangerous extension of the Fonda del Mundo.[7] The proprietress would come out occasionally and stare moodily at them. She never looked at me.

A train would shortly leave for the frontier. I bade farewell to the patrona, and asked her if she could recommend me a hotel in Burgos or in Pontaisandra.[8] When I mentioned Pontaisandra, she said at once, 'You are going to Pontaisandra?' With a sluggish ghost of a smile she turned to a loitering servant and then said, 'Yes, you can go to the Burgalésa at Pontaisandra. That is a good hotel.' They both showed a few ragged discoloured teeth, only appearing in moments of crafty burlesque. The night before I had told her that my destination was Pontaisandra, and she had looked at me steadfastly and resentfully, as though I had said that my destination was Paradise, and that I intended to occupy a seat reserved for her. But that was the night before: and now Pontaisandra appeared to mean something different to her. The episode of the supper-room the night before I now regarded as an emanation of that place. The Fonda del Mundo was a mysterious hotel, though in the day its secrets seemed more obvious. I imagined it inhabited by solitary and hallucinated beings, like my friend the Perfect American—or such as I myself might have become. The large kitchen staff was occupied far into the night in preparing a strange and excessive table d'hôte. The explanation of this afforded in the morning by the sight of the crowding peasants did not efface that impression of midnight though it mitigated it. Perhaps the

1 "Raging blood."

dreams caused by its lunches, the visions conjured up by its suppers, haunted the place. That was the spirit in which I remembered my over-night affair.

When eventually I started for the frontier, hoping by the inhalation of a picadura to dispose my tongue to the ordeal of framing passable castilian, I did not realize that the american adventure was the progenitor of other adventures; nor that the dreams of the Fonda del Mundo were to go with me into the heart of Spain.

Part III

Burgos, I had intended, should be my first stopping place. But I decided afterwards that San Sebastián and León would be better.

This four days' journeying was an *entr'acte* filled with appropriate music; the lugubrious and splendid landscapes of Castile, the extremely self-conscious, pedantic and independent spirit of its inhabitants, met with en route. Fate was marking time, merely. With the second day's journey I changed trains and dined at Venta de Baños, the junction for the line that branches off in the direction of Palencia, León and the galician country.

While travelling, the spanish peasant has a marked preference for the next compartment to his own. No sooner has the train started, than, one after another, heads, arms, and shoulders appear above the wooden partition. There are times when you have all the members of the neighbouring compartment gazing with the melancholy stolidity of cattle into your own. In the case of some theatrical savage of the Sierras, who rears a dishevelled head before you in a pose of fierce abandon, and hangs there smoking like a chimney, you know that it may be some grandiose recoil of pride that prevents him from remaining in an undignified position huddled in a narrow carriage. In other cases it is probably a simple conviction that the occupants of other compartments are likely to be more interesting.

The whole way from Venta de Baños to Palencia the carriage was dense with people. Crowds of peasants poured into the train, loaded with their heavy vivid horse-rugs, gaudy bundles and baskets; which profusion of mere matter, combined with their exuberance, made the carriage appear positively to swarm with animal life. They would crowd in at one little station and out at another a short way along the line, where they were met by hordes of their relations awaiting them. They would rush or swing out of the door, charged with their property or recent purchases, and catch the nearest man or woman of their blood in their arms, with a turbulence that outdid our Northern people's most vehement occasions. The waiting group became twice as vital as average mankind upon the train's arrival, as though so much more blood had poured into their veins. Gradually we got beyond the sphere of this Fiesta, and in the small hours of the morning arrived at León.

Next day came the final stages of the journey to the Atlantic sea-board. We arrived within sight of the town that evening, just as the sun was setting. With its houses of green, rose, and white, in general effect a faded bouquet, its tints a scarcely coloured reminiscence, it looked like some oriental city represented in the nerveless tempera of an old wall. Its bay stretched between hills for many miles to the ocean, which lay beyond an island of scarcely visible rocks.

On the train drawing up in the central station, the shock troops furnished by every little ragamuffin café as well as stately hotel in the town were hurled against us. I had mislaid the address given me at Bayonne. I wished to find a hotel of medium luxury. The different hotel-attendants called hotly out their prices at me. I selected one who named a sum for board and lodging that only the frenzy of competition could have fathered, I thought. Also the name of this hotel was, it seemed to me, the one the patrona at Bayonne had mentioned. I had not then learnt to connect Burgalésa with Burgos: this was my first long visit to Spain. With this man I took a cab and was left seated in it at the door of the station, while he went after the heavy luggage. Now one by one, the hotel emissaries came up; their fury of a few minutes before contrasted oddly with their present listless calm. Putting themselves civilly at my disposition, they thrust forward matter-of-factly the card of their establishment, adding that they were sure that I would find out my mistake.

I now felt in a vague manner a tightening of the machinery of Fate—a certain uneasiness and strangeness, in the march and succession of facts and impressions, like a trembling of a decrepit motor-bus about to start again. The interlude was over. After a long delay the hotel tout returned and we started. My misgivings were of a practical order. The price named was very low, too low perhaps. But I had found it a capital plan on former occasions to go to a cheap hotel and pay a few pesetas more a day for 'extras.' My palate was so conservative, that I found in any case that my main fare lay outside the spanish menu. Extras are very satisfactory. You always feel that a single individual has bent over the extra and carefully cooked it, and that it has not been bought in too wholesale a manner. I wished to live on extras—a privileged existence: and extras are much the same in one place as another. So I reassured myself.

The cabman and the hotel man were discussing some local event. But we penetrated farther and farther into a dismal and shabby quarter of the town. My misgivings began to revive. I asked the representative of the Burgalésa if he were sure that his house was a clean and comfortable house. He dismissed my doubtful glance with a gesture full of assurance. 'It's a spendid place! You wait and see; we shall be there directly,' he added.

We suddenly emerged into a broad and imposing street, on one side of which was a public garden, 'El Paseo,'[9] I found out afterwards, the Town Promenade. Gazing idly at a palatial white building with a hotel omnibus drawn up before it, to my astonishment I found our driver also stopping at its door. A few minutes later, still scarcely able to credit my eyes, I got out and entered this palace, noticing 'Burgalésa' on the board of the omnibus as I passed. I followed the tout, having glimpses in passing of a superbly arrayed table with serviettes that were each a work of art, that one of the splendid guests entertained at this establishment (should I not be among them?) would soon haughtily pull to pieces to wipe his mouth on—tables groaning beneath gilded baskets tottering with a lavish variety of choice fruit. Then came a long hall, darkly panelled, at the end of which I could see several white-capped men shouting fiercely and clashing knives, women answering shrilly and juggling with crashing dishes: a kitchen—the most diabolically noisy and malodorous I had ever approached. We went straight on towards it. Were we going through it? At the very threshold we stopped, and opening the panel-like door in the wall, the porter disappeared with my portmanteau, appearing again without my portmanteau, and hurried away. At this moment my eye caught something else, a door ajar on the other side of the passage and a heavy, wooden, clothless table, with several squares of bread upon it, and a fork or two. In Spain there is a sort of bread for the rich, and a forbidding juiceless papery bread for the humble. The bread on that table was of the latter category, far more like paper than that I had had at Bayonne.

Suddenly the truth flashed upon me. With a theatrical gesture I dashed open again the panel and passed into the pitchy gloom within. I struck a match. It was a cupboard, quite windowless, with just enough room for a little bed; I was standing on my luggage. No doubt in the room across the passage I should be given some cod soup, permanganate of potash and artificial bread. Then, extremely tired after my journey, I should crawl into my kennel, the pandemonium of the kitchen at my ear for several hours.

In the central hall I found the smiling proprietor. He seemed to regard his boarders generally as a gentle joke, and those who slept in the cupboard near the kitchen a particularly good but rather low one. I informed him that I would pay the regular sum for a day's board and lodging, and said I must have another room. A valet accepted the responsibility of seeing that I was given a bedroom. The landlord walked slowly away, his iron-grey side-whiskers, with their traditional air of respectability, giving a disguised look to his rogue's face. I was transferred from one cupboard to another; or rather, I had exchanged a cupboard for a wardrobe—reduced to just half its size by a thick layer of skirts and cloaks, twenty deep, that protruded from all four walls. But still the little open space left in the centre ensured a square foot to wash and dress in, with a quite distinct square foot or two for sleep.

And it was upstairs.

A quarter of an hour later, wandering along a dark passage on the way back to the hotel lounge, a door opened in a very violent and living way that made me start and look up, and a short rectangular figure, the size of a big square trunk, issued forth, just ahead of me. I recognized this figure fragmentarily—first, with a cold shudder, I recognized an excrescence of hair; then with a jump I recognized a hat held in its hand; then, with an instinctive shrinking, I realized that I had seen these flat traditional pseudo-american shoulders before. With a really comprehensive throb of universal emotion, I then recognized the whole man.

It was the implacable figure of my neighbour at dinner, of the Fonda del Mundo.

He moved along before me with wary rigidity, exhibiting none of the usual signs of recognition. He turned corners with difficulty, a rapid lurch precipitating him into the new path indicated when he reached the end of the wall. On the stairs he appeared to get stuck in much the way that a large american trunk would, borne by a sweating porter. At last he safely reached the hall. I was a yard or two behind him. He stopped to light a cigar, still taking up an unconscionable amount of space. I manœuvred round him, and gained one of the doors of the salle à manger. But as I came within his range of vision, I also became aware that my presence in the house was not a surprise to this sandwich-man of Western citizenship. His eye fastened upon me with ruthless bloodshot indignation, an eye-blast as it were crystallized from the episode at Bayonne. But he was so dead and inactive that he seemed a phantom of his former self: and in all my subsequent dealings with him, this feeling of having to deal with a ghost, although a particularly mischievous one, persisted. If before my anger at the trick that had been played on me had dictated a speedy change of lodging, now my anxiety to quit this roof had, naturally, an overwhelming incentive.

After dinner I went forth boldly in search of the wonderful american enemy. Surely I had been condemned, in some indirect way, by him, to the cupboard beside the kitchen. No dungeon could have been worse. Had I then known, as I learnt later, that he was the owner of this hotel, the mediæval analogy would have been still more complete. He now had me in his castle.

I found him seated, in sinister conjunction with the proprietor or manager, as I supposed he was, in the lobby of the hotel. He turned slightly away as I came up to him, with a sulky indifference due to self-restraint. Evidently the time for action was not ripe. There was no pretence of not recognizing me. As though our conversation in the Fonda del Mundo had taken place a half-hour before, we acknowledged in no way a consciousness of the lapse of time, only of the shifted scene.

'Well, colonel,' I said, adopting an allocution of the United States, 'taking the air?'

He went on smoking.

'This is a nice little town.'

'Vous vous plaisez ici, monsieur? C'est bien!'[1] he replied in french, as though I were not worthy even to *hear* his american accent, and that, if any communication was to be held with me, french must serve.

'I shall make a stay of some weeks here,' I said, with indulgent defiance.

'Oui?'

'But not in this hotel.'

He got up with something of his Bayonne look about him.

'No. I shouldn't. You might not find it a very comfortable hotel,' he said vehemently in his mother tongue.

He walked away hurriedly, as a powder magazine might walk away from a fuse, if it did not, for some reason, want to blow up just then.

That was our last encounter that day. The upstairs and less dreadful dungeon with its layer of clothes would have been an admirable place for a murder. Not a sound would have penetrated its woollen masses and the thick spanish walls enclosing it. But the next morning I was still alive. I set out after breakfast to look for new quarters. My practised eye had soon measured the inconsistencies of most of the Pensions of the town. But a place in the Calle Real[10] suited me all right, and I decided to stop there for the time. There too the room was only a cupboard. But it was a human cupboard and not a clothes cupboard. It was one of the four tributaries of the dining-room. My bedroom door was just beside my place at table—I had simply to step out of bed in the right direction, and there was the morning coffee. The extracting of my baggage from the Burgalésa was easy enough, except that I was charged a heavy toll. I protested with the manager for some time, but he smiled and smiled. 'Those are our charges!' He shrugged his shoulders, dismissed the matter, and smiled absent-mindedly when I renewed my objections. As at Bayonne, there was no sign of the enemy in the morning. But I was not so sure this time that I had seen the last of him.

That evening I came amongst my new fellow-pensionnaires for the first time. This place had recommended itself to me, partly because the boarders would probably speak castilian, and so be practice for me. They were mostly not Gallegos, at least, who are the Bretons of Spain, and afford other Spaniards much amusement by their way of expressing themselves. My presence caused no stir whatever. Just as a stone dropped in a small pond which has long been untouched, and has an opaque coat of green decay, slips dully to the bottom, cutting a neat little hole on the surface, so I took my place at the bottom of the table. But as the pond will send up its personal odour at this intrusion, so these people revealed something of themselves in the first few minutes, in an illusive and immobile way. They must all have

---

1 "Do you like it here? Good!"

lived in that Pension together for an inconceivable length of time. My neighbour, however, promised to be a little El Dorado of spanish; a small mine of gossip, grammatical rules and willingness to impart these riches. I struck a deep shaft of friendship into him at once and began work without delay. Coming from Madrid, this ore was at least 30 carat, thoroughly thetaed and castilian stuff that he talked. What I gave him in exchange was insignificant. He knew several phrases in french and english, such as 'If you please,' and 'fine day'; I merely confirmed him in these. Every day he would hesitatingly say them over, and I would assent, 'quite right,' and 'very well pronounced.' He was a tall, bearded man, head of the orchestra of the principal Café in the town. Two large cuffs lay on either side of his plate during meals, the size of serviettes. Out of them his hands emerged without in any way disturbing them, and served him with his food as far as they could. But he had to remain with his mouth quite near his plate, for the cuffs would not move a hair's breadth. This somewhat annoyed me, as it muffled a little the steady flow of spanish, and even sometimes was a cause of considerable waste. Once or twice without success I attempted to move the cuff on my side away from the plate. Their ascendancy over him and their indolence was profound.

But I was not content merely to work him for his mother-tongue inertly, as it were. I wished to see it in use: to watch this stream of castilian working the mill of general conversation, for instance. Although willing enough for himself, he had no chance in this Pension. On the third day, however, he invited me to come round to the Café after dinner and hear him play. Our dinners overlapped, he leaving early. So the meal over, I strolled round, alone.

The Café Pelayo was the only really parisian establishment in the town. It was the only one where the Madrileños and the other Spaniards proper, resident in Pontaisandra, went regularly, I entered, peering round in a business-like way at its monotonously mirrored walls and gilded ceiling. I took up an advantageous position, and settled down to study the idiom.

In a lull of the music, my chef d'orchestre came over to me, and presented me to a large group of people, friends of his. It was an easy matter, from that moment, to become acquainted with everybody in the Café.

I did not approach Spaniards in general, I may say, with any very romantic emotion. Each man I met possessed equally an ancient and admirable tongue, however degenerate himself. He often appeared like some rotten tree, in which a swarm of highly evocative admirable words had nested. I, like a bee-cultivator, found it my business to transplant this vagrant swarm to a hive prepared. A language has its habits and idiosyncrasies just like a species of insect, as my first professor comfortably explained; its little world of symbols and parts of speech have to be most carefully studied and manipulated. But above all it is important to observe their habits and idiosyncrasies, and the pitch and accent that naturally accompanies them. So I had my hands full.

When the Café closed, I went home with Don Pedro, chef d'orchestre, to the Pension. Every evening, after dinner—and at lunch-time as well—I repaired there. This lasted for three or four days. I now had plenty of opportunity of talking castilian Spanish. I had momentarily forgotten my american enemy.

On the fifth evening, I entered the Café as usual, making towards my most useful and intelligent group. But then, with a sinking of the heart, I saw the rectangular form of my ubiquitous enemy, quartered with an air of demoniac permanence in their midst. A mechanic who finds an unaccountable lump of some foreign substance stuck in the very heart of his machinery—what simile shall I use for my dismay? To proceed somewhat with this image, as this unhappy engineer might dash to the cranks or organ stops of his machine, so I dashed to several of my formerly most willing listeners and talkers. I gave one a wrench and another a screw, but I found that already the machine had become recalcitrant.

I need not enumerate the various stages of my defeat on that evening. It was more or less a passive and moral battle, rather than one with any evident show of the secretly bitter and desperate nature of the passions engaged. Of course, the inclusion of so many people unavoidably caused certain brusqueries here and there. The gradual cooling down of the whole room towards me, the disaffection that swept over the chain of little drinking groups from that centre of mystical hostility, that soul that recognized in me something icily antipodean too, no doubt; the immobile figure of America's newest and most mysterious child, apparently emitting these strong waves without effort, as naturally as a fountain: all this, with great vexation, I recognized from the moment of the intrusion of his presence. It almost seemed as though he had stayed away from this haunt of his foreseeing what would happen. He had waited until I had comfortably settled myself and there was something palpable to attack. His absence may have had some more accidental cause.

What exactly it was, again, he found to say as regards me I never discovered. As at Bayonne, I saw the mouth working and experienced the social effects, only. No doubt it was the subtlest and most electric thing that could be found; brief, searching and annihilating. Perhaps something seemingly crude—that I was a spy—may have recommended itself to his ingenuity. But I expect it was a meaningless blast of disapprobation that he blew upon me, an eerie and stinging wind of convincing hatred.[11] He evidently enjoyed a great ascendancy in the Café Pelayo. This would be explained no doubt by his commercial prestige. But it was due, I am sure, even more to his extraordinary character—moulded by the sublime force of his illusion. His inscrutable immobility, his unaccountable self-control (for such a person, and feeling as he did towards me), were of course the american or anglo-saxon phlegm and sang-froid as reflected, or interpreted, in this violent human mirror.

I left the Café earlier than usual, before the chef d'orchestre. It was the following morning at lunch when I next saw him. He was embarrassed. His eyes wavered in my direction, fascinated and inquisitive. He found it difficult to realize that his respect for me had to end and give place to another feeling.

'You know Monsieur de Valmore?' he asked.

'That little ape of a Frenchman, do you mean?'

I knew this description of my wonderful enemy was only vulgar and splenetic. But I was too discouraged to be more exact.[12]

This way of describing Monsieur de Valmore appeared to the chef d'orchestre so eccentric, apart from its vulgarity, that I lost at once in Don Pedro's sympathy. He told me, however, all about him; details that did not touch on the real constituents of this life.

'He owns the Burgalésa and many houses in Pontaisandra. Ships, too—Es Américano,' he added.

Vexations and hindrances of all sorts now made my stay in Pontaisandra useless and depressing. Don Pedro had generally almost finished when we came to dinner, and I was forced to close down, so to say, the mine. Nothing more was to be extracted, at length, except disobliging monosyllables. The rest of the boarders remained morose and inaccessible. I went once more to the Café Pelayo, but the waiters even seemed to have come beneath the hostile spell. The new Café I chose yielded nothing but gallego chatter, and the garçon was not talkative.

There was little encouragement to try another Pension and stay on in Pontaisandra. I made up my mind to go to Coruña. This would waste time and I was short of money. But there is more gallego than spanish spoken in Galicia, even in the cities. Too easily automatic a conquest as it may seem, Monsieur de Valmore had left me nothing but the Gallegos. I was not getting the practice in spanish I needed, and this sudden deprivation of what I had mainly come into Spain for, poisoned for me the whole air of the place. The task of learning this tiresome language began to be burdensome. I even considered whether I should not take up gallego instead. But I decided finally to go to Coruña. On the following day, some hours before the time for the train, I paraded the line of streets towards the station, with the feeling that I was no longer there. The place seemed cooling down beneath my feet and growing prematurely strange. But the miracle happened. It declared itself with smooth suddenness.[13] A more exquisite checkmate never occurred in any record of such warfare.

The terrible ethnological difference that existed between Monsieur de Valmore and myself up till that moment, showed every sign of ending in a weird and revolting defeat for me. The 'moment' I refer to was that in which I turned out of the High Street, into the short hilly avenue where the post office lay. I thought I would go up to the Correo and see for the last time if a letter for which I had been waiting had arrived.

On turning the corner I at once became aware of three anomalous figures walking just in front of me. They were all three of the proportions known in America as 'husky.' When I say they were walking, I should describe their movements more accurately as *wading*—wading through the air, evidently towards the post office. Their carriage was slightly rolling, like a ship under way. They occasionally bumped into each other, but did not seem to mind this. Yet no one would have mistaken these three young men for drunkards. But I daresay you will have already guessed. It would under other circumstances have had no difficulty in entering my head. As it was, there seemed a certain impediment of consciousness or inhibition with me which prevented me from framing to myself the word 'American.' These three figures were three Americans! This seems very simple, I know: but this very ordinary fact trembled and lingered before completely entering into my consciousness. The extreme rapidity of my mind in another sense—in seeing all that this fact, if verified, might signify to me—may have been responsible for that. Then one of them, on turning his head, displays the familiar features of Taffany, a Mississippi friend of mine. I simultaneously recognized Blauenfeld and Morton, the other two members of a trio. A real trio, like real twins, is rarer than one thinks. This one was the remnant of a quartet, however. I had met it first in Paris. Poor Bill (Borden Henneker) was killed in a motor accident. These three had mourned him with insatiable drinking, to which I had been a party for some days the year before. And my first feeling was complicated with a sense of their forlornness, as I recognized their three backs, rolling heavily and mournfully.

In becoming, from any three Americans, three friends of mine, they precipitated in an immediate inrush of the most full-blooded hope the sense of what might be boldly anticipated from this meeting. Two steps brought me up with them: my cordiality if anything exceeded theirs.

'Why, if it isn't Cairo! Look at this! Off what Christmas-tree did you drop? Gee, I'm glad to see you, Kire!' shouted Taffany. He was the irrepressible Irishman of the three.

'Why, it's you, that's swell. We looked out for you in Paris. You'd just left. How long have you been round here?' Blauenfeld ground out cordially. He was the rich melancholy one of the three.

'Come right up to the Correo and interpret for us, Cairo. You know the idioma, I guess. Feldie's a washout,' said Morton, who was the great debauchee of the three.

Optimism, consciousness of power (no wonder! I reflected) surged out of them, my simple-hearted friends. Ah, the kindness! the *overwhelming* kindness. I bathed voluptuously in this american greeting—this real american greeting. Nothing naturalized about *that*. At the same time I felt almost awe at the thought of the dangerous nationality. These good fellows I knew and liked so well, seemed for the moment to have some intermixture of the strangeness of Mondieur de Valmore. However, I measured with enthusiasm their egregious breadth of shoulder, the exorbitance of their 'pants.' I examined with some disappointment these signs of nationality. How english they looked, compared to de Valmore. They were by no means american enough for my taste. Had they appeared in a star-stripe swallow-tail suit like the cartoons of Uncle Sam, I should not have been satisfied.

But I felt rather like some ambitious eastern prince who, having been continually defeated in battle by a neighbour because of the presence in the latter's army of a half-dozen elephants, suddenly becomes possessed of a couple of dozen himself.

I must have behaved oddly. I enquired anxiously about their plans. They were not off at once? No. That was capital. I was most awfully glad that they were not departing at once. I was glad that they had decided to stop. They had booked their rooms? Yes. That was good. So they were here for the night at all events? That was as it should be! You should always stop the night. Yes, I would with very great pleasure interpret for them at the Correo. I cherished my three Americans as no Americans before have ever been cherished. I was inclined to shelter them as though they were perishable, to see that they didn't get run over, or expose themselves unwisely to the midday sun. Each transatlantic peculiarity of speech or gesture I received with something approaching exultation. Morton was soon persuaded that I was tight. All thoughts of Coruña disappeared. I did not ask at the Poste Restante for my letter.[14] First of all, I took my trio into a little Café near the post office. There I told them briefly what was expected of them.

'You have a most distinguished compatriot here,' I said.

'Oh. An American?' Morton asked seriously.

'Well, he deserves to be. But he began too late in life, I think. He hails from the southern part of France, and americanism came to him as a revelation when youth had already passed. He repented sincerely of his misguided early nationality. But his years spent as a Frenchman have left their mark. In the meantime, he won't leave Englishmen alone. He persecutes them, apparently, wherever he finds them.'

'He mustn't do that!' Taffany said with resolution. 'That won't do at all.'

'Why, no, I guess he mustn't do that. What makes him want to do that? What's biting him anyway? Britishers are harmless enough, aren't they?' said Blauenfeld.

—

'I knew you'd look at the matter in that light,' I said. 'It's a rank abuse of authority; I knew it would be condemned at headquarters. Now if you could only be present, unseen, and witness how I, for instance, am oppressed by this fanatic fellow-citizen of yours; and if you could issue forth, and reprove him, and tell him not to do it again, I should bless the day on which you were born in America.'

'I wasn't born there anyway,' said Morton. 'But that's of no importance I suppose. Well, unfold your plan, Cairo.'

'I don't see yet what we can do. Do you owe the guy any money? How does it come that he persecutes you like this?' Taffany asked.

'I'm very sorry you should have to complain, Mr. Ker-Orr, of treatment of that sort—but what sort is it anyway?'

I gave a lurid picture of my tribulations, to the scandal and indignation of my friends. They at once placed themselves, and with a humorous modesty their americanism—any quantity of that mixture in their 'organisms'—at my disposal.

It appeared to me, to start with of the first importance that Monsieur de Valmore should not get wind of what had happened. I took my three Americans cautiously out of the Café, reconnoitring before allowing them outside. As their hotel was near the station and not near the enemy's haunts, I encouraged their going back to it. I also supposed that they would wish to make some toilet for the evening, and relied on their good sense to put on their largest clothes, though Taffany was the only one of the three that seemed at all promising from that point of view. The scale of his buttocks did assure a certain outlandish girth that would at once reveal to M. de Valmore the presence of an American.

My army was in excellent form. A robust high spirits possessed them. I kept them out of the way till nightfall, and then after an early dinner, by a circuitous route, approached the Café Pelayo.

Morton was by this time a little screwed: he showed signs that he might become difficult. He insisted on producing a packet of obscene photographs, which he held before him fan-wise, like a hand of cards, some of them upside down. The confused mass of bare legs and arms of the photographs, distorted by this method of holding them, with some highly indecent details occurring here and there, produced the effect of a siamese demon. Blauenfeld was grinning over his shoulder, and seemed likely to forget the purpose for which he was being brought to the Pelayo.

'I know that coon,' he insisted, pointing to one of the photos. 'I swear I know that coon.'

My idea was that the three Americans should enter the Café Pelayo without me. There they would establish themselves, and I had told them where to sit and how to spot their man. They should become acquainted with

Monsieur de Valmore. Almost certainly the latter would approach his fellow citizens at once. But if there was any ice to break, it must be broken quickly by Taffany. They must ply him with imitation high-balls or some other national drink, which they must undertake to mix for him. For this they could hand the bill to me afterwards. When the ground was sufficiently prepared, Taffany was to sign to me from the door, and I would then, after a further interval, put in my appearance.

Morton was kissing one of the photographs. Should he continue to produce, in season and out of season, his objectionable purchases, and display them, perhaps, to the customers of the Pelayo, although he might gain an ill-deserved popularity, he would certainly convey an impression of a different sort to that planned by me for this all-american evening. After considerable drunken argument I persuaded him to let me hold the photographs until the *coup* had been brought off. That point of discipline enforced, I sent them forward, sheltering, myself, in an archway in an adjoining street, and watched them enter the swing door 'ra-raing,' as ordered. But I had the mortification of seeing Morton fall down as he got inside, tripping, apparently, over the mat. Cursing this intemperate clown, I moved with some stealth to a small gallego Café within sight of the door of the Pelayo to await events.

I fixed my eyes on the brilliantly lighted windows of the Café. I imagined the glow of national pride, the spasm of delighted recognition, that would invade Monsieur de Valmore, on hearing the 'ra-ra' chorus. Apart from the sentimental reason—its use as a kind of battle-song—was the practical one that this noisy entrance would at once attract my enemy's attention. Ten minutes passed. I knew that my friends had located Monsieur de Valmore, even if they had not begun operations. Else they would have returned to my place of waiting. I wallowed naïvely in a superb indifference. Having set the machinery going, I turned nonchalantly away, paying no more attention to it. But the stage analogy affected me, in the sense that I became rather conscious of my appearance. I must await my cue, but was sure of my reception. I was the great star that was not expected. I was the unknown quantity. Meantime I pulled out the photographs and arranged them fantastically as Morton had done. From time to time I glanced idly down the road. At last I saw Blauenfeld making towards me, his usual american swing of the body complicated by rhythmical upheavals of mirth into tramplings, stumblings and slappings of his thigh. He was being very american in a traditional way as he approached me. He was a good actor, I thought: I was grateful to him. I paid for my coffee while he was coming up.

'Is it O.K.? Is he spitted?'

'Yep! we've got him fine! Come and have a look at him.'

'Did he carry out his part of the programme according to my arrangements?'

'Why, yes. We went right in, and all three spotted him at the same time. Taffany walked round and showed himself: he was the decoy. Morty and me coquetted round too, looking arch and *very american*. We could see his old pop-eyes beginning to stick out of his old head, and his old mouth watering. At last he could hold himself no longer. He roared at us. We bellowed at him. Gee, it was a great moment in american history! We just came together with a hiss and splutter of joy. He called up a trayful of drinks, to take off the rawness of our meeting. He can't have seen an American for months. He just gobbled us up. There isn't much left of poor old Taff. He likes him best and me next. Morty's on all fours at present, tickling his legs. He doesn't much care for Morty. He's made us promise to go to his hotel to-night.'

I approached the palmy terrace, my mouth a little drawn and pinched, eyebrows raised, like a fastidious expert called in at a decisive moment. I entered the swing door with Blauenfeld, and looked round in a cold and business-like way, as a doctor might, with the dignified enquiry, 'Where is the patient?' The patient was there right enough, surrounded by the nurses I had sent. There he sat in as defenceless a condition of beatitude as possible. He stared at me with an incredulous grin at first. I believe that in this moment he would have been willing to extend to me a temporary pardon—a passe-partout[1] to his Café for the evening. He was so happy I became a bagatelle. Had I wished, an immediate reconciliation was waiting for me. But I approached him with impassive professional rapidity, my eye fixed on him, already making my diagnosis. I was so carried away by the figure of the physician, and adhered so faithfully to the bedside manner that I had decided upon as the most appropriate for the occasion, that I almost began things by asking him to put out his tongue. Instead I sat down carefully in front of him, pulling up my trousers meticulously at the knee. I examined his flushed and astounded face, his bristling moustache, his bloodshot eyes in silence. Then I very gravely shook my head.

No man surprised by his most mortal enemy in the midst of an enervating debauch, or barely convalescent from a bad illness, could have looked more nonplussed. But Monsieur de Valmore turned with a characteristic blank childish appeal to his nurses or boon companions for help, especially to Taffany. Perhaps he was shy or diffident of taking up actively his great rôle, when more truly great actors were present. Would not the divine America speak, or thunder, through them, at this intruder? He turned a pair of solemn, appealing, outraged dog's-eyes upon Taffany. Would not his master repulse and chastise this insolence?

'I guess you don't know each other,' said Taffany. 'Say, Monsieur de Valmore, here's a friend of mine, Mr. Ker-Orr from London.'

---

[1] Properly "a laissez-passer," a pass.

My enemy pulled himself together as though the different parts of his body all wanted to leap away in different directions, and he found it all he could do to prevent such disintegration. An attempt at a bow appeared as a chaotic movement, the various parts of his body could not come together for it. It had met other movements on the way, and never became a bow at all. An extraordinary confusion beset his body. The beginning for a score of actions ran over it blindly and disappeared.

'Guess Mr. de Valmore ain't quite comfortable in that chair, Morty. Give him yours.'

Then in this chaotic and unusual state he was hustled from one chair to the other, his muffled expostulations being in french, I noticed.

His racial instinct was undergoing the severest revolution it had yet known. An incarnation of sacred America herself had commanded him to take me to his bosom. And, as the scope of my victory dawned upon him, his personal mortification assumed the proportions of a national calamity. For the first time since the sealing of his citizenship he felt that he was only a Frenchman from the Midi—hardly as near an American, in point of fact, as is even a poor god-forsaken Britisher.

The Soldier of Humour is chivalrous, though implacable. I merely drank a bottle of champagne at his expense; made Don Pedro and his orchestra perform three extras, all made up of the most intensely national english light comedy music. Taffany, for whom Monsieur de Valmore entertained the maximum of respect, held him solemnly for some time with a detailed and fabulous enumeration of my virtues. Before long I withdrew with my forces to riot in barbarous triumph at my friends' hotel for the rest of the evening.

During the next two days I on several occasions visited the battlefield, but Monsieur de Valmore had vanished. His disappearance alone would have been sufficient to tell me that my visit to Spain was terminated. And in fact two days later I left Pontaisandra with the Americans, parting with them at Tuy, and myself continuing on the León-San Sebastián route back to France, and eventually to Paris. The important letter which I had been expecting had arrived at last and contained most unexpected news. My presence was required, I learnt, in Budapest.

Arrived at Bayonne, I left the railway station with what people generally regard as a premonition. It was nothing of course but the usual mechanical working of inference within the fancy. It was already night-time. Stepping rapidly across the square, I hurried down the hall-way of the Fonda del Mundo. Turning brusquely and directly into the dining-room of the inn I gazed round me almost shocked not to find what I now associated with that particular scene. Although Monsieur de Valmore had not been there to greet me, as good or better than his presence seemed to be attending me on my withdrawal from Spain. I still heard in this naked little room, as the wash of the sea in the shell, the echo of the first whisperings of his weird displeasure. Next day I arrived in Paris, my spanish nightmare shuffled off long before I reached that humdrum spot.

NOTES

[1] The 1927 proofs gave "humour" here.
[2] The last six words were added to the proofs.
[3] Compare with a similar effect in *Tarr* (IV, 2) : ". . . the large gas-stove, like a safe, its gas stars, on top, blasting away luridly at pans and saucepans with Bertha's breakfast."
[4] The proofs give: "fifty-two."
[5] This "gnashing," absent from the 1917 text, is clearly a Tyro trait.
[6] Compare with "Freud explains everything by *sex*. . ." (page 18).
[7] The proofs gave : "extension of my dubious hotel."
[8] Unlike all the other geographical names in this story, Pontaisandra is an imaginary place, though possibly an echo of Pontevedra, near Vigo in Galicia, where Lewis spent the spring of 1908.
[9] Presumably the "paseo de la Alameda," the main promenade in Vigo.
[10] The main street in the older part of Vigo ; see "A Spanish Household," in part two, below.
[11] The proofs gave : "wind of inexplicable hatred."
[12] The proofs gave : "But often it is necessary to be vulgar or inexact."
[13] The proofs gave : "It comes with a gradual flowering of beauty."
[14] The proofs gave : "The letters remained unposted."

BEAU SÉJOUR

This is the final, completely overhauled version of "The 'Pole,'" the first text ever published by Lewis, but it is excessive to call it "a new story" as the author does in his "Foreword": it is now a real story and no longer a sketch, but the main characters, the setting and atmosphere were already there in 1909. Compared with the earlier sketch, "Beau Séjour" is marked like the other stories in The Wild Body *by the usual dramatization of a static material: most of the secondary characters, described for their own sake, have been, though some of them were quite interesting, eliminated; a potential triangle (Zaborov, Mademoiselle Péronnette and Carl) has materialized, and this situation finally leads, with Zaborov's triumph, to a satisfactory conclusion which was not even suggested in 1909. Moreover dialogue, completely non-existent in "The 'Pole,'" has been systematically introduced. As to the narrator—who remains here a rather peripheral and certainly anonymous observer, probably because of the descriptive weight of the initial sketch—it is said in the "Foreword" that "Beau Séjour" relates his first adventure.*

On arrival at *Beau Séjour*,[1] in the country between Rosnoën[1] and the littoral, I was taken by the proprietress, Mademoiselle Péronnette, for a 'Pole.'[2] She received my first payment with a smile. At the time I did not understand it. I believe that she was preparing to make a great favourite of me.

The 'Poles,' who in this case were mostly Little Russians, Finns and Germans, sat at the table d'hôte, at the head of the table. They smoked large pipes and were served first. They took the lion's share. If it was a chicken they stripped it, and left only the legs and bones for the rest of the company. This was a turbulent community. The quarrels of the permanent boarders with Mademoiselle Péronnette affected the quality of the food that came to the table.

The master-spirit was a man named Zoborov. This is probably not the way to spell it. I never saw it written. That is what I called him, and he answered to it when I said it. So the sound must have been true enough, though as I have written it down possibly no russian eye would recognize it.

This man was a discontented 'Pole.' He always spoke against the 'Polonais,' I noticed, I could not make out why. Especially to me he would speak with great contempt of all people of that sort. But he also spoke harshly of Mademoiselle Péronnette and her less important partner, Mademoiselle Maraude. He was constantly stirring up his fellow pensionnaires against them.

Zoborov at first sight was a perfect 'Pole.' He was exceedingly quiet. He wandered stealthily about and yawned as a cat does. Sometimes he would get up with an abrupt intensity, like a cat, and walk steadily strongly and rhythmically away out of sight. He may have had a date with another 'Pole,' of course, or have wanted exercise. But he certainly did succeed in conveying in a truly polesque manner that it was a more mysterious thing that had disturbed him. Every one has experienced those attractive calls that lead people to make impulsive visits, which result in some occurrence or meeting that, looking back on it, seems to have lain behind the impulse. Scenes and places, at least other things than men, an empty seashore, an old horse tethered in a field, some cavernous armorican lane, under some special aspect and mood, had perhaps the power of drawing these strange creatures towards it, as though it had something to impart. Yet as far as Zoborov was con-

---

[1] Literally, "Beautiful Sojourn" or "Beautiful Abode."

[2] An account of the 'Pole' will be found at the end of this story. The 'Pole' is a national variety of Pension-sponger, confined as far as I know to France, and to the period preceding the Russian Revolution [author's note].

cerned, although certainly he succeeded in conveying the correct sensation at the time, when you thought about it afterwards you felt you had been deceived. The date or exercise seemed more likely in retrospect than the mysterious messages from arrangements of objects, or the attractive electrical dreaming of landscapes. In the truth-telling mind of after-the-event this crafty and turbulent personage was more readily associated with man-traps and human interests than with natural magic.

Zoborov was touchy, and he affected to be more so and in a different sense than actually he was. He wished you to receive a very powerful impression of his *independence.* To effect this he put himself to some pains. First he attempted to hypnotize you with his isolation. Yet everything about him proved 'the need of a world of men' for him. Are not people more apt to bestow things on a person who is likely to spurn them? you suspected him of reflecting: his gesture of spurning imaginary things recurred very often. So you gradually would get a notion of the sort of advantageous position he coveted in your mind.

After dinner in conversing with you he always spoke in a hoarse whisper, or muttered in an affected bass. He scarcely parted his lips, often whistling his words through his teeth inside them. Whether he were telling you what a hypocrite Mademoiselle Péronnette was, or, to give you a bit of romance and savagery, were describing how the Caucasians ride standing on their horses, and become so exultant that they fling their knives up in the air and catch them—he never became audible to any one but you. He had a shock of dark hair, was dark-skinned, his eyes seemed to indicate drugs and advertised a profound exhaustion. He had the smell of a tropical plant: the vegetation of his body was probably strong and rank. Through affecting not to notice people, to be absorbed in his own very important thoughts, or the paper or the book he was reading, the contraction of his eyebrows had become permanent. He squinted slightly. He had bow-legs and protruding ears and informed me that he suffered from haemorrhoids. His breath stank; but as he never opened his mouth more than he could help, this concerned only himself.

He was a great raconteur. He had a strongly marked habit of imitating his own imitations. In telling a story in which he figured (his stories were all designed to prove his independence) he had a colourless formula for his interlocutor. A gruff, half-blustering tone was always used to represent himself. Gradually these two voices had coalesced and had become his normal conversational voice. He was short, thick-set and muscular. His physical strength must have been considerable. He exploited it in various ways. It was a confirmation of his independence. His 'inferiority complex' brought forward his tremendous chest, when threatened, with above it his cat-like face seeming to quizz, threaten and go to sleep all at once, with his mouth drawn to a point, in a purring position. His opponent would be in doubt as to whether he was going to hit him, laugh or sneeze.

French visitors he always made up to. Seeing him with the friend of the moment, talking confidentially apart, making signs to him at table, you would have supposed him an exclusive, solitary man, who 'did not make friends easily.' Aloofness towards the rest of the company was always maintained. You would not guess that he knew them except to nod to. When about to take up with a new-comer, his manner became more severe than ever, his aloofness deepened. As he passed the salt to him, he scarcely showed any sign of realizing what he was doing, or that he had a neighbour at all. His voice became gruffer. As though forcing himself to come out of himself and behave with decent neighbourliness, he would show the new guest a stiff politeness.

He was from twenty-five to thirty years old. In women he took no interest, I think, and disliked exceedingly Mademoiselle Péronnette and Mademoiselle Maraude. I thought he was a eunuch. No homosexuality was evident. He often spoke of a friend of his, a Russian like himself. This man was exceedingly independent: he was also prodigiously strong; far stronger than Zoborov. This person's qualities he regarded as his own, however, and he used them as such. The shadowy figure of this gigantic friend seemed indeed superimposed upon Zoborov's own form and spirit. You divined an eighth of an inch on all sides of the contour of his biceps and pectorals, another contour—the visionary contour of this friend's even larger muscles. And beyond even the sublime and frowning pinnacles of his own independence, the still loftier summits of his friend's pride, of a piece with his.

His friend was in the Foreign Legion. In recent fighting with the Moors he had displayed unusual powers of resistance. Because of his extraordinary strength he was compelled on the march to carry several of his comrades' rifles in addition to his own. Zoborov would read his african letters apart, with an air of absorbed and tender communion, seeking to awaken one's jealousy. He repeated long dialogues between his friend and himself. When it came to his friend's turn to speak, he would puff his chest out, and draw himself up, until the penumbra of visionary and supernatural flesh that always accompanied him was almost filled by his own dilated person. He would assume a debonair recklessness of manner, his moustaches would flaunt upwards over his laughing mouth, and even the sombre character of his teeth and his strong breath would be momentarily forgotten. His gestures would be those of an open-handed and condescending prince. He would ostentatiously make use of the personal pronoun 'thou' (in his french it had a finicky lisping sound), to make one eager to get on such terms with him oneself.

I never got on those terms with him. One day he remained at table after the others had left. He was waiting to be asked to go for a walk. Off my guard, I betrayed the fact that I had noticed this. Several such incidents occurred, and he became less friendly.

Many of Zoborov's tales had to do with Jews. The word 'juif' with him appeared as a long, juicy sound, 'jouiive,' into which, sleepily blinking his eyes, he injected much indolent contempt. When he used it he made a particular face—sleepy, far-away, heavy-lidded, allowing his almost immobile mouth to flower rather dirtily, drawn down to a peculiarly feline point. He mentioned Jews so often that I wondered if he were perhaps a Jew. On this point I never came to any definite conclusion.

My second night at *Beau Séjour* there was a scene outside my room, which I witnessed. My bedroom was opposite that of Mademoiselle Péronnette. Hearing the shattering report of a door and sounds of heavy breathing, I got up and looked out.

'Va-t'en! Tu n'es qu'un vaurien! Va-t'en! Tu m'entends? Tu m'agaces! Va-t'en!'[1]

The voice of the proprietress clappered behind her locked door. A long white black-topped lathe was contorted against it. It was the most spoilt of all our 'Poles,' a german giant, now quite naked. With his bare arms and shoulders he strained against the wood. As I appeared he turned round enquiring breathlessly with farcical fierceness:

'Faurien! Faurien! Elle m'abelle faurien!'[2]

His eyes blazed above a black-bearded grin, with clownesque incandescence. He was black and white, dazzling skin and black patches of hair alternating. His thin knees were unsteady, his hands were hanging in limp expostulation, his grin of protest wandered in an aimless circle, with me for centre.

'Faurien,' he repeated.

'Veux-tu t'en aller? Je te défends de faire un scandale, tu entends, Charles? Va-t'en!'[3] The voice of the proprietress energetically rattled on the other side of the door.

'Sgantal?' he asked helplessly and incredulously, passing one hand slowly in front of his body, with heavy facetious[2] prudery. The floor boards groaned to the right, a stumpy figure in stocking feet, but otherwise clothed, emerged in assyrian profile, in a wrestling attitude, flat hands extended, rolling with professional hesitation, with factitious rudeness seized the emaciated nudity

[1] "Go away! You're just a good-for-nothing! Do you hear me? You get on my nerves! Go away!"

[2] I.e., "Elle m'appelle vaurien" with a German accent: "She calls me a good-for-nothing!"

[3] "*Will* you go away! I forbid you to make a scandal, do you hear, Charles? Go away!"

of the german giant beneath the waist, then disappeared with him bodily down the passage to the left. It was Zoborov in action. The word 'faurien' came escaping out of the dark in a muzzy whistle, while the thump thump of the stocking feet receded. I closed the door.

This gave me an insight at once into the inner social workings of the Pension. Carl had slept with the proprietress from the start, but that was not among Zoborov's accomplishments. He intrigued in complete detachment. Carl and he never clashed, they both sucked up to each other.

Next morning I had a look at Carl. He was about six foot two, with a high, narrow, baldish black head and long black beard. His clothes hung like a sack on his thin body. He gave me an acid grin. Zoborov frowned, blinked stupidly in front of him, and swallowed his coffee with loud, deep-chested relish. He then wiped his moustache slowly, rose, and stamped heavily out into the garden in his sabots, rolling, husky peasant fashion, from side to side. Carl's lank black hair curled in a ridge low on his neck: a deep smooth brow surmounted the settled unintelligent mockery of the rest of his face. The general effect was that of an exotic, oily, south-german Royal Academician. He had an italian name. Essaying a little conversation, I found him surly.

A week later Zoborov, sitting in the orchard with his back against a tree, whittling a stick, obliged me with his views of Carl.

'Where did you take him?' I said, referring to the night scene.

Zoborov knitted his brows and muttered in his most rough and blustering voice:

'Oh, he was drunk. I just threw him on his bed, and told him to shut his head and go to sleep. He bores me, Carl does.'

'He's on good terms with Mademoiselle Péronnette?'

'Is he? I don't know if he is now. He was. She was angry with him that night because she'd found him with the bonne, in the bonne's room. That's why Maria left—the little bonne that waited at table when you came. He sleeps with all the bonnes.'

'I slept with the new one last night,' I said.

He looked up quickly, wrinkling his eyes and puffed out in his sturdiest, heartiest bass, puffed through his closed teeth, that is, in his spluttering buzz:

'Did you? With Antoinette? She's rather a pretty girl. But all bonnes are dirty!' He expressed distaste with his lips. 'A girl who works as a bonne never has time to wash. Maria *stank.* There's no harm in his sleeping with the bonnes. But truly he gets so drunk, too drunk—all the time. He's engaged to Mademoiselle Péronnette, you know.' He laughed softly, gently fluttering his moustaches, heaving up his square protruding chest, and making a gruff rumble in it.

'Engaged—what is that?'

'Why, engaged to be married.' He laughed, throwing his eyes coquettishly up. 'He *was*. I don't know if they're still supposed to be. *He* says she's always trying to marry him. Last year she lent him some money and they became engaged.' He never raised his eyes, except to laugh, and went on whittling the stick.

'She paid him for the engagement?'[3] I said at last.

'Ye-es!' he drawled, with soft shaking chuckles. 'And that's all she'll ever get out of old Carl!—But I don't think she wants to marry him now. I think she wants the money back. I wish he'd take himself off!' He frowned and became gruff. 'He's a good fellow all right, but he's always making scandals. I *think*—he wants her to lend him more money. That's what I think he wants. All these scandals—they disgust me, both of them. I'd leave here to-morrow if I had any money to get out with.'

He hooked his eyebrows down in a calm and formal frown, and surveyed his finger nails. They were short and thick. Putting down the stick he turned his attention to them. He chipped indolently at their edges, then bit the corners off.

I was frequently the witness of quarrels between Carl and Mademoiselle Péronnette. A few days after my conversation in the orchard I entered the kitchen of the Pension, but noticing that Carl was holding Mademoiselle Péronnette by the throat, and was banging her head on the kitchen table, I withdrew. As I closed the door I heard Mademoiselle Péronnette, as I supposed, crash upon the kitchen floor. Dull sounds that were probably kicks followed, and I could hear Carl roaring, 'Gourte! Zale gourte!' When enraged he always made use of the word *gourte*. It was, I think, a corruption of the french word *gourde*, which means a calabash.[1]

As I was leaving Antoinette's bedroom one night I thought I noticed something pale moving in the shadow of the staircase. Five minutes afterwards I returned to her room to remind her to wake me early, and as I got outside I heard voices. She was saying, 'Allez-vous-en, Charles! Non, je ne *veux* pas! J'ai sommeil! Laisse-moi tranquille. Non!'[2] There was a scuffling and creaking of the bed, accompanied by a persuasive and wheedling rumble that I recognized as belonging to Carl.

Then suddenly there was a violent commotion, Antoinette's voice exploded in harsh breton-french:

'Sacré *gars*,[4] fiche-moi donc la paix, veux-tu! *Laisse*-moi tranquille, nom de dieu de dieu——'[3]

The door flew open and Carl, quite naked again, came hotly flopping into

---

[1] I. e., idiot.

[2] "Go away, Charles! No, I don't *want* to! I'm sleepy! Let me alone. No!"

[3] "You dirty fellow, let me alone, will you! Bloody hell—"

my arms, his usual grin opening his beard and suffusing his eyes. He lay in my arms a moment grinning, then stood up.

'Nothing doing to-night?' I said. I was going back to my room when a furious form brushed past me, and I heard a violent slap, followed by the screaming voice of our proprietress:

'Ah, satyre, tu couches avec les bonnes? Tu ne peux pas laisser les femmes tranquilles la nuit, sale bête? C'est ainsi que tu crois toujours débaucher les bonnes après avoir trahi la patronne, espèce de saloperie! Prends ça pour ton rhume—et ça. Fumier! Oui, sauve-toi, sale bête!'[1]

The doors began opening along the passage: a few timid little slav pensionnaires and a couple of Parisians began appearing in their openings; I could see the unsteady nudity of Carl staggering beneath slaps that resounded in him, as though she had been striking a hollow column. I hastened to my room. A moment later the precipitate tread of Zoborov passed my door *en route* for the scene of the encounter. The screaming voice of Antoinette then made itself heard amongst the others. I went to my door: I was glad to hear that Antoinette was giving Mademoiselle Péronnette more than she was receiving, delivering herself of some trenchant reflections on the standard of the *mœurs* obtaining in the *Beau Séjour*, on employers that it was impossible to respect, seeing that they were not respectable, and I then once more closed my door. A few moments later Mademoiselle Péronnette's door crashed, the other doors quietly closed, the returning tread of Zoborov passed my wall. So that night's events terminated.

The two Parisians on our landing left next morning to seek more respectable quarters, and Antoinette the same. Carl was at breakfast as usual. He grinned at me when I sat down. Zoborov frowned at the table, drank his coffee loudly, rose, pushing his chair back and standing for a moment in a twisted overbalanced posture, then, his sabots falling heavily on the parquet floor, his body rolling with the movement of a husky peasant, he went out of the window into the garden. The food grew worse. Two days later I told the proprietress that I was leaving.

Next night I was sitting in the kitchen reading *l'Eclair de l'Ouest*. Mademoiselle Péronnette and Mademoiselle Maraude were sitting near the lamp on the kitchen table and mending the socks of several pensionnaires, when Carl came in at the door, shouted:

'Gourte! Brend za bour don rhume!'[2] . . . and fired three shots from a large

---

1 "Ah, satyr, sleeping with the maids? Can't you leave women alone during the night, you brute? So you intend to debauch the maids after betraying the proprietress, you dirty bastard! Take this—and that as well. Bastard! Beat it, you brute!"

2 "Gourde, prends ça pour ton rhume!" with a German accent: "Take this, you idiot!"

revolver at Mademoiselle Péronnette. Two prolonged screams rose from the women, rising and falling through a diapason at each fresh shot. Mademoiselle Péronnette fell to the floor. Carl withdrew. Mademoiselle Péronnette slowly rose from the floor, her hands trembling, and burst into tears. A little Pole who had been curled up asleep on the bench by the fire, and who no doubt had escaped Carl's notice, got up, and limped towards the table. He had been hit in the calf by a bullet. The women had not been hit, and they rolled up his trousers with execrations of the 'bandit,' Carl, and washed and dressed the wound, which was superficial. I went to look for Zoborov, whose presence I thought was probably required. I found him at the bottom of the orchard with two other 'Poles,' in the moonlight, playing a flute. As he lifted his little finger from a stop and released a shrill squeak, he raised one eyebrow, which he lowered again when, raising another finger, he produced a lower note. I sat down beside them. Zoborov finished the tune he was playing. His companions lay at right angles to each other, their heads propped on their bent forearms.

'Carl has broken out,' I said.

'Ah. He is always doing that,' Zoborov said.

'He's been firing a pistol at the proprietress.'

Zoborov lifted one eyebrow, as he had when he released the squeak on the flute.

'That doesn't surprise me,' he said.

'No one was hurt except a pensionnaire, who was asleep at the time. He hit him in the calf.'

'Who was it?'

'I don't know his name.'

Zoborov turned in my direction, and falling down on his side, propped his head like the other two 'Poles,' on his bent forearm, while he puffed out his heavy chest. His voice became rough and deep.

'Écoutez!' he began, with the sound like a voice blowing in a comb covered with tissue paper. 'Écoutez, mon ami.[1]—This Pension will never be quiet until that imbecile Carl leaves. He's not a bad fellow (il n'est pas mauvais camarade), he's a bad hat (il est mauvais sujet). You understand, he's not straight about money. He's a chap with money, his father's a rich brewer. A brewer, yes, my friend, you may laugh! It's not without its humour. He'd have to brew a lot to satisfy old Carl! He is an inveterate boozer. Why? Why does a man drink so much as that? Why?' His voice assumed the russian sing-song of pathetic enquiry, the fine gnat-like voice rapidly ascending and dropping again in an exhausted complaint. 'Because he is a german brute! That is the reason. He thinks because his father is a rich brewer that people

[1] "Listen, my friend."

should give him drink for nothing—it is a strange form of reasoning! He is always dissatisfied.—Now he has shot a pensionnaire. It is not the first time that he has fired at Mademoiselle Péronnette. But he never hits her! He doesn't want to hit her. He just fires off his revolver to make her excited! Then he tries to borrow more money!'

The three of them now remained quite immobile, stretched out on the dewy grass in different directions. I got up. With a gruff and blustering sigh, Zoborov exclaimed:

'Ah yes, my friend, that is how it is!'

I walked back to the house. As I passed the kitchen, I heard a great deal of noise, and went in.

The little shot pensionnaire was once more back on the bench, by the fire, with his bare leg, bandaged, stretched out horizontally in front of him, his two hands behind his head. At the table sat Carl, his face buried in a large handkerchief, which he held against his forehead, his shoulders heaving. A great volume of sound rose from him, a rhythmical bellowing of grief.

Mademoiselle Péronnette was standing a few yards away from him, a denunciatory forefinger stabbing the air in the direction of his convulsions.

'There he sits, the wretch. Mon dieu, he is a pretty sight! And to reflect that that is a fellow of good family, who comes from a home cracking with every luxury! Ça fait pitié![1]—Is there anything I haven't done for you, Charles? Say, Charles, can you deny I have done all a woman can?' she vociferated. 'I have given you my youth' (tremblingly and tenderly), 'my beauty!—I have shamed myself. I have offered myself to the saucy scorn of mere bonnes, I have made every sacrifice a woman can make! With what result I should like to know? Ah yes, you may well hide your face! You outrage me at every moment, you take my last halfpenny, and when you have soaked yourself in a neighbouring saloon, you come back here and debauch my bonnes! Any dirty peasant girl serves your turn. Is not that true, Charles? Answer! Deny it if you dare! That is what you do! That is how you repay all my kindness!'

Observing my presence, she turned expansively towards me.

'Tenez, ce monsieur-là peut te le dire, il a été le témoin de tes indignes caprices.[2] —Had you not, sir, occasion to observe this ruffian, as naked as he came into the world, issuing from the bedroom of the good-for-nothing harlot, Antoinette? Is not that the case, sir? Without a stitch of clothing, this incontinent ruffian——'

The french tongue, with its prolix dignity for such occasions, clamoured

1 "How pitiful!"

2 "Look, this gentleman here can confirm it. He was a witness to your shameful fancies."

on. As I was drawn into the discussion, a section of Carl's face appeared from behind the handkerchief, enough to free the tail of his eye for an examination of that part of the kitchen that was behind him. Our boche exhibitionist ascertained who it was had witnessed his last nocturnal contretemps. He thrust his head back deeper into the handkerchief. A roar of mingled disapproval and grief broke from him.

'Ah yes, now you suffer! But you never consider how you have made me suffer!'

But her discourse now took a new direction.

'I don't say, Charles, that you are alone—there are others who are even more guilty than you. I could name them if I wished! There is that dirty sneaking individual Zoborov, for instance. Ah, how he irritates me, that man! He is an extremely treacherous personage, that! *I* have heard the things he says about me. He thinks I don't know. I know very well. I am informed of all his manœuvres. *That* is the guilty party in this affair. He is the person who poisons the air of this establishment! I would get rid of him to-morrow if I could! Yes, Charles, I know that you, in comparison with such a crapulous individual as that Zoborov, are at least frank. At least you are a gentleman, a man of good family, accustomed to live in ease—what do I say, in luxury: and your faults are the faults of your station. *Tu es un fils de papa*,[1] mon pauvre garçon—you are a spoilt darling. You are not a *dirty moujik*, like that Zoborov!'

I noticed at this point, the face of Zoborov peering in at the window with his gascon frown, his one hooked-down and angrily-anchored eyebrow, and fluffy cavalier moustache, above his steady inscrutable feline pout. Mademoiselle Péronnette observed him at the same moment.

'Yes, I see you, sir! *Toujours aux écoutes!* Always eavesdropping! What eavesdroppers hear of themselves they deserve to hear. I hope you are satisfied, that's all I can say!'

'La ferme! La ferme!'[2] Zoborov's gruff railing voice puffed in at the window. He made his hand into a duck's bill, and worked it up and down to make it quack, as he turned away.

'He insults me, you know, that dirty *type*, he treats me as though I were the last of creatures! Yet what is he? He is nothing but a dirty moujik! He actually boasts of it. He's not a credit to the house—you should see the Parisians looking at him. He has driven pensionnaires away with his rudeness—and his dirt! He doesn't mind what he says. Then he abuses me to *everybody*, from morning till night. C'est une mauvaise langue!'[3]

---

1 "You're a daddy's boy." The American edition correctly prints "un fils *à* papa."

2 "Shut up!"

3 "He is a malicious gossip!"

'En effet!' Mademoiselle Maraude agreed. 'He has a bad tongue. He does this house no good.'

The 'Pole' with the bandaged leg began giggling. The two women turned to him.

'What is it, mon petit? Is your leg hurting you?'

Carl's head had sunk upon the table. The heat inside the handkerchief, the effects of the brandy he had been drinking, and the constant music of Mademoiselle Péronnette's voice, had overcome him. Now prolonged and congested snores rose from him, one especially vicious and intense crescendo making Mademoiselle Péronnette, who was examining the bandage on the leg of the pensionnaire, jump.

'Mon dieu!' she said. 'I wondered whatever it was.' The door opened, and Zoborov entered, advancing down the kitchen with as much noise as he could extract from his weight, his clumsiness, and the size of his sabots.

As he came, expanding his chest and speaking in his deepest voice, he said, bluff and 'proletarian':

'Écoutez, Mademoiselle Péronnette! I don't like the way you talk about me. You are absurd! What have I done to cause you to speak about me like that? I spend half my time keeping the peace between you and Carl; and when anything happens you turn on me! You are not reasonable!'

He spoke in an indolent sing-song, his eyes half closed, scarcely moving his lips, and talking through his teeth. He knelt down beside his wounded compatriot and put his hand gently upon his bandaged leg, speaking to him in russian.

'I only say what I know, sir!' Mademoiselle Péronnette hotly replied.

Zoborov continued speaking in russian to the injured pensionnaire, who replied in accents of mild musical protest.

'Your intrigues are notorious! You are always making mischief. I detest you, and wish you had never entered this house!'

Zoborov had unwound the bandage. He rose with a face of frowning indignation.

'Écoutez, Mademoiselle! If instead of amusing yourself by blowing off steam in that way, you did something for this poor chap who has just been injured through no fault of his own, you would be showing yourself more humane, yes, more humane! Why have you not at once put him to bed? He should see a doctor. His wound is in a dangerous condition! If it is not attended to blood-poisoning will set in.'

Mademoiselle Péronnette faced him, eye flashing; Mademoiselle Maraude had rised and moved towards the injured figure.

'It isn't true!' Mademoiselle Maraude said. 'He is not seriously hurt——'

'No, you are lying, Zoborov! He has been attended to,' Mademoiselle Péronnette said. 'It doesn't hurt, does it, mon petit?' she appealed coaxingly.

'It was nothing but a scratch, was it?—No. It was nothing but a scratch.'

'For a scratch there's a good deal of blood.' Zoborov said. 'Fetch a basin and some hot water. I will go for a doctor.'

The women looked at each other.

'A doctor? Why? You must be off your head! There's no occasion for a doctor! Do you wish for a doctor, mon petit?'

The injured pensionnaire smiled indulgently, with an amused expression, as though an elder taking part in a children's game, and shook his head.

'No. He does not wish for a doctor. Of course he doesn't! He ought to know best himself.'

'Écoutez!'[1] said Zoborov sleepily. 'It's for your sake, Mademoiselle Péronnette, as much as his—— You don't want anything to happen to him? No. These wounds are dangerous. You should get a doctor.'

Mademoiselle Péronnette stared at him in impotent hatred. She turned quickly to Mademoiselle Maraude, and said:

'Run quickly, Marie, and get some ice—down at Cornic's.'

Zoborov started rolling with ungainly speed towards the door, saying over his shoulder, 'I will go. I shall be back in a few minutes. Bathe his leg.'

As the door closed Mademoiselle Péronnette stared glassily at Mademoiselle Maraude.

'Quel homme! Quel homme! Mon dieu, quel malhonnête individu que celui-là![2] You saw how he put the blame on us? any one would think that we had neglected this poor boy here. My god, what a man!'

An obscene and penetrating trumpeting rose from the prostrate Carl—it rose shrieking and strong, sank to a purr, then rose again louder and stronger, sank to a gurgling purr again, then rose to a brazen crow, higher and higher.

Mademoiselle Péronnette put her fingers in her ears. 'My god, my god! As though it were not enough to have caused all this trouble——'

She sprang over, and seizing Carl by the shoulders shook him nervously.

'Go and sleep off your booze somewhere else—do you hear? Be off! Get out! Allez—vite! Marchez! Assez, assez! Fiche-moi la paix! *Enfin!*'

Carl rose unsteadily, a malevolent eye fixed on Mademoiselle Péronnette, and staggered out of the room. Mademoiselle Péronnette drew Mademoiselle Maraude aside, and began whispering energetically to her. I withdrew.

That night the bedroom door of the proprietress opened and shut it seemed incessantly. Between four and five,[5] as it was getting light, I woke and heard a scuffle in the passage. The voice of Mademoiselle Péronnette insisted in a juicy whisper:

'Dis, Charles, tu m'aimes? M'aimes-tu, chéri? Dis!'[3]

---

1 "Listen!

2 "What a man! What a man! Heavens, what a dishonest fellow!"

3 "Tell me, Charles, do you love me? Do you love me, Darling? Tell me!"

A sickly rumble came in response. Then more scuffling. Sucking and patting sounds and the signs of disordered respiration, with occasional rumbles, continued for some time. I got down to the bottom of the bed and turned the key in the door. I expected our german exhibitionist to enter my room at any moment with the nude form of Mademoiselle Péronnette in his arms, and perhaps edify me with the final phases of his heavy adieus. The sound of the key in the lock cut short whatever it was, and gradually the sounds ceased.

Next evening, at the request of Carl, we all collected in the kitchen for a little celebration. Whether it was to mark the rupture of the engagement, an approaching marriage, or what, was not made clear to us. Carl, with the courtliness of the South of Germany, his thin academic black locks and lengthy beard conferring the air of a function upon the scene, was very attentive to Mademoiselle Péronnette.

Zoborov was the gallant moujik. He toasted, with rough plebeian humour, the happy couple.

'Aux deux tourtereaux!'[1] he rolled bluffly out, lifting his glass, and rolling the r's of 'tourtereau' with a rich russian intensity. Placing his heavy sinewy brown hand before his mouth he whispered to me:

'Old Carl has relieved her of a bit more of her dough!'[6] He shook his shoulders and gurgled in the bass.

"Do you think that's it?'

'*Zurement!*'[2] he lisped. 'He's got the secret of the safe! He knows the combination!' He chuckled, bawdy and bluff. 'Old Carl will clean her out, you see.'

'He's an exceedingly noisy burglar. He woke me up last night in the course of his operations.'

Zoborov chuckled contentedly.

"He's mad!' he said. 'Still, he gets what he goes for. Good luck to him, I say.'

'Is Mademoiselle Péronnette rich?' I asked him. He squinted and hooked his left eyebrow down, then burst out laughing and looked in my face.

'I don't know,' he said. 'I shouldn't think so. Have you seen the safe?' he laughed again.

'No.'

'She has the safe in her bedroom. Carl rattles it when he's very screwed. Once he tried to carry it out of the room.' Zoborov laughed with his sly shaking of his big diaphragm. The recollection of this event tickled him.

---

1 "To the turtle-doves!"

2 Sûrement: "for sure."

Then he said to me: 'If you ask me, all she's got is in that safe, that's what I think.'

A piano had been brought in. A pensionnaire was playing the 'Blue Danube.'

Carl and Mademoiselle Péronnette danced. She was a big woman, about thirty. Her empty energetic face was pretty, but rather dully and evenly laid out. Her back when *en fête*[1] was a long serpentine blank with an embroidered spine. When she got up to dance she held herself forward, bare arms hanging on either side, two big meaty handles, and she undulated her *nuque* and back while she drew her mouth down into the tense bow of an affected kiss. While she held her croupe out stiffly in the rear, in muscular prominence, her eyes burnt at you with traditional gallic gallantry, her eyebrows arched in bland acceptance (a static *'Mais oui, si vous voulez!'*)[2] of french sex-convention, the general effect intended to be 'witty' and suggestive, without vulgarity. I was very much disgusted by her for my part: what she suggested to me was something like a mad butcher, who had put a piece of bright material over a carcase of pork or mutton, and then started to ogle his customers, owing to a sudden shuffling in his mind of the respective appetites. Carl on this occasion behaved like the hallucinated customer of such a pantomime, who, come into the shop, had entered into the spirit of the demented butcher, and proceeded to waltz with his sex-promoted food. The stupid madness, or commonplace wildness, that always shone in his eyes was at full blast as he jolted uncouthly hither and thither, while the proprietress undulated and crackled in complete independence, held roughly in place merely by his two tentacles.

With the exception of Mademoiselle Maraude and the bonne amie of a parisian schoolmaster on his vacation, all the guests were men. They danced together timidly and clumsily; Zoborov, frowning and squinting, stamped over to the schoolmaster's girl, and with a cross gruff hauteur invited her to dance. He rolled his painful proletarian weight once or twice round the room. The 'Blue Danube' rolled on; Carl poured appreciative oily light into Mademoiselle Péronnette's eyes, she redoubled her lascivious fluxions,[3] until Carl, having exhausted all the superlatives of the language of the eyes, cut short their rhythmical advance and, becoming immobile in the middle of the room, clasped her in his arms, where she hung like a dying wasp, Carl devouring with much movement the lower part of her face, canted up with abandon.[7] The pensionnaire at the piano broke into a cossack dance. Zoborov, who had handed the lady back to her schoolmaster again, with ceremony, and had returned to sit at my side, now rose and performed a series of gargantuan movements up and down the kitchen (flinging the less

1 Festive.

2 "Yes, if you wish."

3 Probably "flexions."

weighty couples to left and right) studiously devoid of any element of grace or skill. At regular intervals he stamped in his sabots and uttered a few gruff cries, while the pianist trumped upon the piano. Then, head back and his little moustache waving above his mouth, he trundled down the room, with a knees-up gymnastic movement. Satisfied that he had betrayed nothing but the completest barbaric uncouthness, he resumed his seat, grinning gravely at me.

His compatriots applauded, the piano stopped.

'That is a *typical* dance, mon ami, of the Don Cossacks!' he said, puffing a little. *'Typical'* (Tee-peek!), in his slow mincing french. In using this word his attitude was that I had a well-known curiosity about everything cossack, and that now, by the purest chance, I had heard a characteristic Don dance, and seen it interpreted with a racy savagery that only a Cossack could convey: and that, at the same time, he, Zoborov, had been astonished, he was bound to admit, at this happening in such an informative way as it had. In fine, I was lucky.

'Typical!' he said again. 'But I am out of practice.' Then he dropped the subject. The piano struck up again, with a contemporary Berlin dance-tune, and the floor was soon full of bobbing shapes, attempting to time their feet to the music. Long before the end the forms of Carl and Mademoiselle Péronnette, head and shoulders above the rest of the company, were transfixed in the centre of the room, Carl like a lanky black spider, always devouring but never making an end of his meal provided by the palpitating wasp in his arms while the others bobbed on gently around them.

Zoborov fixed his frown of quizzical reproof upon them, and stuttered thickly in the beard that was not there:

'Les deux tourrterreaux!' [1]

The cider was of good quality, and it was plentiful, being drawn from a large cask. Carl and Mademoiselle Péronnette in the intervals of the music remained in a deep embrace by the side of the fire. At length, when the fête had been in progress for perhaps half an hour, they withdrew, so coiled about one another that they experienced some difficulty in getting out of the door.

Zoborov drew my attention to their departure.

'The two doves are going to their nest to lie down for a little while!' he remarked, with the bluff rolling jocosity of Zoborov celebrating.

Zoborov now took charge, and the party became all-russian. He fetched his flute and another pensionnaire had an accordion: a concert of russian popular music began. The Volga Boat Song was chorally rendered, with Zoborov beating time.

At the end of a quarter of an hour Mademoiselle Péronnette and Carl

---

1 The two doves.

reappeared. Carl was pale and Mademoiselle Péronnette very red. She affected to fan herself. Carl's monotonous grin attached itself to the faces of the company with its unfailing brutal confession, hang-dog to stress its obscene message, while his sleek and shining black hair curled venerably behind, where a hasty brush and comb had arranged it.

'Qu'il fait *chaud!'* [1] exclaimed Mademoiselle Péronnette, and drew down a window.

Zoborov took no notice of the reappearance of the turtle doves, but continued his concert. After a while Mademoiselle Péronnette showed signs of impatience. She got up, and advancing towards her choir of pensionnaires, who were gathered round the fire in a half-circle, she exclaimed:

'What do you say to another dance, now, my friends? Let somebody play the piano. Your russian music is very pretty but it is so sad. It always makes me sad. Let us have something more cheerful.'

A pensionnaire got up and went to the piano. Zoborov remained near the fire. The dance began half-heartedly. Zoborov went on playing the flute to himself, his little peaked mouth drawn down to the mouthpiece, his little finger remaining erect while he sampled the feeble sound.

The 'Poles' of the Pension sat and gazed, like a group of monks bowed down with many vows, at their proprietress and her german lover, while one of their number made music for this voluptuous couple, so strangely different from them. Their leader, Zoborov, continued to draw a few notes out of his flute, the skeleton of a melancholy air. Then two or three rose and embraced each other awkwardly, and began to move round the room, shuffling their feet, out of consideration for their worldly hostess. The parisian schoolmaster and his bonne amie also accommodated.

The kitchen door opened and a group of eleven Russians entered, friends of Zoborov, whom he had invited. They had come over from a neighbouring Pension. He rose and greeted them in impressive gutturals, lurching huskily about. They moved to the bottom of the kitchen, were provided with cups, and drew cider from the barrel. There were now about thirty Russians in the room. A few were dancing languidly. Mademoiselle Péronnette and Carl were indulging in a deep kiss midway in their career. Zoborov, when his visitors had refreshed themselves, crossed the kitchen with them and they left. He was going to show them over the establishment.

'I ask you!' said Mademoiselle Péronnette to Mademoiselle Maraude. 'Quel toupet, quand même!' [2]

Mademoiselle Maraude, to whom I had been talking, gazed after Zoborov.

'En effet!' she said.

---

1 "It's hot in here!"

2 "What cheek!"

'One would think that the house belonged to him!' exclaimed Mademoiselle Péronette. 'He brings a band of strangers in here—— I might not exist at all, for all I am consulted! What an ill-mannered individual!'

'C'est un paysan, quoi!'[1] Mademoiselle Maraude folded her hands in her lap with dignified deliberation. Carl grinned at both of them in turn. Zoborov returned with his friends. Mademoiselle Péronnette burst out:

'Monsieur! One would say that you have forgotten to whom this house belongs! You bring your friends in here and take no more notice of me than if I were the bonne. I am the proprietress of this establishment, gentlemen and this,' turning to Carl, 'my fiancé, is now my partner.'

Zoborov advanced sleepily towards Mademoiselle Péronnette, a blustering complaint blowing from his mouth as he came, rolling and blowing lazily before him.

'But, Mademoiselle Péronnette, I don't understand you, really. You asked us to invite anybody we liked.—These are good friends of mine. I have just shown them over the house out of kindness to *you*. I was advertising your Pension!'

'I'm quite capable of doing that myself, Monsieur Zoborov!'

'You can't have too much advertisement!' said Zoborov genially.

Carl, who had stood with his dark sheepish grin on his face, gave a loud and unexpected laugh. Quickly raising his arm, he brought his hand down on Zoborov's back. He then kneaded with his long white fingers Zoborov's muscular shoulder.

'Zagré[2] Zoborov!' he exclaimed, shaking with guttural mirth, 'that's capital! I and my partner appoint you as our agent!'

Rolling gently in contact with the hearty mannerisms of his german friend, glancing up quickly with shrewd conciliation, Zoborov blustered out pleasantly:

'Good! I'll be your factor. That's fixed.—Congratulations, old fellow, on your promotion!—What is my salary?'

'We pay by results!' grinned Carl.

'Well, here is one gentleman already who wishes to come round and reside here.'

He pointed to a ragged figure lurking absentmindedly in the rear of the group. 'I shall expect my commission when he moves in.'

Mademoiselle did not like this conversation, and now said:

'I've got quite enough Russians here already. I should be more obliged to you if you found a few Parisians or Americans. That's what I should like.'

'En effet!' said Mademoiselle Maraude distinctly, under her breath.

---

1 "He's a peasant, that's all!"

2 I.e., "sacré": "you devil."

The tactful pensionnaire at the piano began playing a viennese waltz. Mademoiselle Péronnette, still boiling, drew Carl away, saying:

'C'est trop fort![1] How that man irritates me, how he irritates me! He's *malin*,[2] also, he is treacherous! He always has an answer, have you noticed? He's never without an answer. He's as rusé[2] as a peasant—but, anyhow, he *is* a peasant, so that's to be expected. How he irritates me!'

Carl rumbled along incoherently beside her, bending down, his arms dangling, his stoop accentuated.

'Oh, he means no harm!' he said.

'Not so. He's a treacherous individual, I tell you!'

Carl put his arm around her waist, and kicking his large flat feet about for a few moments, jerked her into a brisk dance, which with reluctant and angry undulations she followed. As they flew round, in angular sweeps, describing a series of rough squares, a discontented clamour still escaped from her.

A little later the Russians began singing the Volga Boat Song, at the bottom of the room, Zoborov again acting as conductor. Mademoiselle Péronnette put her fingers in her ears.

'Mon dieu, quelle vilaine musique que celle-là!'[3] she exclaimed.

'En effet!' said Mademoiselle Maraude, 'elle n'est pas bien belle!'[4]

'En effet!' said Mademoiselle Péronnette.

Carl was pouring himself out a cognac, and in a blunt and booming bass was intoning the air with the others. Mademoiselle Péronnette left the room. After an interval Carl followed her.

I went over and talked by the fire to the pensionnaire who usually played the piano. Zoborov came up, his chest protruding, and his eyes almost closed, and sat down heavily beside us.

'Well, my friend, what do you think of Mademoiselle Péronnette's new *partner?*' he laughed with a gruff gentle rattle.

'Carl, do you mean?'

'Why, yes, Carl!' he again gave way to soft rumbling laughter. 'I wish them luck of their partnership. They are a likely pair, I am bound to say!'

The pianist gazed into the fire.

'What time do you leave in the morning?' he asked.

'At ten.' We talked about Vannes, to which I was going first. He seemed to know Brittany very well. He gave several yawns, gazing over towards his animated crowd of compatriots.

'It's time we went to bed. I shall get rid of this lot,' he said, getting up.

---

1 "It's too much!"

2 "Cunning, shrewd."

3 "What ugly music that is!"

4 "It certainly isn't very pretty!"

'Come along, my children,' he exclaimed. 'To bed! We're going to bed!'

Several hurried up to him excitedly. They talked for some minutes in russian. Again he raised his voice.

'Let's go to bed, my friends! It's late.'

Mademoiselle Péronnette entered the kitchen. Zoborov, without looking in her direction, put out his hand and switched off the lights. A roar of surprise, laughter and scuffling ensued. The fire lighted up the faces of those sitting near us, and a restless mass beyond.

'Will you be so kind, Monsieur Zoborov, as to put on the lights at once!' the voice of Mademoiselle Péronnette clamoured. 'Monsieur Zoborov, do you hear me? Put on the lights immediately!' Suddenly the lights were switched on again. Mademoiselle Péronnette had done it herself.

'Will you allow me, Monsieur Zoborov, to manage my own house? At last I have had enough of your ways! You are an insolent personage. You are an ill-conditioned individual!'

Zoborov's eyes were now completely closed, apparently with sleep that could not be put off. He blustered plaintively back without opening them:

'But, Mademoiselle! I thought you'd gone to bed! Some one had to get all these people out! I don't understand you. Truly I don't understand you at all! Still, now that you're here I can go to bed! I'm dropping with sleep! Good-night! Good-night!' he sang gruffly as he rolled out, raising his brawny paw several times in farewell.

'Quel homme que celui-là![1] Quel homme!' said Mademoiselle Péronnette, gazing into the eyes of Mademoiselle Maraude, who had come up.

'En effet!' said Mademoiselle Maraude. 'For a pensionnaire who never pays his "pension," he is a cool hand!'

That night the new partners had their first business disagreement in the bedroom of the proprietress. I heard their voices booming and rattling for a long time before the door opened. It burst open at last. Mademoiselle Péronnette shouted:

'Bring me the fifteen thousand francs you have stolen from me, you indelicate personage, and I will then return you your papers. If your father knew of your conduct what would he think? Do you suppose he would like to think that he had a son who was nothing but a crook? Yes, crook! Our partnership begins from the moment of the first *versement*[2] that you have promised, do you understand? And I require the money at once, you hear? At once!'

A furious rumble came from outside my door.

'No, I have heard that before! Enough! I will hear no more.'

A second rumble answered.

---

[1] "What a man!"

[2] "Payment."

'What, you accuse me of that? You ungrateful individual, you have the face to——'

A long explanatory muted rumble followed.

'Never!' she screamed. 'Never, while I live! I will sign nothing! That's flat! I would never have believed it possible——'

A rumble came from a certain distance down the passage.

'Yes, you had better go! You do well to slink away! But I'll see you don't get far, my bird. You will be held for *escroquerie*, yes, *escroquerie!*[1] at the nearest commissariat! Don't make any mistake!'

A distant note sounded, like the brief flatulence of an elephant. I took it to be 'Gourte!'

'Ah yes, my pretty bird!' vociferated Mademoiselle Péronnette. 'Wait a bit! You may vilify me now. That is the sort of person you are! That I should have expected! But we shall see! We shall see!'

There was no answer. There was a short silence. Mademoiselle Péronnette's door crashed to.

The next morning I left at ten.

A year later I went to the Pardon at Rot.[1] I was sitting amongst the masses of black-clothed figures at a minor wedding, when I saw a figure approaching that appeared familiar. Five peasants were rolling along in their best sabots and finest flat black hats, one in the middle holding the rest with some story he was telling, with heavy dare-devil gestures, as they closed in deferentially upon him as they walked. In the middle one I recognized Zoborov. He was now dressed completely as a breton peasant, in black cloth a half-inch thick, of the costliest manufacture. He rocked from side to side, stumbling at any largish cobble, chest up and out, a double chin descending spoon-shaped and hard beneath upon his short neck, formed as a consequence of the muscular arrangements for the production of his deep bass. His mouth protruded like the mouths of stone masks used for fountains.

As he shouldered his way impressively forward, he made gestures of condescending recognition to left and right, as he caught sight of somebody he knew. His fellow peasants responded with eager salutes or flattering obeisances.

As he caught sight of me he stumbled heartily towards me, his mouth belled out, as though mildly roaring, one large rough hand held back in readiness to grasp mine.

'Why, so you are back again in this part of the country, are you? I am glad to see you! How are you?' he said. 'Come inside, I know the patronne here. I'll get her to give us some good cider.'

We all went in. The patronne saw us and made her way through the crowd

---

1 "Swindling."

at once to Zoborov. Her malignant white face, bald at the sides, as usual with the breton woman, shone with sweat; she came up whining deferentially. With his smiling frown, and the gruff caress of his artificial roar, Zoborov greeted her, and went with her into a parlour next to the kitchen. We followed.

'Bring us three bottles of the best cider, Madame Mordouan,' he said.

'Why yes, Monsieur Zoborov, certainly, immediately,' she said, and obsequiously withdrew.

Zoborov was fatter. The great thickness of the new suiting made him appear very big indeed. The newness and stiffness of the breton fancy dress, the shining broadcloth and velvet, combined with the noticeable filling out of his face, resulted in a disagreeable impression of an obese doll or gigantic barber's block.

'You look prosperous,' I said.

'Do you think so? I'm *en breton*[1] now, you see! When are you coming over to see us at *Beau Séjour?* This gentleman was at *Beau Séjour*,' he said, turning to his friends. 'Are you stopping in the neighbourhood? I'll send the trap over for you.'

'The trap? Have they a trap now?'

'A trap? Why yes, my friend. There have been great changes since you were at *Beau Séjour!*'

'Indeed. Of what kind?'

'Of *every* kind, my friend!'

'How is Mademoiselle Péronnette?'

'Oh, she's gone, long ago!'

'Indeed!'

'Why yes, she and old Carl left soon after you.' He paused a moment. 'I am the proprietor now!'

'You!'

'Why yes, my friend, me! Mademoiselle Péronnette went bust. *Beau Séjour* was sold at auction as it stood. It was not expensive. I took the place on.—Mais oui, mon ami, je suis maintenant le propriétaire!'[2] He seized me by the shoulder, then lightly tapped me there. 'C'est drôle, n'est-ce pas?'[3]

I seemed to hear the voice of Mademoiselle Maraude replying, 'En effet.'

'En effet!' I said.

He offered himself banteringly as the comic proprietor. Fancy Zoborov being the proprietor of a french hotel! He turned, frowning menacingly, however, towards the peasants, and raised his glass with solemn eye. I raised mine. They raised their glasses like a peasant chorus.

---

[1] "Dressed as a Breton."

[2] "Yes, my friend, I'm the owner now!"

[3] "Funny, isn't it?"

'What has become of Carl?' I asked.

'Carl? Oh I don't know what's become of Carl! He's gone to the devil, I should think!'

I saw that I was obtruding other histories upon the same footing with his, into a new world where they had no place. They were a part of the old bad days.

'How are the Russians, "les Polonais"?'

He looked at me for a moment, his eyes closing in his peculiar withdrawal or sleep.

'Oh, I've cleared all that rubbish out! I've got a chic hotel now! It is really quite comfortable. You should come over. I have several Americans, there's an Englishman, Kenyon, do you know him? His father is a celebrated architect.—I only have three Russians there now. I kept them on, poor devils. They help me with the work. Two act as valets.—I know what Russians are, being one myself, you see! I have no wish to go bankrupt like Mademoiselle Péronnette.'

I was rather richly dressed at the time, and I was glad. I ordered for the great 'peasant' and his satellites another bottle of the ceremonious cider.

THE POLE[9]

In pre-war Europe, which was also even more the Europe of before the Russian Revolution, a curious sect was established in the watering-places of Brittany. Its members were generally known by the peasants as 'Poles.' The so-called 'Pole' was a russian exile or wandering student, often coming from Poland. The sort that collected in such great numbers in Brittany were probably not politicians, except in the sentimental manner in which all educated Russians before the Revolution were 'radical' and revolutionary. They had banished themselves, for purely literary political reasons, it is likely, rather than been banished. Brittany became a heavenly Siberia for masses of middle-class russian men and women who made 'art' the excuse for a never-ending holiday. They insensibly became a gentle and delightful parasite upon the French. Since the Revolution (it being obvious that they cannot have vast and lucrative estates, which before the Revolution it was easy for them to claim) they have mostly been compelled to work. The Paris taxi-driver of to-day, lolling on the seat of his vehicle, cigarette in mouth, who, without turning round, swiftly moves away when a fare enters his cab, is what in the ancien régime would have been a 'Pole.' If there is a communist revolution in France, this sort of new nomad will move down into Spain perhaps. He provides for the countries of Europe on a very insignificant scale a new version, to-day, of the 'jewish problem.' His indolence, not his activity, of course, makes him a 'problem.'

The pre-war method of migration was this. A 'Pole' in his home in Russia would save up or borrow about ten pounds. He then left his native land for ever, taking a third-class ticket to Brest. This must have become an almost instinctive proceeding. At Brest he was in the heart of the promised land. He would then make the best of his way to a Pension de Famille, already occupied by a phalanstery of 'Poles.' There he would have happily remained until the crack of doom, but for the Bolshevik Revolution. He had reckoned without Lenin, so to speak.

He was usually a 'noble,' very soberly but tactfully dressed. He wore suède gloves: his manners were graceful. The proprietress had probably been warned of his arrival and he was welcome. His first action would be to pay three months' board and lodging in advance; that would also be his last action of that sort. With a simple dignity that was the secret of the 'Pole,' at the end of the trimester, he remained as the guest of the proprietress. His hostess took this as a matter of course. He henceforth became the regular, unobtrusive, respected inhabitant of the house.

If the proprietress of a Pension de Famille removed her establishment from one part of the country to another, took a larger house, perhaps (to make room for more 'Poles'), her 'Poles' went with her without comment or change in their habits. Just before the war, Mademoiselle T. still sheltered in her magnificent hotel, frequented by wealthy Americans, some of these quiet 'Poles,' who had been with her since the day when she first began hotel-keeping in a small wayside inn. Lunching there you could observe at the foot of the table a group of men of a monastic simplicity of dress and manner, all middle-aged by that time, indeed even venerable in several instances, talking among themselves in a strange and attractive tongue. Mademoiselle T. was an amiable old lady, and these were her domestic gods. Any one treating them with disrespect would have seen the rough side of Mademoiselle T.'s tongue.

Their hosts, I believe, so practical in other ways, became superstitious about these pensive inhabitants of their houses. Some I know would no more have turned out an old and ailing 'Pole' who owed them thirty years' board and lodging, than many people would get rid of an aged and feeble cat.

For the breton peasant, 'Polonais' or 'Pole' sufficed to describe the member of any nation whom he observed leading anything that resembled the unaccountable life of the true slav parasite with which he had originally familiarized himself under the name of 'Pole.'

Few 'Poles,' I think, ever saw the colour of money once this initial pin-money that they brought from Russia was spent. One 'Pole' of my acquaintance did get hold of three pounds by some means, and went to spend a month in Paris. After this outing, his prestige considerably enhanced, he came back and resumed his regular life, glad to be again away from the *siècle* and its metropolitan degradation. In pre-war Paris, 'Poles' were to be met, very much *de passage*, seeing some old friends (*en route* for Brest) for the last time.

A woman opened a smart hotel of about thirty beds not far from *Beau Séjour*. I was going over to see it. She advertised that any artist who would at once take up his quarters there would receive his first six months gratis. Referring to this interesting event in the hearing of a 'Pole,' he told me he had been over there the previous day. He had found no less than twelve 'Poles' already installed, and there was a considerable waiting list. 'If you like to pay you can go there all right,' he said, laughing.

The general explanation given by the 'Pole' of the position in which he found himself, was that his hosts, after six or nine months, were afraid to let him go, for fear of losing their money. He would add that he could confidently rely on more and more deference the longer he stopped, and the larger the amount that he represented in consequence. Ordinary boarders, he would tell you, could count on nothing like so much attention as he could.

That such a state of affairs should ever have occurred, was partly due perhaps to the patriarchal circumstances of the breton agricultural life. This new domestic animal was able to insinuate himself into its midst because of the existence of so many there already. Rich peasants, and this applied to the proprietors of country inns, were accustomed in their households to suffer the presence of a number of poor familiars, cousinly paupers, supernumeraries doing odd jobs on the farm or in the stables. The people not precisely servants who found a place at their hearth were not all members of the immediate family of the master.

But there was another factor favouring the development of the 'Pole.' This was that many of them were described as painters. They seldom of course were able to practise that expensive art, for they could not buy colours or canvases: in their visitors' bulletins, however, they generally figured as that. But after the death of Gauguin, the dealer, Vollard, and others, came down from Paris. They ransacked the country for forgotten canvases: when they found one they paid to the astonished peasants, in the heat of competition, very considerable sums. Past hosts of the great french romantic had confiscated paintings in lieu of rent. The least sketch had its price. The sight of these breathless collectors, and the rumours of the sums paid, made a deep impression on the local people. The 'Poles' on their side were very persuasive. They assured their hosts that Gauguin was a mere cipher compared to them.—These circumstances told in favour of the 'Pole.'

But no such explanations can really account for the founding of this charming and whimsical order. Whether there are still a few 'Poles' surviving in Brittany or not, I have no means of knowing. In the larger centres of *villégiature*[1] the *siècle*[2] was already paramount before the war.

The Russian with whom translations of the russian books of tsarist Russia familiarized the West was an excited and unstable child. We have seen this society massacred in millions without astonishment. The russian books prepared every

---

[1] Holiday resorts.

[2] Lit. "century," hence "spirit of the age."

Western European for that consummation. All the cast of the *Cherry Orchard* could be massacred easily by a single determined gunman. This defencelessness of the essential Slav can, under certain circumstances, become an asset. Especially perhaps the French would find themselves victims of such a harmless parasite, so different in his nature to themselves. A more energetic parasite would always fail with the gallic nature, unless very resolute.

NOTES

[1] Rosnoën (spelt Roznoën in *The Wild Body*), a village in Finistère.
[2] The proofs gave "clownesque."
[3] The proofs gave "She bought the engagement, was that it?"
[4] "Sacré *garce*" in the first edition, which is ungrammatical and confusing, because feminine. This is Antoinette speaking to Carl, and not to Mademoiselle Péronnette. See the use of "sacré gars" in "Franciscan Adventures." The error was corrected in the American edition.
[5] The proofs gave "between three and four."
[6] The proofs gave "of her capital!"
[7] An image echoed in *Snooty Baronet:* "I took her over in waspish segments," page 45.
[8] An imaginary place also mentioned in "The Death of the Ankou," "Franciscan Adventures," and the 1922 "Bestre."
[9] On no other occasion did Lewis retain one of his earlier analyses. This is understandable—without such a note, "the myth of the Poles" might appear as a gratuitous figment of the author's imagination.

BESTRE

The history of "Bestre" is more complex than that of any of its companions. Alone it went through three successive stages, appearing in print in 1909, 1922 and 1927. Yet it was eventually less modified than "Beau Séjour," for instance, because of the initial dynamism of its central character.

Bestre is certainly the most powerful inmate of the hallucinated world of The Wild Body, *and from the start he offered a veritable intuition of some central aspects of Lewis's future philosophy and aesthetics. Obviously astonished, the author was first led to ask: "Has Bestre discovered the only type of action compatible with artistic creation?" before finally dismissing him as a degenerate. It is not surprising therefore that Lewis should have interrogated this enigmatic archetype and guide more than once and that he should have affectionately called him "Bertie" in "Writings."*

The passage from "Bestre I" to "Bestre II" (published in The Tyro *no. 2 in 1922) will be discussed in the sectional introduction to "Some Innkeepers and Bestre." The 1927 text did not modify the 1922 "Bestre" in any significant way–it only brought numerous minor alterations, and a few telling additions concerning mostly the building up of Ker-Orr's career as a soldier of humour and the further elucidation of Bestre's techniques of aggression.*

What is really important is that, between the second and final versions, Bestre came to be identified as a "Tyro." Internal evidence shows that the story was not specially rewritten for inclusion in The Tyro, *and probably that Lewis came to visualize this new wild population while rewriting "Bestre." Lewis tended to keep the two forms of expression at his disposal separated into tight compartments, and it may be said that the graphic Tyros were the epigones of the early literary wild bodies, and conversely he did not give ample literary life to this second generation of puppets. When Lewis writes that his graphic Tyros are "at once satires, pictures and stories," he could as well be describing "Bestre."*

But there is even more to the matter. Perpetually finding fresh enemies to attack with his eye, Bestre stands as the vital link between the early Lewis of the Breton illuminations and the mature Lewis of The Enemy. In more sense than one was Bestre father of Lewis.

As I walked along the quay at Kermanac,[1] there was a pretty footfall in my rear. Turning my head, I found an athletic frenchwoman,[2] of the bourgeois class, looking at me.

The crocket-like floral postiches on the ridges of her head-gear looked crisped down in a threatening way: her nodular pink veil was an apoplectic gristle round her stormy brow; steam came out of her lips upon the harsh white atmosphere. Her eyes were dark, and the contiguous colour of her cheeks of a redness quasi-venetian, with something like the feminine colouring of battle. This was surely a feline battle-mask, then; but in such a pacific and slumbrous spot I thought it an anomalous ornament.

My dented *bidon*[3] of a hat—cantankerous beard—hungarian[4] boots, the soles like the rind of a thin melon slice, the uppers in stark calcinous segments; my cassock-like blue broadcloth coat (why was I like this—the habits of needy travel grew this composite shell), this uncouthness might have raised in her the question of defiance and offence. I glided swiftly along on my centipedal boots, dragging my eye upon the rough walls of the houses to my right like a listless cane. Low houses faced the small vasey[5] port. It was there I saw Bestre.

This is how I became aware of Bestre.

The detritus of some weeks' hurried experience was being dealt with in my mind, on this crystalline, extremely cold walk through Kermanac to Braspartz,[6] and was being established in orderly heaps. At work in my untidy hive, I was alone: the atmosphere of the workshop dammed me in. That I moved forward was no more strange than if a carpenter's shop or chemist's laboratory, installed in a boat, should move forward on the tide of a stream. Now, what seemed to happen was that, as I bent over my work, an odiously grinning face peered in at my window. The impression of an intrusion was so strong, that I did not even realize at first that it was I who was the intruder. That the window was not my window, and that the face was not peering in but out, that, in fact, it was I myself who was guilty of peering into somebody else's window: this was hidden from me in the first moment of consciousness about the odious brown person of Bestre. It is a wonder that the curse did not at once fall from me on this detestable inquisitive head. What I did do was to pull up in my automatic progress, and, instead of passing on, to continue to stare in at Bestre's kitchen window, and scowl at Bestre's sienna-coloured gourd of a head.

Bestre in his turn was nonplussed. He knew that some one was looking in at his kitchen window, all right: he had expected some one to do so, some one who in fact had contracted the habit of doing that. But he had mistaken my steps for this other person's; and the appearance of my face was in a measure as disturbing to him as his had been to me. My information on these points afterwards became complete. With a flexible imbrication reminiscent of a shutter-lipped ape, a bud of tongue still showing, he shot the latch of his upper lip down in front of the nether one, and depressed the interior extremities of his eyebrows sharply from their quizzing perch—only this monkey-on-a-stick mechanical pull—down the face's centre. At the same time, his arms still folded like bulky lizards, blue tattoo on brown ground, upon the escarpment of his vesicular middle, not a hair or muscle moving, he made a quick, slight motion to me with one hand to get out of the picture without speaking—to efface myself. It was the suggestion of a theatrical sportsman. I was in the line of fire. I moved on: a couple of steps did it. That lady was twenty yards distant: but nowhere was there anything in sight evidently related to Bestre's gestures. 'Pension de Famille?' What prices?—and how charmingly placed! I remarked the vine: the building, of one storey, was exceedingly long, it took some time to pass along it. I reached the principal door. I concluded this entrance was really disused, although more imposing. So emerging on the quay once more, and turning along the front of the house, I again discovered myself in contact with Bestre. He was facing towards me, and down the quay, immobile as before, and the attitude so much a replica as to make it seem a plagiarism of his kitchen piece. Only now his head was on one side, a verminous grin had dispersed the equally unpleasant entity of his shut mouth. The new facial arrangement and angle for the head imposed on what seemed his stock pose for the body, must mean: 'Am I not rather smart? Not just a little bit smart? Don't you think? A little, you will concede? You did not expect that, did you? That was a nasty jar for you, was it not? Ha! my lapin,[1] that was unexpected, that is plain! Did you think you would find Bestre asleep? He is always awake! He watched you being born, and has watched you ever since. Don't be too sure that he did not play some part in planting the little seed from which you grew into such a big, fine (many withering exclamation marks) boy (or girl). He will be in at your finish too. But he is in no hurry about that. He is never in a hurry! He bides his time. Meanwhile he laughs at you. He finds you a little funny. That's right! Yes! I am still looking!'

His very large eyeballs, the small saffron ocellation in their centre, the tiny spot through which light entered the obese wilderness of his body; his bronzed bovine arms, swollen handles for a variety of indolent little ingenuities; his inflated digestive case, lent their combined expressiveness to say these things; with every tart and biting condiment that eye-fluid, flaunting of fatness (the well-filled), the insult of the comic, implications of indecency, could provide. Every variety of bottom-tapping resounded from

1 "Rabbit," hence "crafty one."

his dumb bulk. His tongue stuck out, his lips eructated with the incredible indecorum that appears to be the monopoly of liquids, his brown arms were for the moment genitals, snakes in one massive twist beneath his mamillary slabs, gently riding on a pancreatic swell, each hair on his oil-bearing skin contributing its message of porcine affront.

Taken fairly in the chest by this magnetic attack, I wavered. Turning the house corner it was like confronting a hard meaty gust. But I perceived that the central gyroduct passed a few feet clear of me. Turning my back, arching it a little, perhaps, I was just in time to receive on the boko [1] a parting volley from the female figure of the obscure encounter, before she disappeared behind a rock which brought Kermanac to a close on this side of the port. She was evidently replying to Bestre. It was the rash grating philippic of a battered cat, limping into safety. At the moment that she vanished behind the boulder, Bestre must have vanished too, for a moment later the quay was empty. On reaching the door into which he had sunk, plump and slick as into a stage trap, there he was inside—this greasebred old mammifer—his tufted vertex charging about the plank ceiling—generally ricochetting like a dripping sturgeon in a boat's bottom[7]—arms warm brown, ju-jitsu of his guts, tan canvas shoes and trousers rippling in ribbed planes as he darted about—with a filthy snicker for the scuttling female, and a stark cock of the eye for an unknown figure miles to his right: he filled this short tunnel with clever parabolas and vortices, little neat stutterings of triumph, goggle-eyed hypnotisms, in retrospect, for his hearers.

'T'as vu? T'as vu? Je l'ai fichu c'es' qu'elle n'attendait pas! Ah, la rosse! Qu'elle aille raconter ça à sa crapule de mari. Si, si, s'il vient ici tu sais——'[2] His head nodded up and down in batches of blood-curdling affirmations; his hand, pudgy hieratic disc, tapped the air gently, then sawed tenderly up and down.

Bestre, on catching sight of me, hailed me as a witness. 'Tiens! Ce monsieur peut vous le dire: il était là. Il m'a vu là-dedans qui l'attendais![3]

I bore witness to the subtleties of his warlike ambush. I told his sister and two boarders that I had seldom been privy to such a rich encounter. They squinted at me, and at each other, dragging their eyes off with slow tosses of the head. I took a room in this house immediately—the stage-box in fact, just above the kitchen. For a week I was perpetually entertained.

---

[1] British slang for "nose."

[2] Ungrammatical: "Did you see? Did you see? I gave her what she didn't expect! Ah, the bitch! Let her report this to her husband, the bastard! Yes, yes, if he ever comes here, you know—" The American edition correctly prints "sa crapule"; the English edition had "son crapule."

[3] "Ah! This gentleman can confirm it. He was there. He saw me inside waiting for her." (The English edition incorrectly printed "attendait.")

Before attempting to discover the significance of Bestre's proceedings when I clattered into the silken zone of his hostilities, I settled down in his house; watched him idly from both my windows—from that looking on to the back—(cleaning his gun in the yard, killing chickens, examining the peas), from the front one—rather shyly sucking up to a fisherman upon the quay. I went into his kitchen and his shed and watched him. I realized as little as he did that I was patting and prodding a subject of these stories.[8] There was no intention in these stoppages on my zigzag course across Western France of taking a human species, as an entomologist would take a Distoma or a Narbonne Lycosa, to study. Later, at the time of my spanish adventure (which was separated by two years from Bestre), I had grown more professional. Also, I had become more conscious of myself and of my powers of personally provoking a series of typhoons in tea-cups. But with my Bretons I was very new to my resources, and was living in a mild and early millennium of mirth.[9] It was at the end of a few months' roaming in the country that I saw I had been a good deal in contact with a tribe, some more and some less generic. And it is only now that it has seemed to me an amusing labour to gather some of these individuals in retrospect and group them under their function, to which all in some diverting way were attached.

So my stoppage at Kermanac, for example, was because Bestre was a little excitement. I had never seen brown flesh put to those uses. And the situation of his boarding-house would allow of unlimited pococurantism, idling and eating,[10] sunning myself in one of my windows, with Berkeley or Cudworth in my hand, and a staring eye that lost itself in reveries that suddenly took on flesh and acted some obstinate little part or other, the phases of whose dramatic life I would follow stealthily from window to window, a book still in my hand, shaking with the most innocent laughter. I was never for a minute unoccupied. Fête followed fête, fêtes of the mind. Then, as well, the small cliffs of the scurfy little port, its desertion and queer train of life, reached a system of very early dreams I had considered effaced. But all the same, although not self-conscious, I went laughing after Bestre, tapping him, setting traps for the game that he decidedly contained for my curiosity. So it was almost as though Fabre[11] could have established himself within the masonries of the bee, and lived on its honey, while investigating for the human species: or stretched himself on a bed of raphia and pebbles at the bottom of the Lycosa's pit, and lived on flies and locusts. I lay on Bestre's billowy beds, drank his ambrosial cider, fished from his boat; he brought me birds and beasts that he had chased and killed. It was an idyllic life of the calmest adventure. We were the best of friends: he thought I slapped him because contact with his fat gladdened me, and to establish contact with the feminine vein in his brown-coated ducts and muscles. Also he was Bestre, and it must be nice to pat and buffet him as it would be to do that with a dreadful lion.

He offered himself, sometimes wincing coquettishly, occasionally rolling his eyes a little, as the lion might do to remind you of your natural dread, and heighten the luxurious privilege.

Bestre's boarding-house is only open from June to October: the winter months he passes in hunting and trapping. He is a stranger to Kermanac, a Boulonnais,[1] and at constant feud with the natives. For some generations his family have been strangers where they lived; and he carries on his face the mark of an origin even more distant than Picardy. His great-grandfather came into France from the Peninsula, with the armies of Napoleon. Possibly his alertness, combativeness and timidity are the result of these exilings and difficult adjustments to new surroundings, working in his blood, and in his own history.

He is a large, tall man, corpulent and ox-like: you can see by his movements that the slow aggrandisement of his stomach has hardly been noticed by him. It is still compact with the rest of his body, and he is as nimble as a flea. It has been for him like the peculations of a minister, enriching himself under the nose of the caliph; Bestre's kingly indifference can be accounted for by the many delights and benefits procured through this subtle misappropriation of the general resources of the body. Sunburnt, with large yellow-white moustache, little eyes protruding with the cute strenuosity already noticed, when he meets any one for the first time his mouth stops open, a cigarette end adhering to the lower lip. He will assume an expression of expectancy and repressed amusement, like a man accustomed to nonplussing: the expression the company wears in those games of divination when they have made the choice of an object, and he whose task it is to guess its nature is called in, and commences the cross-examination. Bestre is jocose; he will beset you with mocking thoughts as the blindfold man is danced round in a game of blind man's buff. He may have regarded my taps as a myopic clutch at his illusive person. He gazes at a new acquaintance as though this poor man, without guessing it, were entering a world of astonishing things! A would-be boarder arrives and asks him if he has a room with two beds. Bestre fixes him steadily for twenty seconds with an amused yellow eye. Without uttering a word, he then leads the way to a neighbouring door, lets the visitor pass into the room, stands watching him with the expression of a conjurer who has just drawn a curtain aside and revealed to the stupefied audience a horse and cart, or a life-size portrait of the Shah of Persia,[12] where a moment ago there was nothing.

Suppose the following thing happened. A madman, who believes himself a hen, escapes from Charenton, and gets, somehow or other, as far as Finis-

---

[1] A native of Boulogne.

tère. He turns up at Kermanac, knocks at Bestre's door and asks him with a perfect stereotyped courtesy for a large, airy room, with a comfortable perch to roost on, and a little straw in the corner where he might sit. Bestre a few days before has been visited by the very idea of arranging such a room: all is ready. He conducts his demented client to it. Now his manner with his everyday client would be thoroughly appropriate under these circumstances. They are carefully suited to a very weak-minded and whimsical visitor indeed.

Bestre has another group of tricks, pertaining directly to the commerce of his hospitable trade. When a customer is confessing in the fullest way his paraesthesias, allowing this new host an engaging glimpse of his nastiest propriums and kinks, Bestre behaves, with unconscious logic, as though a secret of the most disreputable nature were being imparted to him. Were, in fact, the requirements of a vice being enumerated, he could not display more plainly the qualms caused by his rôle of accessory. He will lower his voice, whisper in the client's ear; before doing so glance over his shoulder apprehensively two or three times, and push his guest roughly into the darkest corner of the passage or kitchen. It is his perfect understanding—is he not the only man who does, at once, forestall your eager whim: there is something of the fortune-teller in him—that produces the air of mystery. For his information is not always of the nicest, is it? He must know more about you than I daresay you would like many people to know. And Bestre will in his turn mention certain little delicacies that he, Bestre, will see that you have, and that the other guests will not share with you. So there you are committed at the start to a subtle collusion. But Bestre means it. Every one he sees for the first time he is thrilled about, until they have got used to him. He would give you anything while he is still strange to you. But you see the interest die down in his eyes, at the end of twenty-four hours, whether you have assimilated him or not. He only gives you about a day for your meal. He then assumes that you have finished him, and he feels chilled by your scheduled disillusion. A fresh face and an enemy he depends on for that 'new' feeling—or what can we call this firework that he sends up for the stranger, that he enjoys so much himself—or this rare bottle he can only open when hospitality compels—his own blood?

I had arrived at the master-moment of one of Bestre's campaigns. These were long and bitter affairs. But they consisted almost entirely of dumb show. The few words that passed were generally misleading. A vast deal of talking went on in the different camps. But a dead and pulverizing silence reigned on the field of battle, with few exceptions.

It was a matter of who could be most silent and move least: it was a stark stand-up fight between one personality and another, unaided by adventitious muscle or tongue. It was more like phases of a combat or courtship in the insect-world. The Eye was really Bestre's weapon: the ammunition with which he loaded it was drawn from all the most skunk-like provender, the most ugly mucins, fungoid glands, of his physique. Excrement as well as sputum would be shot from this luminous hole, with the same certainty in its unsavoury appulsion. Every resource of metonymy, bloody mind transfusion or irony were also his. What he selected as an arm in his duels, then, was the Eye. As he was always the offended party, he considered that he had this choice. I traced the predilection for this weapon and method to a very fiery source—to the land of his ancestry—Spain. How had the knife dropped out of his outfit? Who can tell? But he retained the *mirada* whole and entire enough to please any one, all the more active for the absence of the dagger. I pretend that Bestre behaved as he did directly because his sweet forebears had to rely so much on the furious languishing and jolly conversational properties of their eyes to secure their ends at all. The spanish beauty imprisoned behind her casement can only roll her eyes at her lover in the street below. The result of these and similar Eastern restraint develops the eye almost out of recognition. Bestre in his kitchen, behind his casement, was unconsciously employing this gift from his semi-arabian past. And it is not even the unsupported female side of Bestre. For the lover in the street as well must keep his eye in constant training to bear out the furibond jugular drops, the mettlesome stamping, of the guitar. And all the haughty chevaleresque habits of this bellicose race have substituted the eye for the mouth in a hundred ways. The Grandee's eye is terrible, and at his best is he not speechless with pride? Eyes, eyes: for defiance, for shrivelling subordinates, for courtesy, for love. A 'spanish eye' might be used as we say, 'Toledo blade.' There, anyway, is my argument; I place on the one side Bestre's eye; on the other I isolate the iberian eye. Bestre's grandfather, we know, was a Castilian. To show how he was beholden to this extraction, and again how the blood clung to him, Bestre was in no way grasping. It went so far that he was noticably careless about money. This, in France, could not be accounted for in any other way.

Bestre's quarrels turned up as regularly as work for a good shoemaker or dentist. Antagonism after antagonism flashed forth: became more acute through several weeks: detonated in the dumb pyrotechnic I have described; then wore itself out with its very exhausting and exacting violence.—At the passing of an enemy Bestre will pull up his blind with a snap. There he is, with his insult stewing lusciously in his yellow sweat. The eyes fix on the enemy, on his weakest spot, and do their work. He has the anatomical instinct of the hymenopter for his prey's most morbid spot; for an old wound; for a lurking vanity. He goes into the other's eye, seeks it, and strikes. On a physical blemish he turns a scornful and careless rain like a garden hose. If the deep vanity is on the wearer's back, or in his walk or gaze, he sluices it with an abundance you would not expect his small eyes to be capable of delivering.

But the *mise en scène* for his successes is always the same. Bestre is *discovered* somewhere, behind a blind, in a doorway, beside a rock, when least expected. He regards the material world as so many ambushes for his body.

Then the key principle of his strategy is provocation. The enemy must be exasperated to the point at which it is difficult for him to keep his hands off his aggressor. The desire to administer the blow is as painful as a blow received. That the blow should be taken back into the enemy's own bosom, and that he should be stifled by his own oath—*that* Bestre regards as so many blows, and so much abuse, of *his*, Bestre's, although he has never so much as taken his hands out of his pockets, or opened his mouth.

I learnt a great deal from Bestre. He is one of my masters. When the moment came for me to discover myself—a thing I believe few people have done so thoroughly, so early in life and so quickly—I recognized more and more the beauty of Bestre. I was only prevented from turning my eye upon myself even at that primitive period of speculative adolescence by that one-sidedness that only the most daring tamper with.[13]

The immediate quay-side neighbours of Bestre afford him a constant war-food. I have seen him slipping out in the evening and depositing refuse in front of his neighbour's house. I have seen a woman screeching at him in pidgin french from a window of the débit two doors off, while he pared his nails a yard from his own front door. This was to show his endurance. The subtle notoriety, too, of his person is dear to him. But local functionaries and fishermen are not his only fare. During summer, time hangs heavy with the visitor from Paris. When the first ennui comes upon him, he wanders about desperately, and his eye in due course falls on Bestre.

It depends how busy Bestre is at the moment. But often enough he will take on the visitor at once in his canine way. The visitor shivers, opens his eyes, bristles at the quizzing pursuit of Bestre's œillade; the remainder of his holiday flies in a round of singular plots, passionate conversations and prodigious encounters with this born broiler.

Now, a well-known painter and his family, who rented a house in the neighbourhood, were, it seemed, particularly responsive to Bestre. I could not—arrived, with some perseverance, at the bottom of it—find any cause for his quarrel. The most insignificant pretext was absent. The pretentious peppery Paris Salon artist, and this Boulogne-bred Breton inhabited the same village, and they grew larger and larger in each other's eyes at a certain moment, in this armorican wilderness. As Bestre swelled and swelled for the painter, he was seen to be the possessor of some insult incarnate, that was an intolerable factor in the life of so lonely a place. War was inevitable. Bestre saw himself growing and growing, with the glee of battle in his heart, and the flicker of budding affront in his little eye. He did nothing to arrest this alarming aggrandizement. Pretexts could have been found: but they were dispensed with, by mutual consent. This is how I reconstructed the obscure and early phases of that history. What is certain, is that there had been much eye-play on the quay between Monsieur Rivière and Monsieur Bestre. And the scene that I had taken part in was the culmination of a rather humiliating phase in the annals of Bestre's campaigns.

The distinguished painter's wife, I learnt, had contracted the habit of passing Bestre's kitchen window of a morning when Mademoiselle Marie was alone there—gazing glassily in, but never looking at Mademoiselle Marie. This had such a depressing effect on Bestre's old sister, that it reduced her vitality considerably, and in the end brought on diarrhœa. Why did Bestre permit the war to be brought into his own camp with such impunity? The only reason that I could discover for this was, that the attacks were of very irregular timing. He had been out fishing in one or two cases, employed in his garden or elsewhere. But on the penultimate occasion Madame Rivière had practically finished off the last surviving female of Bestre's notable stock. As usual, the wife of the parisian Salon master had looked into the kitchen; but this time she had looked *at* Mademoiselle Marie, and in such a way as practically to curl her up on the floor. Bestre's sister had none of her brother's ferocity, and in every way departed considerably from his type, except in a mild and sentimental imitation of his colouring. The distinguished painter's wife, on the other hand, had a touch of Bestre about her. Bestre did not have it all his own way. Because of this, recognizing the redoubtable and Bestre-like quality of his enemy, he had resorted no doubt to such extreme measures as I suspect him of employing. She had chosen her own ground—his kitchen. That was a vast mistake. On that ground, I am satisfied, Bestre was invincible. It was even surprising that there any trump should have been lavished.[14]

On that morning when I drifted into the picture what happened to induce such a disarray in his opponent? What superlative shaft, with deadly aim, did he direct against her vitals? She would take only a few seconds to pass the kitchen window. He had brought her down with a stupendous rush.[15] In principle, as I have said, Bestre sacrifices the claims any individual portion of his anatomy might have to independent expressiveness to a tyrannical appropriation of all this varied battery of bestial significance by his *eye*. The eye was his chosen weapon.[16] Had he any theory, however, that certain occasions warranted, or required, the auxiliary offices of some unit of the otherwise subordinated mass? Can the sex of his assailant give us a clue? I am convinced in my own mind that another agent was called in on this occasion. I am certain that he struck the death-blow with another engine than his eye. I believe that the most savage and obnoxious means of affront were employed to cope with the distinguished painter's wife. His rejoinder would perhaps be of that unanswerable description, that it would be stamped on the spot, for an adversary, as an authentic last word. No further appeal to arms of that sort would be rational: it must have been right up against litigation and physical assault.[17]

Monsieur Rivière, with his painting-pack and campstool, came along the quay shortly afterwards, going in the same direction as his wife. Bestre was at his door; and he came in later, and let us know how he had behaved.

'I wasn't such a fool as to insult him: there were witnesses; let him do that. But if I come upon him in one of those lanes at the back there, you know . . . I was standing at my door; he came along and looked at my house and scanned my windows' (this is equivalent in Bestre-warfare to a bombardment). 'As he passed I did not move. I thought to myself, "Hurry home, old fellow, and ask Madame what she has seen during her little walk!" *I looked him in the white of the eyes.* He thought I'd lower mine; he doesn't know me. And, after all, what is he, though he's got the Riband of the Legion of Honour? I don't carry my decorations on my coat! I have mine marked on my body. Did I ever show you what I've got here? No; I'm going to show you.' He had shown all this before, but my presence encouraged a repetition of former sucesses. So while he was speaking he jumped up quickly, undid his shirt, bared his chest and stomach, and pointed to something beneath his arm. Then, rapidly rolling up his sleeves, he pointed to a cicatrice rather like a vaccination mark, but larger. While showing his scars he slaps his body, with a sort of sneering rattle or chuckle between his words, his eyes protruding more than usual. His customary wooden expression is disintegrated: this compound of a constant foreboded reflection of the expression of astonishment your face will acquire when you learn of his wisdom, valour, or wit: the slightest shade of sneering triumph, and a touch of calm relish at your wonder. Or he seems teaching you by his staring grimace the amazement you should feel: and his grimace gathers force and blooms as the full sense of what you are witnessing, bearing, bursts upon you, while your gaping face conforms more and more to Bestre's prefiguring mask.

As to his battles, Bestre is profoundly unaware of what strange category he has got himself into. The principles of his strategy are possibly the possession of his libido,[18] but most certainly not that of the bulky and surface citizen, Bestre. On the contrary, he considers himself on the verge of a death struggle at any moment when in the presence of one of his enemies.

Like all people who spend their lives talking about their deeds, he presents a very particular aspect in the moment of action. When discovered in the thick of one of his dumb battles, he has the air of a fine company promoter, concerned, trying to corrupt some sombre fact into shielding for an hour his unwieldy fiction, until some fresh wangle can retrieve it. Or he will display a great empirical expertness in reality, without being altogether at home in it.

Bestre in the moment of action feels as though he were already talking. His action has the exaggerated character of his speech, only oddly curbed by the exigencies of reality. In his moments of most violent action he retains something of his dumb passivity. He never seems quite entering into reality, but observing it. He is looking at the reality with a professional eye, so to speak: with a professional liar's.

I have noticed that the more cramped and meagre his action has been, the more exuberant his account of the affair is afterwards. The more restrictions reality has put on him, the more unbridled is his gusto as historian of his deeds, immediately afterwards. Then he has the common impulse to avenge that self that has been perishing under the famine and knout of a bad reality, by glorifying and surfeiting it on its return to the imagination.

NOTES

[1] The 1909 Kerman*e*c (one of the poles of Lewis's Brittany, see "The Death of the Ankou," "Franciscan Adventures" and "Brotcotnaz") became Kerman*a*c in 1922—probably a mistake. In 1927 Lewis, using the *Tyro* version, did not harmonize the spelling.

[2] The American edition of *The Wild Body* capitalized "frenchwoman," which suggests that Lewis was not responsible for the corrections; however those which correct points of French grammar have been followed in the present text.

[3] Can or milk-churn.

[4] The boots were "Austrian" in 1922—an interesting alteration in view of Ker-Orr's important Hungarian background (see "A Soldier of Humour").

[5] Ambiguous: the proofs had the word corrected into "vasy" followed by a question mark. However, rather than "vase-like," "vasey" is more likely to mean "muddy," as is suggested by the description of the same harbor in "Franciscan Adventures": "Que la vase pue là-bas!" ("How the mud there stinks!").

[6] *The Tyro* gave "Kermanac to Rot." The reasons for this change are obscure. Rot is an imaginary place, which Brasparts is not, though it is located inland some fifteen miles from the sea.

[7] An image reminiscent of "the strong elastic fish" of "Inferior Religions" (see page 151).

[8] Present in the *Tyro* version, this sentence shows that Lewis was already reorganizing the future *Wild Body*.

[9] The preceding three sentences were added in 1927 and confirm what is said in the "Foreword"—that these stories were rewritten "within the last few months."

[10] The section from "sunning myself" down to "fêtes of the mind" was added in 1927.

[11] Lewis's interest in insects and "shells" is certainly indebted to Jean Henri Fabre, whose works regularly appeared in the pre-World War I issues of *The English Review*.

[12] Less prudently *The Tyro* gave: "a life-size portrait of H. G. Wells. . ."
[13] This paragraph was added in 1927.
[14] The proofs gave for the last sentence: "Nevertheless even for him the effect was exceptional." The last three sentences were added in 1927.
[15] The last three sentences read like this in 1922: "What means did he employ during the second or two that she would take in passing his kitchen window, to bring her to her knees?" These alterations make it clear that Bestre is resorting to sexual exhibitionism.
[16] This sentence was added in 1927.
[17] The last two sentences were added in 1927.
[18] A word already used in 1922.

THE CORNAC AND HIS WIFE

First published in 1909 under the title "Les Saltimbanques" (i.e., "The Showmen"), "The Cornac and his Wife" was heavily revised in 1927. Yet of Lewis's first published texts (those which appeared in Ford Madox Hueffer's English Review*) it is the only one not to have been substantially modified in its progression. Its nature being essentially theoretical, and its characters being much less individualized (they are actors involved with a public in a collective ritual), Lewis simply could not dramatize this work by redistributing its episodes so as to emphasize the most striking ones—he had to submit to the discontinuous unfolding of a show. So, on the whole, this remains much more a semi-fictional essay than a real story. And Ker-Orr's presence had to remain what it was in 1909—that of an attentive, intelligent, but hardly individualized, spectator, i.e. the author himself.*

I met in the evening, not far from the last inn of the town, a cart containing the rough professional properties, the haggard offspring, of a strolling circus troupe from Arles, which I had already seen. The cornac[1] and his wife tramped along beside it. Their talk ran on the people of the town they had just left. They both scowled. They recalled the inhabitants of the last town with nothing but bitterness.

Against the people to whom they played they had an implacable grudge. With the man, obsessed by ill-health, the grievance against fortune was associated with the more brutal hatred that almost choked him every time he appeared professionally.

With their children the couple were very demonstrative. Mournful caresses were showered upon them: it was a manner of conspicuously pitying themselves. As a fierce reproach to the onlooker these unhandsome gytes[1] were publicly petted. Bitter kisses rained upon their heads. The action implied blows and ill-treatment at the hands of an anonymous adversary; in fact, the world at large. The children avoided the kisses as though they had been blows, wailing and contorting themselves. The animosity in the brutal lips thrust down upon their faces was felt by them, but the cause remained hidden for their inexperience. Terror, however, they learnt to interpret on all hands; even to particularly associate it with love towards the offspring. When the clown made a wild grimace in their blubbering faces, they would sometimes howl with alarm. This was it, perhaps! They concluded that this must be the sign and beginning of the terrible thing that had so long been covertly menacing them; their hearts nearly hopped out of their throats, although what occurred passed off in a somersault and a gush of dust as the clown hurled his white face against the earth, and got up rubbing his sides to assure the spectators that he was hurt.

Setting up their little tent in a country town this man and his wife felt their anger gnawing through their reserve, like a dog under lock and key. It was maddened by this other animal presence, the perspiring mastodon that roared at it with cheap luxurious superiority. Their long pilgrimage through this world inhabited by 'the Public' (from which they could never escape) might be interpreted by a nightmare image. This was a human family, we could say, lost in a land peopled by sodden mammoths possessed of a deeply-rooted taste for outdoor performances of a particularly depressing and disagreeable nature. These displays involved the insane contortions of an indignant man and his dirty, breathless wife, of whose ugly misery it was required that a daily mournful exhibition should be made of her shrivelled legs, in pantomime hose. She must crucify herself with a scarecrow abandon,

1 Obscure: possibly a version of *get*, a noun meaning "offspring" and colloquially pronounced "git." The *Oxford English Dictionary* gives "gyte" as a Scottish adjective meaning "out of one's senses."

this iron and blood automaton, and affect to represent the factor of sex in a geometrical posturing. These spells were all related in some way to physical suffering. Whenever one of these monsters was met with, which on an average was twice a day, the only means of escape for the unfortunate family was to charm it.[2] Conduct involving that never failed to render the monster harmless and satisfied. They then would hurry on, until they met another. Then they would repeat just the same thing over again, and once more hasten away, boiling with resentment.

The first time I saw them, the proprietress stood straddling on a raised platform, in loose flesh-tights with brown wrinkled knee-caps, *espadrilles*, brandy-green feathers arching over her almost naked head; while clutched in her hands aloft she supported a rigid child of about six. Upon this child stood three others, each provided with a flag. The proprietor stood some distance away and observed this event as one of the public. I leant on the barrier near him, and wondered if he ever willed his family to fall. I was soon persuaded, on observing him for a short while, that he could never be visited by such a mild domestic sensation. He wished steadily and all the time, it was quite certain, that the earth would open with a frantic avulsion, roaring as it parted, decorated with heavy flames, across the middle of the space set aside for his performance;[3] that everybody there would immediately be hurled into this chasm, and be crushed flat as it closed up. The Public on its side, of course, merely wished that the entire family might break their necks one after the other, the clown smash his face every time he fell, and so on.

To some extent Public and Showman understood each other. There was this amount of give and take, that they both snarled over the money that passed between them, or if they did not snarl it was all the worse. There was a unanimity of brutal hatred about that. Producer and consumer both were bestially conscious of the passage of coppers from one pocket to another. The public lay back and enjoyed itself hardly, closely, and savagely. The showman contorted himself madly in response. His bilious eye surveyed its grinning face, his brow sweated for its money, his ill-kept body ached. He made it a painful spectacle; he knew how to make it painful. He had the art of insisting on the effort, that foolish effort. The public took it in the contrary spirit, as *he* felt, on purpose. It was on purpose, as he saw it, that it took its recreation, which was coarse. It deliberately promoted his misery and affected to consider him a droll gay bird.

So this by no means exceptional family took its lot: it dressed itself up, its members knocked each other about, tied their bodies in diabolical knots before a congregation of Hodges, who could not even express themselves in the metropolitan tongue, but gibbered in breton, day in, day out. That was the situation. Intimately, both Showman and Public understood it, and were in touch more than, from the outside, would be at once understood. Each performance always threatened to end in the explosion of this increasing volume of rage. (This especially applied to its fermentation within the walls of the acrobatic vessel known as the 'patron,' who was Monsieur Jules Montort.)[4] Within, it flashed and rumbled all the time: but I never heard of its bursting its continent, and it even seemed of use as a stimulus to gymnastics after the manner of Beethoven with a fiery composition.

So there those daily crowds collected, squatted and watched, 'above the mêlée,' like *aristos* or gentlepeople. But they did pay for their pleasure (and such pleasure!): they were made to part with their sous, strictly for nothing, from the performers' standpoint. That would be the solitary bright spot for the outraged nomad. At least to that extent they were being got the better of. Had you suggested to the Showman that the Public paid for an idea, something it drew out of itself, that would have been a particularly repugnant thought. The Public depends upon him, that the primitive performer cannot question. And if women for instance find it hard to look on their own beauty as their admirer does (so that a great number of their actions might be traced to a contempt for men, who become so passionate about what they know themselves to be such an ordinary matter—namely themselves), so it was perhaps their contempt that enabled this fierce couple to continue as they did.

This background of experience was there to swell out my perception of what I now saw—the advancing caravan, with the familiar forms of its owners approaching one of their most hated haunts, but their heads as yet still full of the fury aroused by the last mid-day encounter. I followed them, attempting to catch what they were saying: but what with the rumbling of the carriages and the thick surge of the proprietor's voice, I could not make out much except expletives. His eye, too, rolled at me so darkly that I fell behind. I reflected that his incessant exercise in holding up his family ranged along his extended arm, though insipid to watch, must cause him to be respected on a lonely road, and his desperate nature and undying resentment would give his ferocity an impact that no feeling I then experienced could match. So I kept my eyes to myself for the time and closed down my ears, and entered the town in the dust of his wagons.

But after my evening meal I strolled over the hill bisected by the main street, and found him in his usual place on a sort of square, one side of which was formed by a stony breton brook, across which went a bridge. Drawn up under the beeches stood the brake. Near it in the open space the troupe had erected the trapeze, lighted several lamps (it was after dark already), and placed three or four benches in a narrow semicircle. When I arrived, a large crowd already pressed round them. 'Fournissons les bancs, et alors nous commençons!'[1] the proprietor was crying.

---

[1] "Take your seats on the benches, ladies and gentlemen, and we'll begin!"

But the seats remained unoccupied. A boy in tights, with his coat drawn round him, shivered at one corner of the ring. Into the middle of this the Showman several times advanced, exhorting the coy Public to make up its mind and commit itself to the extent of sitting down on one of his seats. Every now and then a couple would. Then he would walk back, and stand near his cart, muttering to himself. His eyebrows were hidden in a dishevelled frond of hair. The only thing he could look at without effort was the ground, and there his eyes were usually directed. When he looked up they were heavy—vacillating painfully beneath the weight of their lids. The action of speech with him resembled that of swallowing: the dreary pipe from which he drew so many distressful sounds seemed to stiffen and swell, and his head to strain forward like a rooster about to crow. His heavy under-lip went in and out in sombre activity as he articulated. The fine natural resources of his face for inspiring a feeling of gloom in his fellows, one would have judged irresistible on that particular night. The bitterest disgust disfigured it to a high degree.

But *they* watched this despondent and unpromising figure with glee and keen appreciation. This incongruity of appearance and calling was never patent to them at all, of course. That they had no wish to understand. When the furious man scowled they gaped delightedly; when he coaxed they became grave and sympathetic. All his movements were followed with minute attention. When he called upon them to occupy their seats, with an expressive gesture, they riveted their eyes on his hand, as though expecting a pack of cards to suddenly appear there. They made no move at all to take their places. Also, as this had already lasted a considerable time, the man who was fuming to entertain them—they just as incomprehensible to him as he was to them from that point of view—allowed the outraged expression that was the expression of his soul to appear more and more in his face.

Doubtless they had an inspired presentiment of what might shortly be expected of the morose figure before them. The chuckling exultation with which an amateur of athletics or fight-fan would examine some athlete with whose prowess he was acquainted, yet whose sickly appearance gives no hint of what is to be expected of him, it was with that sort of enlightened and hilarious knowingness that they responded to his melancholy appeals.

His cheerless voice, like the moaning bay of solitary dogs, conjured them to occupy the seats.

'Fournissons les bancs!' he exhorted them again and again. Each time he retired to the position he had selected to watch them from, far enough off for them to be able to say that he had withdrawn his influence, and had no further wish to interfere. Then, again, he stalked forward. This time the exhortation was pitched in as formal and matter-of-fact a key as his anatomy would permit, as though this were the first appeal of the evening. Now he seemed merely waiting, without discreetly withdrawing—without even troubling to glance in their direction any more, until the audience should have had time to seat themselves,—absorbed in briefly rehearsing to himself, just before beginning, the part he was to play. These tactics did not alter things in the least. Finally, he was compelled to take note of his failure. No words more issued from his mouth. He glared stupidly for some moments at the circle of people, and they, blandly alert, gazed back at him.

Then unexpectedly, from outside the periphery of the potential audience, elbowing his way familiarly through the wall of people, burst in the clown. Whether sent for to save the situation, or whether his toilet were only just completed, was not revealed.

'B-o-n-soir, M'sieurs et M'dames,' he chirruped and yodeled, waved his hand, tumbled over his employer's foot. The benches filled as if by magic. But the most surprising thing was the change in the proprietor. No sooner had the clown made his entrance, and, with his assurance of success as the people's favourite, and comic familiarity, told the hangers-back to take their seats, than a brisk dialogue sprang up between him and his melancholy master. It was punctuated with resounding slaps at each fresh impertinence of the clown. The proprietor was astonishing. I rubbed my eyes. This lugubrious personage had woken to the sudden violence of a cheerful automaton. In administering the chastisement his irrepressible friend perpetually invited, he sprang nimbly backwards and forwards as though engaged in a boxing match, while he grinned appreciatively at the clown's wit, as though in spite of himself, nearly knocking his teeth out with delighted blows. The audience howled with delight, and every one seemed really happy for the moment, except the clown. The clown every day must have received, I saw, a little of the *trop-plein*[1] of the proprietor.

In the tradition of the circus it is a very distinct figure, the part having a psychology of its own—that of the man who invents posers for the clown, wrangles with him, and against whom the laugh is always turned. One of the conventions of the circus is, of course, that the physical superiority of this personage should be legendary and indisputable. For however numerous the clowns may be, they never attack him, despite the brutal measures he adopts to cover his confusion and meet their ridicule. He seems to be a man with a marked predilection for evening dress. As a result he is a far more absurd figure than his painted and degenerate opponent. It may be the clown's superstitious respect for rank, and this emblem of it, despite his consciousness of intellectual superiority, that causes this ruffianly dolt to remain immune.

In playing this part the pompous dignity of attitude should be preserved in

---

[1] Overflow.

the strictest integrity. The actor should seldom smile. If so, it is only as a slight concession, a bid to induce the clown to take a more serious view of the matter under discussion. He smiles to make it evident that he also is furnished with this attribute of man—a discernment of the ridiculous. Then, with renewed gusto and solemnity, he asks the clown's *serious* opinion of the question by which he seems obsessed, turning his head sideways with his ear towards his droll friend, and closing his eyes for a moment.

Or else it is the public for whom this smile is intended, and towards whom the discomfited 'swell' in evening dress turns as towards his peers, for sympathy and understanding, when 'scored off' anew, in, as the smile would affirm, this low-bred and unanswerable fashion. They are appealed to, as though it were their mind that was being represented in the dialogue, and constantly discomfited, and he were merely their mouthpiece.

Originally, no doubt, this throaty swell stood in some sense for the Public. Out of compliment to the Public, of course, he would be provided with evening dress. It would be tacitly understood by the courteous management, that although many of those present were in billycocks, blouses and gaiters, shawls and reach-me-downs, their native attire was a ceremonial evening outfit.

The distinguished Public would doubtless still further appreciate the delicacy of touch in endowing its representative with a high-born inability to understand the jokes of his inferiors, or be a match for them in wit. In the better sort of circus, his address is highly genteel, throaty and unctuous.

In the little circuses, such as the one I am describing, this is a different and a very lonely part. There are none of those appeals to the Public—as the latter claim, not only community of mind, but of class, with the clown. It becomes something like a dialogue between mimes, representing employer and employee, although these original distinctions are not very strictly observed.

A man without a sense of humour, the man in the toff's part, finds himself with one whose mischievous spirit he is aware of, and whose ridicule he fears. Wishing to avoid being thought a bore, and racking his brains for a means of being entertaining, he suddenly brings to light a host of conundrums, for which he seems endowed with a stupefying memory. Thoroughly reassured by the finding of this powerful and traditional aid, with an amazing persistence he presses the clown, making use of every 'gentlemanly' subterfuge, to extract a grave answer. 'Why is a cabbage like a soul in purgatory?' or, 'If you had seven pockets in your waistcoat, a hip pocket, five ticket-pockets, and three other pockets, how many extra buttons would you need?' So they follow each other. Or else some anecdote (a more unmanageable tool) is remembered. The clown here had many opportunities of displaying his mocking wit.

This is the rôle of honour usually reserved for the head showman, of course. The part was not played with very great consistency in the case in question. Indeed, so irrepressible were the comedian's spirits, and so unmanageable his vitality at times, that he seemed to be turning the tables on the clown. In his cavernous baying voice, he drew out of his stomach many a caustic rejoinder to the clown's pert but stock wit. The latter's ready-made quips were often no match for his strange but genuine hilarity. During the whole evening he was rather 'hors de son assiette,'[1] I thought. I was very glad I had come, for I had never seen this side of him, and it seemed the most unaccountable freak of personality that it was possible to imagine. Before, I had never spent more than a few minutes watching them, and certainly never seen anything resembling the present display.

This out-of-door audience was differently moved from the audiences I have seen in the little circus tents of the breton fairs. The absence of the mysterious hush of the interior seemed to release them. Also the nearness of the performers in the tent increases the mystery. The proximity of these bulging muscles, painted faces and novel garbs, evidently makes a strange impression on the village clientèle. These primitive minds do not readily dissociate reality from appearance. However well they got to know the clown, they would always think of him the wrong way up, or on all-fours. The more humble suburban theatre-goer would be twice as much affected at meeting the much-advertised star with whose private life he is more familiar than with her public display, in the wings of the theatre, as in seeing her on the stage. Indeed, it would be rather as though at some turning of an alley at the Zoo, you should meet a lion face to face—having gazed at it a few minutes before behind its bars. So the theatre, the people on the stage and the plays they play, is part of the surface of life, and is not troubling. But to get behind the scenes and see these beings out of their parts, would be not merely to be privy to the workings and 'dessous'[2] of the theatre, but of life itself.

Crowded in the narrow and twilight pavilion of the saltimbanques at the breton Pardon, the audience will remain motionless for minutes together. Their imagination is awakened by the sight of the flags, the tent, the drums, and the bedizened people. Thenceforth it dominates them, controlling their senses. They enter the tent with a mild awe, in a suggestive trance. Then a joke is made that requires a burst of merriment, or when a turn is finished, they all begin moving themselves, as though they had just woken up, changing their attitude, shaking off the magnetic sleep.

Once I had seen this particular troupe in a fair with their tent up. I had gone in for a short while, but had not paid much attention to them individually and soon left.[5] But the clown, I remember, conducted everything—

1 "Out of sorts."

2. "Hidden side."

acting as interpreter of his own jokes, tumbling over and getting up and leading the laugh, and explaining with real conscientiousness and science the proprietor's more recondite conundrums. He took up an impersonal attitude. He was a friend who had dropped in to see the 'patron'; he appreciated quite as one of the public the curiosities of the show. He would say, for instance: 'Now this is very remarkable: this little girl is only eleven, and she can put both her toes in her mouth,' etc., etc. Had it not been for his comments, I am persuaded that the performance would have passed off in a profound, though not unappreciative, silence.

Returning to the present occasion, some time after the initial bout between the clown and his master, and while some chairs were being placed in the middle of the ring, I became aware of a very grave expression on the latter's face. He now mounted upon one of the chairs. Having remained impressively silent till the last moment, from the edge of the chair, as though from the brink of a precipice, he addressed the audience in the following terms:

'Ladies and gentlemen! I have given up working for several years myself, owing to ill-health. As far as some of my most important tricks are concerned, my little girl has taken my place. But Monsieur le Commissaire de Police would not give the necessary permission for her to appear.—Then I will myself perform!'

A grievance against the police would, of course, any day of the week, drive out everything else with any showman. The Public momentarily benefited. At these words M. Montort jerked himself violently over the back of the chair, the unathletic proportions of his stomach being revealed in this moment, and touched the ground with his head. Then, having bowed to the audience, he turned again to the chairs and grasping them, with a gesture of the utmost recklessness, heaved his body up into the air. This was accompanied by a startling whir proceeding from his corduroys, and a painful crepitation of his joints. Afterwards he accomplished a third feat, suspending himself between two chairs; and then a fourth, in which he gracefully lay on all three, and picked up a handkerchief with his face reversed.[6] At this sensational finish, I thought it appropriate to applaud: a *feu nourri*[1] of clapping broke from me. Unfortunately the audience was spellbound and my demonstration attracted attention. I was singled out by the performer for a look of individual hatred. He treated all of us coldly: he bowed stiffly, and walked back to the cart with the air of a man who has just received a bullet wound in a duel, and refusing the assistance of a doctor walks to his carriage.

He had accomplished the feats that I have just described with a bitter dash that revealed once more the character that from former more casual visits I recognized. He seemed courting misfortune. 'Any mortal injury sustained

[1] A sustained burst.

by me, M. le Commissaire, during the performance, will be at your door! The Public must be satisfied. I am the servant of the Public. You have decreed that it shall be me (all my intestines displaced by thirty years of contortions) that shall satisfy them. Very well! I know my duty, if you don't know yours. Good! It shall be done as you have ordered, M. le Commissaire!'

The drama this time was an *internal* one, therefore. It was not a question of baiting the public with a broken neck. We were invited to concentrate our minds upon what was going on *inside*. We had to visualize a colony of much-twisted, sorely-tried intestines, screwed this way and that, as they had never been screwed before. It was an anatomical piece.

The unfortunate part was that the public could not *see* these intestines as they could see a figure suspended in the air, and liable to crash. A mournful and respectful, a *dead* silence, would have been the ideal way, from his point of view, for the audience to have greeted his pathetic skill. Instead of that, salvos of muscular applause shook the air every time he completed one of the phases of this painful trick. Hearing the applause, he would fling himself wildly into his next posture, with a whistling sneer of hatred. The set finished, the last knot tied and untied, he went back and leant against the car, his head in the hollow of his arm, coughing and spitting. A boy at my side said, 'Regarde-donc; il souffre![1] This refusal of the magistrate to let his little girl perform was an event that especially outraged him: it wounded his french sense of the dignity of a fully-enfranchised person. His wife was far less affected, but she seconded him with a lofty scowl. Shortly afterwards, she provided a new and interesting feature of the evening's entertainment.

Various insignificant items immediately succeeded the showman's dramatic exploit, where he deputized for his daughter. A donkey appeared, whose legs could be tied into knots. The clown extracted from its middle-class comfortable primness of expression every jest of which it was susceptible. The conundrums broke out again; they only ceased after a discharge that lasted fully a quarter of an hour. There was a little trapeze. For some time already we had been aware of a restless figure in the background. A woman with an expression of great dissatisfaction on her face, stood with muffled arms knotted on her chest, holding a shawl against the cold air. Next, we became aware of a harsh and indignant voice. This woman was slowly advancing, talking all the while, until she arrived in the centre of the circle made by the seats. She made several slow gestures, slightly raising her voice. She spoke as a person who had stood things long enough. 'Here are hundreds of people standing round, and there are hardly a dozen sous on the carpet! We give you entertainment, but it is not for nothing! We do not work for nothing! We have our living to make as well as other people! This is the third

[1] "Look. He is in pain!"

performance we have given to-day. We are tired and have come a long way to appear before you this evening. You want to enjoy yourselves; but you don't want to pay! If you want to see any more, loosen your purse-strings a little!'

While delivering this harangue her attitude resembled that seen in the London streets, when women are quarrelling—the neck strained forward, the face bent down, and the eyes glowering upwards at the adversary. One hand was thrust stiffly out. In these classes of action the body, besides, is generally screwed round to express the impulse of turning on the heel in disgust and walking away. But the face still confronts whoever is being apostrophized, and utters its ever-renewed maledictory post-scriptums.

Several pieces of money fell at her feet. She remained silent, the arms fiercely folded, the two hands bitterly dug into her sides. Eventually she retired, very slowly, as she had advanced, as it were indolently, her eyes still flashing and scowling resentfully round at the crowd as she went. They looked on with amiable and gaping attention. They took much more notice of her than of the man; she thoroughly interested them, and they conceded to her unconditionally their sympathy. There was no response to her attack—no gibing or discontent; only a few more sous were thrown. Her husband, it appeared, had been deeply stimulated by her speech. One or two volcanic conumdrums followed closely upon her exit. The audience seemed to relish the entertainment all the more after this confirmation from the proprietress of its quality, instead of being put in a more critical frame of mind.

Her indignant outburst carried this curious reflection with it; it was plain that it did not owe its tone of conviction to the fact that she conceived a high opinion of their performance. Apparently it was an axiom of her mind that the public paid, for some obscure reason, not for its proper amusement, but for the trouble, inconvenience, fatigue, and in sum for all the ills of the showman's lot. Or rather did *not* pay, sat and watched and did not pay. Ah ça!—that was trying the patience too far. This, it is true, was only the reasoning every gesture of her husband forcibly expressed, but explicit, in black and white, or well-turned forcible words.

Peasant audiences in latin countries, and no doubt in most places, are herded to their amusements like children; the harsh experts of fun barbarously purge them for a few pence. The spectacles provided are received like the daily soup and weekly cube of tobacco of the convict. Spending wages, it seems, is as much a routine as earning them. So in their entertainment, when buying it with their own money, they support the same brow-beating and discipline as in their work. Of this the outburst of the proprietress was a perfect illustration. Such figures represent for the spectators, for the moment, authority. In consequence a reproof as to their slackness in spending is received in the same spirit as a master's abuse at alleged slackness in earning it.

I have described the nature of my own humour—how, as I said, it went over into everything, making a drama of mock-violence of every social relationship. Why should it be so *violent*—so mock-violent—you may at the time have been disposed to enquire? Everywhere it has seemed to be compelled to go into some frame that was always a simulacrum of mortal combat. Sometimes it resembled a dilution of the Wild West film, chaplinesque in its violence. Why always *violence*? However, I have often asked that myself.

For my reply here I should go to the modern Circus or to the Italian Comedy, or to Punch. Violence is of the essence of *laughter* (as distinguished of course from smiling wit): it is merely the inversion or failure of *force*. To put it in another way, it is the *grin* upon the Deathshead. It must be extremely primitive in origin, though of course its function in civilized life is to keep the primitive at bay. But it hoists the primitive with its own explosive. It is a realistic firework, reminiscent of war.

These strolling players I am describing, however, and their relation to their audience, will provide the most convincing illustration of what I mean. The difference and also the inevitable consanguinity between my ideal of humour, and that of any other man whatever, will become plain. For the primitive peasant audience the comic-sense is subject to the narrowest convention of habit. Obviously a peasant would not see anything ridiculous in, or at least never amuse himself over his pigs and chickens: his constant sentiment of their utility would be too strong to admit of another. Thus the disintegrating effect of the laughing-gas, and especially the fundamentals of the absurd, that strike too near the life-root, is instinctively isolated. A man who succeeds in infuriating us, again, need never fear our ridicule, although he may enhance our anger by his absurdity. A countryman in urging on his beast may make some disobliging remark to it, really seizing a ludicrous point in its appearance to envenom his epithet: but it will be caustic and mirthless, an observation of his intelligence far removed from the irresponsible emotion of laughter. It will come out of his anger and impatience, not his gaiety. You see in the peasant of Brittany and other primitive districts of France a constant tendency to sarcasm. Their hysterical and monotonous voices—a variety of the 'celtic' screech—are always with the Bretons pitched in a strain of fierce raillery and abuse. But this does not affect their mirth. Their laughter is sharp and mirthless and designed usually to wound. With their grins and quips they are like armed men who never meet without clashing their weapons together. Were my circus-proprietor and his kind not so tough, this continual howl or disquieting explosion of what is scarcely mirth would shatter them.

So (to return to the conventions of these forms of pleasure) it could be said that if the clown and the manager consulted in an audible voice, before cracking each joke—in fact, concocted it in their hearing—these audiences would respond with the same alacrity. Any rudiment of décor or makeshift property, economy in make-up, or feeble trick of some accredited acrobat, which they themselves could do twice as well, or mirthless patter, is not enough to arouse criticism in them, who are so critically acute in other matters. To criticize the amusements that Fate has provided, is an anarchy to which they do not aspire.

The member of a peasant community is trained by Fate, and his law is to accept its manifestations—one of which is comic, one of love, one of work, and so on. There is a little flowering of tenderness for a moment in the love one. The comic is always strenuous and cruel, like the work. It never flowers. The intermediary, the showman, knows that. He knows the brutal *frisson*[1] in contact with danger that draws the laughter up from the deepest bowel in a refreshing unearthly gush. He knows why he and the clown are always black and blue, his children performing dogs, his wife a caryatid. He knows Fate, since he serves it, better than even the peasant.

The educated man, like the true social revolutionary, does not *accept* life in this way. He is in revolt, and it is the laws of Fate that he sets out to break. We can take another characteristic fatalism of the peasant or primitive man. He can never conceive of anybody being anything else but just what he is, or having any other name than that he is known by. John the carpenter, or Old John (or Young John) the carpenter, is not a person, but, as it were, a fixed and rigid communistic convention. One of our greatest superstitions is that the plain man, being so 'near to life,' is a great 'realist.' In fact, he seldom gets close to reality at all, in the way, for instance, that a philosophic intelligence, or an imaginative artist, does. He looks at everything from the outside, reads the labels, and what he *sees* is what he has been told to see, that is to say, what he expects. What he does not expect, he, of course, does not see. For him only the well-worn and general exists.

That the peasant, or any person living under primitive conditions, does not appreciate the scenery so much as, say, John Keats, is a generally accepted truth, which no available evidence gives us any reason to question. His contact with the quickest, most vivid, reality, if he is averagely endowed, is muffled, and his touch upon it strangely insensitive; he is surrounded by signs, not things. It is for this reason that the social revolutionary, who wishes to introduce the unexpected and to awaken a faculty of criticism, finds the peasant such unsatisfactory material.

Just as the peasant, then, has little sense of the beauty of his life, so his laughter is circumscribed. The herd-bellow at the circus is always associated with mock-violent events, however, and his true laughter is always torn out of a tragic material. How this explains my sort of laughter is that both our patterns are cut or torn out of primitive stuff. The difference is that pure physical action usually provides him with his, whereas mine deal with the

---

1 Shudder.

phantoms of action and the human character. For me *everything* is tragically primitive: whereas the peasant only feels 'primitively' at stated times. But both our comedies are comedies of action, that is what I would stress.

This particular performance wound up rather strangely. The showman's wife had occasion to approach and lash the public with her tongue again, in the final phase. As the show approached its conclusion, the donkey was led in once more, pretended to die, and the clown made believe to weep disconsolately over it. All was quiet and preparation for a moment.

Then, from an unexpected quarter, came a sort of dénouement to our evening. Every one's attention was immediately attracted to it. A small boy in the front row began jeering at the proprietor. First, it was a constant muttering, that made people turn idly to that quarter of the ring. Then it grew in volume and intensity. It was a spontaneous action it appeared, and extremely sudden. The outraged showman slouched past him several times, looking at him from the tail of his eye, with his head thrust out as though he were going to crow. He rubbed his hands as he was accustomed to do before chastizing the clown. Here was a little white-faced clown, an unprofessional imp of mischief! He would slap him in a moment. He rubbed his horny hands but without conviction. This had no effect: the small voice went steadily on like a dirge. This unrehearsed number found him at a loss. He went over to the clown and complained in a whisper. This personage had just revealed himself as a serious gymnast. Baring his blacksmith's arms, and discarding his ludicrous personality, he had accomplished a series of mild feats on the trapeze. He benefited, like all athletic clowns, by his traditional foolish incompetence. The public were duly impressed. He now surveyed them with a solemn and pretentious eye. When his master came up to him, supposing that the complaint referred to some disorderly booby, he advanced threateningly in the direction indicated. But when he saw who was the offender, finding a thoughtful-looking little boy in place of an intoxicated peasant, he was as nonplussed as had been his master. He looked foolishly round, and then fell to jeering back, the clown reasserting itself. Then he returned with a shrug and grimace to his preparations for the next and final event.

It is possible that this infant may never have thought comically before. Or he may, of course, have visited travelling shows for the purpose of annoying showmen, advertising his intelligence, or even to be taken on as a clown. But he may have been the victim of the unaccountable awakening of a critical vein, grown irresponsibly active all at once. If the latter, then he was launched on a dubious career of offence. He had one of the handsome visionary breton faces. His oracular vehemence, though bitterly sarcastic, suggested the more romantic kind of motivation. The showman prowled about the enclosure, grinning and casting sidelong glances at his poet: his vanity tickled in some fashion, perhaps: who knows? the boy persevering blandly, fixing him with his eye. But suddenly his face would darken, and he would make a rush at the inexplicable juvenile figure. Would this boy have met death with the exultation of a martyr rather than give up his picture of an old and despondent mountebank—like some stubborn prophet who would not forgo the melodrama forged by his orderly hatreds—always of the gloom of famine, of cracked and gutted palaces, and the elements taking on new and extremely destructive shapes for the extermination of man?

At last that organism, 'the Public,' as there constituted, fell to pieces, at a signal: the trapeze collapsed, the benches broke the circle described for the performance, and were hurried away, the acetylene lamps were extinguished, the angry tongues of the saltimbanques began their evil retrospective clatter. There had been *two* Publics, however, this time. It had been a good show.[7]

NOTES

[1] ''Cornac (meaning ''mahout; guide'') is French and commonly used, whereas the English ''carnac'' is rare.

[2] ''By flinging their bodies about and grimacing for several hours'' was deleted on the proofs.

[3] With the conclusion of the story, this is the first manifestation in Lewis's works of the apocalyptic theme.

[4] The proofs gave ''Jules Cromagne,'' obviously modelled on Cro-Magnon. ''Montort,'' just like ''Brotcotnaz'' (in opposition to ''Brobdingnag'') is less suggestive.

[5] See ''A Breton Journal,'' pp. 195-196.

[6] The proofs gave ''with his back teeth.''

[7] This last paragraph was added in August 1927 on the proofs.

THE DEATH OF THE ANKOU

This tale of death, blindness and paradoxical fascination was not, apparently, published before its inclusion in The Wild Body. *That is strange because in "Beginnings"* (see pp. 373-374, below), *Lewis revealed that "The Ankou" had been the very first story he ever wrote:*

> *It was the sun, a Breton instead of a British, that brought forth my first short story—*The Ankou *I believe it was. . . The "short story" was the crystallization* of what I had to keep out of my consciousness while painting. . . *As I squeezed out* everything *that smacked of literature from my vision of the beggar, it collected at the back of my mind. It imposed itself upon me as a complementary creation.*

One may understand why Lewis never illustrated his own books. A certain blindness seems for him inseparable from literary creation—which is surprising with so visual an artist. But this may well explain the spectral quality of his writing at its best. In this sense "The Death of the Ankou" sheds light on the nature of the Lewisian vision—a light confirmed by what was said much later in "The Sea-Mists of the Winter."

To go back to the circumstances of the appearance of this story, it is always possible that an early publication may have passed unnoticed by the bibliographers, though it is unlikely, because, had it been completed when he first wrote it, Lewis would probably have given it to Ford Madox Hueffer for The English Review, *or a little later to Douglas Goldring for* The Tramp. *This is apparently corroborated by the absence of "The Death of the Ankou" from "Writings." In 1916 the story must still have been a draft or a group of notes, which Lewis picked up in 1927.*

'And Death once dead, there's no more dying then.'
—William Shakespeare[1]

Ervoanik Plouillo—meaning the death-god of Ploumilliau;[2] I said over the words, and as I did so I saw the death-god.—I sat in a crowded inn at Vandevennec,[3] in the *argoat*, not far from Rot,[4] at the Pardon, deafened by the bitter screech of the drinkers, finishing a piece of cheese. As I avoided the maggots I read the history of the Ankou, that is the armorican death-god. The guide-book to the antiquities of the district made plain, to the tourist, the ancient features of this belief. It recounted how the gaunt creature despatched from the country of death traversed at night the breton region. The peasant, late on the high-road and for the most part drunk, staggering home at midnight, felt around him suddenly the atmosphere of the shades, a strange cold penetrated his tissues, authentic portions of the *Néant*[1] pushed in like icy wedges within the mild air of the fields and isolated him from Earth, while rapid hands seized his shoulders from behind, and thrust him into the ditch. Then, crouching with his face against the ground, his eyes shut fast, he heard the hurrying wheels of the cart. Death passed with his assistants. As the complaint of the receding wheels died out, he would cross himself many times, rise from the ditch, and proceed with a terrified haste to his destination.

There was a midnight mass at Ploumilliau, where the Ankou, which stood in a chapel, was said to leave his place, pass amongst the kneeling congregation, and tap on the shoulders those he proposed to take quite soon. These were memories. The statue no longer stood there, even. It had been removed some time before by the priests, because it was an object of too much interest to local magicians. They interfered with it, and at last one impatient hag, disgusted at its feebleness after it had neglected to assist her in a deadly matter she had on hand, introduced herself into the chapel one afternoon and, unobserved by the staff, painted it a pillar-box red. This she imagined would invigorate it and make it full of new mischief. When the priest's eyes in due course fell upon the red god, he decided that that would not do: he put it out of the way, where it could not be tampered with. So one of the last truly pagan images disappeared, wasting its curious efficacy in a loft, dusted occasionally by an ecclesiastical *bonne*.

Such was the story of the last authentic plastic Ankou. In ancient Brittany the people claimed to be descended from a redoubtable god of death. But long

1 Nothingness.

passed out of the influence of that barbarity, their early death-god, competing with gentler images, saw his altars fall one by one. In a semi-'parisian' parish, at last, the cult which had superseded him arrived in its turn at a universal decline, his ultimate representative was relegated to a loft to save it from the contemptuous devotions of a disappointed sorceress. Alas for Death! or rather for its descendants, thought I, a little romantically: that chill in the bone it brought was an ancient tonic: so long as it ran down the spine the breton soul was quick with memory. So, *alas!*

But I had been reading after that, and immediately prior to my encounter, about the peasant in the ditch, also the blinding of the god. It was supposed, I learnt, that formerly the Ankou had his eyesight. As he travelled along in his cart between the hedges, he would stare about him, and spot likely people to right and left. One evening, as his flat, black, breton peasants' hat came rapidly along the road, as he straddled attentively bolt-upright upon its jolting floor, a man and his master, in an adjoining field, noticed his approach. The man broke into song. His scandalized master attempted to stop him. But this bright bolshevik continued to sing an offensively carefree song under the nose of the supreme authority. The scandal did not pass unnoticed by the touchy destroyer. He shouted at him over the hedge, that for his insolence he had eight days to live, no more, which perhaps would teach him to sing etcetera! As it happened St. Peter was there. St. Peter's record leaves little question that a suppressed communist of an advanced type is concealed beneath the archangelical robes. It is a questionable policy to employ such a man as doorkeeper, and many popular airs in latin countries facetiously draw attention to the possibilities inherent in such a situation. In this case Peter was as scandalized at the behaviour of the Ankou as was the farmer at that of his farm-hand.

'Are you not ashamed, strange god, to condemn a man in that way, *at his work?*' he exclaimed. It was the *work* that did it, as far as Peter was concerned. Also it was his interference with work that brought his great misfortune on the Ankou. St. Peter, so the guide-book said, was as touchy as a captain of industry or a demagogue on that point. Though how could poor Death know that work, of all things, was sacred? Evidently he would have quite different ideas as to the attributes of divinity. But he had to pay immediately for his blunder. The revolutionary archangel struck him blind on the spot—struck Death blind; and, true to his character, that of one at all costs anxious for the applause of the *muchedumbre*,[1] he returned to the field, and told the astonished labourer, who was still singing—because in all probability he was a little soft in the head—that he had his personal guarantee of a very long and happy life, and that he, Peter, had punished Death with

[1] The crowd (Spanish).

blindness. At this the labourer, I daresay, gave a hoarse laugh; and St. Peter probably made his way back to his victim well-satisfied in the reflection that he had won the favour of a vast mass of mortals.

In the accounts in the guide-book, it was the dating, however, connected with the tapping of owls, the crowing of hens, the significant evolutions of magpies, and especially the subsequent time-table involved in the lonely meetings with the plague-ridden death-cart, that seemed to me most effective. If the peasant were overtaken by the cart on the night-road towards the morning, he must die within the month. If the encounter is in the young night, he may have anything up to two years still to live. It was easy to imagine all the calculations indulged in by the distracted man after his evil meeting. I could hear his screaming voice (like those at the moment tearing at my ears as the groups of black-coated figures played some game of chance that maddened them) when he had crawled into the large, carved cupboard that served him for a bed, beside his wife, and how she would weigh this living, screaming, man, in the scales of time provided by superstition, and how the death damp would hang about him till his time had expired.

I was persuaded, finally, to go to Ploumilliau, and see the last statue of the blind Ankou. It was not many miles away. *Ervoanik Plouillo*—still to be seen for threepence: and while I was making plans for the necessary journey, my mind was powerfully haunted by that blind and hurrying apparition which had been so concrete there.

It was a long room where I sat, like a gallery: except during a Pardon it was not so popular. When I am reading something that interests me, the whole atmosphere is affected. If I look quickly up, I see things as though they were a part of a dream. They are all penetrated by the particular medium I have drawn out of my mind. What I had last read on this occasion, although my eyes at the moment were resting on the words *Ervoanik Plouillo*, was the account of how it affected the person's fate at what hour he met the Ankou. The din and smoke in the dark and crowded gallery was lighted by weak electricity, and a wet and lowering daylight beyond. Crowds of umbrellas moved past the door which opened on to the square. Whenever I grew attentive to my surroundings, the passionate movement of whirling and striking arms was visible at the tables where the play was in progress, or a furious black body would dash itself from one chair to another. The 'celtic screech' meantime growing harsher and harsher, sharpening itself on caustic snarling words, would soar to a paroxysm of energy. 'Garce!'[1] was the most frequent sound. All the voices would clamour for a moment together. It was a shattering noise in this dusky tunnel.—I had stopped reading, as I have said, and I lifted my eyes. It was then that I saw the Ankou.

---

1 "Bitch!"

With revulsed and misty eyes almost in front of me, an imperious figure, apparently armed with a club, was forcing its way insolently forward towards the door, its head up, an eloquently moving mouth hung in the air, as it seemed, for its possessor. It forced rudely aside everything in its path. Two men who were standing and talking to a seated one flew apart, struck by the club, or the sceptre, of this king amongst afflictions. The progress of this embodied calamity was peculiarly straight. He did not deviate. He passed my table and I saw a small, highly coloured, face, with waxed moustaches. But the terrible perquisite of the blind was there in the staring, milky eyeballs: and an expression of acetic[5] ponderous importance weighted it so that, mean as it was in reality, this mask was highly impressive. Also, from its bitter immunity and unquestioned right-of-way, and from the habit of wandering through the outer jungle of physical objects, it had the look that some small boy's face might acquire, prone to imagine himself a steam-roller, or a sightless Juggernaut.

The blinded figure had burst into my daydream so unexpectedly and so pat, that I was taken aback by this sudden close-up of so trite a tragedy. Where he had come was compact with an emotional medium emitted by me. In reality it was a private scene, so that this overweening intruder might have been marching through my mind with his taut convulsive step, club in hand, rather than merely traversing the eating-room of a hotel, after a privileged visit to the kitchen. Certainly at that moment my mind was lying open so much, or was so much exteriorized, that almost literally, as far as I was concerned, it was inside, not out, that this image forced its way. Hence, perhaps, the strange effect.

The impression was so strong that I felt for the moment that I had met the death-god, a garbled version with waxed moustaches. It was noon. I said to myself that, as it was noon, that should give me twelve months more to live. I brushed aside the suggestion that day was not night, that I was not a breton peasant, and that the beggar was probably not Death. I tried to shudder. I had not shuddered. His attendant, a sad-faced child, rattled a lead mug under my nose. I put two sous in it. I had no doubt averted the omen, I reflected, with this bribe.

The weather improved in the afternoon. As I was walking about with a fisherman I knew, who had come in twenty miles for this Pardon, I saw the Ankou again, collecting pence. He was strolling now, making a leisurely harvest from the pockets of these religious crowds. His attitude was, however, peremptory. He called out hoarsely his requirements, and turned his empty eyes in the direction indicated by his acolyte, where he knew there was a group who had not paid. His clothes were smart, all in rich, black broadcloth and black velvet, with a ribboned hat. He entered into every door he found open, beating on it with his club-like stick. I did not notice any

Thank you! pass his lips. He appeared to snort when he had received what was due to him, and to turn away, his legs beginning to march mechanically like a man mildly shell-shocked.

The fisherman and I both stood watching him. I laughed.

'Il ne se gêne pas!'[1] I said. 'He does not *beg*. I don't call that a *beggar*.'

'Indeed, you are right.—That is Ludo,'[6] I was told.

'Who is Ludo, then?' I asked.

'Ludo is the king of Rot!' my friend laughed. 'The people round here spoil him, according to my idea. He's only a beggar. It's true he's blind. But he takes too much on himself.'

He spat.

'He's not the only blind beggar in the world!'

'Indeed, he is not,' I said.

'He drives off any other blind beggars that put their noses inside Rot. You see his stick? He uses it!'

We saw him led up to a party who had not noticed his approach. He stood for a moment shouting. From stupidity they did not respond at once. Turning violently away, he dragged his attendant after him.

'He must not be kept waiting!' I said.

'Ah, no. With Ludo you must be nimble!'

The people he had left remained crestfallen and astonished.

'Where does he live?' I asked.

'Well, he lives, I have been told, in a cave, on the road to Kermarquer.[7] That's where he lives. Where he banks I can't tell you!'

Ludo approached us. He shouted in breton.

'What is he saying?'

'He is telling you to get ready; that he is coming!' said my friend. He pulled out a few sous from his pocket, and said: 'Faut bien! Needs must!' and laughed a little sheepishly.

I emptied a handful of coppers into the mug.

'Ludo!' I exclaimed. 'How are you? Are you well?'

He stood, his face in my direction, with, except for the eyes, his mask of an irritable Jack-in-office, with the waxed moustaches of a small pretentious official.

'Very well! And you?' came back with unexpected rapidity.

'Not bad, touching wood!' I said. 'How is your wife?'

'Je suis garçon! I am a bachelor!' he replied at once.

'So you are better off, old chap!' I said. 'Women serve no good purpose, for serious boys!'

'You are right,' said Ludo. He then made a disgusting remark. We

---

[1] "He's rather cheeky!"

laughed. His face had not changed expression. Did he try, I wondered, to picture the stranger, discharging remarks from empty blackness, or had the voice outside become for him or had it always been what the picture is to us? If you had never seen any of the people you knew, but had only talked to them on the telephone—what under these circumstances would So-and-So be as a voice, I asked myself, instead of mainly a picture?

'How long have you been a beggar, Ludo?' I asked.

'Longtemps!'[1] he replied. I had been too fresh for this important beggar. He got in motion and passed on, shouting in breton.

The fisherman laughed and spat.

'Quel type!'[2] he said. 'When we were in Penang, no it was at Bankok, at the time of my service with the fleet, I saw just such another. He was a blind sailor, an Englishman. He had lost his sight in a shipwreck.—He would not beg from the black people.'

'Why did he stop there?'

'He liked the heat. He was a *farceur.*[3] He was such another as this one.'

Two days later I set out on foot for Kermarquer. I remembered as I was going out of the town that my friend had told me that Ludo's cave was there somewhere. I asked a woman working in a field where it was. She directed me.

I found him in a small, verdant enclosure, one end of it full of half-wild chickens, with a rocky bluff at one side, and a stream running in a bed of smooth boulders. A chimney stuck out of the rock, and a black string of smoke wound out of it. Ludo sat at the mouth of his cave. A large dog rushed barking towards me at my approach. I took up a stone and threatened it. His boy, who was cooking, called off the dog. He looked at me with intelligence.

'Good morning, Ludo!' I said. 'I am an Englishman. I met you at the Pardon, do you remember? I have come to visit you, in passing. How are you? It's a fine day.'

'Ah, it was you I met? I remember. You were with a fisherman from Kermanec?'

'The same.'

'So you're an Englishman?'

'Yes.'

'Tiens!'[4]

I did not think he looked well. My sensation of mock-superstition had passed. But although I was now familiar with Ludo, when I looked at his

1 "For a long time."
2 "Quite a character."
3 "A joker."
4 "Well, well!"

staring mask I still experienced a faint reflection of my first impression, when he was the death-god. That impression had been a strong one, and it was associated with superstition. So he was still a feeble death-god.

The bodies of a number of esculent frogs lay on the ground, from which the back legs had been cut. These the boy was engaged in poaching.

'What is that you are doing them in?' I asked him.

'White wine,' he said.

'Are they best that way?' I asked.

'Why, that is a good way to do them,' said Ludo. 'You don't eat frogs in England, do you?'

'No, that is repugnant to us.'

I picked one up.

'You don't eat the bodies?'

'No, only the thighs,' said the boy.

'Will you try one?' asked Ludo.

'I've just had my meal, thank you all the same.'

I pulled out of my rucksack a flask of brandy.

'I have some eau-de-vie here,' I said. 'Will you have a glass?'

'I should be glad to,' said Ludo.

I sat down, and in a few minutes his meal was ready. He disposed of the grenouilles with relish, and drank my health in my brandy, and I drank his. The boy ate some fish that he had cooked for himself, a few yards away from us, giving small pieces to the dog.

After the meal Ludo sent the boy on some errand. The dog did not go with him. I offered Ludo a cigarette which he refused. We sat in silence for some minutes. As I looked at him I realized how the eyes mount guard over the face, as well as look out of it. The faces of the blind are hung there like a dead lantern. Blind people must feel on their skins our eyes upon them: but this sheet of flesh is rashly stuck up in what must appear far outside their control, an object in a foreign world of sight. So in consequence of this divorce, their faces have the appearance of things that have been abandoned by the mind. What is his face to a blind man? Probably nothing more than an organ, an exposed part of the stomach, that is a mouth.

Ludo's face, in any case, was *blind*; it looked the blindest part of his body, and perhaps the deadest, from which all the functions of a living face had gone. As a result of its irrelevant external situation, it carried on its own life with the outer world, and behaved with all the disinvolture of an internal organ, no longer serving to secrete thought any more than the foot. For after all to be lost *outside* is much the same as to be hidden in the dark *within*.—What served for a face for the blind, then? What did they have instead, that was expressive of emotion in the way that our faces are? I supposed that all the responsive machinery must be largely readjusted with them, and directed to some other part of the body. I noticed that Ludo's hands, all the movement of his limbs, were a surer indication of what he was thinking than was his face.

Still the face registered something. It was a health-chart perhaps. He looked very ill I thought, and by that I meant, of course, that his *face* did not look in good health. When I said, 'You don't look well,' his hands moved nervously on his club. His face responded by taking on a sicklier shade.

'I'm ill,' he said.

'What is it?'

'I'm indisposed.'

'Perhaps you've met the Ankou.' I said this thoughtlessly, probably because I had intended to ask him if he had ever heard of the Ankou, or something like that. He did not say anything to this, but remained quite still, then stood up and shook himself and sat down again. He began rocking himself lightly from side to side.

'Who has been telling you about the Ankou, and all those tales?' he suddenly asked.

'Why, I was reading about it in a guide-book, as a matter of fact, the first time I saw you. You scared me for a moment. I thought you might be he.'

He did not reply to this, nor did he say anything, but his face assumed the expression I had noticed on it when I first saw it, as he forced his way through the throngs at the inn.

'Do you think the weather will hold?' I asked.

He made no reply. I did not look at him. With anybody with a face you necessarily feel that they can see you, even if their blank eyes prove the contrary. His fingers moved nervously on the handle of his stick. I felt that I had suddenly grown less popular. What had I done? I had mentioned an extinct god of death. Perhaps that was regarded as unlucky. I could not guess what had occurred to displease him.

'It was a good Pardon, was it not, the other day?' I said.

There was no reply. I was not sure whether he had not perhaps moods in which, owing to his affliction, he just entered into his shell, and declined to hold intercourse with the outside. I sat smoking for five minutes, I suppose, expecting that the boy might return. I coughed. He turned his head towards me.

'Vous êtes toujours là?'[1] he asked.

'Oui, toujours,' I said. Another silence passed. He placed his hand on his side and groaned.

'Is there something hurting you?' I asked.

He got up and exclaimed:

---

1 "Are you still there?"

'Merde!'[1]

Was that for me? I had the impression, as I glanced towards him to enquire, that his face expressed fear. Of what?

Still holding his side, shuddering and with an unsteady step, he went into his cave, the door of which he slammed. I got up. The dog growled as he lay before the door of the cave. I shouldered my rucksack. It was no longer a hospitable spot. I passed the midden on which the bodies of the grenouilles now lay, went down the stream, and so left. If I met the boy I would tell him his master was ill. But he was nowhere in sight, and I did not know which way he had gone.

I connected the change from cordiality to dislike on the part of Ludo with the mention of the Ankou. There seemed no other explanation. But why should that have affected him so much? Perhaps I had put myself in the position of the Ankou, even—unseen as I was, a foreigner and, so, ultimately dangerous—by mentioning the Ankou, with which he was evidently familiar. He may even have retreated into his cave, because he was afraid of me. Or the poor devil was simply ill. Perhaps the frogs had upset him: or maybe the boy had poisoned him. I walked away. I had gone a mile probably when I met the boy. He was carrying a covered basket.

'Ludo's ill. He went indoors,' I said. 'He seemed to be suffering.'

'He's not very well to-day,' said the boy. 'Has he gone in?'

I gave him a few sous.

Later that summer the fisherman I had been with at the Pardon told me that Ludo was dead.

---

1 "Shit!"

NOTES

1 The last line of Sonnet CXLVI.

2 A village in the Côtes-du-Nord where the celebrated statue of the Ankou can still be seen. Lewis's account of its removal in the next paragraph is based on fact. (Gwenc'hlan Le Sconëzec, *Bretagne Terre* Sacrée, Paris, Editions Albatros, 1977.)

3 An imaginary name, which also appears in "Franciscan Adventures."

4 This imaginary place with an evocative name (i. e. "a belch," as noticed by Lewis) also appears in "Beau Séjour," in the 1922 "Bestre," and in "Franciscan Adventures."

5 The proofs bear a correction to "ascetic," but Lewis deleted this and restored "acetic" (meaning "vinegary").

6 The name was changed on the proofs from the very Breton "Gabik" to the popular "Ludo."

7 An imaginary name.

FRANCISCAN ADVENTURES

"Franciscan Adventures," published for the first time in 1910 under the title "Le Père François (A Full-Length Portrait of a Tramp)," was the most heavily revised of the 1927 texts, because the chaotic utterances which constitute the subject of the story could be reshuffled ad lib *to give an indeterminate fictional patchwork—an opportunity Lewis could not resist. Lewis, who may have had Joyce at the back of his mind (see his drawing, "The Duc de Joyeux Sings,"), had retitled his story "The Musician," probably to avoid the irritating exoticism of one more French title. The final title was introduced in the proofs in August 1927. As usual the main modifications concern the systematic introduction of dialogue, the heightening of style (though more moderately than in "Bestre") and the elimination of excessive generalizations—this in order to make the central character more vivid, which was a necessity as the narrator here remains rather passive and impersonal. This was certainly a major improvement, integrating form and matter in a story of music and words which demonstrates how a man can be defeated by singing—a Lewisian theme illustrated by this sentence in* The Revenge for Love: *". . . just as some men are undone by women and some by wine and a very few by song." (II, 2).*

I found him in front of a crowd of awestruck children, the french vagabond, hoisting a box up under his arm, strapping it over his shoulder, and brandishing three ruined umbrellas. 'Ah, yes, say what you will, music, that is the art for me! Do you know, shall I tell you?' (he approached a little girl, who shrank abashed from his confidences). 'Shall I tell you, my little chicken?' he whispered, his voice sustaining in a sepulchral vibration the *dise* of 'veux-tu que je te *dise*?' and slobbering at 'poule,' which he puffed out from his vinous lips, eyes sodden, fixed and blank.

'I am musical!'

Waggling his head, he turned away and started down the road. Then he wheeled at their jeers. In big strides he hurried back: he saw himself as a giant in a fairy tale. The group of small children backed in a block, all eyes centering on the figure stalking towards them. He brought himself to a sudden halt, stiffened to lift himself still further above their lilliputian stature. 'Music!' he exclaimed: 'ah, yes, I am' (he paused, kneading them with his fiery eyes; then in a very confidential key) *'musical!'* He proceeded with that theme, but conversationally. In making use of certain expressions such as *pianissimo* and *contralto*, he would add, as a polite afterthought, 'that is a term in music.' Then, towering over his puny audience, arms extended, head thrown back, he would call out menacingly his maxims—all on the subject of music. Afterwards, dropping his voice once more, and turning his pompous and knowing eyes upon the nearest infant, he would add, in a manner suggestive of a favoured privacy, some further information or advice, 'Remember, the stomach is the womb! L'estomac, c'est la matrice! it is the stomach that sings! It comes out here.' Tall, slender and with graceful waving limbs, he wore a full beard, growing in a lustreless, grey-green cascade, while hair fell, curling at the ends, upon his shoulders. He had a handsome, fastidiously regular, thin and tanned face, in which his luminous black eyes recognized the advantage of their position; they rolled luxuriously on either side of his aristocratic nose. He would frequently pass his hands, of a 'musical' tenuity, over his canonical beard.

I thought I would stop and interrogate this shell. I watched his performance from a distance. He soon saw me and left the children. He passed, his hat struck down over his eyes, a drunken pout of watchful defiance lying like a burst plum in a nest of green bristle and mildewed down, his nose reddening at its fine extremity. From beneath the hat-brim he quizzed me, but offering alternatives, I thought.

I smiled at him broadly, showing him my big, white, expensive teeth, in perfect condition.

'Good-day!' I nodded.

He might pull up, or perhaps he was too drunk, or not in the mood: I thought I would leave it at that. He was not sure: the tail of his eye interrogated.

'Good-day!' I nodded more sharply, reassuringly.

An arch light replaced the quizzing scowl, but still he did not stop.

'Good-day!' I exclaimed. 'Yes!' I nodded with pointed affirmative.

'Good-day!'

He went on, his eyes trained sideways on me. I gave a salvo of emphatic nods in quick succession.

'Yes!' I coaxed. I showed my teeth again. 'Why yes!'

He was repelled by my shabby appearance, I saw. I opened my coat and showed him a rich coloured scarf. I smiled again, slowly and hypnotically, offering to his dazzled inspection the dangling scarf.

He suddenly wheeled in my direction, stopped, stretched out the hand with the scarecrow umbrellas, and began singing a patriotic song. I stopped. A half-dozen yards separated us. His voice was strong: it spent most of its time in his throat, wallowing in a juicy bellow. Sometimes by accident the sinuses were occupied by it, as it charged up the octave, and it issued pretty and flute-like from the well-shaped inside of his face. As he sang, his head was dramatically lowered, to enable him to fish down for the low notes; his eyes glared fixedly up from underneath. His mouth was stretched open to imitate the dark, florid aperture of a trumpet: from its lips rich sputum trickled. He would stop, and with an indrawn wheeze or a quick gasp, fetch it back as it was escaping. Then he would burst out violently again into a heaving flux of song. I approached him.

'That was not at all bad,' I remarked when he had done, and was gathering up stray drops the colour of brandy with his tongue.

'No?'

'Not at all. It was very musical. Quite good!'

'Ah!' he exclaimed, and his eyes rested blankly on my person. 'Musical! Ah!'

'Yes, I think so.'

'Ah!'

'By God and the Devil and what comes between, you have a voice that is not at all bad.'

'You are of that opinion?'

'My God, yes!'

'Truly?'

'That is what I hold for the moment. But I must hear more of it.'

He retreated a step, lowered his head, took a deep breath, and opened his mouth, deflated his chest, and raised his head.

'Have a cigarette,' I said.

He eyed my luxurious new morocco cigarette case. He perceived the clean, pink shirt and collar as I drew it out. With a clear responsive functioning to delight 'Behavior,' he swung his box off his shoulder, put it down upon the road, and placed his umbrellas upon it. He felt stiff when that was off. He rattled himself about circumspectly.

'Thanks! Thanks!'

His fine amber and ebony finger-tips entered the case with suspicious decorum, and drew out the little body of a cigarette nipped between thumb and index.

'Thank you, old chap!'

The cigarette was stuck into the split plum, which came out in the midst of his beard—its dull-red hemispheres revolving a little, outward and then inward, to make way, gently closing upon it. I lighted it; he began sucking the smoke. A moment later it burst from his nostrils.

'What is the time, mon petit?' he asked.

He wanted to see my watch.

'Half-past hanging time,' I said. 'Will you have a drink? Tu prendras un petit coup, n'est-ce pas?'[1]

'Mais!—je-ne-demande-pas-mieux!'[2]

It was done. I led him to the nearby débit. We sat down in the excessive gloom and damp. I rattled on the tin table with the soucoupe of the last drinker.

I examined this old song-bird with scorn. Monotonous passion, stereotyped into a frenzied machine, he irritated me like an aimlessly howling wind. Had I been sitting with the wind, however, I should not have felt scorn. He was at the same time elemental and silly, that was the reason. What emotions had this automaton experienced before he accepted outcast life? In the rounded personality, known as Father Francis, the answer was neatly engraved. *The emotions provoked by the bad, late, topical sentimental songs of Republican France.* You could get no closer answer than that, and it accounted completely for him. He had become their disreputable embodiment. In his youth the chlorotic heroine of the popular lyrical fancy must have been his phantom mate. He became her ideal, according to the indications provided by the lying ballad. So he would lose touch more and more with unlyricized reality, which would in due course vomit him into the outcast void. That was the likeliest story of this shell I had arrested and attracted in here to inspect.

I settled down to watch. I flashed a few big smiles at him to warm him up. But he was very businesslike. A stranger would have supposed us engaged in

---

1 "Just a drop, won't you?"

2 "Well! Why not?"

some small but interesting negotiation. My rôle would have seemed that of a young, naïve, enthusiastic impresario. Francis was my 'find.' (I was evidently a musical impresario.)

After having been shown his throat, and having failed in my attempt to seize between my thumb and forefinger an imaginary vessel, which he insisted, with considerable violence, I should locate, our relations nearly terminated out of hand. I had cast doubt, involuntarily, upon a possession by which he set great store. He frowned. But he had other resources. I pursued song across this friend's anatomy to its darkest springs. Limited, possibly, to the field of his own body, he was a consummate ventriloquist. I have heard the endocrines uttering a C sharp, and there is nowhere in the intestines from which for me musical notes have not issued. Placing his hand upon his stomach, and convulsing himself solemnly, as though about to eat, his chin on his chest, he and I would sit and listen, and we would both hear a rich, musical sound an inch or so above the seat of the stool on which he sat.

He would then look up at me slowly, with a smile of naïve understanding.

I got tired of this, and said irrelevantly:

'Your hair is very long.'

He pushed in a brake—he had heard—he slowed down his speech, his eye doubtfully hooked on to mine: some sentences still followed. Then after a silence, releasing as it were with a snap all his face muscles so that his mask dropped into lines of preternatural gravity, he exclaimed:

'T'as raison mon pauv' gosse![1]—I will tell you. Here, I say, I will tell you. It's too long. My hair is too long!'

How vastly this differed from my own observation, though the words were the same, it is difficult to convey. If he had with irrefragable proofs confuted my statement for ever, it could not have been more utterly wiped out.

What was I? That did not exercise him. Once or twice he looked at me, not certainly with curiosity, but with a formal attention. An inscrutable figure had beckoned to him, and was now treating him for no reason beyond that he was. (This might be a strange circumstance. But it possessed no monopoly of strangeness.) His cigarettes, though not strong, were good. He was a foreigner. That was sufficient. François was not interested in other people, except as illustrations of elementary physics. Some people repelled him, violently on occasion, and set up interferences, resulting in hunger and thirst. He lived in outer space, outcast, and only came to earth to drink and get a crust. There people mattered, for a moment, but without identity.

The obstacles to be overcome if you were to establish profitable relations with this at first sight inaccessible mind, were many. Between it and the

---

[1] "You're right, my poor boy!"

outer world many natural barriers existed. His conversation was obscure. My ignorance of the theory of music, the confusion caused in my mind by his prolonged explanation of difficult passages (full of what I supposed to be musicians' slang, confounded with thieves' slang and breton idiom); the destructive hiccups that engulfed so many of his phrases, and often ruined a whole train of thought, even nipped in the bud entire philosophies, the constant sense of insecurity consequent upon these repeated catastrophes, these were only a few of the disappointments. Another obstacle was that he spoke the major part of the time in a whisper. When I could not catch a single word, I yet often could judge, by the glances he shot at me, the scornful half-closing of his eyes, screwing up his mouth and nose, all the horrid cunning of his expression and nodding of his head, the sort of thing that was occurring. At other times, his angry and defiant looks showed me that my respect was being peremptorily claimed. But it remained dumb show, often, his voice was pitched so low.

'Speak up, Francis. On Tibb's-eve you'll have to be louder than that.'

'I'm sorry, my poor friend.—It's the vocal cords. They function badly to-day.'

'Are you dry? Fill up.'

He forgot the next moment, and renewed his muttering.

The remembrance of injuries constantly stirred in him. Excited by his words, when he had found some phrase happier than another to express his defiant independence, he felt keenly the chance he had lost. But enemies melted into friends, and vice versa, in his mind, as they had in his experience. He turned and frankly enjoyed his verbal triumphs at my expense.

We had been together some time, and he had drunk a bottle of wine, when his thoughts began to run on a certain hotel-keeper of the neighbourhood, whom he suspected of wishing to sell his present business. The day before, or the week before, he had observed him looking up at a newly-constructed building in the main street of Rot.[1]

When he first began about this, I supposed he was referring to the coarse eructations of some figure whom we had imperceptibly left, although I thought we were still with him. He dropped his voice, and looked behind him when he said 'Rot.' (Rot is a breton commune, and it also means a belch.) I sat over him with knitted brows for some time.

'Oui. Pour moi, c'est sa dame qui ne veut plus de Kermanec.[2]—Que la vase pue là-bas—oh, là là! Quel odeur! Elle a raison! Qu'il aille à Rot! Qu'il y aille! Moi, je m'en fous. Tant pis pour lui. C'est un malin, tu sais.'[1] He drank

[1] "Yes. I think it's his missus who is opposed to Kermanec.—The mud there, what a stench! How it stinks! She's right! Let him go to Rot! Let him go! I don't care! Too bad for him! He knows a thing or two, you know." (The English first edition gave "je m'en foute," corrected in the American edition.)

fiercely and continued (I will translate the sort of rigmarole that followed): 'He's like that. Once he gets an idea in his head. What's he want to leave Kermanec for? It's a good place: he has a fine trade. He's my cousin. He doesn't know me. I got behind the wall. It's not a bad house. It's been in that state for two years. What? Two years, I say, for certain; it may be three or four. There's no roof, but its first floor is in:—no staircase. It's dry. I don't say it's a Régina! They put a *flic* [1] at the corner, but we got in the back way. There's waste-land—yes, waste. Of course. *Naturally.* I saw him. He was going in at the gate. I hid. He paced the frontage.' He put one sabot in front of the other to show the method. This was the innkeeper—not the *flic*—measuring the frontage of the half-built house, in the sheltered part of which tramps were accustomed to spend the night, under the nose of the sergent de ville. And this was the house on which, so it seemed, the landlord had his eye.

In the course of his recital, he repeatedly reverted to the proud spirit of this publican. On my catching the word 'vermin,' and showing interest, he repeated what he was saying a little louder.

'Any one seeing me as I am, without profession, poor, might suppose that I had vermin in my beard. Yes,' he added softly. We fell into a conversation at this point upon matters connected with the toilet. What a bore it was to wash! No great men had ever washed. There was a great sage in England called Shaw, I told him, he never washed. Doctor Johnson, another british sage, found washing repugnant. It was very unusual, I said, for *me* to wash, though I had, I said, washed that morning. Searching stealthily behind the unorganized panels of rags, which could be seen symmetrically depending when his great-coat was opened, he produced the middle section of a comb. With this he made passes over his beard—without, however, touching it—which he shook scornfully. He looked at me steadily. I showed I was impressed. He replaced the comb. The dumb-show had been intended to reveal to my curiosity a characteristic moment of his toilet.

'Zut!' [2] he said, coughing, 'I had a good brush. That rogue Charlot (ce chenapan de Charlot!) pinched it!' 'Charlot,' I heard, was so named among his brother vagabonds on account of his resemblance to Chaplin.

A story intervened in which he gave a glimpse of his physical resource and determination in moments of difficulty. The landlords of inns, and farmers, were his principal enemies. He told me how he treated them. First, it was in general, then particular figures suggested themselves. He dealt with them one by one.

'Je lui disais: Monsieur!' (Like Doctor Johnson all his addresses began with an emphatic and threatening 'Sir!') 'I said: Your views are not mine. It's no

---

1 "A cop."

2 "Damn!"

use my affecting to be in agreement with you. You say I'm a "Rôdeur." I give you the lie. (—*I don't beat about the bush!* he said in an aside to me.) Je n'ai jamais rôdé.—Je ne bouge pas, moi—jamais! J'y suis, j'y reste!—[1] That is my motto! That is my way, sir!'

A scene of considerable violence shortly took place. He stamped on the floor with his great sabots to render more vivid to himself this scene, also to supply the indispensable element of noise. Owing to emotion, his voice was incapable of providing this. He spoke with a dreadful intensity, glaring into my face. Eventually he sprang up; struggling and stamping about the room (overmatched at first) with an indomitable heave of the shoulders, and an irresistible rush, he then made believe to fling his antagonist out of the door. While engaged in this feat, panting and stamping, he had exclaimed where the action suggested it, 'Ah! veux-tu! Sale bête! Ah sacré gars! Et puis alors, quoi? Es-tu fou? Tu crois pétrir avec tes mains un tel que moi! Allons donc! Tu plaisantes! Ah! Je vois bien ton jeu!—Ah bah! le voilà foutu! Tant mieux! Con! Oui! Con! Sale con! Ah!'[2] He came back and sat down, his chest heaving, looking at me for a long time silently, with an air of insolent triumph.

It would have been difficult to blame him for the steps he had taken, for he evidently experienced a great relief at the eviction of this imaginary landlord. Probably he had thrown him out of every bar along the road. Ever since we had entered he had been restless. I was not sorry he had rid us of this phantom; but I looked with a certain anxiety towards the door from time to time. He now seemed enjoying the peace that he had so gallantly secured for himself. His limbs relaxed, his eyes were softer. The lips of the voluptuary were everted again, moving like gorged red worms in the hairs of his moustache and beard. He delicately fed them from his wine-glass. He proceeded now to show me his mild side. He could afford to. He assured me that he did not like turbulent people. 'J' n'aime pas l' monde turbulent!' And then he raised his voice, making the gesture of the teacher: 'Socrates said, "Listen, but do not strike!"' ('Socrate a dit: "Ecoutez, mais ne frappez pas."')

He abounded in a certain kind of catch-word (such as 'Il ne faut pas confondre la vitesse avec la preécipitation![3] Non! Il ne faut pas confondre la vitesse avec la précipitation!'). These sayings occurred to him hors d'à propos.[4] Sometimes, finding them there on his tongue, he would just use

---

[1] "I never prowled.—I don't move about! Here I am and here I stay!" The last words are a famous saying of General MacMahon after the capture of Malakoff (1855).

[2] Various insults and exclamations, and a typically Lewisian image: "You believe your hands can knead someone like me! . . . I can see through you!"

[3] "Haste and speed should not be confused."

[4] Properly "hors *de* propos": "untimely."

them and leave it at that. Or he would boldly utter them and take them as a text for a new discourse. Another perhaps would turn up: he would drop the first and proceed triumphantly at a tangent.

'Do you go to Rumengol?[3] I asked him.

'Rumengol? Why, yes, I have gone to Rumengol.'

'It is the Pardon for men of your profession.'

He looked at me, saying absent-mindedly:

'Why, yes, perhaps.'

'It is called *le Pardon des chanteurs*, "the singers' Pardon," is not that so, I believe?'

His face lit up stupidly.

'Ah, is it called that?' he said. 'I didn't know it was called that. *Pardon des chanteurs.* That's jolly! Pardon des chanteurs!'

He began singing a catch.

'Is your beat mostly on the *armor*, or is it in the *argoat*?'

'Argouate?' he asked blankly. 'What is that? Argouate! I don't know it.'

Those are the terms for the littoral and the interior respectively. I was surprised to find he did not know them.

'Where do you come from?' I asked.

'I don't know.—Far from here,' he said briefly.

So he was not breton. The historic rôle of the vagabond in Armorica has almost imposed on him the advertisement of a mysterious origin. It was so much to his advantage, in the more superstitious centuries, to be a stranger, and seem not to know the breton tongue, if not deaf and mute. So he could slip into the legendary framework, and become, at need, Gabik or Gralon.

Something had struck his fancy particularly. This was connected with his name François. He told me how he had slept in the château of François I. at Chambord. It appeared that it was in giving information against his *bête noire,* the local innkeeper, that he had come to sleep there. I could not discover what connection these two facts might have. I expect they had none. It began suddenly with a picture of a wintry night in the forest. It was very cold and it blew. An inn put in its appearance. There an 'orgie' was in progress. He introduced himself. Without being exactly welcomed, he was suffered to remain. The account at this point became more and more fantastic and uncertain. He must have got drunk almost immediately. This I put down to his exposure to the cold: so I picked my way through his disordered words. His story staggered and came in flashes. He could not understand evidently why the material had, all of a sudden, grown so intractable. Once or twice he stopped. Living it again, he rolled his eyes and even seemed about to lose his balance on the stool. He wanted to go on telling it: but it began to sound absurd even to him. It still did not occur to him that at this point he had fallen down drunk. He gave it up.

But the inevitable wicked landlord put in his appearance, robbed him of his tobacco and other articles. He resisted this exploitation. Then we certainly reached the château. He became more composed. I asked him where he had slept in the château. He answered he had slept on a mattress, and had had *two* blankets. On second thoughts he concluded that this would tax my credulity too much, and withdrew one of the blankets. It was in the Château de Chambord that Molière played for the first time *Le Bourgeois Gentilhomme*,[4] under the splendid ceiling covered then with freshly painted salamanders. But how did this Francis come to lodge there, if he ever did? Flaubert's indignant account of the neglect into which, in his time, this celebrated castle had fallen, may afford some clue. He says of it: 'On l'a donné à tout le monde, comme si personne n'en voulait le garder. Il a l'air de n'avoir jamais presque servi et avoir été toujours trop grand. C'est comme une hôtellerie abandonnée où les voyageurs n'ont pas méme laissé leurs noms aux murs.'[1]

As it has been 'given to everybody,' and yet 'nobody has ever wanted it,' perhaps this 'derelict inn' was given to le père François for a night. When Flaubert and Maxime du Camp, already in a state of bellicose distress, gaze over the staircase into the central court, their indignant gaze falls on a humble female donkey, giving milk to a newly-born colt. 'Voilà ce qu'il y avait dans la cour d'honneur du Château de Chambord!' exclaims Flaubert: 'un chien qui joue dans l'herbe et un âne qui tette, ronfle et brait, fiente et gambade sur le seuil des rois. . . .'[2] Could Flaubert have observed le père François installed beneath his sumptuous blanket in the entrance court of kings, or addressing himself to his toilet, I feel certain that that impetuous man would have passionately descended the staircase and driven him out with his cane. But this account of Flaubert's does make the franciscan adventure of the Château de Chambord more likely: for if a dog and a donkey, why not a tramp?

There was no break in the story; but the château grew dim. He evidently rapidly fell asleep, owing to the unaccustomed blanket. He forgot the last landlord. He had been a robust man. He ran after the bonnes. He melted into a farmer. The farmer was robust. He ran after François. There was a dog. It fixed its teeth in his leg. He struggled madly with the dog, his back against the débit wall. Afterwards, when it was all over, he rolled up his trousers and we attempted to find a cicatrice. He wetted his thumb, with that he abraded a

1 "It has been handed over to everybody, as if nobody wanted it or could keep it. It seems never to have been used, and to have been always too vast. It is like an abandoned inn on the walls of which travellers have not even left their names."[5]

2 "This is what was to be seen in the main courtyard of Chambord. A dog playing on the grass, and a donkey sucking and snoring and braying and excreting and leaping about the threshold of kings. . ."

rectangular strip near the ankle: there was a little weal.

The saloon-keeper passed the table several times during this chain of stories. Once he said, stopping to listen for a moment, 'Ouf, a pack of lies!' 'Non pas!' replied Francis. 'You lie. You love falsehood! I can see it. Go away.' The man shrugged violently and went back to the bar. Some customers had come in. One sat listening to François with a heavy grin. I turned to him and said:

'He is original, le père François, don't you find that so?'

'Why, yes. He's mad.' The steady eyes of the smiling peasant continued to follow his movements with lazy attention.

'Yes, *original*, I am original!' François eagerly assented, as though in fear, then, that I should be converted to this other man's opinion.

'Original!' he insisted. 'I am original.'

Suddenly turning to me with rapid condescension, he remarked:

'Je suis content de toi! I am satisfied with you!'

However, the horizon became anew overclouded. With him it never stood at Fair for long. He grew more and more violent. Often he sprang up and whirled round without reason, with the ecstasy of a dervish, his ruined umbrellas shaken at arm's length. Afterwards he sat down suddenly. He held his arm out stiffly towards me, looked at it, then at me, wildly, contracting his muscles, as if searching for some thought that this familiar instrument suggested, without finding it. Stretching his arm back swiftly as though about to strike, drawing his breath between his teeth, with the other hand he seized his forearm as though it were an independent creature, his fingers its legs, and stared at it. What did this mad arm want? Allons donc! He dropped it listlessly at his side, where it hung.

Night had fallen: the landlord had lighted the lamp over the bar. Francis grew steadily more noisy, singing and using the window as a drum, his arms on either side of it, tattooing and banging it, his head turned towards us. The landlord shouted at him at last, with great violence, 'Tais-toi, vieil imbécile!'[1] The landlord was vexed. His wife slouched out from the kitchen, and directing the fine hostility of her gaze toward Francis, muttered heatedly with her husband for some minutes. They were afraid they would have to give him a night's lodging in the barn. Not long after this we were turned out. Francis went meekly: he ridiculed the event, in sotto voce conversation with himself. I was ready to go. At the door he cut a caper, and shouted at the landlord, bolder out of doors:

'Je vous remercie! Monsieur, adieu! Me v'là qui va me chauffer à la cheminée du roi René.'[2]

---

1 "Shut up, you old fool!" (The English first edition gave "vieux imbécile," corrected in the American edition.)

2 "Thank you! Good bye! I'll get warm by King René's fireplace."

'Plutôt à belle étoile, mon pauv' viou!'[1]

Francis looked up into the sky overhead and saw a bright star.

'Plutôt, en effet,' he said. 'Mais oui-da, t'as raison—il fait nuit! T'es intelligent, tu sais! N'est-ce pas, mon petit, qu'il est intelligent, le patron, quand même? Il n'en a pas l'air, parbleu! Pauv' 'colas, va! Ah, bah! Tant pis! Les paysans de par ici sont d'une bêtise!—c'est fantastique! Oui-dame: mais écoute! C'môme-là, tu sais: il n'est pas méchant; *mais* non! Il est trop bête! C'est à peine qu'il sait lire et écrire. C'est une brute, quoi! Tant pis! Ah! merde alors, où sont donc mes photos——?'[2]

He stood drawn up to his full height, his hands hurrying dramatically into all the hiding places of his person. First one hand, then the other, disappeared beneath his rags and leapt out empty.

'Rien! Ils ne sont pas là! Nom d'un nom! On m'a volé!'[3]

He made as though to rush back to the débit. I held him by the arm.

'Come on! I'll give you a franc. You can buy some more.'

He was about to put into execution the immemorial tactic of the outcast in such a situation. Eviction from an eating and drinking house, first: then comes the retort of an accusation of theft. The indignant customary words raced on his tongue. He had been robbed! All his photographs had been pinched! What a house! What people! It was not safe for honest men to drink there! He would inform the Commissioner of Police when he reached Saint-Kaduan.[6] They would see if he was to be robbed with impunity!

He shook his fist at the débit while I held him. The landlord had left the door. The road was deserted; a gilt moon (it was that he had mistaken for the sun, in a condition of partial eclipse) hung over the village a hundred yards away. Our shadows staggered madly for a moment, then the thought of the franc cut short this ceremony, and he came away towards the village. I gave him the franc. He came half way, then left me. Standing in the middle of the road, the moonlight converting him into a sickly figure of early republican romance, he sang to me as I walked away. With the franc, I supposed it was his intention to return to the débit.

In the 'granges' at the various farms, tramps usually find a night's lodging. They make arrangements to meet, and often spend several nights together in this way. The farm people take their matches and pipes away from them. Or

---

1 "Under the stars, rather, my poor old chap!"

2 "True. Right you are—it's dark! You're intelligent, you know! After all the landlord is intelligent, isn't he, my lad? He doesn't look it, by God! Poor Nick! . . . The peasants round here are so stupid!—it's incredible. Indeed—but listen! This guy is not nasty, you know; not at all! He's too stupid! He can hardly read and write. He is a brute, that's all! . . . Damn it, where are my photos——"

3 "Nothing! They're not here! Damnation! I've been robbed!" (Should be "Elles ne sont pas là!")

they put them in the stable among the cattle, making a hole in the wet straw like a cradle for them. Two days later I saw him through an inn window for a moment, outside Braspartz.[7] He was dancing in his heavy sabots, his shoulders drawn up to his ears, arms akimbo. 'I saw an Italian dance this way,' I heard him exclaim. 'It's true! This is the way the Italians dance!' A group of sullen peasants watched him, one laughing, to show he was not taken in. On noticing me, he began singing a love song, in a loud strong voice. Without interrupting the song, he stretched his hand through the window for a cigarette. There was no recognition in his face while he sang: his lips protruded eloquently in keeping with the sentiment. That is the last I saw of him.

NOTES

[1] An imaginary place also mentioned in "Beau Séjour," "The Death of the Ankou" and the 1922 "Bestre."

[2] An imaginary place which also appears in "Bestre," "The Death of the Ankou" and "Brobdingnag." The proofs gave "Vandevennec" (see "The Death of the Ankou," page 107).

[3] A village near Rosnën.

[4] The play was performed there on October 14, 1670.

[5] This quotation taken from the first chapter (written by Flaubert) of *Par les champs et par les grèves* (1886) is imperfect and should read: "comme si personne n'en voulait ou ne pouvait le garder. Il semble n'avoir jamais servi et avoir été toujours trop grand. . ." Partly corrected in the American edition.

[6] An imaginary name.

[7] "Braspartz" (Brasparts) was added in 1927.

BROTCOTNAZ

"Brotcotnaz," first published in 1911 under the title of "Brobdingnag," may seem at first sight to follow the main lines of the earlier story in spite of considerable rewriting. As usual a few short factual sentences were in 1927 expanded into several full-length scenes complete with dialogue and visual effects. Ker-Orr's presence was fortified and, after "A Soldier of Humour," this story—with "Bestre" and "The Death of the Ankou"—is the one in which he plays the most active part, though his relation with the Brotcotnaz—a combination of provocative mock-naïveté and voyeurism—appears mysteriously elliptical: Ker-Orr's mother and Madame Brotcotnaz are associated through their drinking habits, and Julie's final triumph is suggested to be at Ker-Orr's expense as well, which would associate him implicitly with Monsieur Brotcotnaz. In fact the conclusions of 1911 are reversed with Julie's triumph which was not even suggested in the earlier version. Hence the new and much more explicit reasons given for Brotcotnaz' disarray. In 1911 he was the victim of an abstract enigmatic collision between reality and fiction, whereas in 1927 his confusion is largely attributed to his no longer being in a position to suppress Julie with impunity. "Brobdingnag" concluded on "nocturnal rites growing more and more savage and desperate," whereas Brotcotnaz is left petrified by an inner "blankness." A clarification of motivations is typical of the final stage of The Wild Body. *That the Wild Body sequence should end up with this story, rather than with the more eschatological "Death of the Ankou" or the more existential "Franciscan Adventures," suggests the persistence and importance of the parental fuscination.*

Madame Brotcotnaz is orthodox: she is the breton woman at forty-five, from la basse Bretagne,[1] the heart of Old Brittany, the region of the great Pardons. Frans Hals also would have passed from the painting of the wife of a petty burgess to Madame Brotcotnaz without any dislocation of his formulas or rupture of the time-sense. He would still have seen before him the black and white—the black broadcloth and white coiffe or caul; and for the white those virgated, slate-blue surfaces, the cold ink-black for the capital masses of the picture, would have appeared without a hitch. On coming to the face Frans Hals would have found his favourite glow of sallow-red, only deeper than he was accustomed to find in the flemish women. He would have gone to that part of the palette where the pigment lay for the men's faces at forty-five, the opposite end to the monticules of olive and sallow peach for the *juniores*, or the virgins and young wives.

The distillations of the breton orchard have almost subdued the obstinate yellow of jaundice, and Julie's face is a dull claret. In many tiny strongholds of eruptive red the more recent colour has entrenched itself. Her hair is very dark, parted in the middle, and tightly brushed down upon her head. Her eyebrows are for ever raised. She could not depress them, I suppose, any more, if she wanted to. A sort of scaly rigor fixes the wrinkles of the forehead into a seriated field of what is scarcely flesh, with the result that if she pulled her eyebrows down, they would fly up again the moment she released the muscles. The flesh of the mouth is scarcely more alive: it is parched and pinched in, so that she seems always hiding a faint snicker by driving it primly into her mouth. Her eyes are black and moist, with the furtive intensity of a rat. They move circumspectly in this bloated shell. She displaces herself also more noiselessly than the carefulest nun, and her hands are generally decussated, drooping upon the ridge of her waist-line, as though fixed there with an emblematic nail, at about the level of her navel. Her stomach is, for her, a kind of exclusive personal 'calvary.' At its crest hang her two hands, with the orthodox decussation, an elaborate ten-fingered symbol.

Revisiting the home of the Brotcotnazes this summer, I expected to find some change: but as I came down the steep and hollow ramp leading from the cliffs of the port, I was reassured at once. The door of the débit I perceived was open, with its desiccated bush over the lintel. Julie, with her head bound up in a large surgical bandage, stood there peering out, to see if there were any one in sight. No one was in sight, I had not been noticed; it was not from the direction of the cliffs that she redoubted interruption. She quickly withdrew. I approached the door of the débit in my noiseless *espadrilles* (that is, the hemp and canvas shoes of the country), and sprang quickly in after her. I snapped her with my eye while I shouted:

'Madame Brotcotnaz! Attention!'[1]

She was behind the bar-counter, the fat medicine-glass was in the air, reversed. Her head was back, the last drops were trickling down between her gum and underlip, which stuck out like the spout of a cream-jug. The glass crashed down on the counter; Julie jumped, her hand on her heart. Beneath, among tins and flagons, on a shelf, she pushed at a bottle. She was trying to get it out of sight. I rushed up to her and seized one of her hands.

'I am glad to see you, Madame Brotcotnaz!' I exclaimed. 'Neuralgia again?' I pointed to the face.

'Oh, que vous m'avez fait peur, Monsieur Kairor!'[2]

She placed her hand on her left breast, and came out slowly from behind the counter.

'I hope the neuralgia is not bad?'

She patted her bandage with a sniff.

'It's the erysipelas.'

'How is Monsieur Brotcotnaz?'

'Very well, thank you, Monsieur Kairor!' she said in a subdued sing-song. 'Very well,' she repeated, to fill up, with a faint prim smile. 'He is out with the boat. And you, Monsieur Kairor? Are you quite well?'

'Quite well, I thank you, Madame Brotcotnaz,' I replied, 'except perhaps a little thirsty. I have had a long walk along the cliff. Could we have a little glass together, do you think?'

'Why, yes, Monsieur Kairor.' She was more reserved at once. With a distant sniff, she turned half in the direction of the counter, her eyes on the wall before her. 'What must I give you now?'

'Have you any *pur jus*, such as I remember drinking the last time I was here?'

'Why, yes.' She moved silently away behind the wooden counter. Without difficulty she found the bottle of brandy, and poured me out a glass.

'And you, Madame? You will take one with me, isn't that so?'

'Mais, je veux bien!'[3] she breathed with muted dignity, and poured herself out a small glass. We touched glasses.

'A votre santé, Madame Brotcotnaz!'

'A la vôtre, Monsieur Kairor!'

She put it chastely to her lip and took a decent sip, with the expression reserved otherwise for intercourse with the sacrament.

---

1 "Careful!"

2 "Oh, you've given me a nasty turn!"

3 "Yes, with pleasure!"

'It's good.' I smacked my lips.

'Why, yes. It is not at all bad,' she said, turning her head away with a faint sniff.

'It's good *pur jus*. If it comes to that, it is the best I have tasted since last I was here. How is it your *pur jus* is always of this high quality? You have taste where this drink is concerned, about that there can be no two opinions.'

She very softly tossed her head, wrinkled her nose on either side of the bridge, and appeared about to sneeze, which was the thing that came next before a laugh.

I leant across and lightly patted the bandage. She withdrew her head.

'It is painful?' I asked with commiseration.

My father, who, as I believe I have said,[2] is a physician, once remarked in my hearing at the time my mother was drinking very heavily, prior to their separation, that for the management of alcoholic poisoning there is nothing better than koumiss.

'Have you ever tried a mixture of fermented mare's milk? Ordinary buttermilk will do. You add pepsin and lump sugar and let it stand for a day and a night. That is a very good remedy.'

She met this with an airy mockery. She dragged her eyes over my face afterwards with suspicion.

'It's excellent for erysipelas.'

She mocked me again. I told myself that she might at any moment find koumiss a useful drink, though I knew that she was wounded in the sex-war now only, and so required a management of another sort. I enjoyed arousing her veteran's contempt. She said nothing, but sat with resignation on the wooden bench at the table.

'I remember well these recurrent indispositions before, Madame Brotcotnaz,' I said. She looked at me in doubt for a moment, then turned her face quickly towards the door, slightly offended.

Julie was, of course, secretive, but as it had happened, she was forced to hug her secrets in public like two dolls that every one could see. I pretended to snatch first one, then the other. She looked at me and saw that I was not serious. She was silent in the way a child is: she just silently looked at me with a primitive coquetry of reproach, and turned her side to me.—Underneath the counter on the left hand of a person behind it was the bottle of eau-de-vie. When every one else had gone to the river to wash clothes, or had collected in the neighbouring inn, she approached the bottle on tiptoe, poured herself out several glasses in succession, which she drank with little sighs. Everybody knew this. That was the first secret. I had ravished it impetuously as described. Her second secret was the periodic beatings of Brotcotnaz. They were of very great severity. When I had occupied a room there, the crashing in the next apartment at night lasted sometimes for twenty minutes. The next day Julie was bandaged and could hardly limp downstairs. That was the erysipelas. Every one knew this, as well: yet her secretiveness had to exercise itself upon these scandalously exposed objects. I just thought I would stroke the second of them when I approached my hand to her bandaged face. These intrusions of mine into a *public* secret bored her only. She knew as well as I did when a thing was secret and when it was not. *Qu'est-ce qu'il a, cet homme?*[1] she would say to herself.

'When do you expect Nicholas?' I asked.

She looked at the large mournful clock.

'Il ne doit pas tarder.'[2]

I lifted my glass.

'To his safe return.'

The first muscular indications of a sneeze, a prim depression of the mouth, and my remark had been acknowledged, while she lifted her glass and took a solid sip.

Outside it was a white calm: I had seen a boat round the corner, with folded sails, beneath the cliff. That was no doubt Brotcotnaz. As I passed, they had dropped their oars out.

He should be here in a moment.

'Fill up your glass, Madame Brotcotnaz,' I said.

She did not reply. Then she said in an indifferent catch of the breath.

'Here he is!' Hands folded, or decussated as I have said they always were, she left him to me. She had produced him with her exclamation, 'Le v'là!'

A footfall, so light that it seemed nothing, came from the steps outside. A shadow struck the wall opposite the door. With an easy, dainty, and rapid tread, with a coquettishly supple giving of the knees at each step, and a gentle debonair oscillation of the massive head, a tall heavily-built fisherman came in. I sprang up and exclaimed:

'Ah! Here is Nicholas! How are you, old chap?'

'Why, it is Monsieur Kairor!' came the low caressing buzz of his voice. 'How are you? Well, I hope?'

He spoke in a low indolent voice. He smiled and smiled. He was dressed in the breton fashion.

'Was that you in the boat out there under the cliff just now?' I asked.

'Why, yes, Monsieur Kairor, that must have been us. Did you see us?' he said, with smiling interest.

I noted his child's pleasure at the image of himself somewhere else, in his boat, observed by me. It was as though I had said, Peep-oh! I see you, and we were back in the positions we then had occupied. He reflected a moment.

---

1 "What's the matter with this man?"

2 "He shouldn't be long."

'I didn't see you. Were you on the cliff? I suppose you've just walked over from Lopérec?'[1]

His instinct directed him to account for my presence, here, and then up on the cliff. It was not curiosity. He wished to have cause and effect properly displayed. He racked his brains to see if he could remember having noticed a figure following the path on the cliff.

'Taking a little walk?' he added then.

He sat on the edge of a chair, with the symmetrical propriety of his healthy and powerful frame, the balance of the seated figure of the natural man, of the european type, found in the quattrocento frescoes. Julie and he did not look at each other.

'Give Monsieur Brotcotnaz a drink at once,' I said.

Brotcotnaz made a deprecatory gesture as she poured it, and continued to smile abstractedly at the table.

The dimensions of his eyes, and their oily suffusion with smiling-cream, or with some luminous jelly that seems still further to magnify them, are very remarkable. They are great tender mocking eyes that express the coquetry and contentment of animal fats. The sides of his massive forehead are often flushed, as happens with most men only in moments of embarrassment. Brotcotnaz is always embarrassed. But the flush with him, I think, is a constant affluence of blood to the neighbourhood of his eyes, and has something to do with their magnetic machinery. The tension caused in the surrounding vessels by this aesthetic concentration may account for it. What we call a sickly smile, the mouth remaining lightly drawn across the gums, with a slight painful contraction—the set suffering grin of the timid—seldom leaves his face.

The tread of this timid giant is softer than a nun's—the supple quick-giving at the knees at each step that I have described is the result no doubt of his fondness for the dance, in which he was so rapid, expert, and resourceful in his youth. When I first stayed with them, the year before,[3] a man one day was playing a pipe on the cliff into the hollow of which the house is built. Brotcotnaz heard the music and drummed upon the table. Then, lightly springing up he danced in his tight-fitting black clothes a finicky hornpipe, in the middle of the débit. His red head was balanced in the air, face downwards, his arms went up alternately over his head, while he watched his feet like a dainty cat, placing them lightly and quickly here and there, with a ceremonial tenderness, and then snatching them away.

'You are fond of dancing,' I said.

His large tender steady blue eyes, suffused with the witchery of his secret juices, smiled and smiled: he informed me softly:

'J'suis maître danseur. C'est mon plaisir!'

The buzzing breton drawl, with as deep a 'z' as the dialect of Somerset, gave a peculiar emphasis to the *C'est mon plaisir!* He tapped the table, and gazed with the full benignity of his grin into my face.

'I am master of all the breton dances,' he said.

'The aubade,[4] the gavotte—?'

'Why, yes, the breton gavotte.' He smiled serenely into my face. It was a blast of innocent happiness.

I saw as I looked at him the noble agility of his black faun-like figure as it must have rushed into the dancing crowd at the Pardon, leaping up into the air and capering to the *biniou*[1] with grotesque elegance, while a crowd would gather to watch him. Then taking hands, while still holding their black umbrellas, they would spread out in chains, jolting in a dance confined to their rapidly moving feet. And still like a black fountain of movement, its vertex the flat, black, breton hat, strapped under the chin, he would continue his isolated performance.—His calm assurance of mastery in these dances implied such a position in the past in the festal life of the pagan countryside.

'Is Madame fond of dancing?' I asked.

'Why, yes. Julie can dance.'

He rose, and extending his hand to his wife with an indulgent gallantry, he exclaimed:

'Viens donc, Julie! Come then. Let us dance.'

Julie sat and sneered through her vinous mask at her fascinating husband. He insisted, standing over her with one toe pointed outward in the first movement of the dance, his hand held for her to take in a courtly attitude.

'Viens donc, Julie! Dansons un peu!'

Shedding shamefaced, pinched, and snuffling grins to right and left as she allowed herself to be drawn into this event, she rose. They danced a sort of minuet for me, advancing and retreating, curtseying and posturing, shuffling rapidly their feet. Julie did her part, it seemed, with understanding. With the same smile, at the same pitch, he resumed his seat in front of me.

'He composes verses also, to sing,' Julie then remarked.

'Songs for gavotte-airs, to be sung——?'

'Why, yes. Ask him!'

I asked him.

'Why, yes,' he said. 'In the past I have written many verses.'

Then, with his settled grin, he intoned and buzzed them through his scarcely parted teeth, whose tawny rows, he manipulating their stops with his tongue, resembled some exotic musical instrument.

Brotcotnaz is at once a fisherman, débitant or saloon-keeper, and 'cultivator.' In spite of this trinity of activities, he is poor. To build their present home he dissipated what was then left of Julie's fortune, so I was told by the

---

1 The Breton bagpipe.

postman one evening on the cliff. When at length it stood complete, beneath the little red bluff hewn out for its reception, brightly whitewashed, with a bald slate roof, and steps leading up to the door, from the steep and rugged space in front of it, he celebrated its completion with an expressive house-warming. Now he has the third share in a fishing boat, and what trade comes his way as a saloon-keeper, but it is very little.

His comrades will tell you that he is a 'charmant garçon, mais jaloux.'[1] They call him 'traître.'[2] He has been married twice. Referring to this, gossip tells you he gave his first wife a hard life. If this is true, and by analogy, he may have killed her. In spite of this record, poor Julie 'would have him.' Three times he has inherited money which was quickly spent. Such is his bare history and the character people give him.

The morning after a beating—Julie lying seriously battered upon their bed, or sitting rocking herself quietly in the débit, her head a turban of bandages, he noiselessly attends to her wants, enquires how she feels, and applies remedies. It is like a surgeon and a patient, an operation having just been successfully performed. He will walk fifteen miles to the nearest large town and back to get the necessary medicines. He is grave, and receives pleasantly your commiserations on her behalf, if you offer them. He has a delicate wife, that is the idea: she suffers from a chronic complaint. He addresses her on all occasions with a compassionate gentleness. There is, however, something in the bearing of both that suggests restraint. They are resigned, but none the less they remember the cross they have to bear. Julie will refer to his intemperance, casually, sometimes. She told me on one occasion, that, when first married, they had had a jay. This bird knew when Brotcotnaz was drunk. When he came in from a wake or 'Pardon,' and sat down at the débit table, the jay would hop out of its box, cross the table, and peck at his hands and fly in his face.

The secret of this smiling giant, a year or two younger, I daresay, than his wife, was probably that he intended to kill her. She had no more money. With his reputation as a wife-beater, he could do this without being molested. When he went to a 'Pardon,' she on her side knew he would try to kill her when he came back. That seemed to be the situation. If one night he did succeed in killing her, he would sincerely mourn her. At the fiançailles with his new bride he would see this one on the chair before him, his Julie, and, still radiating tolerance and health, would shed a melancholy smiling tear.

'You remember, Nicholas, those people that called on Thursday?' she now said.

---

1 "A charming fellow, but jealous."

2 "Treacherous."

He frowned gently to recall them.

'Ah, yes, I know—the Parisians that wanted the room.'

'They have been here again this afternoon.'

'Indeed.'

'I have agreed to take them. They want a little cooking. I've consented to do that. I said I had to speak to my husband about it.—They are coming back.'

He frowned more heavily, still smiling. He put his foot down with extreme softness:

'Julie, I have told you that I won't have that! It is useless for you to agree to do cooking. It is above your strength, my poor dear. You must tell them you can't do it.'

'But—they are returning. They may be here at any moment, now. I can do what they wish quite easily.'

With inexorable tenderness he continued to forbid it. Perhaps he did not want people in the house.

'Your health will not permit of your doing that, Julie.'

He never ceased to smile, but his brows remained knit. This was almost a dispute. They began talking in breton.

'Nicholas, I must go,' I said, getting up. He rose with me, following me up with the redoubled suavity of his swimming eyes.

'You must have a drink with me, Monsieur Kairor. Truly you must! Julie! Another glass for Monsieur Kairor.'

I drank it and left, promising to return. He came down the steps with me, his knee flexing with exaggerated suppleness at each step, placing his feet daintily and noiselessly on the dryest spaces on the wet stones. I watched him over my shoulder returning delicately up the steps, his massive back rigid, inclined forward, as though he were being steadily hauled up with a cord, only feet working.

It was nearly three weeks later when I returned to Kermanec.[1] It was in the morning. This time I came over in a tradesman's cart. It took me to the foot of the rough ascent, at the top of which were Brotcotnaz's steps. There seemed to be a certain animation. Two people were talking at the door, and a neighbour, the proprietress of the successful débit, was ascending the steps. The worst had happened. Ça y est.[1] He had killed her! Taking this for granted, I entered the débit, framing my *condoléances.* She would be upstairs on the bed. Should I go up? There were several people in the room. As I entered behind them, with a start of surprise I recognized Julie. Her arm was in a large sling. From beneath stained cloths, four enormously bloated and discoloured fingers protruded. These the neighbours inspected. Also one of

1 "That was it."

her feet had a large bandage. She looked like a beggar at a church door: I could almost hear the familiar cry of the 'droit des pauvres!'[1] She was speaking in breton, in her usual tone of 'miséricorde,' with her ghostly sanctimonious snigger. In spite of this, even if the circumstances had not made this obvious, the atmosphere was very different from that to which I had been accustomed.

At first I thought: She has killed Brotcotnaz, it must be that. But that hypothesis was contradicted by every other fact that I knew about them. It was possible that he had killed himself by accident. But, unnoticed, in the dark extremity of the débit, there he was! On catching sight of his dejected figure, thrust into the darkest shadow of his saloon, I received my second shock of surprise. I hesitated in perplexity. Would it be better to withdraw? I went up to Julie, but made no reference to her condition, beyond saying that I hoped she was well.

'As well as can be expected, my poor Monsieur Kairor!' she said in a sharp whine, her brown eyes bright, clinging and sad.

Recalling the events of my last visit and our conversation, in which I had tapped her bandages, I felt these staring fingers, thrust out for inspection, were a leaf taken out of my book. What new policy was this? I left her and went over to Brotcotnaz. He did not spring up: all he did was to smile weakly, saying:

'Tiens! Monsieur Kairor, vous voilà. Sit down, Monsieur Kairor!'

I sat down. With his elbows on the table he continued to stare into space. Julie and her women visitors stood in the middle of the débit; in subdued voices they continued their discussion. It was in breton, I could not follow it easily.

This situation was not normal: yet the condition of Julie was the regular one. The intervention of the neighbours and the present dejection of Brotcotnaz was what was unaccountable. Otherwise, for the cause of the mischief there was no occasion to look further; a solution, sound, traditional, and in every way satisfying, was there before me in the person of Nicholas. But he whom I was always accustomed to see master of the situation was stunned and changed, like a man not yet recovered from some horrid experience. He, the recognized agent of Fate, was usually so above the mêlée. Now he looked another man, like somebody deprived of a coveted office, or from whom some privilege had been withheld. Had Fate acted without him? Such necessarily was the question that at this point took shape.

Meanwhile I no doubt encountered in turn a few of the perplexities, framing the same dark questions, that Brotcotnaz himself had done. He pulled himself together now and rose slowly.

---

[1] "The Poor Tax!" (Literally, "the right of the poor.")

'You will take something, Monsieur Kairor!' he said, habit operating, with a thin unction.

'Why, yes, I will have a glass of cider,' I said. 'What will you have, Nicholas?'

'Why, I will take the same, Monsieur Kairor,' he said. The break or give at the knee as he walked was there as usual, but mechanical, I felt. Brotcotnaz would revive, I hoped, after his drink. Julie was describing something: she kept bending down to the floor, and making a sweeping gesture with her free hand. Her guests made a chuckling sound in their throats like 'hoity-toity.'

Brotcotnaz returned with the drinks.

'A la vôtre, Monsieur Kairor!' He drank half his glass. Then he said:

'You have seen my wife's fingers?'

I admitted guardedly that I had noticed them.

'Higher up it is worse. The bone is broken. The doctor says that it is possible she will lose her arm. Her leg is also in a bad state.' He rolled his head sadly.

At last I looked at him with relief. He was regaining his old composure. I saw at once that a very significant thing had happened for him, if she lost her arm, and possibly her leg. He could scarcely proceed to the destruction of the trunk only. It was not difficult at least to appreciate the sort of problem that might present itself.

'Her erysipelas is bad this time, there is no use denying it,' I said.

A look of confusion came into his face. He hesitated a moment. His ill-working brain had to be adjusted to a past time, when what now possessed him was not known. He disposed himself in silence, then started in an astonished voice, leaning over the table:

'It isn't the erysipelas, Monsieur Kairor! Haven't you heard?'

'No, I have heard nothing. In fact, I have only just arrived.'

Now I was going to hear some great news from this natural casuist:[5] or was I not? It was *not* erysipelas.

Julie had caught the word 'erysipelas' whispered by her husband. She leered round at me, standing on one leg, and tossed me a desperate snigger of secretive triumph, very well under control and as hard as nails.

Brotcotnaz explained.

The baker had asked her, on driving up the day before, to put a stone under the wheel of his cart, to prevent it from moving. She had bent down to do so, pushing the stone into position, but suddenly the horse backed: the wheel went over her hand. That was not all. At this she slipped on the stony path, blood pouring from her fingers, and went partly under the cart. Bystanders shouted, the horse started forward, and the cart went over her arm and foot in the reverse direction.

He told me these facts with astonishment—the sensation felt by him when he had heard them for the first time. He was glad to tell me. There was a misunderstanding, or half misunderstanding, on the part of his wife and all the others in this matter. He next told me how he had first heard the news.

At the time this accident had occurred he had been at sea. On landing he was met by several neighbours.

'Your wife is injured! She has been seriously injured!'

'What's that? My wife injured? My wife seriously injured!'—Indeed I understood him! I began to feel as he did. 'Seriously' was the word stressed naïvely by him. He repeated these words, and imitated his expression. He reproduced for me the dismay and astonishment, and the shade of overpowering suspicion, that his voice must originally have registered.

It was now that I saw him encountering all the notions that had come into my own mind a few minutes before, on first perceiving the injured woman, the visiting neighbours and his dejected form thrown into the shade by something.

'"Your wife is seriously injured!" I stood there altogether upset—tout à fait bouleversé.'

The familiar image of her battered form as seen on a *lendemain de Pardon*[1] must have arisen in his mind. He is assailed with a sudden incapacity to think of injuries in his wife's case except as caused by a human hand. He is solicited by the reflection that he himself had not been there. There was, in short, the effect, but not the cause. Whatever his ultimate intention as regards Julie, he is a 'jaloux.' All his wild jealousy surges up. A cause, a rival cause, is incarnated in his excited brain, and goes in an overbearing manner to claim its effect. In a second a man is born. He does not credit him, but he gets a foothold just outside of reason. He is a rival!—another Brotcotnaz; all his imagination is sickened by this super-Brotcotnaz, as a woman who had been delivered of some hero, already of heroic dimensions, might naturally find herself. A moment of great weakness and lassitude seizes him. He remains powerless at the thought of the aggressive actions of this hero. His mind succumbs to torpor, it refuses to contemplate this figure.

It was at this moment that some one must have told him the actual cause of the injuries. The vacuum of his mind, out of which all the machinery of habit had been momentarily emptied, filled up again with its accustomed furniture. But after this moment of intense void the furniture did not quite resume its old positions, some of the pieces never returned, there remained a blankness and desolate novelty in the destiny of Brotcotnaz. That was still his state at present.

I then congratulated Julie upon her escape. Her eyes peered into mine with derision. What part did I play in this? She appeared to think that I too had

---

1 The morning after the Pardon.

been outwitted. I sauntered over to the counter and withdrew the bottle of eau-de-vie from its hiding-place.

'Shall I bring it over to you?' I called to Brotcotnaz. I took it over. Julie followed me for a moment with her mocking gaze.

'I will be the débitant!' I said to Brotcotnaz.

I poured him out a stiff glass.

'You live too near the sea,' I told him.

'Needs must,' he said, 'when one is a fisherman.'

'Ahès!' I sighed, trying to recall the famous line of the armorican song, that I was always meeting in the books that I had been reading. It began with this whistling sigh of the renegade king, whose daughter Ahès was.

'Why, yes,' Brotcotnaz sighed politely, supposing I had complimented the lot of the fisherman in my exclamation, doing the devil's tattoo on the table, as he crouched in front of me.

'Ahès, *brêman* Mary Morgan.'[6] I had got it.

'I ask your pardon, Monsieur Kairor?'[7]

'It is the lament of your legendary king for having been instrumental in poisoning the sea. You have never studied the lore of your country?'

'A little,' he smiled.

The neighbours were leaving. We three would now be alone. I looked at my watch. It was time to rejoin the car that had brought me.

'A last drink, Madame Brotcotnaz!' I called.

She returned to the table and sat down, lowering herself to the chair, and sticking out her bandaged foot. She took the drink I gave her, and raised it almost with fire to her lips. After the removal of her arm, and possibly a foot, I realized that she would be more difficult to get on with than formerly. The bottle of eau-de-vie would remain no doubt in full view, to hand, on the counter, and Brotcotnaz would be unable to lay a finger on her: in all likelihood she meant that arm to come off.

I was not sorry for Nicholas; I regarded him as a changed man. Whatever the upshot of the accident as regards the threatened amputations, the disorder and emptiness that had declared itself in his mind would remain.

'To your speedy recovery, Madame Brotcotnaz,' I said.

We drank to that, and Brotcotnaz came to the door. Julie remained alone in the débit.

NOTES

[1] There is some uncertainty as to the exact location of this story. "La basse Bretagne" (incorrectly given as "La Basse-Bretagne" in the first edition) may mean the coast, or else Southern Brittany. The setting seems to be in the same district as "Bestre"

(whose hero is mentioned in "Brobdingnag"), since "Bestre" mentions Kermanec and Brasparts—and "Brotcotnaz" Kermanec and Lopérec (in the vicinity of Brasparts). However Quimperlé which appears in "Brobdingnag" would place the story in quite another part of Brittany—that associated with "A Breton Journal."

[2] See "A Soldier of Humour," page 18.

[3] The proofs gave: "After some days when I first stayed there . . ."

[4] The aubade is not a dance.

[5] The proofs gave "from this enraged mass of subtlety. . ."

[6] "Ahès" and "Morgan le Fay," Breton princesses associated with water.

[7] The typescript in the Buffalo archive gives "Monsieur Barnard" instead of "Monsieur Kairor" throughout the story, but the proofs give "Kairor." Clearly Lewis opted for "Ker-Orr" at a late stage in his revisions.

INFERIOR RELIGIONS

This important essay was most probably meant at first as an introduction to the overall collection of stories (see page 314). T. S. Eliot called it "the most indubitable evidence of genius, the most powerful piece of imaginative thought, of anything that Mr. Lewis has written" ("Tarr," The Egoist, *September 1918). It was first published in September 1917, and heavily revised in 1927. Since it was a critical essay it was not structurally rehandled as the stories were. The alterations were more matters of detail, generally affecting the literary allusions, as well as the capitalizing of abstractions which was toned down in 1927.*

I

To introduce my puppets, and the Wild Body, the generic puppet of all, I must project a fanciful wandering figure to be the showman to whom the antics and solemn gambols of these wild children are to be a source of strange delight. In the first of these stories he makes his appearance. The fascinating imbecility of the creaking men machines, that some little restaurant or fishing-boat works, was the original subject of these studies, though in fact the nautical set never materialized.[1] The boat's tackle and dirty little shell, or the hotel and its technique of hospitality, keeping the limbs of the men and women involved in a monotonous rhythm from morning till night, that was the occupational background, placed in Brittany or in Spanish Galicia.

A man is made drunk with his boat or restaurant as he is with a merry-go-round: only it is the staid, everyday drunkenness of the normal real, not easy always to detect. We can all see the ascendance a 'carousal' has on men, driving them into a set narrow intoxication. The wheel at Carisbrooke imposes a set of movements upon the donkey inside it, in drawing water from the well, that it is easy to grasp. But in the case of a hotel or fishing-boat, for instance, the complexity of the rhythmic scheme is so great that it passes as open and untrammelled life. This subtle and wider mechanism merges, for the spectator, in the general variety of nature. Yet we have in most lives the spectacle of a pattern as circumscribed and complete as a theorem of Euclid. So these are essays in a new human mathematic. But they are, each of them, simple shapes, little monuments of logic. I should like to compile a book of forty of these proportions, one deriving from and depending on the other. A few of the axioms for such a book are here laid down.

These intricately moving bobbins are all subject to a set of objects or to one in particular. Brotcotnaz is fascinated by one object, for instance; one at once another vitality. He bangs up against it wildly at regular intervals, blackens it, contemplates it, moves round it and dreams. He reverences it: it is his task to kill it. All such fascination is religious. The damp napkins of the inn-keeper are the altar-cloths of his rough illusion, as Julie's bruises are the markings upon an idol; with the peasant, Mammon dominating the background. Zoborov and Mademoiselle Péronnette struggle for a Pension de Famille, unequally. Zoborov is the 'polish' cuckoo of a stupid and ill-managed nest.

These studies of rather primitive people are studies in a savage worship and attraction. The inn-keeper rolls between his tables ten million times in a realistic rhythm that is as intense and superstitious as are the figures of a war-dance. He worships his soup, his damp napkins, the lump of procreative flesh probably associated with him in this task. Brotcotnaz circles round Julie with gestures a million times repeated. Zoborov camps against and encircles Mademoiselle Péronnette and her lover Carl. Bestre is the eternal watchdog, with an elaborate civilized ritual. Similarly the Cornac is engaged in a death struggle with his 'Public.' All religion has the mechanism of the celestial bodies, has a dance. When we wish to renew our idols, or break up the rhythm of our naïveté, the effort postulates a respect which is the summit of devoutness.

II

I would present these puppets, then, as carefully selected specimens of religious fanaticism. With their attendant objects or fetishes they live and have a regular food and vitality. They are not creations, but puppets. You can be as exterior to them, and live their life as little, as the showman grasping from beneath and working about a Polichinelle.[1] They are only shadows of energy, not living beings. Their mechanism is a logical structure and they are nothing but that.

Boswell's Johnson, Mr. Veneering, Malvolio, Bouvard and Pécuchet, the 'commissaire' in *Crime and Punishment*, do not live; they are congealed and frozen into logic, and an exuberant hysterical truth. They transcend life and are complete cyphers, but they are monuments of dead imperfection. Their only significance is their egoism. So the great intuitive figures of creation live with the universal egoism of the poet. This 'Realism' is satire. Satire is the great Heaven of Ideas, where you meet the titans of red laughter; it is just below intuition, and life charged with black illusion.

III

When we say 'types of humanity,' we mean violent individualities, and nothing stereotyped. But Quixote, Falstaff, and Pecksniff attract, in our memory, a vivid following. All difference is energy, and a category of humanity a relatively small group, and not the myriads suggested by a generalization.

A comic type is a failure of a considerable energy, an imitation and standardizing of self, suggesting the existence of a uniform humanity,—creating, that is, a little host as like as nine-pins; instead of one synthetic and

[1] The puppet Punchinello or Punch.

various ego. It is the laziness that is the habit-world or system of a successful personality. It is often part of our own organism become a fetish. So Boswell's Johnson or Sir John Falstaff are minute and rich religions.

That Johnson was a sort of god to his biographer we readily see. But Falstaff as well is a sort of english god, like the rice-bellied gods of laughter of China. They are illusions hugged and lived in; little dead totems. Just as all gods are a repose for humanity, the big religions an immense refuge and rest, so are these little grotesque fetishes. One reason for this is that, for the spectator or participator, it is a world within the world, full of order, even if violent.

All these are forms of static art, then. There is a great deal of divine olympian sleep in english humour, and its delightful dreams. The most gigantic spasm of laughter is sculptural, isolated, and essentially simple.

IV

I will catalogue the attributes of Laughter.

1. Laughter is the Wild Body's song of triumph.
2. Laughter is the climax in the tragedy of seeing, hearing, and smelling self-consciously.
3. Laughter is the bark of delight of a gregarious animal at the proximity of its kind.
4. Laughter is an independent, tremendously important, and lurid emotion.
5. Laughter is the representative of tragedy, when tragedy is away.
6. Laughter is the emotion of tragic delight.
7. Laughter is the female of tragedy.
8. Laughter is the strong elastic fish, caught in Styx, springing and flapping about until it dies.
9. Laughter is the sudden handshake of mystic violence and the anarchist.
10. Laughter is the mind sneezing.
11. Laughter is the one obvious commotion that is not complex, or in expression dynamic.
12. Laughter does not progress. It is primitive, hard and unchangeable.

V

The Wild Body, I have said, triumphs in its laughter. What is the Wild Body?

The Wild Body, as understood here, is that small, primitive, literally antediluvian vessel in which we set out on our adventures. Or regarded as a brain, it is rather a winged magic horse, that transports us hither and thither, sometimes rushing as in the chinese cosmogonies, up and down the outer reaches of space. Laughter is the brain-body's snort of exultation. It expresses its wild sensation of power and speed; it is all that remains physical in the flash of thought, its friction: or it may be a defiance flung at the hurrying fates.

The Wild Body is this supreme survival that is us, the stark apparatus with its set of mysterious spasms: the most profound of which is laughter.[2]

VI

The chemistry of personality (subterranean in a sort of cemetery, whose decompositions are our lives) puffs up in frigid balls, soapy Snowmen, arctic carnival-masks, which we can photograph and fix.

Upwards from the surface of existence a lurid and dramatic scum oozes and accumulates into the characters we see. The real and tenacious poisons, and sharp forces of vitality, do not socially transpire. Within five yards of another man's eyes we are on a little crater, which, if it erupted, would split up as would a cocoa-tin of nitrogen. Some of these bombs are ill-made, or some erratic in their timing. But they are all potential little bombs. Capriciously, however, the froth-forms of these darkly-contrived machines twist and puff in the air, in our legitimate and liveried masquerade.

Were you the female of Bestre or Brotcotnaz and beneath the counterpane with him, you would be just below the surface of life, in touch with a tragic organism. The first indications of the proximity of the real soul would be apparent. You would be for hours beside a filmy crocodile, conscious of it like a bone in an X-ray, and for minutes in the midst of a tragic wallowing. The soul lives in a cadaverous activity; its dramatic corruption thumps us like a racing engine in the body of a car. The finest humour is the great play-shapes blown up or given off by the tragic corpse of life underneath the world of the camera. This futile, grotesque, and sometimes pretty spawn, is what in this book is snapshotted by the imagination.

Any master of humour is an essential artist; even Dickens is no exception. For it is the character of uselessness and impersonality which is found in laughter (the anarchist emotion concerned in the comic habit of mind) that makes a man an 'artist.' So when he begins living on his laughter, even in spite of himself a man becomes an artist. Laughter is that arch complexity that is really as simple as bread.

VII

In this objective play-world, corresponding to our social consciousness, as opposed to our solitude, no final issue is decided. You may blow away a man-of-bubbles with a burgundian gust of laughter, but that is not a personality, it is an apparition of no importance. But so much correspondence it has with its original that, if the cadaveric travail beneath is vigorous and bitter, the dummy or mask will be of a more original grotesqueness. The opposing armies in the early days in Flanders stuck up dummy-men on poles for their enemies to pot at, in a spirit of ferocious banter. It is only a shell of that description that is engaged in the sphere of laughter. In our rather drab revel there is a certain category of spirit that is not quite inanimate and yet not very funny. It consists of those who take, at the Clarkson's situated at the opening of their lives, some conventional Pierrot costume. This is intended to assure them a minimum of strain, of course, and so is a capitulation. In order to evade life we must have recourse to those uniforms, but such a choice leaves nothing but the white and ethereal abstraction of the shadow of laughter.

So the King of Play is not a phantom corresponding to the sovereign force beneath the surface. The latter must always be reckoned on: it is the Skeleton at the Feast, potentially, with us. That soul or dominant corruption is so real that he cannot rise up and take part in man's festival as a Falstaff of unwieldy spume. If he comes at all it must be as he is, the skeleton or bogey of veritable life, stuck over with corruptions and vices. As such he could rely on a certain succès d'estime:[3] nothing more.

VIII

A scornful optimism, with its confident onslaughts on our snobbism, will not make material existence a peer for our energy. The gladiator is not a perpetual monument of triumphant health: Napoleon was harried with Elbas: moments of vision are blurred rapidly, and the poet sinks into the rhetoric of the will.

But life is invisible, and perfection is not in the waves or houses that the poet sees. To rationalize that appearance is not possible. Beauty is an icy douche of ease and happiness at something *suggesting* perfect conditions for an organism: it remains suggestion. A stormy landscape, and a pigment consisting of a lake of hard, yet florid waves; delight in each brilliant scoop or ragged burst, was John Constable's beauty. Leonardo's consisted in a red rain on the shadowed side of heads, and heads of massive female aesthetes. Uccello accumulated pale parallels, and delighted in cold architecture of distinct colour. Korin found in the symmetrical gushing of water, in waves like huge vegetable insects, traced and worked faintly, on a golden pâte, his business. Cézanne liked cumbrous, democratic slabs of life, slightly leaning, transfixed in vegetable intensity.

Beauty is an immense predilection, a perfect conviction of the desirability of a certain thing, whatever that thing may be. It is a universe for one organism. To a man with long and consumptive fingers, a sturdy hand may be heaven. We can aim at no universality of form, for what we see is not the reality. Henri Fabre was in every way a superior being to a Salon artist, and he knew of elegant grubs which he would prefer to the Salon painter's nymphs.—It is quite obvious though, to fulfil the conditions of successful art, that we should live in relatively small communities.

NOTES

[1] The only remains of the "nautical set" are a few sentences in "Brotcotnaz," the description of Lorient in the "Breton Journal," one painting (Michel P1) and one drawing (Michel 19, reproduced on page 191 below).

[2] See note 3 page 319, which suggests that his section added in 1927 might have been accidentally dropped in 1917. But it may be that this wrong numbering suggested to Lewis in 1927 the possibility of adding one more section. The object of this section—an explicit definition of the Wild Body quite in the mood of "The Meaning of the Wild Body"—makes this hypothesis very probable. This is further confirmed by the Buffalo archives which have a manuscript of this section associated with a revised copy of *The Little Review:* though heavily corrected, this manuscript seems to have been written at one go.

[3] The change from "succès d'hystérie" ("hysteria" being one of Lewis's favourite pre-War I words, see *Tarr*) seems expressive of his fresh acquaintance with Freud.

THE MEANING OF THE WILD BODY

Following "Inferior Religions," "The Meaning of the Wild Body," as is made clear in the 1927 "Foreword" ("the notes attached to it, which are new material. . ."), presents the final conclusive identification of the Wild Body. It was probably written early in 1927. It has none of the incantatory quality of "Inferior Religions" because it offers a satisfactory logical definition of both "The Meaning of the Wild Body" and "The Root of the Comic"—and that definition is absurdity. In some seven pages the word "absurd" occurs no less than seven times, "absurdity" occurs four times, not to speak of the repeated presence of "ludicrous" or "ridiculous." Lewis is clearly conscious he is making a point which has not been made before—hence his reversal of Bergson's definition of the comic as "du mécanique plaqué sur du vivant." This does not mean of course that the absurd was until now absent from Lewis's vision—it was certainly there at the very inception of The Wild Body, but the identification and the naming of this feeling or Weltanschauung as a critical idiom certainly makes Lewis a precursor. Of course he was not the first great modernist to use the word "absurd": Anne P. Freeman in her dissertation, Joseph Conrad and the Absurd (1974), noted that the word "absurd" and its derivatives occur no less than 638 times in Conrad's works. In fact Schopenhauer (mentioned here and as early as the first Tarr) was, with Shakespeare, one of the great inspirers of both Conrad and Lewis. However Lewis's ferociously external absurd appears more formal and advanced than Conrad's more lyrical and existential absurd—and this is more than a question of style. In that sense "The Meaning of the Wild Body" does stand as a landmark in the history of the theory of the comic—somewhere between Le Rire and André Breton's Anthologie de l'Humour Noir—but it is true too that, in practice, The Revenge for Love and Under Western Eyes share the same grotesque expressionism.

'From man, who is acknowledged to be intelligent, non-intelligent things such as hair and nails originate, and . . . on the other hand, from avowedly non-intelligent matter (such as cow-dung), scorpions and similar animals are produced. But . . . the real cause of the non-intelligent hair and nails is the human body, which is itself non-intelligent, and the non-intelligent dung. Even there there remains a difference . . . in so far as non-intelligent matter (the body) is the abode of an intelligent principle (the scorpion's soul) while other unintelligent matter (the dung) is not.'

Vedânta-Sûtras.
II Adhyáya. I Pâda, 6.[1]

1. THE MEANING OF THE WILD BODY

First, to assume the dichotomy of mind and body is necessary here, without arguing it; for it is upon that essential separation that the theory of laughter here proposed is based. The essential us, that is the laugher, is as distinct from the Wild Body as in the Upanisadic account of the souls returned from the paradise of the Moon, which, entering into plants, are yet distinct from them. Or to take the symbolic vedic figure of the two birds, the one watching and passive, the other enjoying its activity, we similarly have to postulate *two* creatures, one that never enters into life, but that travels about in a vessel to whose destiny it is momentarily attached. That is, of course, the laughing observer, and the other is the Wild Body.

To begin to understand the totality of *the absurd,* at all, you have to assume much more than belongs to a social differentiation. There is nothing that is animal (and we as bodies are animals) that is not absurd. This sense of the absurdity, or, if you like, the madness of our life, is at the root of every true philosophy. William James delivers himself on this subject as follows:—

'One need only shut oneself in a closet and begin to think of the fact of one's being there, of one's queer bodily shape in the darkness (a thing to make children scream at, as Stevenson says), of one's fantastic character and all, to have the wonder steal over the detail as much as over the general fact of being, and to see that it is only familiarity that blunts it. Not only that *anything* should be, but that *this* very thing should be, is mysterious. Philosophy stares, but brings no reasoned solution, for from nothing to being there is no logical bridge.'

It is the chasm lying between being and non-being,[2] over which it is impossible for logic to throw any bridge, that, in certain forms of laughter, we leap. We land plumb in the centre of Nothing. It is easy for us to see, if we are french, that the German is 'absurd,' or if german, that the French is 'ludicrous,' for we are *outside* in that case. But it was Schopenhauer (whom James quotes so aptly in front of the above passage), who also said: 'He who is proud of being "a German," "a Frenchman," "a Jew," can have very little else to be proud of.' (In this connection it may be recalled that his father named him 'Arthur,' because 'Arthur' was the same in all languages. Its possession would not attach him to any country.) So, again, if we have been at Oxford or Cambridge, it is easy to appreciate, from the standpoint acquired at a great university, the absurdity of many manners not purified or intellectualized[3] by such a training. What it is far more difficult to appreciate, with any constancy, is that, whatever his relative social advantages or particular national virtues may be, every man is profoundly open to the same criticism or ridicule from any opponent who is only different enough. Again, it is comparatively easy to see that another man, as an animal, is absurd; but it is far more difficult to observe oneself in that hard and exquisite light. But no man has ever continued to live who has observed himself in that manner for longer than a flash. Such consciousness must be of the nature of a thunderbolt. Laughter is only summer-lightning. But it occasionally takes on the dangerous form of absolute revelation.

This fundamental self-observation, then, can never on the whole be absolute. We are not constructed to be *absolute observers.* Where it does not exist at all, men sink to the level of insects. That does not matter: the 'lord of the past and the future, he who is the same to-day and to-morrow'—that 'person of the size of a thumb that stands in the middle of the Self'—departs. So the 'Self' ceases, necessarily. The conditions of an insect communism are achieved. There would then no longer be any occasion, once that was completely established, to argue for or against such a dichotomy as we have assumed, for then it could no longer exist.

2. THE ROOT OF THE COMIC

The root of the Comic is to be sought in the sensations resulting from the observations of a *thing* behaving like a person. But from that point of view all men are necessarily comic: for they are all *things,* or physical bodies, behaving as *persons.* It is only when you come to deny that they are 'persons,' or that there is any 'mind' or 'person' there at all, that the world of appearance is accepted as quite natural, and not at all ridiculous. Then, with a denial of 'the person,' life becomes immediately both 'real' and very serious.

To bring vividly to our mind what we mean by 'absurd,' let us turn to the plant, and enquire how the plant could be absurd. Suppose you came upon an orchid or a cabbage reading Flaubert's *Salammbô*, or Plutarch's *Moralia*, you would be very much surprised. But if you found a man or a woman reading it, you would *not* be surprised.

Now in one sense you ought to be just as much surprised at finding a man occupied in this way as if you had found an orchid or a cabbage, or a tom-cat, to include the animal world. There is the same physical anomaly. It is just as absurd externally, that is what I mean.—The deepest root of the Comic is to be sought in this anomaly.

The movement or intelligent behaviour of matter, any autonomous movement of matter, is essentially comic. That is what we mean by comic or ludicrous. And we all, as human beings, answer to this description. We are all autonomously and intelligently moving matter. The reason we do not laugh when we observe a man reading a newspaper or trimming a lamp, or smoking a pipe, is because we suppose he 'has a mind,' as we call it, because we are accustomed to this strange sight, and because we do it ourselves. But because when you see a man walking down the street you know why he is doing that (for instance, because he is on his way to lunch, just as the stone rolling down the hillside, you say, is responding to the law of gravitation), that does not make him less ridiculous. But there is nothing essentially ridiculous about the stone. The man is ridiculous fundamentally, he is ridiculous *because he is a man*, instead of a thing.

If you saw (to give another example of intelligence or movement in the 'dead') a sack of potatoes suddenly get up and trundle off down the street (unless you were at once so sceptical as to think that it was some one who had got inside the sack), you would laugh. A couple of trees suddenly tearing themselves free from their roots, and beginning to waltz: a 'cello softly rubbing itself against a kettle-drum: a lamp-post unexpectedly lighting up of its own accord, and then immediately hopping away down to the next lamp-post, which it proceeded to attack[4] all these things would appear very 'ridiculous,' although your alarm, instead of whetting your humour, might overcome it. These are instances of miraculous absurdities, they do not happen; I have only enumerated them, to enlighten us as regards the things that do happen.

The other day in the underground, as the train was moving out of the station, I and those around me saw a fat but active man run along, and deftly project himself between the sliding doors, which he pushed to behind him. Then he stood leaning against them, as the carriage was full. There was nothing especially funny about his face or general appearance. Yet his running, neat, deliberate, but clumsy embarkation, *combined with the coolness of his eye*, had a ludicrous effect, to which several of us responded. His *eye* I decided was the key to the absurdity of the effect. It was its detachment that was responsible for this. It seemed to say, as he propelled his sack of potatoes—that is himself—along the platform, and as he successfully landed the sack in the carriage:—'I've not much "power," I may just manage it:—yes *just*!' Then in response to our gazing eyes, 'Yes, that's me! That was not so bad, was it? When you run a line of potatoes like ME, you get the knack of them: but they take a bit of moving.'

It was the detachment, in any case, that gave the episode a comic quality, that his otherwise very usual appearance would not have possessed. I have sometimes seen the same look of whimsical detachment on the face of a taxi-driver when he has taken me somewhere, in a very slow and ineffective conveyance. *His taxi for him stood for his body.* He was quite aware of its shortcomings, but did not associate himself with them. He knew quite well what a taxi ought to be. He did not identify himself with his machine.[5]

Many cases of the comic are caused by the reverse of this—by the *unawareness* of the object of our mirth: though awareness (as in the case of comic actors) is no hindrance to our enjoyment of the ludicrous. But the case described above, of the man catching the train, illustrates my point as to the root of the sensation of the comic. It is because the man's body was not him.

These few notes, coming at the end of my stories, may help to make the angle from which they are written a little clearer, in giving a general rough definition of what 'Comic' means for their author.

NOTES

[1] As shown in the late '50s by the vogue of Zen Buddhism, when the Theatre of the Absurd was at its peak, the connection between Eastern mysticism and the Western absurd is not fortuitous. A good example of this conjunction is offered by the opening paragraph of Michel Foucault's *Les Mots et les Choses,* based on a text comparable to this epigraph.

[2] *The Wild Body* gave: ". . . lying between non-being, over which. . ." The obvious omission of "being" is confirmed by Lewis's correction in his own copy of *The Wild Body* (see Omar S. Pound, and Phillip Grover, *Wyndham Lewis: A Descriptive Bibliography,* page 17).

[3] The proofs gave "reinforced with. . ."

[4] Lewis's long-standing interest in cartoons and burlesque films was clear as early as the first *Tarr* which mentioned the Vitagraph (page 1).

[5] Taxis, from "The Taxi-Cab-Driver-Test" to "The Sea-Mists of the Winter," were to occupy a privileged place in Lewis's imagination.

SIGISMUND

Most probably written after the war, and first published in the Art and Letters *issue for Winter 1920, "Sigismund" was revised in 1927, but the fairly numerous alterations (only the most significant variants are indicated here) only concerned minor stylistic details and in no way affected the substance of the story.*

Possibly Lewis's funniest story, and—outside the mainstream of the Wild Body—one of his most ambitious efforts with "Cantleman's Spring-Mate," "Sigismund" has been ignored by the critics, with the exception of Robert Chapman. Altogether no more than two or three sentences—this shows how unduly selective the criticism of Lewis remains after half a century!

This story, as is made clear in the author's "Foreword," obviously belongs to a world quite removed from that of the Breton stories, hence its location in a sort of appendix. Yet its inclusion in The Wild Body *is in no way artificial as—with its hyper-conscious exploitation of all the resources of the absurd—it offers an excellent illustration of the later developments of the philosophy and aesthetics constructed round the Wild Body. The Body asserts itself triumphantly in the reductio ad absurdum leading from an aggressive dog (the canine theme, from "The French Poodle" to "The Man Who Was Unlucky With Women," "My Disciple" and the unpublished "Creativity," was a fairly continuous one with Lewis), through a Hellzapoppinesque obsession with race and the enormous Deborah (a feature noticed by Geoffrey Wagner in* Wyndham Lewis, *p. 55), to infatuation with historical clichés and final confinement in a mental asylum. From the savagery of the primitive Bretons, Lewis passed naturally to the grotesqueries of these other primitives, the English County Society. This certainly is in keeping with the evolution leading from "Our Wild Body" through "Inferior Religions" to "The Meaning of the Wild Body," and later* The Apes of God. *The satire on collecting as an activity—be it dogs, evidence of lineage, or pictures—is typical of Lewis, the impecunious artist and observer of alienations, who naturally opposes the collector to the creator.*

Sigismund's bulldog was called Pym. He believed implicitly in his pedigree.[1] And every one understood that the names of famous dogs to be found on Pym's family tree constituted a genealogical crop which did great credit to him and his master. This lifted Pym for Sigismund into the favoured world of race. He staggered and snorted everywhere in the company of Sigismund, with a look that implied his intention to make the most of being a bulldog, and a contemptuous curl of his chop for the world in which that appeared to signify so much.

Now Pym was really rather peak-headed. Far from being 'well broken up,' his head was almost stopless. His nostrils were perpendicular,[2] the lay back of the head unorthodox:[3] he would have been unable to hold anything for more than twenty seconds, as his nose would have flattened against it as well as his muzzle, his breathing automatically corked up by his prey. His lips were pendent, but his flews were not: his tusks were near together, and like eyes too closely set, gave an air of meanness. The jaws as well were level: in short he was both 'downfaced' and 'froggy' to an unheard-of degree. As to his ears, sometimes he had the appearance of being button-eared, sometimes tulip-eared: he was defective in dewlap, his brisket was shallow, he had a pendulous belly and a thick waist.

As to the back, far from being a good 'cut-up,' he had a very bad 'cut-up' indeed. He had *no* 'cut-up.' He was 'swamp-backed' and 'ring-tailed.' He also possessed a disgusting power of lifting his tail up and waggling it about above the level of his disgraceful stern, anomalously high up on which it was placed. His pasterns were too long, his toes seemed glued together: his stifles were wedge-shaped, and turned in towards the body. His coat was wiry, of the most questionable black and tan.

He was certainly the ugliest, wickedest, most objectionable bulldog[4] that ever trod the soil of Britain.[5] In the street he conducted himself like the most scurvy hoodlum ever issued from a nameless kennel. But he was a *bulldog*. His forebears had done romantic things. They had fixed their teeth in the noses of bulls. Sigismund was very proud of him. He insisted that the blood of Rosa flowed in his veins. All Sigismund's friends thumped and fingered him, saying what a splendid dog he was. To see Sigismund going down the road with Pym, you would say, from the dashing shamble of his gait, that he was bound for the Old Conduit Fields, or the Westminster Pit.

This partnership continued very uneventfully for several years, to Sigismund's perfect satisfaction. Then a heavy cantrip, of the most feudal ingredients, was cast upon Sigismund. He became deeply enamoured of a deep-chested lady. He pursued her tirelessly with his rather trite addresses. She had the slightest stagger, reminiscent of Pym. She was massive and mute.

And when Sigismund mechanically slapped her on the back one day, she had a hollow reverberation such as Pym's swollen body would emit. Her eyes flickered ever so little. Sigismund the next moment was overcome with confusion at what he had done: especially as her pedigree was like Pym's, and he had the deepest admiration for race. A minute or two later she coughed. And he could not for the life of him decide whether the cough was admonitory—possibly the death-knell of his suit—or whether it was the result of his premature caress.

The next day, grasping the stems of a bushel of new flowers inside a bladder of pink paper, he called. A note accompanied them:

> DEAR MISS LIBYON-BOSSELWOOD,—There are three flowers in this bouquet which express, by their contrite odour, the sentiments of dismay which I experience in remembering the hapless slap which I delivered upon your gorgeous back yesterday afternoon. Can you ever forgive me for this good-for-nothing action?—Your despondent admirer.
>
> SIGISMUND.

But when they next met she did not refer to the note. As she rose to her thunderous stature to go over to the vase where the bushel of flowers he had brought was standing, and turned on him her enormous and outraged back, Sigismund started. For there, through a diaphanous négligé, he saw a blood-red hand upon her skin. His hand! And in a moment he realized that she had painted it to betray her sentiments, which otherwise would have remained, perhaps for ever, hidden. So he sprang up and grasped her hand, saying:

'Deborah!'

She fell into his arms to signify that she would willingly become his bride. In a precarious crouch he propped her for a moment, then they both subsided on to the floor, she with her eyes closed, rendered doubly heavy by all the emotion with which she was charged. Pym, true to type, 'the bulldog' at once, noticing this contretemps, and imagining that his master was being maltreated by this person whom he had disliked from the first, flew to the rescue. He fixed his teeth in her eighteenth-century bottom. She was removed, bleeding, in a titanic faint. Sigismund fled once more in dismay.

The next day he called unaccompanied by Pym. He was admitted to Deborah's chamber. She lay on her stomach. Her swollen bottom rose in the middle of the bed.[6] But a flat disc of face lay sideways on the pillow, a reproachful eye slumbering where her ear would usually be.

He flung himself down on the elastic nap of the carpet and rolled about in an ecstasy of dismay. She just lisped hoarsely: 'Sigismund!' and all was well between them.

But she stipulated that Pym should be eliminated from their nuptial arrangements. So he sold Pym and wedded Deborah.

On returning from the church—husband, at length, of the Honourable Deborah Libyon-Bosselwood—Sigismund's first action was to rub a little sandal-wood oil into both her palms. As she had stood beside him at the altar, her heavy hand in his, he had wondered what lay concealed in this prize-packet he was grasping. As the gold ring ploughed into the tawny fat of her finger, descending with difficulty toward the Mount of the Sun, he asked himself if this painful adjustment contained an augury. Appropriately for the golden mount, however, the full-bellied ring, of very unusual circumference, settled down on this characteristic Bosselwood paw as though determined to preside favourably over that portion of the hand.

Having oiled her palms, much to her surprise, he flew with Deborah to a steaming basin, drew out a sheet of dental wax, and planted her hand firmly on it. But, alas, the Libyon hairiness had invaded even the usually bald area of the inside of the hand. And when Sigismund tried to pull her hand off the wax, Deborah screamed. She had not at all understood or relished his proceedings up to this point. And now that, adhering by these few superfluous hairs to the inadequately heated wax, she felt convinced of the malevolence of his designs, she gave him such a harsh buffet with her free hand that he fell at full length at her feet, a sound shaken out of him that was half surprise and half apology. He soon recovered, rushed to fetch a pair of scissors, and snipped her hand free of the wax cast. His bride scowled at him, but the next moment bit his ear and attempted to nestle, to show that he was forgiven.

'Deborah! Will you ever *really* forgive me?' He gasped in despair, covering her injured hand with kisses and a little blood, the result of her impulsive blow. The great Bosselwood motto 'Never Forgive' made him shake in every limb as he thought of it. How *uncanny* to be united to such a formidable offshoot of such an implacable race!

'Say you *can* forgive!'

But she only murmured in sulphurous Latin the words 'Nunquam ignoscete.'[1]

For she read his heart and remembered the motto (with some difficulty). She always read his heart, but could not always remember the heraldic and other data required properly to prostrate him. On these occasions, she would confine herself to smiling enigmatically. This redoubled his terror. She in

---

1 "Never forgive!"

due course observed this, too. After that she did nothing but grin at him the whole time.

But now came the moment that must be considered as the virtual consummation of Sigismund's vows. The ordinary brutal proclivities of man were absent in the case of Sigismund. The monstrous charms of the by-now lisping and blushing Deborah he was not entirely unaffected by: but the innermost crypt of this cathedral of a body Sigismund sought in a quite public place. The imminence of her brown breasts was hidden to him. They were almost as remote as the furniture of the Milky Way. Enormous mounts, he saw them as (but of less significance than) those diminutive ones of Saturn or the Sun at the base of her fingers. The real secrets of this highly-pedigreed body lay at the extremities of her limbs. The Mount of Venus, for him, was to be sought on the base of the thumb, and nowhere else. The certain interest he felt for her person, heavy with the very substance of Race, that made it like a palpitating relic, was due really to the element of reference that lay in every form of which it was composed, to the clear indications of destiny that enlivened to such an incredible degree the leathery cutis of her palm. Her jawbone, the jutting of her thighs, the abstract tracts of her heavily-embossed back, meant so many mitigations or confirmations of the Via Lasciva or her very 'open' line of head. Surely the venustal pulp of her thumb, the shape of a leg of mutton, had a more erotic significance than any vulgarer desiderata of the bust or belly? The desmoid bed of her great lines of Race, each 'island' a poem in itself, adapted for the intellectual picnicking he preferred, was a more suitable area for the discreet appearance of such sex-aims as those of Sigismund.

So, still bleeding slightly from the feudal buffet he had lately encountered, he seized her hand, and slowly forced it round with the air of a brutal ravisher, until it lay palm uppermost. The pudeur and mystery of these primitive tracings sent a thrill down his spine. It had been almost a point of honour with him not to ravish the secrets of her hand until now. 'Silent upon a peak in Darien' was nothing to the awe and enthusiasm with which he peeped over the ridge of her palm as it gradually revolved.

But now occurred one of the most substantial shocks of Sigismund's career. Deborah's palm was almost *without* lines of any sort. Where he had expected to find every foray of a feudal past marked in some way or another, every intrigue with its zig-zag, every romantic crime owning its little line, there was nothing but a dumbfounding, dead, distressing *blank*. Sigismund was staggered. The Palmer Arch, it is true, had its accompanying furrow, rather yellow (from which he could trace the action of Deborah's bile) but clear. The Mars line reinforced it. Great health: pints of blood: larders full of ox-like resistance to disease. It was the health sheet of a bullock, not the flamboyant history of a lady descended from armoured pirates.

All the mounts swelled up in a humdrum way. But from the Mount of the Sun to the first bracelet, and from the Mount of Venus to Mars Mental, it was, O alas, for his purposes, an empty hand! Her life had never been disturbed by the slightest emotional spasm: the spasms of her ancestors were seemingly obliterated from the recording skin. Nature had made an enigma of her hide! The life-line flowed on and on. He followed it broodingly to the wrist. It actually seemed to continue up the arm. Sigismund turned in dismay from this complacent bulletin of unchequered health.

He set to work, however, on the sparse indications that his noble bride was able to provide. He made the little insular convolutions of the line of heart spell simply 'Sigismund.' Kisses followed: coquettish and minute kisses attempted to land on each island in turn. Deborah glared in surly amusement.

A sinister stump where the head-line should have been disturbed him. It had a frayed ending. (More uneasiness.) Although in quantity this hand possessed few marks, those that were there were calculated to electrify any cheiromancer. It was a penny-shocker of a hand.

But most disquieting of all was a peculiar little island that mated a similar offensive little irregularity in his own hand. He had never seen it on the hand of any other being. And it was backed up by a faint but very horrible Star. This star furthermore was situated in the midst of Jupiter. But, worse still, a cross on another part of the hand completely unnerved him. He paced twice from one end of the room to the other. He was so abstracted that it was with a new anxiety and amazement that he found in a minute or two, that Deborah had disappeared.

He rushed all over the house. At last he came upon her in the dining-room, finishing a stiff whisky-and-soda. A rather cross squint was levelled at him across the whisky. Five minutes later she again vanished. Fresh alarmed pursuit. This time he discovered her in their bedroom, as naked as your hand (though he would never have used this expression, having an intense delicacy[7] about everything relating to the hand), in bed, and trumpeting in a loud, dogmatic, and indecent way. The palliasse purred, and the bed creaked beneath her baronial weight. The eiderdown rose and fell with a servile gentleness. Her face was calm and forbidding. It was the dreamless, terrible sleep of the Hand he had just fled from. Yes. It was the Hand sleeping! He was united for better or for worse with this empty, sinisterly-starred, well-fed, snoring Hand.

Their honeymoon was uneventful. Sigismund went about with an ephemeris of the year of Deborah's birth, with Tables of Eclipses. He had the moon's radical elongation, and the twenty-two synods that represented his wife's life up to date. The mundane ingress of planets, their less effectual zodiacal ingress, had all been considered in their bearing on the destinies of Deborah and himself. But as on her hand, so in the heavens, the planets and Houses appeared to behave in a peculiarly non-committal, dull and vacant manner. The Spheres appeared to have slowed down their dance, and got in to some sort of clodhopping rustic meander, to celebrate the arrival of his wife upon the earth. But still the sinister star placed where her forefinger plunged into the palm perplexed him.

Back in London, he took her about as he had formerly taken Pym. He explained her pedigree. He pointed to her nose, which was heavy and flat, and told his friends that underneath was the pure Roman curve of the Bosselwoods. Also he detected a blue glint in her eye. That was the blue of the Viking! The Bosselwoods, it was gathered, were huge, snake-headed, bull-horned, armour-plated norse buccaneers. She would give him a terrifying leer when this transpired. It was her only histrionic effort. Her feet, on the other hand, were purely Libyon. If his friend could only see their jolly little well-oiled knuckles! A world of race slumbered in her footwear.

'Race is so poetic, don't you agree?' he would say.

All agreed with Sigismund that race was the most romantic thing imaginable, and that it lent a new interst not only to the human skeleton, but also the the smallest piece of fat or gristle. There were three friends especially of Sigismund's who felt things very much as he did. The four of them would sit around Deborah and gaze at her as connoisseurs in race. They all agreed that they had never met with quite so much race in anybody—so much of it, so exquisitely proportioned, or carried about with so much modesty.

'Deborah is amazing!' Sigismund would lisp. 'Her blood is the bluest in the land. But it might be green, she is so natural.'

'She is natural!' Fireacres said, with the emphasis proper to his years.

'Her language is sometimes—he! he!—as blue, I promise you, as her blood!'

They all shuffled and a break of merriment went on cannoning for about a minute. It ended in a sharp crack crack from Gribble-Smith. She scowled at them with a look of heavy mischief. She felt like a red, or perhaps blue, ball, among several very restless white ones. She liked laughter about as little as a Blackfoot brave of romantic fiction. Her tongue appeared to be dallying, for a moment, with the most mediæval malediction. They hushed themselves rapidly and looked frightened.

'You should have heard her to-day. A taxi-driver—he! he!—you should have seen the fellow stare! He wilted. He seemed to forget that he had ever known how to say "Dash it!"'

Deborah plucked at her chin, and spat out the seeds of her last plate of jam.

'How extremes meet!' said a newcomer.

A great insolence was noticeable in this man's carriage. He swung himself about like a famous espada. But when he tossed his locks off his brow, you saw that his bull-ring must be an intellectual one, where he would no doubt dispose of the most savage ideas.[8] He was followed about by the eyes of the little group. Sigismund whispered to Deborah. 'He's a Mars Mental man.' An uninitiated person would probably, after being plunged for a little in this atmosphere, have thought of the Mars Mental man as possessed of phenomenally large muscular mental mounts, whatever they might be. The slender elevation on the side of his palm opposite to the thumb affected these simple people in the same way as athletic potentialities affect the schoolboy. In fingering his hand, as they sometimes did, it was with visible awe, and an eye fixed on the negative mount in question, as though they expected it to develop an eruption.

Deborah scratched her off leg. All were ravished. The Bosselwoods had no doubt always been great Scratchers: 'mighty scratchers before the Lord' Sigismund's mind proceeded.

Deborah bent her intelligence painfully for a moment on the riddle of this company. Could a stranger have glanced into her mind, the scene would have struck him as at once arid and comic. Sigismund's friends would have appeared as a group of monoliths in a frigid moonlight, or clowns tumbling in sacks in an empty and dark circus. Her mind would be seen to construct only rudimentary and quasi-human shapes: but details of a photographic precision arbitrarily occurring: bits of faces, shoes, moustaches and arms, large hands, palm outward, scarred with red lines of life, head and heart, all upside down. Stamped on one of these quasi-human shapes the stranger would have read 'Socialist' in red block letters. This was:

'Tom Fireacres. Awfully good family you know. Fire-acres. Pronounced Furrakers. Jolly old bird. He is a queer fellow. A Socialist——' He would shake his head of rather long political hair from time to time over his young friend's aristocratic excess. But there was a light of kindly mansuetude that never left his eye.

The next of these dismal shapes would be a suit of clothes, not unlike Deborah's brother's: but a palpably insignificant social thing, something inside it, like its spirit jerking about, and very afraid of her. The form its fear seemed to take was that of an incessant barking, just like a dog, with the same misunderstanding of human nature. For it seemed to bark because it thought she liked it. This was:—

'Reddie Gribble-Smith. Been in the Army—Senior Captain. Awful nice feller.' This particular cliché propelled itself through life by means of a sort of Army-laugh.

One of these shapes was rather disreputable. To our hypothetic observer it would have looked like abstract Woman, Sex and its proper Tongue, in a Rowlandson print.[9] The reason for this would be that when she looked at Jones—'Jones: Geoffrey Jones. Charming fellow. He was up at Oxford with me. Very psychic. He's got a lot in him'—she always saw in his place a woman on whose toe she had once stepped in Sloane Square. Abuse had followed. The voice had been like an advertisement. Sounds came up from its sex machinery that were at once réclame and aggression. She felt she had trodden on the machinery of sex, and it had shouted in some customary 'walk-up' voice, 'Clumsy cat! Hulking bitch! Sauce!' Whatever Jones said reached her, through this medium, as abuse. She did nothing: but she threw knives at him sometimes with her eyes.

Sigismund appeared to know dense masses of such men. As far as she could she avoided encounters. But there seemed no escape. So they all lived together in a sort of middle-class dream. Therein she played some rôle of onerous enchantment, on account of her beautiful extraction. They smoked bad tobacco, used funny words, their discourse was of their destiny, that none of them could have any but the slenderest reasons for wishing to examine. They very often appeared angry, and habitually used a chevaleresque jargon: ill-bred, under-bred, well-bred; fellow, cad, boor, churl, gentleman; good form, bad form, were words that came out of them on hot little breaths of disdain, reprobation, or respect. Had she heard some absent figure referred to as a 'swineherd,' a 'varlet,' or 'villein,' she would not have felt surprised in any way. It would have seemed quite natural. You would have to go to[10] Cervantes and his self-invested knight for anything resembling the infatuation of Sigismund and his usual companions.

In more bilious moments Deborah framed the difficult question in the stately mill of her mind, taking a week to grind out one such statement: *What is all this game about, and what are these people that play it?* Deborah could not decide. She abandoned these questions as they dropped, one by one.

Her noble attributes assumed in her mind fantastic proportions. Everything about herself, her family, her name, became unreal. One day she pinched Lord Victor Libyon-Bosselwood to see if he was a figment of Sigismund's brain or a reality. She caused him, by this unprovoked action, so much pain and surprise, that he shouted loudly. Sigismund was in ecstasy. Obviously the war-cry of the Bosselwoods, the old piratic yell! But Sigismund could not leave it at that. Possibly Lord Victor was the last Bosselwood who would ever utter that particular sound. He hesitated for some time. Then one day when Lord Victor was deeply unconscious of his peril, Sigismund led him up the bell-shaped funnel of a gramophone recorder. He approached it jauntily, flower in buttonhole, haw-hawing as he went. As his face was a few inches off the recording mouth, Sigismund ran a large pin into his eminent relative's leg. The mask *à la* Spy vanished in a flash. And sure enough from a past, but a past much further back than that of the successful pirate, another man darted like a djinn into Lord Victor's body. This wraith contracted the rather flaccid skin of Lord Victor's face, distended its nostrils, stuck a demoniacal glint in each of Lord Victor's eyes, and finally curled the skin quickly back from his teeth, and opened his mouth to its fullest extent. Not the romantic battle-cry of the operatic pirate, but a hyena-like yelp, smote the expectant ears of the Boswell-like figure behind him: and the machine had recorded it for all time. But the next moment first the machine and then Sigismund crashed to the floor, as it took about thirty seconds for the pain to ebb and the djinn to take his departure. This period was spent by the ferocious nobleman in kicking the gramophone-box about the floor, then turning upon the ingenious Sigismund, whom he kicked viciously about the head and body.[11] Even when no longer possessed of this dark spirit that had entered along with Sigismund's pin, he still continued to address our hero in a disparaging way.

'Necromancing nincompoop: what does that signify—to run a pin into a man's leg, and then stand grinning at him like a Cheshire cat? Half-witted, flat-faced, palm-tickling imbecile, you will get yourself locked up if you go round sticking pins into people's legs, and telling them to beware of gravel, that they have spatulate hands, and will be robbed by blonde ladies!'

The doors of Lord Victor's dwelling were in future guarded against Sigismund. He found it difficult to satisfy Deborah when she heard of his doings.

They spent a month at Bosselwood Chase.

The first book that Sigismund picked up in the library enthralled him. It seemed to betray such an intelligent interest in Race. He read, for instance, aloud to Deborah the following passage:

> These luckily-born people have a delicious curve of the neck, not found in other kinds of men, produced by their habit of always gazing *back* to the spot from which they started. Indeed they are trained to fix their eyes on the Past. It is untrue, even, to say that they are unprogressive: for they desire to progress backwards more acutely than people mostly desire to progress forwards. And when you say that they hold effort in abhorrence, more inclined to take things easily, that also is not true: for it requires just as much effort to go in one direction as in the other.

The thoroughfares of life are sprinkled with these backward gazing heads, and bodies like twisted tendrils. It is the curve of grace, and challenges nobly the uncouth uprightness of efficiency.

That class of men that in recent years coined the word 'Futurist' to describe their kind, tried to look forward, instead. This is absurd. Firstly, it is not practical: and, secondly, it is not beautiful. This heresy met with bitter opposition, curiously enough, from those possessing the tendril-sweep. Unnecessary bitterness! For there are so many more people looking *back,* than there are looking forward, and in any case there is something so vulgar in looking in front of you, the way your head grows, that of course they never had much success. Here and there they have caused a little trouble. But the people have such right feelings *fundamentally* on these subjects. They realize how very uncomfortable it must be to hold yourself straight up like a poker. Through so many ages they have developed the habit of not looking where they are going. So it is all right. It is only those whom the attitude of grace has rendered a little feeble who are at all concerned at the antics of the devotee of this other method of progressing.

The training of these fortunate people—ancient houses, receding lines of pictures, trophies, books, careful crystallization of memories and forms, quiet parks, large and massive dwellings—all is calculated to make life grow backward instead of forward, naturally, from birth. This is just as pleasant, and in some ways easier. The dead are much nicer companions, because they have learnt not to expect too much of existence, and have a lot of nice habits that only demise makes possible. Far less cunning, only to take one instance, is required to be dead than to live. They respect no one, again, for they know, what is universally recognized, that no one is truly great and good until he is dead: and about the dead, of course, they have no illusions. In spite of this they are not arrogant, as you might expect.[12]

'I think that is divinely well put, don't you agree, darling?' asked Sigismund closing the book. Deborah looked straight at him with genuine hatred: with the look of a dog offered food about which he feels there is some catch.

Some months later, settled in the midst of a very great establishment, Sigismund's fancy found a new avenue of satisfaction. He resolved to make a collection of pictures. His newly-awakened sensibility where pictures were concerned was the servant of his ruling passion, and admirably single-minded. His collection must be such as a nobleman would wish to possess. And again in this fresh activity his instinct was wonderfully right.

But Deborah grew blacker day by day. The dumb animal from the sacred Past felt by now that there was something exceedingly queer about her husband. The fabulous sums of money that Sigismund got through in the prosecution of his new fad awoke at last her predatory instincts. Solid bullion and bank balances was what she had wedded: not a crowd of fantastic and rather disturbing scenes. She secretly consulted with Lord Victor.

However, Sigismund proceeded to fill the house with pictures, engravings, drawings and pieces of sculpture. They all had some bearing on the Past. Many were historical pieces. They showed you Henry VIII., the king of the playing card, divorcing Catherine. He appeared, in the picture, to be trying to blow her away. They disclosed the barons after their celebrated operation at Runnymede, thundering off with the Charter: or William the Conqueror tripping up as he landed. There were pictures celebrating Harry Page's doings, 'Arripay': episodes on the Spanish main. There was an early lord earning his book-rights with an excellent ferocity: and a picture of a lonely geneat[1] on his way to the manor with his lenten tribute of one lamb.

A rather special line depicted a runaway labourer being branded upon the forehead with a hot iron, at the time of the Labour Statutes of the fourteenth century: and sailors being bastinadoed after unusually violent mutinies. Stock and thumb-screw scenes. There was a picture of a Kentish churchyard, John Ball preaching to a rough crowd. As Sigismund gazed at this terrible picture, he experienced perhaps his richest thrill.

When Adam delved and Eve span
Who was then the gentleman?

He could see these unhallowed words coming out of the monk's lips and the crowd capering to them.

He had the six English regiments at Minden, mechanical red and accoutred waves, disposing of the French cavalry: and Hawke in Quiberon Bay, pointing with a grand remote pugnacity to the French flagship: the old ceremonious ships, caught in a rather stormy pathos of the painter's, who had half attempted, by his colouring and arrangement, to find the formula for an event very remote in time from the day of the artist depicting it.

Charles II. dying—('do not let poor Nelly starve')—Sigismund's model of how to die: 'forgive me, Deborah, for protracting this insignificant scene.' He was not sure about 'insignificant' and sometimes substituted 'tedious.' The word 'unconscionable,' he felt, was the prerogative of dying princes.

The masked executioner holding up the head of Charles I., whose face, in the picture, although severed from the body, still wore a look of great dignity

[1] A type of feudal yeoman.

and indifference to the little trick that had been played upon it by the London Magnificos. ('Eikon Basilike' drew as many tears from Sigismund's susceptible lids as it did from many honest burgesses at the time of its publication.)

Mary Queen of Scots over and over again: Fotheringay: many perfect deaths: the Duke of Cumberland holding the candle for the surgeon amputating his leg.

Gildas, Kemble's 'Saxons in England,' the life of Wilfrid, by Eddi, were three of his favourite books. And pictures dealing with this period he concentrated in a room, which he called the 'Saxon' room. In these pieces were seen:

The Crowning of Cedric.

Guthlac of Crowland vomiting at the sight of a bear.

The Marriage of Ethelbert with Bertha, daughter of King Charibert.

The Merchants telling Gregory that the angelic slaves came from 'Deira.'

Constantine on the chalk cliffs, Minster below, knees jutting out, for the first time, in a bluff english breeze; and Ethelbert, polite, elevated, but postponing his conversion with regal procrastination, or possibly leisureliness.

Eumer's dagger reaching Edwine through Lilla's body.

Coifi, the priest, at Godmanham, making his unexpected attack on an obsolete temple.

Aidan with a bag of hairy converts in the wilds of Bernicia.

Penda looking at the snowy fist blessed by Aidan after he had defeated the Northumbrians.

Alfred singing psalms and turning cakes, and Caedmon writing verses in his stable.

These were only a few of the many scenes that Sigismund roamed amongst: standing in front of them (when he could prevail on her to come with him) with his arm round Deborah's waist.

The pictures that Deborah hated most were those most economically noxious. These were pictures by masters contemporary with the Past. Van Dyck was his great favourite, at once a knight, a Belgian, and a painter. He reflected with uncertainty, 'a foreign title, obviously!' Contemporary painters who were at the same time knights, or even lords, he thought less of, it may be mentioned in passing: though he never grudged them, on account of their good fortune, the extra money he had to pay for their pictures.

His instinct manifested itself more subtly, though, in his choice of modern works. Burne-Jones was perhaps his favourite artist not belonging, except in spirit, to the wonderful Past. He recognized the tendril or twist he had read about in the book found at Bosselwood. Also the unquestionable proclivity to occupy himself with very famous knights and queens struck Sigismund as a thing very much in his favour. But our hero was an incomparable touchstone. His psychic qualities had their part in this. You could have taken him up to a work of art, watched his behaviour, and placed the most entire confidence in the infallibility of his taste in deciding as to the really noble qualities, or the reverse, of the artist. The Man in the Savage State propensity always met with a response. And you would not be surprised, if going further along the gallery with Sigismund, you came upon a work by the same painter of a very tender description, showing you some lady conceived on a plane of rhetorical spirituality. The Animal and the Noble, you would know, are not so far apart: and the savage or sentimental and the impulses to high-falute very contiguous.

Suffocated by this avalanche of pictorial art, Deborah had been constantly sending up S.O.S.'s, and Lord Victor had hurried to her assistance, unknown to Sigismund. This very 'natural' female splinter from a remote eruption grew more violent every day. The more animal she grew the better pleased was Sigismund. One day when as usual he strolled round his galleries, he was only able to examine his acquisitions with one eye, the other having been 'poached' overnight by his wife.

Then one day the end came with a truly savage unexpectedness.

Sigismund lay along the wall, nails in his mouth, on a pair of library steps. He was filling up the last space in his room of Prints with an engraving showing Ben White running his Bulldog Tumbler and Lady Sandwich's Bess at the head of Bill Gibbons' Bull. He was startled a little at the sound of a distant hurly-burly, and a bellow that something told him must be Deborah. Shrieks then rose, it seemed of dismay. Then a very deep silence ensued.

Sigismund scratched his head, and blinked discontentedly. But as the silence remained so dead as to be in the full technical sense a dead silence, he stepped down to the floor, and went out into the vast passages and saloons of his establishment, looking for the cause of this mortuary hush.

Deborah was nowhere to be found. But a group of servants at the foot of the main staircase were gathered round her prostrate maid. He was informed that this young lady was dead, having been flung from the top of the stairs with great force by his wife. A doctor had been telephoned for: the police were to be notified.

Sigismund was enraptured. He dissimulated his feelings as best he could. There was indeed a Bosselwood for you! ('The police' meant nothing to him. He never read Oppenheim.)[13] He stood with a sweet absorption gazing at the inanimate form of the maid. He was brought to a consciousness of his surroundings by a tap on his shoulder. A strange man, two strange men, had in some way insinuated themselves amongst his retainers. The first man whispered in his ear: he was evidently under the impression that Sigismund was the author of this tragedy. He modestly disclaimed all connexion with it. But the man smiled, and he could not be sure, but he thought *winked* at him.

What was this fellow murmuring? If he had annihilated his entire domestic staff, he seemed to be saying, with a chuckle, it would have been all the same! Privilege, something about privilege: 'last little fling,' ha! ha! 'Fling' referred, he supposed, to the act of 'flinging' the maid. He held strange views, this newcomer! He was drawing Sigismund aside. He wanted to have a word with him apart. He was rather a nice sort of man, for he seemed to take quite a different sort of view of the accident from the servants. Where was he going? He wanted to show Sigismund something outside. Sell him a car? At a moment like this? No, he could not buy any more cars: and he must see Deborah at once. What was this strange fellow doing? He had actually pushed him inside the car.

Lord Victor had plotted with Deborah for some weeks past. But he had not counted on the Bosselwood fierceness manifesting itself almost simultaneously with the Libyon cunning. A few minutes after Sigismund had been driven off to an asylum, Deborah was also removed to a jail. After a trial that Sigismund would have keenly enjoyed (many a feudal flower in the gallery; the court redolent of the Past, and thundering to the great name of Libyon-Bosselwood), she also found her way to an asylum.

On thinking matters over in his new but very comfortable quarters, Sigismund concluded that that was what the two islands meant: and that that was also the signification of the star upon Jupiter.[14]

NOTES

[1] 1920: "His pedigree was really a myth for his masters. But generally men associate bulldogs with romantic breeding, so everyone understood. . ."

[2] 1920: "lamentably perpendicular."

[3] 1920: "head atrocious."

[4] 1920: "abject-looking bull-dog."

[5] 1920: "He was an understinker of the most wretched type: he was unduly libidinous."

[6] This sentence was added in 1927 on the proofs.

[7] 1920: "having a pudeur about. . ."

[8] 1920: "the most redoubtable monsters of thought."

[9] 1920: "It looked like an arch-female, not of a successful type."

[10] 1920: "Such complacency and lack of sense proportion accompanied all their words and proceedings that you would have to go . . ."

[11] 1920: "about the floor and belabouring Sigismund."
[12] Three sentences were deleted in 1927: "They are quite nice about the living. So it is clear that a dead sparrow is with a live eagle any day. And this is always found to hold good."
[13] 1920: "Oppenheimer" (E. Phillips Oppenheim, English author of popular thrillers).
[14] The influence of the stars and the dream-like aspect of life and confinement suggest that the hero of this story may have been ironically named after the central figure of Calderón's *La Vida es Sueño*.

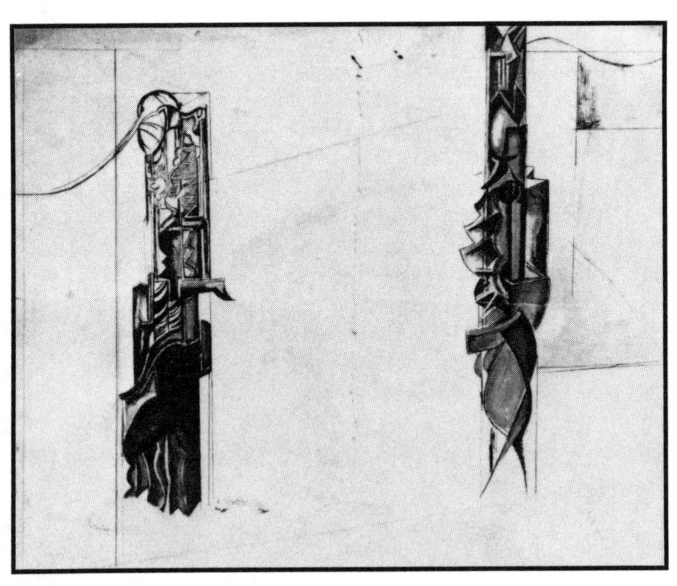

YOU BROKE MY DREAM, OR AN EXPERIMENT WITH TIME

"You Broke My Dream" has a complex history which remains largely hypothetical. Its opening (about one third of the final story) was published in the 1922 first issue of The Tyro *as "Will Eccles (A Serial)." It was discontinued in the second issue with no reason given. It seems probable that the rather flimsy conversation between Will and the two A.B.C. waitresses simply led nowhere, and that Lewis, who had expected too much from the vivid scene of a Young Ape's awakening, just found it impossible to go on with his serial.*

The conclusion had to wait till the Spring of 1927 when the story was unearthed and revised to become a skit on J. W. Dunne's An Experiment with Time, *just published in March of the same year. In spite of the customary numerous alterations, the 1922 opening remained identical but for the addition of a few paragraphs parodying Dunne's method of noting down, and having friends and relatives note down, their dreams on awakening so as later to check "déja vu" events.*

Dominated—like "Sigismund," in fact—by a satirical treatment of temporal aspects, clearly this story has little in common with the current vein of The Wild Body. *The "body" is certainly less present and not really affected by the absurd (as it still was in "Sigismund") which here is essentially verbal and demonstrative, corresponding to the new interests expressed in* Time and Western Man *(completed at the same time and which also mentions Dunne in part II, chapter 5, though the quotation given is not from* An Experiment with Time*). In view of all this it appears probable that Lewis included this last-minute effort—surely a hybrid—just to increase the length of his book.*

Do not burst, or let us burst, into Will Blood's[1] room! (I will tell you why afterwards.) Having flashed our eyes round the passages with which this sanctuary[2] is surrounded, lurched about in our clumsy endeavours, as unskilled ghosts, not to get into the one door that interests us, we do at last blunder in (or are we blown in; or are we perhaps sucked in?) and there we stand at Will Blood's bedside.

You are surprised, I hope, at the elegant eton-cropped purity of the young painter's head (he has been a young painter now for many years, so his head is a young painter's head). It lies serenely upon the dirty pillow, a halo of darkish grey, where the hair-oil has stained the linen, enhancing its pink pallor. Its little hook-nose purrs, its mouth emits regularly the past participle of the french irregular verb 'pouvoir,'[1] as though training for an exam. The puckered lids give the eye-sockets a look of dutiful mirth.[3]

However, his lips twitch, his eyelids strain like feeble butterflies stuck together in some flowery contretemps, then deftly part. The play begins. Will's dream bursts, and out pops Will; a bright enough little churlish flower to win a new encomium every morning from his great Creator! But the truth is, that he has been a slight disappointment to his Creator, on account of his love for Art, and general Will-fulness. Therefore this great Gardener frowns always as he passes the bed where Will modestly blows. Will has to depend on stray sensitive young ladies. But they are usually not very moved by him. The fact is that he does not smell very nice. Quite satisfactory as regards shape, indeed a roguish little bobbing bud of a boy, his smell is not that of a thing of beauty, but is more appropriate to a vegetable. This causes a perpetual deception in the path, the thorny path, in which Will blows.

The Creator has given him this smell as a sign of his displeasure, because of his fondness for Art, and his Will-fulness! But that is a figure.[4]

As his eyes open, the pupils rolling down into the waking position, Will violently closes them again, tightly holding them shut. For a few minutes he lies quite still, then cautiously slips his hand beneath the pillow, searches a moment, draws out a small notebook and pencil. Now he circumspectly opens his eyes, and, propped upon his elbow, turning over several leaves, he begins writing in his notebook.

'A dark wood,' he writes—'I am lying in the shadow of an oak. I want to get up. I find I cannot. I attempt to find out why.—Children are playing in the meadow in front of me. One is tall and one short. One is full of sex. The other has less sex. Both girls. They are picking dandelions—pissenlits.—I find I can get on my hands and knees. I begin crawling into the wood. This

---

[1] I.e. "pu."

makes me feel like an animal. I turn out to be an anteater. I attempt to make water. This owing to lack of practice is unsuccessful. I wake up.'

Poised above the notebook, he strains. Then at top speed he dashes down: *'A man with a hump.'*

He snaps-to the notebook and tosses it onto a chair at his bedside. Sliding two sensitive pink little feet out of the clothes, they hang stockstill above the carpet for a moment, then swoop daintily, and he is up. Pertly and light-heartedly he moves in dainty semi-nudity hither and thither. With a rustle, no more, he dresses extempore.[5] He is soon ready, the little black-curled, red-bearded bird of talent, in his neat black suit, his blue eyes drawing him constantly to the mirror, and rolling roguishly about like kittens there. Oh, how he wondered what to do with them! A blue eye! Why should his lucky craftsman's eye be blue? All his visions of things accouched on a blue bed! The red road he knows through his blue eye! Who had had the job of pigmenting that little window? Some grandmother, at the back of yesterday, who brought her red cavalier to bed through her azure casement.[6] No doubt that was it, or it was the result of some confusion in a ghetto, something sturdy and swarthy ravished by something pink and alert. A pity that Mr. Dunne's time-tracts are so circumscribed, thinks he, or I'd find out for myself!

But where was his waist-strap?

'Goot heavens, Archivelt,
Vere is your Knicker-belt?'—
'I haf no Knicker-belt,'
The little Archie said.

These famous lines passed off the unacceptable hitch: else he might certainly have displayed temper; for he was shrewish when thwarted by things, as who will not be at times.[7] But, once assembled, they fitted him to perfection.

He crossed his fat short legs and made his tie. Out to the A.B.C. for the first snack of the day. The top of the morning to the Norma Talmadge of the new Buszard's counter. He felt as lively on his springy legs as a squirrel. Now for the A.B.C.

A.B.C. The alphabet of a new day! A child was Will. Tootytatoot, for the axe-edged morning, the break of day! Was it an amateur universe after all, as so many believed? Oh, I say! is it an amateur world? It muddled along and made itself, did it, from day to day? At night it slept. He at least believed that was it. Believing *that,* you could not go far wrong. Every morning he comes up as fresh as paint: it is evidently *creative,* is all-things. Oh, it is decidedly a novel, a great creative, rough-and-ready affair: about that there can be no mistake. He throws his hat up in dirty Kentish Town air, as he dances forward. 'Give me the daybreak!' his quick actions say as plain as words. Any one could see he was just up. It is ten o'clock. 'Isn't this the time for rogues,' says he, 'not the night, but the day?'—He feels roguish and fine, and is all for painting the first hours red, in his little way. And also he must remember Mr. Dunne.[8]

The A.B.C. is cold. It has been sluiced by the chars, it faces north, its tiles marble and china repel the heat. It is an agreeable chill. He faces north, pauses and flings himself south and downwards onto the black leather seat at the bottom of the smoking-room. For some minutes he rides the springs, gentle as a bird on the wave, the most buoyant customer ever seen there.—A few blacksacks round the fire, like seamews on a Cornish Sabbath surveying their chapel of rock. Slovenly forces moved black skirts like wings. He is a force, but of course he needs his A.B.C.[9]

But who will bring Will his burning eggs and hot brown tea? Who will bring the leaden fruit, the boiling bullet from the inoffensive serpentine backside of the farmyard fowl? Why, Gladys, the dreary waitress, in her bored jazz.

'I—hi! Gladys, what bonny thought for my name day?'

'What is your name?'

'Will, you know.'

Oh, what a peppery proud girl she is, with her cornucopia of hair the colour of a new penny. He observes it as a molten shell, balanced on the top of the black trunk. He models her with his blue eye into a bomb-like shape at once, associating with this a disk—a marble table—and a few other objects in the neighbourhood.

'Will!' What's in a name? Little for the heart of the mechanical slattern who bears the burning fruit of the fowl where it can be eaten by sweet Will Blood.

Will's a sprucer,[10] thinks May, and tells Gladys so, as they sit side by side, like offended toys, at the foot of the stairs.[11]

'I don't think he's right,' says Gladys. A combative undulation traverses her with dignity from toe to head. Her legs lie rather differently after its passage. She pushes down the shortened apron, upon her black silk sticks.

'He's balmy.' May cocks her eye Willwards, and lowers her voice. 'Yesterday he came to my table. 'Ere! What do you think he had the sauce to ask me?'

They eye each other with drifting baby-gazes.

'He asked me to go to his studio-flat, and be his nude-model!'

'I should say so! Then you wake up!' Gladys tosses her chin and nose-tip. 'He hasn't half got a sauce! I know what *I* should have said.'

'Chance would be a fine thing, I said: and he said he'd—I couldn't keep a straight face—there was an old girl at the next table who heard what he said. She didn't half give me a look——!' A few faint contortions ruffled May tenderly. She sheltered her mouth for a moment with her hand. 'He said he'd give me a strawberry leaf if I was a shy girl! He said all artists kept a stock, all different sizes.' May falls into faint convulsions.

'Soppy-fool! I told you he's not right. I'd soon tell him off if he came any of it with me. I do hate artists. They're all rotters. Young Minnie works with an artist now—you know, Minnie Edmunds.'

'*He's* not an artist. He's sprucing. He's a student. Ernie says he's in the hospital.'

'In the hospital? Noaa! That's not right. Was that Ernie told you that? He must have meant he was a patient.'

Will has the two waitresses in his bright-eye-closet, where he makes them up into a new pattern. He sees them twittering their cowardly scandal, he flattens their cheeks meanwhile, matches their noses, cuts out their dresses into unexpected shapes at every living moment.

The attention of May and Gladys drifts to the extremity of the shop farthest from Will. May's head slowly turns back, vacillates a little, veers a few points either way, then swings back sharply onto Will. Gladys is nudged by May.

'Look at him counting his mouldy coppers!'

Will arranges two columns on the marble table, silver and copper.

'Solidi: Ten. Denarii: Eleven. Must go to the Belge for lunch: supply myself with the pounds—the pence will look after themselves.'

He signs to May, who nudges Gladys. Gladys looks at May.

'He wants you.'

The great copper-red queen of the A.B.C. approaches with majestic reluctance.

'Goot heavens, Archivelt,
Fere ist you Knicker-pelt!'

(She says, in her mind, to May: 'He said something about my knickers, in poetry. I gave him such a look.')

Standing at the side of the table, she traces perfunctory figures on her ticket-block. She redraws them blacker.

'I say, Miss. One of those eggs you brought me smelt high.'

('He said: one of the eggs was high. I said I would have got him another if he'd said.')

'It was blue.'

('Blue, he said it was.')

'We don't often have the customers complain of the eggs,' she observed.

'That was a red egg. Red eggs are always a bit off.'

('He said his egg was red. All red eggs is a bit off, he said. He's crackers.')

'I like them a little *faisandé*.'[1]

---

[1] "High" (game or meat).

('He said something in latin, he gave me a funny look. If he gave me much of his old buck——!')

'All people should be a little *faisandé*, I think, don't you: so why not eggs?'

'I don't see the conjunction.'

'Not between eggs and people? She sees no connection between eggs and people! Oh, lucky girl, oh, how I envy you! where ignorance is bliss!'

Ignorant! Blood rushes to the face of the proud and peppery girl.

'I should be sorry to be as ignorant as some people! Do you want another egg?'

'Oh, don't be angry Mabel. I admire your style of beauty.' He drops a bashful eye into his tea-cup, computing the percentage of vegetable dregs in what remains. 'I can imagine you quite easily in a beautiful oriental bath, surrounded by slaves. You step in. I am your eunuch.'

'Fancy goes a long way, as Nancy said when she kissed the cow.'

'I could easily be your eunuch. I don't understand your last remark. What cow?'

A bright and sudden light flashes in Will's eye. He leaps up. The blood has left the cheek of Gladys, and she steps back with apprehension.

'*Cow!* You've broken my dream? What colour was it?'

With a gesture with her fingers as though to bore into her temple, the haughty waitress returns to her chair by the side of May. Will follows eagerly. Standing over May and Gladys he exclaims:

'You broke my dream! What sort of cow was it?'

Gladys half looks disdainfully at May.

'He's not right.'

Will touches a variety of brakes; he has rushed into an impasse. He turns slowly round. That dream-double has been flustered, she who holds the secret of life and death. 'Gently does it!' thinks he and hoods his eyes. 'How horribly he squints!' thinks Gladys. Slowly up on to the surface steals a dark sugary grin. He leans against a table, nonchalant, crosses one shoe stealthily over the other shoe.

'I know it must sound funny to you, Miss Marsh.' (May smiles, and Gladys pricks up her languid ears. Miss Marsh! the sauce!) 'But you did say something about *kissing a cow,* didn't you, just now? It's this way. I dreamt last night *I kissed a cow.* I know it *is* a funny thing to dream. But that's why I sort of want to know, being of an enquiring turn. The cow I kissed last night is my first cow. That's important. Don't run away with the idea, Miss Marsh, that *every* night——!'

'Oh no-oo!' Lofty withering lady.

'That's right, don't run away.'

May laughs and peers at Gladys. 'Oh, how I hate that man!' thinks Gladys, for he has put her in the wrong with all these cows.

'Of course I made a note of it when I woke up.'

Oh, what a hateful man! and that cat May. What's the girl looking at me for, I should like to know?

'You broke my dream!'

'Oh! fancy that!'

A customer calls and May jumps up: away she hurries, for what, she wonders, has that Gladys been saying about kissing a cow?

Gladys looks after May. She has been put in the wrong. Why does he stop there? Why doesn't he go, I should like to know? he's got his bill.

She won't say, thinks little Will, that she said 'kissed a cow.' I've torn it. I shouldn't have seemed so anxious. Now I've put her back up. Something else must be found. Let's see. He looks round inside his mind. Ah, ha, the very thing! for he catches sight of a red egg, blue inside, and at the same time a faint familiar smell glides into his nostril. He coughs.

'Did you charge me with that egg?'

Gladys immediately alters: her colour jumps up, her eyes fill with dignity. She is back in her classy shell instanter.

'Yes. But if you like I'll deduct it, as you say it was bad.'

'No, please don't: it's quite all right, Miss Marsh.'

'Not at all. If you're not satisfied, I'll deduct it.'

With great dignity she rises and holds out her hand for the check.

'No, I really couldn't let you do that. I meant I hoped that you *had* charged me. That's what I meant.'

'Yes, I did. But I'll deduct it,' she drawls. Every minute she is farther off. He looks at her with his sheep's grin of foolish offence: she bridles and gazes away. He is baffled. What next?

May returns: she settles herself stealthily.

'Won't you tell me before I go about the cow?' Gladys does not mind, she *did* say 'kiss the cow.' She looks away from May, very bored.

'It's an old country saying. My mother uses it. Haven't you ever heard it?'

'So you *did* say "kiss the cow"?' he shouts, standing on tip-toe.

Glady's best proud manner is not proof against his shout quite. She will not relax towards May, but she cannot keep her eyes from casting a quick glance. That cat May's laugh, I do think it's soppy! 'No, I said "kissed the cow."'

May acts a spasm of pent-up mirth, the potty cat: 'kissed the cow! kissed the cow!' she rocks herself from side to side, droning to herself, she dies of laughing; she is dead.

'That's what I wanted to know.—Well, I must pony up with your firm, now. That's another old expression! Tralala!'

'Is it really!' A lady's simple bored reply, the last shot.

May has developed hysteria. Gladys rises in offended silence and goes over to the table. Will has left. But Will darts swiftly to the desk. An amiable oblique jewish face that has only one flat side at a time, or else is an animated projecting edge, receives with flattering vampish slowness his ticket on which the half-crown lies, and bakes him slowly with a cinema smile. 'A nice morning, isn't it? *Thank you,*' softly sliding three coppers and a shilling towards him.

He thanks the innocent bird in her cage at the receipt of custom, and darts erect through the door, out on to the shining pavement, where he skids through the dazzling light to the nearby P.O. Buying a postcard, he goes to the writing-desk and fills in the morning bulletin:

> Last night I dreamt that in crossing a tiny meadow I met two dappled cows. As I passed the second of the two I took its muzzle in my hands, and before it could say *knife*, I had kissed it between the horns. Going as usual this morning to the A.B.C. for my breakfast, I happened to engage in conversation there with a waitress, known as Miss Gladys Marsh. (I can obtain her address if you require it.) Being quite full of blarney, since it was so early in the day, I remarked to this high-spirited girl that I could see in my mind's eye her graceful perfumed form in a turkish setting descending into a beautiful bath. I represented myself as a eunuch (not to alarm her) participating in this spectacle at a discreet distance. At this she remarked:
>
> 'Fancy goes a long way, as Nancy said *when she kissed the cow*!'
>
> For the accuracy of this statement I am prepared to vouch. Time is vindicated! I offer you my warmest congratulations. It is certain that in our dreams the future is available for the least of us. Time *is* the reality. It is as fixed as fixed. Past, Present and Future is a territory over which what we call *I* crawls, and in its dreams it goes backwards and forwards at will. Again, my congratulations! Hip! Hip!—Further Bulletin to-morrow.
>
> *Signed,* WILLIAM BLOOD.

This he addressed to

R. DUNNE, ESQ.[12]

NOTES

[1] The hero was named Will Eccles in *The Tyro.*

[2] *The Tyro:* "sanctuary of young life. . ."

[3] This paragraph was expanded in 1927.

[4] The next three paragraphs were added in 1927.

[5] *The Tyro:* "Now he rose pertly from his bed and dressed extempore."

[6] The next two sentences were added in 1927.

[7] *The Tyro* had this sentence deleted in 1927: "(What, not with the flat, thick button, shying at its appointed slit?)"
[8] A paragraph considerably expanded in 1927.
[9] Most of this paragraph was added in 1927.
[10] *The Tyro* had this sentence deleted in 1927: "There was something about Will that folks despised."
[11] The *Tyro* text ends here.
[12] In *Time and Western Man*, J. W. Dunne's initials are correctly given.

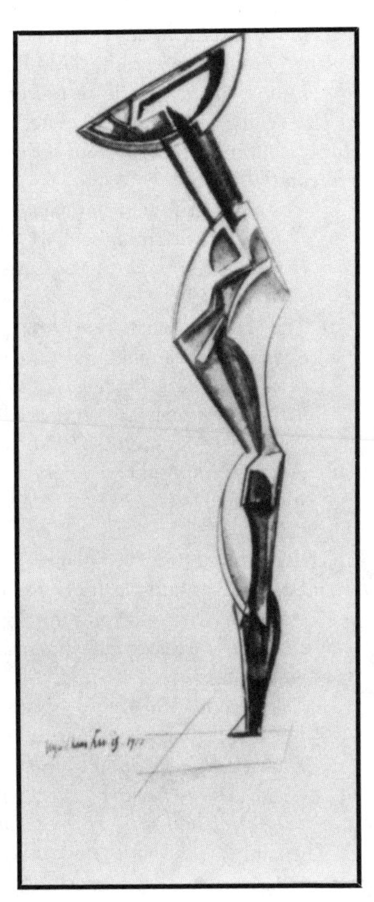

THE ARCHAEOLOGY OF THE WILD BODY

Hardly noticed by the critics, a singular phenomenon marks the first twenty years of Lewis's literary production. Everything had to be repeated or reformulated. The different versions of Tarr; "Cantleman's Spring-Mate" duplicated by "The War Baby"; the two versions of "Enemy of the Stars"—and above all The Wild Body, which, with its profusion of texts, offers indeed a stratigraphy of Lewis's evolution.

Five main periods can be observed in the history of The Wild Body, and most of them can be further subdivided. This is made clear by the organization of this "archaeology," with its distinct strata.

A) The "Prehistory" of The Wild Body. A diary and a sketch carefully preserved by the author, but which he certainly did not intend to publish (1908–09).

B) The Wild Body "Haute Epoque." The richest and most interesting period with twelve texts, probably written in the order of publication, and forming a number of intermediate layers:

- a) The English Review layer with three long and ambitious sketches (1909).
- b) A thin transition with "Our Wild Body," Lewis's first identification of his theme—though this essay was not directly connected with the preceding sketches (1910).
- c) The Tramp layer, revealing a spectrum leading from travelogues ("A Spanish Household" and "A Breton Innkeeper") to semi-fictional constructions ("Le Père François" and "Brobdingnag") finally to attain complete fictional status with "Unlucky for Pringle," and the probably contemporary "Soldier of Humour" (1910–17).
- d) Another thin but strongly contrasted layer with "Inferior Religions," marked by the influence of Vorticism and Lewis's experience as a bombardier (1917).

C) The Wild Body "Basse Epoque." It is characterized by a much greater intellectual and aesthetic sophistication, and again successive layers appear:

- a) A first layer corresponds to "Sigismund," marked by a conscious, systematic use of the absurd, and the second "Bestre," marked by stylistic inflation (1920–22).
- b) The second "Bestre" seems to have initiated the "Tyros," a brief and essentially pictorial period ("Will Eccles" petered out and "Tyronic Dialogues. —X. and F." was a socratic reductio ad absurdum rather than a play). Altogether the "Tyros" moved away from the depiction of primitives to that of ludicrous aesthetes prefiguring the "Apes" (1921–22).

D) The adult Wild Body. The last stage had to wait for another five years when, early in 1927, Lewis began rewriting all the texts included in The Wild Body. This was generally done in a less extreme manner than for "Bestre." A greater lucidity is also apparent in the final identification of the absurd (with "The Meaning of the Wild Body"), in the clarification of motives and behaviours, and in the shaping of Ker-Orr as narrator and coordinator. The Wild Body had found its final hard shell.

E) The offspring of The Wild Body. Absent from this book, they are innumerable, and more or less recognizable as such—from the Gossip Star of The Apes of God and the Carr-Orr/Kell-Imrie of Snooty Baronet to Percy Hardcaster and Vincent Penhale. But one thing is certain: beyond these mutations, the Wild Body remained with Lewis to the very end, as was explicitly stated in Rude Assignment.

A BRETON JOURNAL

*This untitled diary—if it can be called that, as it includes only two entries—forms part of the Lewis archive at Cornell. It was first published in 1982 in a bilingual edition (*Le Corps Sauvage*). The edition of this holograph manuscript was made particularly difficult by Lewis's spidery scrawl, numerous corrections and deletions. The staff of the Rare Book Department of the Olin Library at Cornell had produced a transcript, which was improved by the Age d'Homme edition, which in turn this edition further improves. Most difficulties are now solved and the few remaining uncertainties have been indicated in the notes. The more interesting misspellings have been retained (gallicisms, the use of capitals, etc.). So have the punctuation (here dominated by the ",—" heralding the "=" of the first* Tarr*) and the often obscure syntax.*

Unlike "Crossing the Frontier," which is a fairly elaborate series of vignettes, these remarkable notes were hastily jotted down just after the event, on two successive evenings, in a mood of quasi-mystical lyricism. They obviously do not pretend to literary perfection, and the numerous corrections seem to have all been made at once. That these very rough leaves should have been preserved confirms their importance for the author who probably had read them again much later before stating in Rude Assignment *that Brittany offered him a sort of illumination. "A Breton Journal" may therefore be seen as the very inception of The Wild Body, since it transfers the sombre abstract mood of Lewis's early sonnets into the more concrete observation of primitive celebrations. In these rituals a vitalist phenomenology regularly discovers expressionistic gaps—and this contains the essence of Lewis's future vision.*

August 17. Monday. 1908.[1] Quimperlé. evening. To Pouldhu[2] to-day with Mother and Castells to look for rooms. We stay here, Lion d'or, till Friday, will then go to Plouhinec for 4 or 5 days, then go to Faouët[2] for a week or so.

Returned by way of Clohars: there was a Pardon there today. Found the "Place" dispeopled. We learnt later that there were wrestling matches in a field on the road to Moëlan and most of the people had gone to see them. There were several tables in the vicinity of beer-shops however, still occupied by hideous topers, deep in desperate and interminable conversations, not conscious of the lull in the fête or the deserted square; the group of four or five men come together inevitably, rapt in a mysterious brotherhood, that brotherhood of chance acquaintanceship of an hour ripened, having now created their own and particular atmosphere, each man still robed, physically and spiritually in the garment of strangeness or rather in the *nakedness* of strangeness—for after a day's companionship with a man he will succeed in hiding his real self from you for ever,—the strangeness essential to all perfect relationship between men. They had begun doubtless in a state of general solidarity in their amusement, dependent on the "decors" of the fête, on the concourse of people, etc.—their imagination was dependent on this. Their imagination had long outstrip'd[3] these conventional foundations and essentials of the state of soul required, however, and now rapt them in an ardent abstraction that had no need of these things; but now as a child long held on either side in its efforts to walk, first forgoing one support and then another, and at last walking alone,—as something a man balances with his hands, until he finds, after various trials, that it will stand, and finds the exact position in which it poises, so the fête had so to speak fallen away from them, become no longer part of them—even before the concourse of people had left the village empty,—and these groups of four or five men would move about, or sit at the tables thenceforward no longer a part of the great gathering around them, self-sufficient. These were older men; the younger peasants wander'd aimlessly and gravely about, gazing at one thing and then another. These elders had learnt to despise these gatherings and anything that was to be seen there,—that is to despise their world,—and only went that, with the one or two men necessary to them, and with a brief acceptation of their human weakness and dependance,[4] consciously with fatalism finding the starting point there of their orgies in the clamour, the multitude of the fête,—using this as a man uses food to live, such as a gourmet,—each time with more abandon, found there the acrid savour of their own personality and pursued their flagrant ego like a dog in heat,—a self wonderfully fertilized in these circumstances;—they enjoy'd their self voluptuously, they enjoy'd the enjoyment that others had in them, and with that enjoyment. It is not always the same men that get together in each successive gathering. These people have learnt the secret of finding a complete world, a synthesis of beings, always a small number that satisfy sympathetically.

A man, according to the degree of his intelligence, may comprehend a great many people in an intellectual orgie; might, in the realization of his personality, through the medium of his intelligence, discover an infinitely greater scope. But all men in the satisfaction of their passionate nature,—and in the case of that people it is only so that they realize themselves,—make up their world with, at the most, a very few of their fellows; they could count them on the hand. These fêtes,—Pardons, fiestas, regattas in the ports of these coasts, the fête of the fishing populations,—whatever it may be, beneath the pretexts of "things to be seen," sideshows, stalls, dances, circuses etc., at which the younger and inexperienced folk "se laissent prendre" always, allow themselves to be taken in by, and occupy themselves too long and needlessly with, has for its chief use the gathering together of a vast and orderless concourse of people, a formless society, a gathering together of all the elements of the population that true and ideal societies may be form'd; it is not to make one vast society and make every one that comes to these fêtes a member of a vast society, but, as he comes from his farm or hamlet, where he makes one of a society composed of ten souls, so he may go to the gathering of thousands of people and make one of a society even smaller than his home circle.

These fêtes are essentially *orgies*. It is the renunciation and dissipation at stated times, of everything that a peasant has of disorder'd, exalted, that in us that will not be contain'd in ordinary life; all that there is left of rebellion against life, fate, routine in the peasant. All these people bring all their indignations, all their revolts, and bewilder'd dreams, and sacrifice them here, pay their supreme tribute to Fate, instead of keeping jealously their passions and reveries hidden in their hearts, they come here and fling all to the winds, leave themselves bare, make a bonfire of what the intelligence tells us is most precious. But while the smoke of all this is going up, and their sacrifices are accomplish'd unconsciously amid the clamours of their crowds, certain of their emanations strain to each other as they perish; that theatre[5] "debordant"[1] in each nature,—that that is most delicate, most inspir'd in each nature, and for that reason to be sacrificed as superfluous, as it were a spirit, catches at some other, before its life is extinct, and is thrill'd in this bitter companionship. Many in these fêtes, in the society of their comrades or of some one met there, know the sweetness of this union and a melancholy at this death,—this dissipation, this gross throwing away of something born to the ideal, without knowing the cause of either. The artist, in his defiance of

[1] "Outflowing."

Fate, has always remain'd a recluse, and the enemy of such orgaic[6] participation of life, and often lives without knowing[6] this emotion felt in the midst of its wastefulness.

(The character of each people's music at these gatherings; the sombre fatalism of the Bretons in their dances.)[7]

[Clohar]s. the circus.[8]

The square did not seem to take on easily an air of festivity. On other days it seems inhospitable, desolate and chaste with its large, irregularly built low white church that looks as though it were several separate chapels built together and having a common beneath its small central spire of wood; this square that seems too large for the village, though evidently not made so with any pretentious thought, with its large, waste spaces,—as it seem'd too big for the daily life of the town, so it seem'd too big for its fête, cast a chill upon the people moving at their ease, and was awkward in this case by its very commodiousness: for a feature and essential of all country fêtes is a certain uncomfortableness, crowds that stand closely pack'd, dancers that have hardly room to turn in, with shocks in midcareer—as it is also the charm of these improvised gatherings in a student's room where the dancers at every minute turning riotously between the narrow walls threaten to unseat the pianist. Were they placed in a well-proportion'd hall, their gaiety would vanish. The world must not distend with our spirits, if we are to be gay: if material life grew larger and fairer materially and not only by the spell of our imagination, in our moments of inspiration, we should not feel the interior change, and have no measure by which to judge the greatness of our souls: and for the proper explosion of our animal spirits, on occasions of festivity, cramped material conditions is almost an essential. The air of improvisation is necessary: the fête passes amongst the scenes of their ordinary life, and in streets and houses built for the sober days of work: air of preparation, forethought method in amusement absent.

When I pass'd through Clohars later, the square was almost empty: the stalls of the sweet stuff, and gewgaw sellers, and of the drapers, were still there; a few tables placed near the houses were occupied by groups of men. The barrels of cider stood at the café doors, each with its servant and guardian, but the mass of the fêters seemed to have dispersed.

On the stony ground near the church were two caravans and a little cart; empty boxes, shafts, bundles, etc., were strewn about; a round tent had been set up beside the encampment, at the entrance of which, on a platform fitted with steps stood a woman about forty five, dark and sallow, and without any of the customary powder or rouge, hair tied in a slovenly knot, but dress'd in a complete circus rigout, dark faded purple "tights", embroider'd vest, and skirt halfway down her thighs: it was she that took the money, and cried out the different events, with elogious references to what was passing within the tent. She was quite devoid of any "gêne"[1] or special airs such as old or young women customarily affect when they find themselves in a costume so deliberately design'd as a uniform of their sex. In her gestures and glance and in every way in fact she was just as though she were dress'd as those around her;—a keen business woman, she eyed the occasional passers, noting if their eyes dwelt with the vacillation of a listless conflict within on the door that led to the arena. In the deserted place behind the circus, and near the empty caravans, two children, a boy of four and a girl of nine or ten, in the tights, the vest and drawers of acrobats, had come out from the tent, their turns finish'd. They strain'd in uneasy poses, the little boy with his frowning head, his face turn'd brusquely to his shoulder, look'd like one of Michael[9] Angelo's children,—one of those forms so full of the passion of life, but full of that restraint imposed by their dreaming or whose attitudes are like the rythmic[10] contortions of the dreamer trying to wake from the terror of his dream.[11]

[Lo]rient.[12]

After the march[13] militaire and visit to the Librairie[2] and the daughter of spanish hidalgo to be found there, went down to port. Passed two large breton barges beside quay that look'd like derelicts, lean and storm-swept. Cross'd the bridge in sudden shower of rain, that drove the dock workers under shelter of wood-piles; large Sweedish[14] steamer, red and black hull, with wood tightly pack'd on its decks, over narrow bridge deck, no larger than a wild beast's cage, that he seldom leaves on the voyage, and now that land is there, seldom leaves also, but despite his imprison'd condition, having also one thing that the wild beast has not, the gift of speech—indeed if the wild beast had it, would he not be able to cow us from his cage and drive us away huddled together?, despite the restricted area in which his days are past,[14] succeeding in instilling fear, or obedience at least, in his men, a chetif,[3] bird-faced, scowling captain. Beside him a man, seemingly the mate, holding a pipe stiffly and with a firm grip, as a child holds something she has been sent to fetch,—something not understood of a world not understood, but only her duty as regards it, as though he had been given a pipe and smoked it mechanically, as he saw other people doing, but could never get accustom'd to *anything*, to possessing anything, and with thoughts as with things, used

1 "Embarrassment."

2 Bookshop.

3 Puny.

them always with the first gaucherie and tenacity that one shows with use of something new;—in his yellow head the blue eyes fixed always in front of him, as though looking at something he didn't see very distinctly. Several groups of Sweedish sailors from the boat and breton dock hands were working on the quay, and the harsh celtic tongue, passionate and abrupt, was mixed with the wearisome drawl of the scandinavians. Certain languages,—Russian, sweedish, breton,—apart from the distinct sound of them, are spoken with a distinct tone of voice, suggesting a particular and invariable *mood* in the speaker,—the fluctuation in the voice in Russian, in the speech of Russians of the better classes, suggesting an eager and sensitive nature, almost feminine, and the tone being that of a person reasoning, the voice maintained at a pitch and then suddenly dropp'd, and this constantly repeated gives the effect of a monotonous *expostulation,* reasoning at once; Sweedish is spoken with the tone of a "lourdeau" or ninny, with little accents of self-satisfaction, etc., that make it the best language one would chose for one's mother tongue, if one had to choose again. For it is bad enough to be born to speak an inharmonious tongue—English spoken without effort or "recherche,"[1]—or as it ought to be spoken!—is not one of the most harmonious languages, without being born, apart from one's character, to speak always with the tone of voice of a weak-minded simpleton! Breton is a solemn, rude, patriarchal, monotonous tongue, with long and sudden bursts of wild, impetuous speech, with sentences coming to a dead halt, which is not a breaking off as it seems, but the excited pitch of the voice is kept up till the last syllable and so there is no drop of the voice at the end of the phrase; there seems to be a ring of joy—not benevolent,—and recklessness, hysterical, timbre drawn out, and then sudden harsh and trenchant tones, and grating emphasis.

From these inner quays and the work of unloading cargo, the emptying of drays and barges, I pass'd to the mouth of the mercantile port and the outer quays in the direction of the harbour and bay, where several large steamers and more electric launches were loading up with passengers, crowds of soldiers and sailors for Port Louis, Lac Mort,[15] the villages round the bay and the ships out in the roads. Beside and mingled with these trading vessels, moving boats, etc. The dark rout of clouds that fill'd the skies, pouring eastward,—sweeping like desperate hosts driven onward by their fear, that bracing them prevented them from falling where they were to weep their losses and defeat and realize their despair,—the clouds steam'd on silently above, and the people, spur'd by the late shower, were hurrying in swarms in all directions. The first clouds of the flood, perhaps as then carried on by their very weight and swiftness and sparing the earth for a moment, caused little

1 Elegance.

more concern, no doubt, in men, than grasp their umbrellas and with eyes fix'd on the ground, hurry a little faster about their affairs, and like prophecies and dreams, the clouds, unnoticed, fill the heavens with their shadows, and chill the livid air with the wind of their flight. All the "âcre"[1] and burning life of the port, the workmen with their warm bodies; the crowds of workers on the quays, the hot sweat washed off their arms by the rain, the boats with their heated hulls, and the throbbings of the engines within, the dark oily water, the profusion of the fine tar, all in this damp cold atmosphere and grey tragic light and with the purple gleam of the wet houses, pavements etc., render'd more intense.

From the quays of the mercantile port, one passes onto a long jetty, that extends beyond the entrance of the military port, vis-à-vis. In looking at the large, damp-looking buildings, over the water, belonging to the Admiralty, I was reminded of the scandal that had filled the papers some weeks previously; in the workshops there, since that time suppress'd,—the workmen habitually every morning after having done a short spell of work, got out a pack of cards and play'd interminable "parties de manille"[2] for the rest of the day, leaving a couple of young apprentices to hammer plates of iron with various sounding articles, and generally make such an infernal noise that any one in authority appearing to be within earshot would be more than reassured of the patriotic assiduity of those sons of France within.

[1] "Acrid."

[2] "Games of manille."

NOTES

[1] The Cornell manuscript consists of seven leaves. On top of the first one there is a sketchy map of the triangle Lorient-Quimperlé-Pont-Aven in Southern Brittany. A facsimile of this page is included in Mary F. Daniels, *Wyndham Lewis: A Descriptive Catalogue,* Cornell, 1972, page 3.

[2] Should be "Le Pouldu," and "Le Faouët."

[3] Such old-fashioned contractions are typical of Lewis's early romanticism, as can be seen in the unpublished sonnets.

[4] Depend*a*nce: sic. A French influence probably.

[5] An uncertain reading.

[6] Sic (cf. French "orgiaque" and "fêtard").

[7] The parenthesis suggests this is a note for a further development.

[8] The left hand top corner of the page was torn off. An "s" followed by a full stop appears before "the circus."

[9] Sic.

[10] *Ry*thmic: sic. A French influence probably.

[11] A few details suggest that this last paragraph may have inspired "Les Saltimbanques," in which Lewis was to declare that he had met this circus for the first time "at a small town near Quimperlé." The "Blue Period" atmosphere is similar in both texts, and related to the contemporary "The Theatre Manager," obviously influenced by Picasso (see page 235).
[12] The top left-hand corner of the page was torn off. These impressions of Lorient apparently correspond to the aborted "nautical set" mentioned in the first section of "Inferior Religions" (see page 149), and they help us understand what Lewis may have been after—i.e., a man living in a cage-like space turning his activities into a mechanism.
[13] Should be "marche."
[14] Sic.
[15] In fact "Larmor." See the indexed map in the Appendix.

CROSSING THE FRONTIER

This work was first published in 1978, as a separate volume, to accompany the special limited edition of A Bibliography of the Writings of Wyndham Lewis. *Its composition can be assigned to the years 1909-1910. Lewis spent the Spring of 1908 in Spain and returned to England late that year, after his prolonged stay in Brittany. The typescript in the Cornell archive makes it unlikely that it should have been written—at least in its present state—in Spain, as Lewis had probably no typewriter with him, and no use then of a typist. This is corroborated by internal evidence. The "Ley del Terrorismo" associated with Maura (the Spanish Prime Minister between 1907 and 1909) certainly refers to the aftermath of the riots of July 1909, which culminated in the notorious execution of Francisco Ferrer (mentioned in* The Revenge for Love, *I, 3). On the other hand a* terminus ad quem *is provided by "A Spanish Household" which fictionalizes the episode of "the young man with his arms tied behind his back." "Crossing the Frontier," which records the raw material, must have been written some time before mid-1910, when "A Spanish Household" was published in* The Tramp. *But of course this piece may as well reflect other Spanish experiences previous to 1908. In any case the connection with "A Spanish Household" justifies its inclusion in the corpus of The Wild Body.*

All this sheds light on Lewis's method of composition—the apparent immediate freshness of these notes should not hide the fact that they are not a spontaneous first sketch taken from a diary. This Defoe-esque hybrid of story and travel memoir is typically Lewisian in the attention it pays to character-revealing minutiae and haunting situations or images over which Lewis will go on ruminating—notably the dangerous Spanish frontier, Spanish gestural idiosyncrasies, the Spanish sense of hospitality and picturesque Spanish trains (see "Bestre," "A Spanish Household," "A Soldier of Humour," The Revenge for Love *and the unpublished* Twentieth Century Palette*). Certainly Spain and its obscure fascinations played a determining role in the shaping of Lewis's vision and "philosophy of the eye."*

Amongst the Spaniards crowding into the train at the frontier station, Hendaye, came a youth whose cigarette I destroyed. Having asked him for a light, with my hard, tightly wrapped French cigarette, I burrowed into and shattered his unstuck, loose Spanish one. Over the ruins of this emblem of his country, a friendship sprang up between us. I offered him my case and, when my own cigarette was finished, accepted, dubiously, one of his, knowing well the weary struggle that awaited me. These cigarettes, sold unstuck and unstickable, although rolled up in packets, are extremely difficult to smoke. To succeed in making the glueless paper stick, to prevent the tobacco from straggling into one's mouth and hanging down raggedly at the other end, or to circumvent the fire from creeping down the dry paper, usually underneath, and burning one's finger, requires a combination of very complex and special gifts which only the Spaniard possesses.

After a few minutes of resistance, I left the cigarette to its own devices, throwing all my energy into the conversation. And, left to itself, it soon ceased to be a cigarette. It became a gaping mass of crumbling tobacco and crumpled half-burnt paper. There is a bravado and arrogant carelessness in smoking an unstuck cigarette, like riding a horse bare-back. There can be no practical reason for having cigarettes done up in packets but not properly glued. I exposed some of these views to my new friend.

This young man spoke with the deliberate and argumentative intonation of his race, especially when describing anything that does not call for dramatic treatment. A consummate calm and reasonableness is suggested by this national trick of manner. But besides mannerisms that were essentially national, he had an air of dazed resignation and a sort of self-restraint that seemed weighing on him—a lump in his throat that made speech difficult and his gestures rather languid. We discussed the details of the country we were passing through and the "Ley del Terrorismo" that Señor Maura had just sprung upon his countrymen. He told me that if this law were passed the whole country would be in revolt on the following day.

At an intervening station the guard came for our tickets, and my friend, instead of tendering his, pointed out of the carriage towards the back of the train, saying something about a "carabinero," or "gendarme," to be found there. At the next station the guard returned, puzzled and impatient, and said that he could not find the carabinero, and that my friend must pay for his ticket if he had not got one. The latter's watery blue eyes grew a shade more watery, his air of oppressive fatalism deepened, his tone grew more argumentative, reasonable and deliberate than ever, as he continued to perplex the guard by his imperturbable assertion that there *was*, nevertheless, a carabinero, down there, at the other end of the train, to whom he must apply. I understood little of all this. At last we arrived at San Sebastián, and I got out to secure a porter. On looking round to say good-bye to the young Spaniard, he was nowhere to be seen.

I crossed the bridge into the town, on the look-out for a hotel. Approaching an imposing looking café in a square facing the bridge, I asked a lonely waiter, standing before the door, the rate of accommodation. It was above my means. On asking him if he could recommend me a cheaper place, he at once indicated a neighbouring street where he thought I should find "mon affaire."[1] Both his thick arched eyebrows were drawn down, and his eyes oddly opened, as when the muscles are contracted to retain an eyeglass. This gave a funny dandified expression to his face. His moustaches sprouted upwards, and he was spruce and nervous. He now, on my thanking him for his courtesy, began strutting up and down, evidently pleased and excited by his magnanimity, and elaborately disclaiming it, shrugging his shoulders constantly in expressing his overpowering sense of the ordinariness of his action. "You come to me, you ask me the price of board here. It is more than you want to pay. What more natural than that I should tell you of a cheaper place? What more natural? I quite understand the situation. You have so much to spend. If you have a little more, you come here: a little less, you go there. It is quite normal and natural!" A huge shrug of enormous wisdom considering itself lightly out of excessive pride, and he resumes his nervous strutting little walk, as though he had delivered himself so epigrammatically that nothing more remained to be said. I lingered within earshot as long as I considered it necessary, as a return for his politeness, slowly and courteously retreating, feeling that although he was discoursing no longer, reduced to silence by triumph, a sense of fitness and pride, that nevertheless he wanted to say a great deal more. When I was half way across the square he shouted after me the directions anew, "fourth door down the street," etc. He was evidently woken up for the rest of the day. His delight in his reasonableness, and his energetic deprecating of the word "courteous" as applied to his action, had definitely dispelled the listless state in which I had discovered him.

The hotel recommended was just what I wanted. I deposited my bag and ordered dinner. While this was preparing, I strolled out into the town. I had not gone far when I was struck by the unusual spectacle of a young man with his arms tied behind his back conducted along the street by a man in plain clothes with a large stick.[1] I was astonished on nearer view to find this was my travelling companion. On seeing me he bent his head lower and his tears fell faster. I stopped them. He made a hopeless unexplanatory gesture, and gazed at me with his watery eyes now deluged. I asked him if I could do

---

[1] "What I wanted."

anything for him. He said it was too late: it was nothing, a matter of a few pesetas, but that they wouldn't take it now. His captor said I could come to the Gendarmerie if I liked. So we started off again. Neither of them was very explicit about his crime. As we approached our destination, the boy stopped and said it was no use my coming, that it was too late, and bid me good-bye. The other confirmed this by a gesture. With thanks, a promise to see me again and a despairing, naturally theatrical, adios, he staggered away, and left me hesitating in the street. As I returned to my hotel, I thought at first that he had been merely crossing the frontier without a ticket. But he may have been a young man who had exiled himself after some unlawful proceeding or other, and was now entering his country again to give himself up.

In the hotel everything was very much to my liking. The landlord was a fat, energetic little man from Valladolid. His pronunciation of this word was a guttural explosion: Balladoleeth, roughly, is the form it takes. It came out of his mouth like the rapid twanging of the deepest chords of a cello. All his fat seemed to vibrate dully with the sound.

At the next table sat a man of about thirty-five, that I discovered later to be an officer in mufti. With a curved bronze coloured beard, with two wings, as it were, growing to a point on either side, wide-browed with large, childish, fierce blue eyes, and an expression of perfect solemnity, he had the appearance of a Palladin, and altogether, was wonderfully and subtly anachronistic. This solemnity was pervaded by a smile, so that at first one thought he was smiling: but it was only the form of his face, and the chivalrous curve of his moustache. This splendid person was shortly giving me "tips" as to how to live, what places to visit, where to buy a donkey and many other things. While I recapitulated some of his advice, he sat there in front of me quite silent, with an occasional deep "si!" in affirmation. Then he rose, his serviette in his hand, and advanced upon me, as it were, I still demanding his confirmation on some of the points. His "si's" came quicker and deeper and with more tragic vibrations.

The Spaniard is very proud. Where the Frenchman would be chattering, he remains silent, impassible, with only an occasional "yes." But his vitality is even greater, and behind this silent mask, and this solitary word, entire speeches of cataclysmic violence are clamouring and surging for utterance. So, standing over me, he continued to listen; but, in addition to the "si!" another word at last escaped; a word, it is true, that often goes with "si!"; the word "hombre," meaning "man." This was all he would allow himself: "Si hombre!" "Yes man!"[2] Now that I had verified all the points of his advice that had remained obscure for me, and waited silent, for further discussion on his side, he denied himself, with characteristic austerity, the satisfaction of speech. Having re-seated himself, he remained without moving or speaking for some time. A fine specimen of his race, I was glad to meet this man on my entrance into Spain.

NOTES

[1] See in *The Revenge for Love* (VII, 1) the description of the two plain-clothes policemen "with heavy walking sticks."

[2] See the very first words of *The Revenge for Love:* "Claro," said the warder, "Claro, hombre!"

THE "POLE"

"The 'Pole,'" Lewis's first story, was published in The English Review *of May 1909. It is not a traditional short story concerned with a crisis or a "moment," but rather a series of stills introduced by a sociological account of "The Poles," which will reappear at the end of "Beau Séjour." The first still presents an already quite elaborate portrait of Isoblitsky (the future Zaborov); the next still, abandoned in 1927, describes the "farceur," an important intimation, in view of Lewis's future conception of the absurd, in which farce, not seen as something superficial, appears inseparable from the topsy-turvidom of degraded rituals. The portrait of the future Carl (anonymous here) and the account of the horseplay which will make up most of "Beau Séjour" are briefly evoked: the German's firing of a pistol is dealt with in one sentence and the dance scene in a single paragraph. Then the story seems to move to a conclusion with the German's farewell, but it proves to be a sham exit, and—to stress what can be seen as a sort of post-modernist unconclusiveness—the text peters out with the delicate, very Pont-Avenesque, description of "the only real Pole," a Chaplinesque child-man. This last vignette, as well as that of the "farceur," confers a rare charm—perhaps superior to that of the more polished final product—on this very first effort.*

A young Polish or Russian student, come to the end of his resources, knows two or three alternatives. One is to hang himself—a course generally adopted. But those who have no ties, who take a peaceful pleasure in life, are of a certain piety and mild disposition, borrow ten pounds from a friend and leave their country for ever—they take a ticket to Brest. They do this dreamily enough, and of late years almost instinctively. Once arrived there, they make the best of their way to some one of the many *pensions* that are to be found on the Breton coast. The address had been given them perhaps by some "Pole" who had strayed back to his own country prior to his own decease or to hasten somebody else's.

They pay two or three months' board and lodging, until the ten pounds is finished, and then, with a simple dignity all their own, stop paying. Their hosts take this quite as a matter of course. They henceforth become the regular, unobtrusive, respected inhabitants of the house.

If the proprietress (these establishments are usually run by women) removes her business to another town, or takes a larger house, her "Poles" go with her without comment or change in their habits.

In one of the show towns of Brittany, frequented by rich Americans and *gens du monde*,[1] Mademoiselle Tartarin still shelters in her magnificent hotel, some of these quiet "Poles" that were with her when she started in the little country inn.

If you lunch there you will find, at the foot of the table. a group of men of a monastic simplicity of dress and manner, talking among themselves in a strange and attractive tongue. One or two of them are quite venerable. These are the household gods of this amiable old lady.

I believe the Bretons get superstitious about these pensive inhabitants of their houses, and that some would no more turn out of doors an old and ailing "Pole," who owed them thirty years' board and lodging, than most old women would get rid of a blind and callous old black cat.[2]

The Slav cares little what his material environment may be, so wrapt is he in his thoughts. Many a young Polish student heretofore, confronted with starvation, did not affect the first alternative I have cited above. He would work himself up into a fury with the policeman whose beat lay before his window. He would exasperate himself by some fanciful dislike of the shape of this functionary's hat—repeat to himself monotonously and with deadly

---

[1] Society people.

[2] "Polonais" or "Pole," means to a Breton peasant the member of no particular nation, but merely the kind of being leading the life that I am here introducing cursorily to the reader. [Author's note]

earnest that a man with such a nose deserved death—who was a policeman *par-dessus le marché*[2]—until the mere sound of his approaching footsteps revolted him, and one fine morning he would blow him up.

With the aureole of a political crime he would then retire, in company with a scowling band of fellow heroes, to Siberia. And even yet many of severer temperament choose this way. But Brittany is becoming more and more fashionable, and may end not only by eclipsing Siberia, and dispeopling its mines, but by corrupting the redoubtable austerity of the Slav character.

One of the "Poles" I met in Brittany last summer managed to borrow another three pounds from a friend in Poland, and went to spend a month in Paris; after this little outing he returned and settled down to his regular life again. But it is few that ever see the colour of money, their initial ten pounds once spent. In Paris I have sometimes met "Poles" that were there only for a day or two, to see some friends *en passant*—for the last time. They take little interest in the new sights around them—one can see that it is not for this that they are travelling. They are going to Brittany, one is told.

A woman opened a smart little hotel the other day, rather out of the beaten track, and advertised that any artists who would at once take up their quarters there should have their first six months' board for nothing. One of our "Poles," who had grown discontented with the cooking of late, was absent all the following day, and turned up in the evening manifestly disappointed. He told us he had found no less than eight "Poles" already installed there, and he was not the only one that had arrived too late. But our landlady was never the same with him afterwards. Their hosts quite justly consider a breach of faith or loyalty unpardonable in a "Pole."

The "Pole's" own explanation of the astonishing position in which he finds himself, if by chance he realise the abnormality of it, is that they are afraid to let him go for fear of losing their money. He adds that they treat him with more deference than the ordinary boarders, who pay regularly, for the same reason. This would be quite in keeping with the unreasoning avarice of the Breton peasant, and perhaps it was the cause in the first place. The idea that the patriarchal life still surviving in Brittany keeps alive in people helps to account for the introduction of this new domestic animal into their households. Rich peasants keeping a large house have been used to seeing poor familiars—supernumeraries doing odd jobs on the farm—find a place by their hearth. Also, a good many "Poles" are painters—at least until the ten pounds is spent, and they can no longer get colours. The Bretons have never yet quite got over the shock Monsieur Vollard and others gave them in coming down from Paris *en coup de vent*[2] and offering them a thousand

---

[1] Into the bargain.

[2] On a flying visit.

francs—without a word of warning or a preliminary low offer to *ménager*[1] their nerves—for Gauguin's sketches that these hosts of his had confiscated in lieu of rent. The sight of a constant stream of breathless gentlemen, with the air of private detectives, but with the restless and disquieting eyes of the fanatic, often hustling and tripping each other up, and scrambling and bidding hoarsely for these neglected pictures, moved deeply their imagination. These enthusiasts indeed defeated their own ends. For months they could induce no one to part with the veriest scrap of paper. The more they offered, the more consternated and suspicious the peasants became. After the visit of one of these gentlemen the peasant would go into the church and pray. After that, feeling stronger, he would call a family council, get drunk, and wake up more bewildered and terrified than ever. I think that many Gauguins must have been destroyed by them, in the belief that there was something uncanny, devilish and idolatrous about them—they determining that the anxious connoisseurs suing for these strange images were worshippers of some inform divinity.

However, many of them did at last part with the pictures, receiving very considerable sums. The money once in their pockets they forgot all about Gauguin. This new *fact* engrossed them profoundly and exclusively for a time—they pondering over it, and turning it about in their minds in every direction. At last, with their saving fatalism, they accepted it all. These matters have been no small factor in the establishing of the "Pole." Gauguin might almost have claimed to be the founder of their charming and whimsical order.

On first arriving, I was taken for a "Pole," and the landlady received my first payment with a smile that I did not at the time understand. I think she was preparing to make a great favourite of me.

My hosts at Languenec[1] spoil their "Poles" out of all manner and reason. If too much petted, they will become as dainty and capricious as a child, and those in our *pension* had as many drawbacks as ordinary human beings.

At the *table d'hôte* the "Poles" sat at the head of the table, smoked large pipes and were served first, taking the lion's share. One who had been there for ten years smoked the biggest pipe and had the most authority. Sometimes they quarrelled with Mademoiselle Batz, and then we fed abominably for some days.

Isoblitsky, one of the inmates of this *pension*, was a spoilt "Pole," and yet some traits of his character none but a "Pole" could possess. He wandered stealthily about and yawned as a cat does. He got up sometimes with an abrupt air of resolution, like a cat, and walked away steadily to east, west, north or south, as the case might be. And yet you could never discover what

---

1 Show consideration for.

had determined him to this, or what he had to do there, wherever he went. And this was quite distinct from his conscious posing, for I have said that in some respects he was a degenerate "Pole."

Telepathic attraction, that has been experienced by most men, will lead them under the guise of caprice to somebody's house or a certain quarter of the town, where they meet, as it seems by accident, a friend. I really began to fancy in Brittany that other things than men—that scenes and places—had this power over a "Pole." That an empty seashore, an old horse tethered in a field, some cavernous Breton lane under some special aspect and mood, had the power of drawing these strange creatures towards it, as though it had something to impart.

One always speaks of the Slav as of the most irresolute race existing; that the Slav can never make up his mind. On the contrary, the Slav has a positive genius for making up his mind. And all the month-long psychical struggles and agonies that the hero of a Russian novel goes through are merely the desperate battle of his will against this tyrannous propensity of his nature, whose instinct he cannot trust: they are his frenzied attempt to thwart himself from making up his mind. And usually what the reader hails with a sigh of relief, as his final conquest over the indecision of his character—be the upshot of the struggle only that he will hang, draw and quarter his maternal grandmother, instead of putting her in the oven to bake, the reader having been bewildered through many chapters with the many genial and conclusive reasons that suggest themselves to the hero in favour of each of these alternatives in turn—this final "making up of his mind" is in truth nothing less than the ultimate and utter defeat of his reasoned will by this calamitous genius of his.

The moment an aunt's life grows distasteful to him this tremendous genius of resolve, this elemental gift of the Slav, sweeps down upon the unfortunate hero, and seizing the first thought that happens to be uppermost in his mind, galvanises it and lifts it at once to the pitch of an obsession. But he is *raffiné* and knows that ruin waits him if he lets this blind energy conduct his business. He struggles madly against this power, and will often resist it for weeks, going without food and sleep and writhing on his bed through interminable chapters as though in a physical paroxysm. And when he is offering one of the most heroic spectacles imaginable of force of character, he is regarded by the exasperated reader, entirely misapprehending the situation, as a monster of indecision.

Isoblitsky disliked our proprietress: and he was imbued with several passions more common and proper to men *dans le siècle*[1] than to a "Pole." He wanted one to believe, for some reason or other, that he was tremend-

[1] Worldly.

ously independent. He put himself to great pains to prove it. He must have possessed some such simple axiom as: One is much more apt to bestow things upon a person who dislikes accepting anything, than upon one who would take all you offered him. He coveted excessively this advantageous position in your mind.

After dinner in conversing with you he always spoke in a hoarse whisper, or muttered in an affected bass, hardly parting his lips, and often hissing through his teeth. Whether he were telling you what a hypocrite the landlady was, or describing how the Caucasians ride standing on their horses and become so exultant that they fling their knives up in the air and catch them—he never became audible to any one but you.

He had a shock of dark hair and was dark-skinned; his eyes had grown strengthless, and his expression rather sombre and sickly as the plants in the shadow of a wood. In pretending not to notice people, to be absorbed in his own thoughts, the paper or the book he was reading, the contraction of his eyebrows had become permanent. His preoccupation to appear independent and strong-minded did not permit of any other conscious sentiment: but he had the suavity and natural coquetry of a pretty brute, that—as he was not aware of it—was constantly baffling him and relaxing his stern purposeful independent expression, sometimes at a crucial moment. His nature was the darkest of mysteries[2] for him, and this enemy in the camp, this something that was constantly corrupting his implacable self under its very nose, perplexed him somewhat, and he mused about it.

He had the strangest habit of imitating his own imitations. In telling a story in which he figured (his stories were all designed to prove his independence) he had a conventional type of imitation for the voice and manner of his interlocutor, and a gruff, half-blustering tone to imitate his own voice in these dramatic moments. And gradually these two tones, mixed into each other, had become his ordinary tone in conversation.

A thick-set and muscular little man, he was the second individual I met this summer with the same odd principle of self-assertion. He made a constant display of his physical strength—regarding it merely as an accident that might be put to account and taking no personal pride in it. He had only begun to appreciate it when he found that other people appreciated it, and that it could be exploited. Also, it was a considerable confirmation of his independence, or made it seem more likely. He became intimate with several of the visitors, one after the other. Any one arriving there and seeing him with the friend of the moment—talking confidentially apart, or making signs to him at table, his general attitude of aloofness and reticence maintained towards the rest of the company—would have supposed him an exclusive, solitary man, who had never had any friend in his life but *that* friend. When he intended to "take up" with a new-comer his manner became severer and aloofer than ever, but he would perhaps show them some gruff and stiff politeness, as though forced and forcing himself to be so. He took no interest in women whatever, but when, by some remark I made, he became aware how he had neglected his good looks in his stories, he made the clumsiest attempts on the following days to give me some record of his many successes.

He constantly spoke of a friend of his, a "Pole" also—not because he was rich, or famous or aristocratic, but because he was apparently a fellow who showed a great and startling independence of spirit, and who was prodigiously strong; far stronger than he, Isoblitsky. He looked upon this person's qualities as his own, and used them as such. This shadowy figure of the friend seemed indeed superimposed on Isoblitsky's own form and spirit. One divined an eighth of an inch on all sides of the contour of his biceps and pectorals, another contour—the visionary contour—of this friend's even larger muscles. And beyond even the sublime and frowning pinnacles of his own independence, the still loftier summits of his friend's pride, of a piece with his.[3]

This friend, from all accounts—and such even transpired in Isoblitsky's eulogies—would yield to few in rascality. I entertained a lively admiration for him, and Isoblitsky, mistaking this for a tribute to himself, looked upon me as a person of considerable discernment. And like most continental scamps of their career at one time or other, he had found his way into the French foreign legion in Africa. It is in the distant garrison-rooms of Biribi[4] that the *élite* of the criminal youth of an epoch come together, exchange ideas, and get the polish that is to fit them in after life to occupy envied positions. It is there that they acquire the justest conception of the criminal tone of their time, and are profoundly moved and fired by the sight of so many scalliwags all together. It is very often their bad records in these regiments that lay the foundation of their reputation. But one must not dogmatise on this point. Many a world impostor gained in his African service a corporal's *galons*[1]—and was almost as proud of them as of his most nefarious achievement—and got such a smug conduct-sheet as took the efforts of a whole lifetime of consequent rapine and bloodshed to wipe out.

In the late fighting with the Moors Isoblitsky's friend underwent great hardships. Because of his extraordinary strength he was compelled on the march to carry several of his comrades' rifles in addition to his own. Isoblitsky would read his African letters apart, with an air of absorbed and tender communion, seeking to awaken one's jealousy. He repeated long dialogues between his friend and himself. When it came to his friend's turn to speak, he would puff his chest out, and draw himself up, until the penumbra of visionary and supernatural flesh that always accompanied him was almost

---

1 Stripes.

filled by his own dilated person. He would assume a debonair recklessness of manner, his moustaches would flaunt upwards over his laughing mouth, and even the sombre character of his teeth would be momentarily forgotten. His gestures would be those of an open-handed and condescending prince. He would ostentatiously make use of the personal pronoun "thou," to make one eager to get on such terms with him oneself. I never did, for I offended him. One day he remained at table after the others had left. He was waiting to be asked to go for a walk with me. Off my guard for a moment, my eyes betrayed the fact that I had noticed this, although my expression in no way commented upon it, but registered it only. It was a mere mental observation in the assimilation of which my customarily impassive servants, the eyes, had shared. But this piece of ill-breeding he never forgave.

One among the "Poles" they pointed out to me especially as a great *farceur.* [1] For instance, he once found himself in a railway carriage immediately in front of a sleeping man—a young French officer—with his mouth open. He at once introduced his forefinger between the sleeper's lips, who, waking up with a man's finger in his mouth, spat it out, sprang up, and trembled with rage. But the "Pole" (whose advances the young officer had rejected in this unequivocal fashion, and whose face he had found on waking up near his own, with an expression of mild courtesy imprinted on it) now stammered in a startled voice: "No makey angry! no makey angry! Polish custom, Polish custom!" And the narrator added that they became fast friends.

All his exploits, as recounted by his friends, were well-known stories. He was a simple, expansive, hysterical little man; and although I could imagine him excitedly putting his finger into somebody else's mouth by mistake, I did not credit his doing it in the way narrated. It seemed much more likely that somebody else would put their finger in *his.* At the same time I could hardly believe in his mendacity. I finally concluded that he was a lunatic, and that from having allowed his mind to dwell too much on his friends' anecdotes, he had at length come to believe himself the hero of those that appealed to him most.

A real *farceur* that I once knew resembled this man somewhat; although he was a more credible one. He was voluble, with astonished eyes and no sense of property. The *farceur* of this sort abounds, I believe, in Poland, which must be one of the most perilous contries, on the whole, that has ever been heard of; of just *how* appallingly full it is of police-traps, man-traps, Nihilist-traps, booby-traps and mouse-traps—to mention only some of the snares that yawn at every step there—no mere statistics could ever give one an idea.

---

1 Practical joker.

The practical joker is a degenerate, who is exasperated by the uniformity of life. Or he is one who mystifies people, because only when suddenly perplexed or surprised do they become wildly and startlingly natural. He is a primitive soul, trying to get back to his element. Or it is the sign of a tremendous joy in people, and delight in seeing them put forth their vitality, and in practical joking of a physical nature a joy in the grotesqueness of the human form. Or it is the sadness of the outcast, the spirit outside of life because his nature is fit only for solitude, playing hobgoblin tricks with men that cannot sympathise with him: just as I have no doubt that some anarchist outrages are the work of very violent and extreme snobs, who lie in wait for some potentate, and shoot him, that in the moment of death the august eyes shall become more expressive and show more interest in him than they have ever shown in anybody before. The *farceur* has often many friends and admirers who brave the terrors of his friendship, but he remains peculiarly little understood. He is a lonely hero.

Another of my fellow boarders last summer, a "Pole" in the Breton sense, though a German by birth, was the most spoiled of all the "Poles" at our *pension.* He used to throw Mademoiselle Batz down in the kitchen and stamp on her. One night he fired at her two or three times, wounding in the calf a little "Pole" curled up in the corner near the fire. This was a very odd fellow. He measured about six feet two, and was spare and nervous. With his dark eyes and long black hair curling up at the bottom, scant on the front and leaving a deep smooth brow—with his large melancholy features and handsome elongated black beard—he had the impressive and "distinguished" head of a prosy, though rather wicked, Royal Academician of Celtic origin. He also accompanied his speech with a French grace of gesture—a clumsy imitation—just the way one imagines the really cultivated Royal Academician to speak. He bore an Italian name, and his exotic appearance wad due, as a matter of fact, to his southern ancestry. His dyspepsia was constantly sowing strife between his Teuton sloth and his Latin nervousness—compounds that in his case did not agree. They remained distinct, strong and alternatively assertive. Mademoiselle Batz had tried to marry him, he would tell us. He had not fallen in with her idea. Nevertheless, he bitterly resented the withdrawal of those favours and wiles that she had lavished upon him while engaged in this enterprise.

Without the least intention of marrying her, he tried by constant scenes and agitations, and the *épanchement,*[1] the tenderness of consequent reconciliations, to renew the old state of things, to be coquetted with and petted again: to make her think he was in love with her or could become so. This succeeded once or twice. Mademoiselle Batz thought that perhaps he would

---

[1] Effusion.

fall into his own trap, or his nerves give way: or for fear of losing her favours again, concede a little, and then a little more. She would reinstate him entirely in her good graces, restore all the grateful signs of her predilection. Then one by one she would deprive him of them again—slowly grow colder—first omit one little *prévenance* [1] and then another, let his newfound dominion over her die a slow death by torture. She hoped in this way to bring him up to the point. Besides, violent withdrawals of all prerogatives and considerations at once did not convince him of his loss. But she concluded that her chances of triumphing were very small.

When she had quite cured herself of this hope, however, a period of comparative success attended the German's efforts. She now gave herself up frankly for a few weeks to the pleasure of quarrelling with him, being hurled down on the floor—her Breton nature thoroughly appreciating this side of his character—or having frightful-sounding German words hissed and spat at her, in company with his favourite French word of abuse, *gourt* as he pronounced it. Then the making it up, with its glows and titillations.

After one of their quarrels, they organised a dance to celebrate its completion; their two gaunt and violent forms whirling round the narrow room, quite indifferent to the other dancers, giving them terrible blows with their driving elbows, their hair sweeping on the ceiling. His blazing drunkard's eyes were fixed on hers, striving in the intoxication of the dance, as his German nature taught him, to win her imagination, then malleable as a child's—to seal it with his seal, at a height where no succeeding excitement of every day could reach, with its melting heat, and dethrone him, or efface this image to which he could always appeal. He felt that she was in an extremely sensitive and impressionable state. He seemed to be holding fast and immobilising in his set intensity of expression some forceful mood. In his rigid and absorbed manner, with his smiling mask, he looked as though a camera's recording and unlidded eye were in front of him, and if he stirred or his expression took another tone, the spell would be broken, the plate blurred, his chance lost.

Then came a day when at the word *gourt* she merely shrugged her shoulders, and her unmistakable indifference protected her as completely as though she were bodily out of his reach. He only threw her down when she was already down spiritually—he may have feared that the anomaly of her upright position as to the flesh might provoke a reaction in the spirit—knowing her dependence on physical parallels.

That evening he came down to dinner very white, and afterwards made a short speech, saying that things had arisen that compelled him to seek another roof: he would like us all to take a farewell glass with him. We chose

---

[1] Special attention.

our drink, and the conversation took a lugubrious and sentimental turn, out of consideration for him, though no mention was made of the reason for his departure. I drank my grog with relish, and wished him heartily God-speed, for the vacillations in the quality of the food had been daily of late—nay, hourly—for some disobliging remark of his while the meat was being served—at once repeated to her mistress by the *bonne*—and the sweets were withheld or skilfully spoiled at the last moment. But the next morning he was there as usual, and offered no explanation for this resurrection. He only left some weeks later, his box remaining as security for the bill—twenty thousand francs, I suppose.

But I came to the conclusion that, however good a "Pole," a stray German, Lapp, Esquimau or other dim and hyperborean personage who had found his way to these parts might become, it took an authentic Slav to make a real "Pole."

There was only one real "Pole" there. He was a little child-like man that lived on the ground floor of the tower, with windows on three sides of him, without blinds or obstructions to the view of any sort, and there, passing on their way to meals, the *pensionnaires* could see him in his bare room like a fish in an aquarium. A great friendship for a brother had long absorbed him; and, left alone at his friend's death, he had become a "Pole," as some people take monastic vows in cases of bereavement. He was very fond of children, and had never found out that the Breton children were unimaginative and ill-natured, immature counterparts of their parents. They once rolled him into a ditch while he was painting, and I have seen him running with sobs of laughter across the fields after a little boy who had got away with his paint brushes.

NOTES

1 An imaginary name.

2 Identified as an "inferiority complex" in 1927.

3 An image echoed later in the opening page of *The Revenge for Love:* "he spoke from the bleak, socratic peak of his wisdom to another neighbouring peak."

4 "Biribi" is not a place name but French military slang for the disciplinary or punishment companies of the Bataillons d' Afrique.

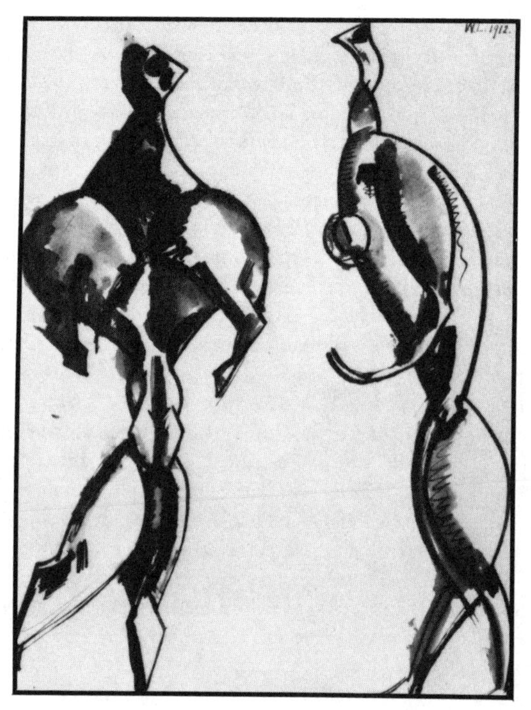

SOME INNKEEPERS AND BESTRE

"Some Innkeepers and Bestre," the second "story" to be published by Lewis, appeared in the June 1909 issue of The English Review. *Quite advanced in its apprehension of Modernism, it is a wayward hybrid made up of a sociological analysis of the commerical mind ("Some Innkeepers") followed, as an illustration, by a portrait ("Bestre"), which is the germ of the future story published in* The Tyro. *The remarkable introductory essay which seems as much to anticipate structuralism as to revisit the then unknown Marxian analysis of reification, was not used again. Yet it shows how, from the start with Lewis, structure and superstructure collide in fictions and rituals. "Some Innkeepers" stands as the original impulse behind such books as* The Art of Being Ruled *or* The Lion and the Fox.

As a result, "Bestre" appears as both the most static and the most seminal of the early stories. Though revised after the war (sometime between 1919 and 1922, the date of its publication in The Tyro, *as may be deduced from the introduction of the word "libido" suggesting fresh acquaintance with Freudian theory), most of the earlier version was retained in the second. But dramatization was introduced, style intensified and motivation further explored. Expanding a single sentence buried in the initial text, the new story starts dramatically* in medias res. *Couched in Vorticist prose at the height of ludicrous abstraction, the 1922 "Bestre" is one of Lewis's most extreme efforts—and the author was certainly conscious of this when he wrote in* Rude Assignment *that "out of Bestre . . . grew . . . the aged 'Gossip Star' at her toilet." Such intensity led Lewis to look more closely into Bestre's behaviour. Where at first he had assigned his victory to the exceptional expressiveness of his eye, he was in 1922 led to assume—which suggests that he had probably been a witness to such a scene—that Bestre must have resorted to another engine than the eye. As seen before with "A Soldier of Humour," satire and humour, because of their savage ancestry, are inseparable from sex—even if Lewis pretends to oppose this.*

To those inns scattered up and down through fiction and history all men have taken either their dreams, their indigestions, their passions, or the thread of their stories—the latter principally occupied with their hero or heroine, who happened to be sojourning there, and chiefly concerned with using them as a trysting-place of alarms, surprises, misadventures, brawls, and flight. In fact, they used the inn as a mere convenience, and in the strict sense as a "public-house"—a place where they would conduct their characters when the story was flagging, and there set the plot going again in a whirl of adventures of the high-road, that would be sufficient to carry them without further effort to the last page. Or else they would choose it as the scene of their comic interludes, and trysting-place of all the drunken characters in their book! And often they allowed these ruffians to behave most scandalously there, when they would have severely rebuked them if it had occurred anywhere else.

How many an obtuse traveller has been entertained by an angel unawares, or, less metaphorically, at least by an amazing and startling personage. But I have entered my inns with none of these preoccupations; with the result that I have discovered that even the most visionary of customers—the Knight of La Mancha himself—could not be more so than many a provincial French innkeeper that I have met with, though in what is often a very different way. Some of these men have made of innkeeping an astonishing art. It has its brilliant and eccentric exponents, who live not only unrecognised, but scorned. So subtle is their method and manner of charming the public that it has an opposite effect; the latter becomes furious, thinking that it is being trifled with. It needs a public as imaginative as the landlord to appreciate what is often the most bold and revolutionary scheme of hospitality. Besides, although the *clientèle* be in view to begin with, this art, in its abnormal development, leaves all thought of its original aim far behind, greatly transcends it. It would be difficult to decide which is the more heroic figure, the artist of genius starving in his garret or the landlord starving in his inn. I have seen the public turning away in rage and loathing from a certain landlord's door, but still he refused to modify one jot his manner and technique of hospitality; and after years spent in its lonely reception-rooms the house was sold to some mediocre person who brought custom flooding back; and he, the true artist, in the ruin of his fortunes, went down into the inhospitable grave. It is for such figures as this that we look in vain in many famous books that have exploited the romance of public-houses. With these innkeepers it is usually an obstinate belief in and cultivation of some personal, perhaps physical, attribute that dictates their conduct. A man is convinced that his oiliness of manner is more ineffably and exquisitely oily than any other man's, and from that moment, if his is not a popular oil, he is lost. Or another will spend his last halfpenny in exploiting and speculating on his breeziness, convinced that there is untold wealth in it; or nothing will shake a belief in a wife's pomposity, or her rotundity. I once knew a landlord who placed all his hopes in his wooden leg, in its at once laughable and friendly effect, and would not have had his old leg back again if he could.

There is a similar phenomenon very often to be met with among servants. Many a domestic is so proud and unbending in his servility, in the particular character and colour of obsequiousness that is his, that if it be unacceptable to those served, in general he passes much of his time out of work. He has become so overweeningly proud of the splendid rigour of his abjection, this starved sentiment of pride growing more monstrously and fiercely in the utter meanness of his life than it has ever done in the souls of the greatest despots and conquerors, that he regards his employer as the merest pretext for abasement. And the master, often blind to all this, such an intensity of feeling being incomprehensible to him, imagines that that stiff back has cast out all limpness in his honour, and that those calves bulge for him.

A young French *hôtelier* setting up business in the provinces forms himself rather in this way. To regulate his attitude towards his customers, he first imagines an ideal customer, and this is inevitably more or less himself. Also, in each hotel of the more modest sort it is the proprietor's idea of comfort that decides its disposition. But in the manner that he finally adopts there will be, apart from his accommodating his nature to what he considers the needs and demands of the ideal customer, another element, caused by his personal conception or mirage of the ideal hotel proprietor. Sometimes the inchoate landlord within him is not that most fitted for the incipient customer likewise emanating from the depths of his consciousness. This is a situation of no little delicacy and embarrassment. But fortunately it is of rare occurrence.

The truest type of innkeeper is to be found in France. And as these papers deal with some of my experiences in Brittany last summer it is chiefly with France that I am concerned.[1]

The Frenchman considers commercial life as the type of all life. And money is the one romantic element in this essentially scientific mind. He becomes mystical about nothing else. The most sceptic and penetrating of Frenchmen, brought face to face with this problem, with this hereditary weakness of their nature, give up in despair, and consent to make an exception in the case of money, to regard it poetically and sentimentally. When they approach this subject they lose their Latin precision and materialness, and one would think it were some northern dreamer speaking.

I can imagine a Frenchman discoursing somewhat in the following manner, when worked up into rather an exalted frame of mind by some of the

Ring music, say. Although probably ignorant of the theme and story of the Nibelungen, still his spirit would feel instinctively that gold, that money in some form or other, had a lot to do with it, was the key of the matter. "It is common for a man to settle substantial sums on his wife, and if I could I would pay all my friends heavy salaries. If you are paying an *employé* a large income, you think better of him, just as you prefer goods that you have acquired at great expense. If my bosom friend were receiving a couple of thousand a year from me in recognition of the extraordinary position he occupied as regards me, I should probably think better of him and enjoy his affection more than if I paid him nothing for it, and generally be extremely proud of him. It is human nature to be delighted with that for which one has paid largely in money, kind, or labour or sorrow. *Parfaitement!* And here I come to a very important point. One always wishes to bestow things on those one loves, admires, be it one's vitality, one's gifts, or one's goods. If a Spaniard, for example, gets particularly enthusiastic about you while out for a walk, it is all you can do to prevent him from undressing there and then and giving you everything down to his socks. As it is, you come home your pockets bulging with presents—handkerchiefs, cigarette-boxes, stilettos, newspapers, cravats, and probably, like a clown in a circus, his hat jammed down on top of your own. But this Spaniard's impulse to bestow things on him that he feels peculiar sympathy for is exactly the same as my, the Frenchman's, impulse to bestow money upon my friends. It would be equally natural in Spain, although it would be more abstract, and not touch the imagination so much, if a Spaniard, meeting you at dinner and being pleased with you, in the heat of the moment gave you a five-pound note. As it is, the Spaniard insists on my accepting all his rings. But whereas his fingers are long, fine, and active, mine are corpulent, sleek, and meditative. So his rings are of no use to me except to pawn. Likewise his hat would fit me ill. But if he were to give me a thousand dollars I could provide myself with a costume analogous to his, but made to my measure, a hat to match, and spacious rings for all my fingers. In the same way one's gifts, one's susceptibilities, more essentially personal, cannot be given away, or always be assimilated and used by another. So man has developed a kind of abstract factor in his mind and self, a social nature that is the equivalent of money, a kind of conventional, nondescript, and mongrel energy, that can at any moment be launched towards a friend and flood him up to the scuppers, as one might cram his pockets with gold. One cannot give him one's own gifts or thoughts, but one bestows upon him this impersonal, social vitality, with which he can acquire things fitted to his particular nature. Because the front that a gentleman of our day shows to the world is conventionalised and uniform, people do not usually recognise that a high state of civilisation and social development is also that of individualism *par excellence*. The characterless, subtle, protean social self of the modern man, his wit, his sympathies, are the moneys of the mind. When the barter of herds, tools, and clothing gave place to coinage this sort of fellow began to exist. And this artificial and characterless go-between, this common energy, keeps the man's individual nature all the more inviolable and unmodified. Why people have this inalterable passion for bestowing things on their friends is because the richer these friends be, spiritually or materially, according to the desire of the person, the more he feels his own love and power. A man would ripen his friend like the sun—not impose on him his own forms and characteristics, but merely his vitality, his heat: he would have his friend's individual personality strongly fructify. And such a result can only be achieved by this modern ideal of abstracting energy from a purely personal and coercive form, and making it a fluid, unaccented medium—the civilised man, in short. This is the modern man's ideal of realising himself in others; that is, the *degree* of himself, and not the specific character, which is inalienable. Those of the ancients that were not moderns, their personality not having become a medium of this sort, could not realise it in others, since it could not be assimilated raw; their way was to subdue and tyrannise over others, and in the mere power of destruction and of subjecting find self-realisation. I personally am terrified if a man wishes to be my friend and shows a dark and obstinate tendency to disregard this conventional, civilised abstraction of social life, this money of such relationship—wishes, in short, to deal with me very self to very self. My savage and inner being has been used so long to solitude, and to having a puissant and protean shadow between it and the world, that it has become more savage than the bushman's naked spirit, and at this sudden and direct contact with another human being it retreats hastily still deeper into its seclusions. Civilisation has resulted in the modern man becoming, in his inaccessibility, more savage than his ancestors of the Stone Age. I feel also that I am being hurried by this stranger into the Dark Ages, that he will make me some costly spiritual present, in 'kind'—and not in 'money,' as I should much prefer—and then squabble with me over the worth of my return present and his dignity, and probably end by cutting my throat. Just as when a woman's thoughts are set upon me the only form of covetousness as regards myself or my person that I receive benevolently or in any way encourage is that having merely my friendship for its object—when it is the social man that she is setting her nets for. Love is an abyss; as a basis for such a contract as she proposes it is inadmissible. A marriage for friendship or for money is the only possible one, and there is room over and above the business part of the matter in either case for love."

At this point, perhaps, the music will swell up again, and the Frenchman, still more moved, will continue, with a fanatic expression in his eyes: "But money (to speak no longer of its equivalents, but of itself!) has a mystical and magnetic power over man. It draws out of him everything that is mean, interested, calculating. English people cry out at the mercenary character of the Frenchwoman, and of all our sexual relations. But as much, and more, 'true sentiment,' exists between French lovers as between their unmercenary English cousins. Mean and worldly interests creep into all relationships that are not purified by money. It obviates many a baseness. It is sanitary, bracing, necessary. It is like an inoculation undergone at the outset. It clears the air. All the mercenary and mean sentiments go into the gold piece—that represents them and absorbs them; it purges the spirit. We Frenchmen merely pay the evil and deceitful and scheming spirits to keep away. Pay that we and the woman may enjoy each other's society without hindrance, hypocrisy, mistrust, or preoccupation—may love each other, if our natures tend that way. In short, pay so that interest should be dragged to the light in the first place, and pensioned at once, so that it should not work secretly and impalpably, as it otherwise does, and spread and infect the whole with its poison. Money is great in evil. But it is nothing compared with the greater iniquity of human nature, that we use it against. It is like the slight indisposition of an inoculation compared with the disease itself. Money is the one thing that saves us from our mean and mercenary passions, whose boundless and obscure anarchy would come in its place."

Here the eloquent Frenchman might draw breath, and by this time you, infected with his ardour, would continue yourself: "Yes; what you say, although the merest truism, is often forgotten in our country. The Englishman has a business self and a private self. He calls the Frenchman's intimacy of shop manners hypocrisy. But the Englishman, in dividing himself up in this way, breeds a much deeper hypocrisy. It is a result of this arbitrary partition of his life that has made the nation a byword in Europe. In insisting that the relations of his private life have nothing but an unselfish, sincere, and heroic nature he leaves unmolested and uncurbed the element of selfishness that battens on the really heroic qualities left in its obscure company. So that in this arrangement, by virtue of which he considers himself a frank and above-board sort of man, he becomes the very type of the impostor. Or else, if he become anything but merely formal in his business manners, it is to affect his private self, who is wholly unselfish in his eyes. The result is that people who have only business intercourse with him—such as foreign nations with whom he is bargaining—consider him of the most disgusting hypocrite that ever lived. His Latin neighbour has not two selves, but one self for public and for private life. He does not divide his nature crudely into a purely business person, and another and second person, purely high-minded, affectionate, &c. He mixes these two persons into each other, and is always the same man. Both in his bed and his banque his attitude is made up half of calculation and half of sentiment, and always he is noisy and cajoling and magnanimous." The Frenchman is becoming uneasy at the direction your discourse is taking, and here I suggest that you should subside into silence again, having had your say, and relieved yourself of some of the burden of thought induced in you by your eloquent neighbour.

French people, it is true, make much more use of their personality in commerce than the English; also of their idiosyncrasies—nay, their affections and tenderest feelings. A French shopkeeper gets quite sentimental about a customer that is in the habit of buying extensively in his shop. I was astonished once to see real feeling in a barber's face, whom I had accidentally deserted—a pale, pretty, inhuman sadness, such as his block in the window might have displayed, it is true, but still feeling. Another time I found myself involved in the most theatrical of friendships with a furniture remover and cabinet-maker.[2] His charges became more and more exorbitant, and his feeling for me almost hysterical. I felt that he was impelled to raise his prices in the interests of our friendship, and as I was touched at this I did not protest. I had occasion to change my quarters several times. He regarded my restlessness as a very beautiful and touching trait in my character, and very closely allied to the profoundest of human sentiments. And also he was moved sometimes at the thought of me. Touched suddenly while engaged in carrying my things up one flight of stairs and down another, through Gothic portals one month, along airy galleries the next; past *concierges* whose "lodge" is always vacant, with a notice informing one that they are on the staircase, but whom one never sees—mysterious and *insaisissables*[1] *concierges!*—past truculent *concierges* who placed a thousand obstacles in his way—who had insisted on seeing not only the receipt for the rent, but all the twenty-three different vouchers for his honesty that never leave a Frenchman's breast-pocket whether he be honest or not, and who, after prying lengthily into his life, allowed him in, still protesting; past drunken *concierges*, waking up and frenziedly attempting to do their duty, with an inarticulate and vehement cry and mad surging of the body and seething of the face, but relapsing into ignominious sleep; groping in shadowy vistas with my chest of drawers on his back, whose weight he knew to an ounce; pausing a moment on the edge of cloud-high balconies, from which the Panthéon could be seen, a flight of doves, the fresh world of the roofs—I would see his face grow pinched and staring of a sudden. Or in some dark corner of the ascent, his forehead bent nearly to the floor, dripping with sweat, during the measured and excessive labour his mind exceptionally active, this thought would assail him. Or seeing the furniture settle down awkwardly, whimsically, forming sad lines and unhappy masses, in the new abode, every piece of it connected in the mind with some spacing or character

---

[1] Elusive.

of the last room, he would stand for a moment involuntarily discouraged and oppressed before its strangeness, and would regard this emotion as one inspired for me. Or the erratic life led by my furniture—its lack of harmony and cheerlessness in that particular moment, rather—suddenly revealed to him, by analogy, the way that he ought to regard its owner. And he saw dimly a spirit that, with its ideal surroundings, made no harmonious whole; something uprooted and forlorn. These feelings were a new bond between us, and of course the bill gave a generous leap at the same time, attaining an unprecedented figure.

Because of this close association of the pocket and the heart in the Frenchman's arduous life of gain, one of these strange tradesmen would not improbably die of heartbreak were his best customer to leave him. This platonic love of the French tradesman for his customer is very curious. I expect when the French laws become a little more consistent there will be added to the *crime passionnel* a *crime commercial,* with the same attenuating circumstances attached. One will then be compelled to distribute one's purchases or a large area, and avoid anything approaching a *liaison* with one's grocer or tailor. Such an affair as that I have mentioned above with the furniture remover might have fatal consequences.

The principle I indicated above, of applying forms of private life to public life in France, is naturally in particular characteristic of the innkeeper. For if a draper in his shop welcomes you as a friend, the innkeeper, with the clearer analogy of his business to "the home," welcomes you as the guest of his hearth, to the house where you are to eat, sleep, and live. The fact that you pay does not in any way modify the primitive feeling of hospitality, the sentiment of benevolence towards the guest that God has sent, the friend entertained at his board. Quite the contrary. Only these feelings of hospitality, of necessity rarely exercised in private life, are strenuously exercised every day in his business. These emotions, like the body, develop if constantly used. Develop, in this case, to prodigious proportions; until, to pursue the physical simile, the original frame and structure is no longer discernible beneath a bulging mass of the strangest excrescences. The innkeeper's soul is a monstrosity of hospitality.

So the study of the French innkeeper is especially fruitful for he veritably puts his whole soul into his part, everything in him blossoms out prodigiously within the conventional limits of his trade. And if any one should say that the affections and things of the heart bloom but artificially in this atmosphere of commerce, I would reply that it is equally undeniable that, as some of the most odd and beautiful varieties of flowers and fruit come to life in the hothouse, so the strangeness and enormity of this soul's hospitable development is often unequalled. These loves and generosities, "forced" as it were in a commercial air, are to some more interesting than the flowers of the field of the affections and other more "natural" products. The Parisienne is a very extraordinary person. But the French innkeeper is of the same stock.

BESTRE

Bestre keeps a boarding-house for Parisians and other strangers in one of the remotest fishing villages of the Breton coast. It is only open in the summer, and he passes the winter months in hunting. He is a stranger to the place himself, a "Boulonnais," and at constant feud with the inhabitants. Bestre's great-grandfather came into France from the Peninsula, with the armies of Napoleon, and his Spanish origin is visible in his face. He is a large man, grown naïvely corpulent: one can see by his movements that the gradual and insidious growth of his stomach has not preoccupied him in the least. Like some king perfectly aware and yet indifferent to the fact that one of his nobles is deliberately and scandalously enriching himself under his nose—some Minister keeping in his own pocket the revenues entrusted to him for distribution throughout the realm—indifferent from superb carelessness for such matters, and also owing to the fact that this subtle courtier procures him many pleasures and benefits—somewhat in this way has Bestre regarded his increase of girth and the organ concerned. But in any case things have not gone very far. Sunburnt, with a large yellow-white moustache, his little eyes protrude with a cute strenuosity of expression. When he meets any one for the first time his mouth remains open, with his cigarette-end adhering to the lower lip; he assumes an expression of expectancy and repressed amusement, like a man accustomed to nonplussing and surprising people—the expression the company wears in those games of divination when they have made the choice of an object, and he whose task it is to find out is called into the room and commences his cross-questioning; or the look with which, in the game of blind man's buff, the pursued follow their groping and erratic pursuer. Bestre shows in his whole attitude a similar arrogant calm and attentive nonchalance; and his remarks, in addition to their mysterious profundity, are delivered with a provoking jocoseness, in the tone of those taunting cries with which his companions seek to exasperate the blindfolded man; as though he would cause the new-comer's mind to whirl round and dart frantically to left and right, without, however, managing to seize any of these mocking thoughts that beset him. Bestre gazes at a new acquaintance as though the latter, all unconscious, were entering a world full of astonishing things, of which he had not yet become aware. A would-be boarder arrives and asks him if he has a room with two beds. Without uttering a single word, he will lead the way to a neighbouring door and let the visitor pass into the room, with the expression of a conjurer who draws the curtain aside and reveals to the dumfounded audience a peacock or a horse and cart where a moment ago there was nothing.

If a madman who believed himself a hen had asked Bestre solemnly for a large, airy room, with a comfortable perch to roost on, and a little straw in the corner where he might sit—Bestre a few days before having been visited by this very idea of arranging such a room, and all were ready—then this habitual manner of his would have been *à propos*—thoroughly appropriate.

Indeed, Bestre, in common with many innkeepers when a customer is explaining what he especially prizes in the way of cooking or comfort, behaves as though the latter were confiding some shameful secret, or explaining the requirements of a ghastly vice or madness. He will lower his voice, whisper in the visitor's ear, and before doing so glance over his shoulder half apprehensively. If some day all men are afflicted with mental derangement, as will certainly be the case unless inspectors are appointed to safeguard the sense for reality and combat Bestre and his kind,[3] a man arriving at an inn and making no secret of the fact that he is a polar bear will be met by the Bestre-like landlord with a wink, his host making his eyes gleam with amusement and enthusiasm, and casting them admiringly over his form, saying, "I guess I shouldn't like a hug from *you!*"—and on chilly days pretending to feel the cold very much indeed, to give the bear all the more advantage over him.

It is the air of *understanding*, of being the only hotel-keeper or other man that *does* understand your particular idiosyncrasies, and consequently the air of being privy to something, of mystery and conspiracy, that is accountable for the strange effect of Bestre's bearing on the most commonplace occasions.

Bestre conducts long and bitter campaigns with some neighbour, that will consist almost entirely of dumb show, a few words only being exchanged—antagonisms that will become more and more acute through several weeks, burst forth and wear themselves out with their own violence—all without words, or even actions that could be remarked as distinctively hostile by an uninitiated observer. It is a most weird sensation to find oneself in the midst of one of these conflicts: like a war in which two armies should take up successive strategical positions, move round each other, push each other back, have drawn battles and overwhelming victories, without ever closing or exchanging a shot. At the passing of an enemy Bestre will pull up his blind with the defiant enthusiasm with which men raise aloft the standard of their country: one is meant to see, or rather hear, in his springy walk a chant of victory, in his immobility intimidation.

Probably Bestre's great principle, however, is that of provocation: to irritate his enemy to such a degree that the latter can hardly keep his hands off him—till the desire to give the blow is as painful as a blow received. To outrage, in his intangible fashion, some unfortunate man, who refrains from striking for fear of the criminal penalties of such an act, and who takes the blow back into his own bosom, as it were, and is stifled by his own oath—*these* Bestre looks upon as so many blows, and so much abuse, of *his*, Bestre's, although he has never taken his hands out of his pockets, or so much as opened his mouth. Bestre is terrible, in his way. To what extent all his manœuvres are effective it would be difficult to say, but in their grand lines they succeed. The gamut of his hostilities this summer was not confined to innkeepers, local functionaries, &c. Several visitors disapproved of him also, chiefly out of boredom; for time hangs heavy on the hands of the *mondain*[1] at Kermanec. When the first great *ennui* came upon them they would walk about desperately, and their eyes would in due course fall on Bestre. At first puzzled by his eye and manner, after a moment of perplexed observation, as a dog dismayed by a doubtful odour belonging to something that he has been suspiciously approaching backs and barks angrily, they suddenly bristled, the remainder of their time flying in a round of petty plots, indignant conversations, alarms and panics. For this extraordinary man with a mere nothing, seemingly, could cause a veritable panic.

Notably a well-known painter and his family were angrily responsive to this something in Bestre that seemed to make the human animal uneasy, as though in his composition were elements derived from the fauna of another planet.

Bestre is partly conscious of his strange attributes, and he shows the same self-consciousness as a man who is queerly dressed; also the subtle notoriety of his person is dear to him.

Undoubtedly one of his greatest victories was won over the distinguished painter's wife. She had the habit of passing the kitchen window every morning when Mademoiselle Marie was alone there—gazing glassily in, but never looking at Mademoiselle Marie. This had such a depressing effect on Bestre's old sister that she began to look quite seedy in a day or two. On the fourth morning, as his sister's aggressor cast her eyes into the kitchen as usual, there stood Bestre himself, alone, quite motionless, looking at *her;* looking with such a nauseating intensity of what seemed meaning, but in truth was nothing more than, by a tremendous effort of concentration, the transference to features and glance of all the unclean contents of his mind, that had he suddenly laid bare his entrails she could not have felt more revolted. He would, in the security of his kitchen, even have ventured on speech, had he not known how much more effective was his silence. She paled, rendered quite speechless—in Bestre's sense, that is expressionless, her glassy look shivered to atoms—hurried on and home, and was laid up for several days.

---

1 The society man.

At other times he would come in and tell his boarders of the way in which he had routed the distinguished painter. "I wasn't such a fool as to insult him—there were witnesses; let him do that. But if I come upon him in one of those lanes at the back there! I was standing at my door; he came along and looked at my house and scanned my windows" (this is equivalent in Bestre warfare to a bombardment). "As he passed I did not move: I looked him in the white of the eyes: he thought I'd lower mine; he doesn't know me. And, after all, what is he, though he's got the Riband of the Legion of Honour? I don't carry *my* decorations on my coat! I have mine marked on my body. Yes, I fought in 1870: did I ever show you what I've got here? No; I'm going to show you." And while he is speaking he jumps up, quickly undoes his shirt, bares his chest and stomach, and points to something beneath his arm; then rapidly rolls up his sleeve and points to a cicatrice rather like a vaccination mark, but larger. While he is showing his scars he slaps his body, with a sort of sneering rattle or chuckle between his words, and with his eyes protruding more than usual. His customary immobile expression is disintegrated, which is a compound of a constant foreboded reflection of the expression of astonishment that will appear in your face when you learn of his wisdom, valour, or wit, mixed with the slightest shade of sneering triumph, and a touch of calm relish at your wonder. Or he seems teaching you in his look the amazement you should feel, and his own expression gathers force and blooms as the full sense of what you are witnessing, hearing, bursts upon you, while your gaping face conforms more and more to Bestre's prefiguring expression.

Has Bestre discovered the only type of action compatible with artistic creation, assuring security and calm to him that holds the key of the situation, in a certain degree compelling others to accept your rules? But Bestre is perhaps alone in the possession of such a physique as is his.

I must here remark that Bestre is perfectly unconscious of this weird dumb-passive method of his, and, quite on the contrary, considers himself on the verge of a death struggle at any moment when in the presence of one of his enemies.

Like all people who spend their lives talking about their deeds, he presents a very particular aspect in the moment of action. When discovered in the midst of one of those silent battles of which he enjoys so much being the historian, he has the air of a company promoter of genius, cornered, and trying to corrupt some sombre fact into shielding for the moment his gigantic and not easily hidden fiction, until some yet greater brother can relieve it. Or sometimes he will show a wonderful empirical expertness in reality, without being altogether at home in it: such skill as some great virtuoso in his own trade might show, forced by circumstances to take up the tools of a kindred industry.

Bestre in the moment of action feels as though he were already talking, and his action has the exaggerated character of his speech, but strangely curbed by the exigencies of reality. He always has in his moments of most violent action something of his dumb-passivity—he never seems quite entering into reality, but observing it; he is looking at the reality with a professional eye, so to speak, with a professional liar's.

Often I have noticed that the more cramped and meagre his action has been, the more exuberant and exaggerated his account of the affair is afterwards, as a man escaping from a period of bondage and physical or mental restriction bursts into riot and dissipation; the more the restricting forces and forms of reality have tried him, the more joy he takes in his liberty as historian of his deeds immediately afterwards.

Then he has the common impulse of avenging that self that was starved and humiliated by the reality, in glorifying and satiating the self that exists by his imagination.

A survival of certain characteristics of race, that I recognised as Spanish, is particularly curious in Bestre.

Bestre is an enormously degenerate Spaniard, all the virilities of the Spanish character being softened in this vapid Gallican atmosphere, and all the weaknesses, especially those akin to French weaknesses, intensified. However, one Spanish virtue has survived, a negative one: Bestre is in no way grasping, a thing not to be accounted for in any other way.

As to his dumb-passive method I traced this also to the Spanish strain in him, the more so that I have met certain South Americans (a South American is an enormously degenerate Spaniard) who had many analogous eccentricities.

A Spanish *caballero* had an extravagant belief in the compelling quality of his eye, of his glance: he would choose to shrivel up a subordinate, daunt a rival, coerce a wavering adherent, rather by this dumb show than by words.

Then, again, the only means that the rigidly secluded daughters of Spain have had for centuries of conveying their messages of passion and desire to their lovers has been in their glances.

Bestre, stationed in his kitchen, and waiting to intercept the baleful stare of the distinguished painter's wife, was helped to his success by the fact that in his vein ran the blood of so many women who, behind their casements at the half-drawn curtain, gazing at their lover in the street below, have put into their glance all the intolerable expression of a love that has never been eased in words.

The *mirada* of the Spanish beauty, her *œillade*, has become traditional. But all Spaniards are peculiarly sensitive to that speech of glance, gesture, and action independent of speech. Spaniards are always trying to master each other by the magnetism of their glance. This heritage, we will admit, must have been for something in the peculiar method of warfare so satisfying to Bestre.

As to the *raison d'être* of these campaigns at all, of his pugnacity, I think this is merely his degeneracy—the irritable caricature of a warlike original.

NOTES

[1] This places Lewis's meeting with Bestre during the summer of 1908, but this is in contradiction with Ker-Orr's statement (see page 80) that this encounter took place "Two years before" the Spanish adventures of "A Soldier of Humour" which at the latest must have occurred during the spring of 1908.

[2] Removals, a typically Lewisian theme (see "Unlucky for Pringle" and *Tarr*).

[3] Heralds "an Ogpu hunting party of *anti-romance* inspectors" (*The Revenge for Love*, II, 2).

LES SALTIMBANQUES

This—Lewis's third sketch—was published in the August 1909 issue of The English Review *and revised in 1927 under the new title "The Cornac and His Wife." Like "Some Innkeepers," but in a more serious mood, it reflects the new intellectual interests of the age in anthropology and sociology. Not only did Lewis attend Bergson's lectures at the Collège de France, he must have been acquainted in some way or other with the work of Durkheim and Frazer, and possibly with that of Lévy-Bruhl and Van Gennep, all part and parcel of the new Zeitgeist. The pictural sensibility of the age—from the "blue" and "pink" periods of Picasso to Augustus John's immoderate enthusiasm for gypsies—also combined to mould Lewis's interest in little shabby circuses. In fact this piece is clearly a sequence to and a development of an experience related in the "Breton Journal" of 1908 which shows the same combination of mystical primitivism and Picasso-esque "misérabilisme." A similar mood finds expression in "The Theatre Manager" (see preceding page), a drawing of the same period, though it appears to be less sentimental than "Les Saltimbanques" in which the romantic side of Lewis's nature appears clearly, especially in an apocalyptic outlook of which this is the first manifestation.*

I met in the evening, not far from the last *débit* of the town, a cart containing all the mingled impedimenta and progeny of a strolling circus troupe from Arles that I had already seen. The cornac and his wife tramped along beside it. Their talk ran on the people of the town they had just left, and they were both scowling.

This couple had a standing grudge against their audiences, in the case of the man superadded to his grievance against fortune for trouble with his health—this last ill complicated alarmingly with laziness. They were very demonstrative with their children on all occasions, giving them mournful caresses—a way of indirectly and publicly pitying themselves. There was something defiant in their affection. They talked to and treated them always as one does a child that has just been ill-used or hurt. As a result the children became extremely morbid and depressed, and the more pathetic kisses they received the more melancholy they became, and seemed in a constant state of gloomy astonishment. They felt that something awful was in the air. When the painted clown made a sinister grimace to amuse them they concluded this must be the sign and beginning of the terrible thing that had so long been covertly menacing them, and their hearts nearly hopped out of their throats for fright. This was the family whose lot it was to dress itself up every day—the first time I saw the proprietress she was standing astride on a raised platform in tights and feathers—and knock each other about and tie their bodies up in knots before an astounded congregation of country people.

The merriment of the public that their unhappy fate compelled them to provoke, was nevertheless a constant source of irritation to these people. Their spirits became sorer and sorer at the recreation and amusement that the public got out of their miserable existence. Its ignorance as to their true sentiments helped to swell their disgust. They looked upon the public as a vast beast, with a very simple but perverse character, differing from any separate man's, the important trait of which was an insatiable longing for their performances. For what man would ever go *alone* to see their circus, they might have argued? And as they knew no other means of gaining a livelihood, if they ceased to propitiate it, it would inevitably destroy them. The brute in us always awakens at the contact of a mob of people. When they set up their tent in a town, and opened to its multitudinous form this tabernacle dedicated to "the many-headed beast," they felt their anger gnawing through their reserve, like a dog under lock and key, yet maddened by this other brutal presence. Or their long pilgrimage through this world inhabited by the public, that they could never get free of, would suggest a nightmare image. It was as though they were lost in a land peopled by mastodon and rhinoceri. Whenever they met one of these monsters—which was on an average twice a day—their only means of escape was by charming it with their pipes, which never failed to render it harmless and satisfied. They then would hurry on, until they met another, when they would again play to it and flee away.

The reflection that all these people parted with their sous for so little would be the only bright spot in the gloomy Adrien Brower[1] of their minds. They felt that they were getting the better of them in some way. That the public was paying for an idea, for something that it gave itself, did not occur to them, but that it was paying for the performance as seen and appreciated by them, the performers. For it is most difficult to realise the charm of something we possess. Women find it so hard to look on their own beauty and desirableness as their admirer does, that a great number of their actions might be traced to a contempt for men, who become so passionate and set so much store by what they know themselves to be such an ordinary matter—namely themselves. But in their shallowness they often become incredibly vain and inconceivably self-assured, because they are praised for certain qualities—although these seem to them, when thinking frankly, purely illusory.

A little later on I re-found these folks in the square of the "Basse-Ville" at Quimperlé.

Drawn up under the beeches stood their brake, and near it in the open space they had erected the trapeze, lighted several lamps (it was after dark already) and placed three or four benches in a narrow semicircle. When I arrived, a large crowd already pressed around them. "Fournissons les bancs, Messieurs et M'dames, fournissons les bancs, et alors nous commençons," the proprietor was crying. But the seats remained unoccupied. A boy in tights, with his coat drawn round him, shivered at one corner of the ring, into the middle of which the showman several times advanced with this exhortation on his lips. He would then walk back, and stand near his cart, muttering to himself. His eyebrows were hidden in a dishevelled frond of hair. The only thing he could look at without effort was the ground, and there his eyes were usually directed. When he looked up they were heavy—vacillating painfully beneath the weight of their lids. The action of speech with him resembled that of swallowing: the dreary pipe from which he drew so many distressful sounds seemed to stiffen and swell, and his head to strain forward like a rooster about to crow. His heavy under-lip went in and out in a sombre activity.

The fine natural resources of his face for inspiring a feeling of gloom in his fellows one would have judged irresistible on that particular night, reinforced by an expression of the bitterest disgust with his audience.

But *they* watched this despondent and unpromising figure with glee and pride. That they did not understand this incongruity of appearance and calling only added the piquancy of something not understood. When he scowled they gaped delightedly; when he coaxed they became grave and sympathetic. All his movements were followed with minute attention. When he called upon them to occupy their seats, with an expressive gesture, they riveted their eyes on his hand as though expecting a pack of cards to suddenly appear there. But they made no move to take their places. Also as this had already lasted a considerable time, the man who was fuming to entertain them—they just as incomprehensible to him as he was to them—allowed the outraged expression that was the expression of his soul to appear more and more in his face.

Doubtless this public had, what I had not, an inspired presentiment of what might shortly be expected of this morose figure. Some rare spirit among them may have gazed on him with the same chuckling exultation that sportsmen do on an athlete whose worth they know, and whose debile or gauche appearance is a constant source of delight to them.

His cheerless voice, that sounded like the moaning bay of solitary dogs, conjured them to occupy the seats, and again he retired. This time the exhortation had been pitched in as formal and matter-of-fact a key as his peculiar anatomy would permit, as though this were the first appeal of the evening. And now he seemed merely waiting, without even troubling to glance in their direction, until the audience should have had time to seat themselves, absorbed in briefly rehearsing to himself, just before beginning, the part he was to play. But these tactics did not alter things a whit. At last he was compelled to take note of his failure: no words more issued from his mouth. He glared stupidly for some moments at the circle of people, and they, blandly alert, gazed back at him.

Suddenly from the side, elbowing his way through the wall of people, burst in the clown. Whether sent for to save the situation, or his toilette were only just completed, I did not discover. "B-o-n-soir, M'sieurs et M'dames," he chirped, waved his hand, tumbled over his employer's foot; the benches filled as by magic. But the most surprising thing was the change in the proprietor. No sooner had the clown made his entrance, and, with his assurance of success as the people's favourite, and comic familiarity, told the hangers-back to take their seats, than a brisk dialogue sprang up between him and his melancholy master, punctuated with resounding slaps at each fresh impertinence of the clown. The proprietor was truly astonishing. I rubbed my eyes. This lugubrious personage had woken to the sudden violence of an automatic figure set in motion. His nature is evidently subject to great extremes. In administering the chastisement so often merited by his irrepressible friend, he sprang nimbly backwards and forwards as though engaged in a boxing match, and grinned appreciatively at the clown's wit, as though in spite of himself, while nearly knocking his teeth out with delighted blows.

The audience howled with delight, and every one seemed really happy for the moment, except the clown.

In the tradition of the circus it is a very distinct figure, the part having a psychology of its own—that of the man who invents posers for the clown, wrangles with him, and against whom the laugh is always turned.

One of the conventions of the circus is that the physical superiority of this personage should be legendary and indisputable among his friends. For however numerous the clowns may be they never attack him, despite the brutal measures he adopts to cover his confusion and ridicule. Like the Germans, he seems to be a man with a predilection for evening dress, the result being that he is a far more absurd figure than his gaping and bedecked opponent. It may be the clown's superstitious respect for rank, and this emblem of it, despite his consciousness of intellectual superiority, that causes this ruffianly dolt to remain immune.

In playing this part the pompous dignity of attitude should be preserved in the strictest integrity. The actor should seldom smile. If so, it is only as a slight concession, and bid to induce the clown to take a more serious view of the matter under discussion. He smiles to make it evident that he also is furnished with this attribute of man—a discernment of the ridiculous. Then, with renewed gusto and solemnity, asks the clown's *serious* opinion of the question by which he seems obsessed, turning his head sideways with his ear towards his friend, and closing his eyes for a moment.

Or else it is the public for whom this smile is intended, and towards whom the discomfited "swell" in evening dress turns as towards his peers, for sympathy and understanding, when "scored off" anew, in, as the smile would affirm, this low-bred and unanswerable fashion. They are appealed to as though it were their mind that was being represented in the dialogue, and constantly discomfited, and he were merely their mouthpiece.

Without doubt this figure originally stood for the public. Out of compliment to the public, of course, they would provide him with evening dress. It would be tacitly understood by the courteous management, that although many of those present were in billycocks, that their native attire was evening clothes, or at least "smokking," as it is called abroad.

Also the distinguished public would doubtless appreciate the delicacy of touch of endowing its representative with a high bred inability to understand the jokes of his inferiors, or be a match for them in wit. In the better sort of circus he speaks in an obviously gentlemanlike voice—throaty, unctuous and rounding his periods.

In the little circuses, such as the one I am describing, his is a very lonely part. There are none of these appeals to the "auditoire"—as the latter claim, not only community of mind, but of class, with the clown. It becomes something like a dialogue between mimes representing employer and employee. But these original distinctions are not very strictly adhered to.

A man without a sense of humour, he finds himself with one of whose mischievous spirit he is aware, and whose ridicule he fears. Wishing to avoid being thought a bore, and racking his brains for a means of being entertaining, he suddenly brings to light a host of conundrums, for which he seems endowed with a positively stupefying memory. Thoroughly reassured by the finding of this powerful and traditional aid, with an amazing persistence he presses the clown, making use of every "gentlemanlike" subterfuge to extract a grave answer. "Why is a cabbage like a soul in purgatory?" "If you had seven pockets in your waistcoat, a rump pocket, a ticket pocket, and three bogus pockets, how many stripes would there be in your trousers?" And so they follow each other. It is dreadful to think how many conundrums he may know! Or else some anecdote (a more unmanageable tool) is remembered. The clown here has many opportunities for displaying his mocking wit.

This is the rôle of honour usually reserved for the head showman. I always look out for this figure with special interest in the circus.

In this case the part was not played with very great consistency. Indeed so irrepressible were the comedian's spirits, and so unmanageable his vitality at times, that he seemed to be turning the tables on the clown. In his hollow lugubrious voice he drew out of his stomach many a caustic rejoinder to the clown's pert but stock wit, and the latter's ready-made quips were often no match for his strange but genuine hilarity.

During the whole evening he was rather "hors de son assiette"—hardly master of himself.

This out-of-door audience was differently moved to the audiences that I have seen in the little circus tents of the Breton fairs. The absence of the mysterious hush of the interior seemed to release them. Also the nearness of the performers in the tent increases the mystery. The proximity of these bulging muscles, painted faces and novel garbs impresses them strangely. They do not readily dissociate reality from appearance. Why primitive people are more imaginative is because everything for their mind retains its apparent diversity. However well they got to know the clown they would always think of him the wrong way up, or on all-fours. The more humble suburban theatre-goer would be twice as much affected if meeting the rouged and bewigged "prima donna" in the wings of the theatre, as in seeing her on the stage. Indeed it would be rather as though at some turning of an alley at the Zoo, he should meet a lion face to face—having gazed at it a few minutes before behind its bars. On the stage, and as seen from the pit, Othello is an ephemeral figure—a man that, like certain summer insects, never lives longer than two hours and a half. Met in the "coulisses"[1] of the playhouse the actor would still be Othello for him, or more Othello than anything else, but in the flesh and in the same conditions of life as himself. The Moor might

---

1 "Wings."

now have an intrigue with his sister Jane at any minute! The theatre, the people on the stage and the plays they play, is part of the surface of life, and is not troubling. But to get behind the scenes and see these beings out of their parts, would be not merely to be privy to the workings and "dessous"[1] of the theatre, but of life itself. Is the illusion of a man's greatness diminished by reading anecdotes and biographies about him? It is only then that for his devotee the poignancy of the romance begins. The commonest detail—the sight of the most apocryphal pocket handkerchief or most dubious ink-pot, will excite his admirer more than a new work discovered from his hand. For with these humble, and even undignified, objects, the breathing man, life and all its boundless possibilities, is evoked, and all the volumes of the master's completed works could not move so much the devout imagination. The desire for intercourse and fleshly acquaintance with God that has always tormented man he has satisfied in the "great man" of these later times. In earlier epochs there were no "great men"; God was the Great Man. The Jewish people did not feel a much deeper personal awe for their prophets than the British people do for Mortimer Mempes, the biographer of Whistler, or any other man whose name we recall especially in connection with some master. The moment it was known that they had quarrelled with God, "that the spirit of God had forsaken them," they became ordinary people again. These servants of God were often severely criticised for their misrepresentations (doubtless unjustly) as are sometimes the servants of great men. But not seldom they were an impertinent and meddling type of fellow, and rank toadies of the Almighty. The possessors of strange destinies never lose by coming down among the people. Suddenly to be able to touch and to feel the breath of a thing of the imagination is a confirmation and reinforcement of the imagination. It is never so powerful in a man as in those moments when he first holds his love in his arms. Instinct of sex or genius is only that which may from hour to hour force any man to return to primitive vision. The cleverest fellow is only human, and runs the risk of being overtaken by genius at any moment, and having his best laid plans upset.

Crowded in the narrow and twilight pavilion of the Saltimbanques at the Breton "pardons," the audience will remain motionless for minutes together. Their imagination is awoken by the sight of the flags, the tent, the drums, and the bedizened people. Thenceforth it rules them, controlling the senses. They enter the tent with a feeling almost of awe. They are "suggestionné,"[2] and in a dream the whole time. All they see they change, add to, and colour. When a joke is made that requires a burst of merriment, or when a turn is finished, they all begin moving themselves as though they had just woken up, changing their attitude, shaking off a magnetic sleep.

[1] "Hidden side."

[2] "Influenced by suggestion."

I first saw this circus troupe at a small town[2] near Quimperlé. They had set up their tent. The clown conducted, so to speak, everything—acting as interpreter of his own jokes, tumbling over and getting up and leading the laugh, and explaining with real conscientiousness and science the proprietor's more recondite and tenebrous conundrums. He took up an impersonal attitude, as a friend who had dropped in to see the "patron," and who appreciated quite as one of the public the curiosities of the show. He would say for instance: "Now this is very remarkable: this little girl is only eleven, and she can put both her toes in her mouth," &c. &c. If it hadn't been for his comments, I am persuaded that the performance would have passed off in a profound, though not unappreciative, silence.

To return to my description of their evening at Quimperlé, some hour after the initial bout between the clown and his master, and while some chairs were being placed in the middle of the ring, I became aware of a very grave expression on the latter's face. He now mounted on to one of the chairs. Having remained impressively silent till the last moment, from the edge of the chair, as though from the brink of a precipice, he addressed the audience in the following terms. "Ladies and Gentlemen, I have given up working for several years myself, owing to ill-health. My little girl has taken my place. But Monsieur le Commissaire de Police of Quimperlé would not give the necessary permission for her to appear. Then I will myself perform." At these words he jerked himself violently over the back of the chair, the unathletic proportions of his stomach being revealed in this movement, and touched the ground with his head. Then having bowed to the audience he turned again to the chairs and grasping them, with a gesture of the utmost recklessness, heaved his body up into the air. This was accompanied by a blood-curdling whirr sent forth by his corduroys, and a creaking and cracking of his joints of a most alarming nature. Afterwards he accomplished a third feat, suspending himself between two chairs, and a fourth in which he gracefully lay on all three and picked up a handkerchief with his back teeth. At this sensational finish, my enthusiasm knew no bounds, and I applauded vociferously. But when my ardour had a little cooled I felt confused to find that I had attracted some attention, and astonished at perceiving the performer glancing in my direction with a mixture of dislike and reproof. However, he treated all of us rather coldly, bowed stiffly and walked back to the cart with the air of a man who has just received a bullet wound in a duel, and refusing the assistance of his friends, walks to his carriage.

He had accomplished the feats that I have just described with a bitter dash and a desperate "entrain"[1] truly surprising. "Be it on your own head, M. le Commissaire, if I do myself an injury." He seemed courting misfortune. A

---

1 "Gusto."

mournful, solemn and respectful, a *dead* silence would have been the ideal way, from his point of view, for the audience to have greeted his pathetic skill. And I can understand now that our applause had seemed impertinent and unfeeling. He went back and leant against the cart, his head in the hollow of his arm, coughing and spitting. A boy at my side said, "Regarde-donc; il souffre' (look how ill he is!). This refusal of the magistrate to let his little girl perform, was an event that touched him very deeply. His remarkable behaviour all through the evening came from this no doubt. That his right to make his own child stand on her head, and put her leg round her neck should be questioned wounded his French sentiment of liberty to the quick, and struck at certain dim patriarchal bases of his spirit. His wife also was affected, but less profoundly, as I judged, and was more usual and consistent in her way of showing it. She, indeed, provided, shortly afterwards, a new and interesting feature of the evening's entertainment.

Various items immediately succeeded the showman's dramatic exploits. A donkey appeared, whose legs could be tied into knots, and the clown extracted from its middle-class and comfortable primness of expression every jest of which it was susceptible. The conundrums broke out again, and only ceased after a discharge that lasted fully a quarter of an hour. There was a little trapeze. I had noticed for some time already a restless figure in the background. A woman with an expression of great dissatisfaction on her face, stood with muffled arms knotted on her chest, holding a shawl against the cold. Next I became aware of a harsh and indignant voice, and saw this woman slowly advancing and talking the while until arrived in the middle of the circle, when she made several slow gestures, slightly raising her voice. She spoke as a person who had stood things long enough. "Here are hundreds of people standing round, and there are hardly a dozen sous on the carpet. We give you entertainment, but it is not for nothing. We do not work for nothing! We have our living to make as well as other people. This is the third performance we have given to-day. We are tired and have come a long way to appear before you this evening. You want to enjoy yourselves but don't want to pay. If you want to see any more loosen your purse-strings a little!"

While delivering this harangue, her attitude resembled that seen in the London streets when women are quarrelling—the neck strained forward, the face bent down, and the eyes glowing upwards at the adversary—or in this case on the people in front—and one hand thrust out in a remonstrative gesture. Also the body is generally screwed round to express the impulse of turning on the heel in disgust and walking away, while the face still confronts whoever is being apostrophised, and utters its ever-renewed maledictory post-scriptums.

Several pieces of money fell at her feet, and eventually she slowly retired, her eyes still flashing, and scowling resentfully round at the crowd. They looked on with amiable and gaping attention, evidently thoroughly interested in her and sympathising with her unconditionally. There was no response to the hostile declamation—no jibing or discontent; only a few more sous were thrown. Her husband evidently felt stirred at her speech, and one or two volcanic conundrums followed closely upon her exit. The audience seemed to relish the entertainment all the more after this confirmation from the proprietress of its quality, instead of being put in a more critical frame of mine.

Her indignant outburst did not owe its tone of conviction to the fact that she conceived a high opinion of their performance. In her harangue she spoke as though the public paid, for some inexplicable reason, not for its proper amusement, but for the trouble, inconvenience, fatigue, and in sum for all the ills of their, the circus people's, existence; or rather did *not* pay. It was this that so bitterly incensed her.

The people (or the people that I chiefly know, these Bretons) are spiritually herded to their amusements as prisoners are served out their daily soup, and weekly square inch of tobacco. The spending of their wages is as much a routine as the earning of them. Also in their pleasures—and when buying them with their own money—they support the same brow-beating and discipline as in their work. The circus proprietor and his wife represented for the moment the principle of authority, and they received the reproof as to their slackness in spending their money, as they would a master's just abuse if they showed a slackness in earning it.

The comedy, or possibility of it, that an educated man sees existing in everything, the people only feel in a restricted number of persons and things, and this is subject to the narrowest convention of habit. A peasant would never see anything ridiculous, or at least never amuse himself over, his pigs and chickens. The donkey that helps to get his living would never be a cause of amusement to him, as his constant sentiment of its utility would be too strong to admit of another; as a man who succeeds in revolting or angering us need never fear our ridicule, although he may increase the other emotion by his absurdity.

A countryman in urging on his beast may make some disobliging remark to it, really seizing a ludicrous point in its appearance to envenom his epithet with, but it will be caustic and dry, and an observation of his intelligence far removed from an hilarious emotion. Or it will come out of his anger and impatience and not his gaiety. One sees in the Breton peasant a constant tendency to sarcasm. Their hysterical and monotonous voices are always pitched in a strain of fierce raillery and abuse. But this does not infect their mirth. Their laughter is forced and meant to be wounding, and with their grins and quips they are like armed men who never meet without clashing their swords together.

They dance, work and amuse themselves fatalistically. There is a time for dancing and for working. Also there is a place, occasion and certain people marked out to entertain others, and fate has ordained that these people shall be the most diverting and comic folk that exist, else they would not be public entertainers. And if the clown and the manager consulted in an audible voice before cracking each joke, concocted it, in fact, in their hearing, they would laugh at it with the same fervour. Any tawdry makeshift for scenery, any stupid trick done by one of these accredited acrobats that they themselves could do twice as well, is not enough to destroy their illusion, and drive them into revolt. It would be a revolt against Fate to criticise the amusements that Fate has provided for them, and it would be a sign of imminent anarchy in all things if they looked solemn while the clown was cracking a joke.

They are accustomed to look upon all conditions of life as inevitable. They can never conceive of a man being anything else but what he is. They have this primitive wisdom. A man is a carpenter or shoemaker. He may be lazy or unskilful, and they will say he is not as good as his rival, but he is as irretrievably a carpenter or shoemaker as his name is John or William, and just as no man with another name could become John or William, so no baker could usurp the place that he fills. This is not the same as the conscious argument that because he has learnt this trade he is to be respected and accepted in that capacity. He possess it as indisputably as though it were a physical attribute; he is for them *"John* the *carpenter."*

The showman's wife had occasion to again sally forth and lash the public in the course of the evening. Towards the end of the performance the donkey was led in once more, pretended to die, and the clown pretended to weep over it. All was quiet and preparation for a moment.

Then a strange thing happened. A little boy in the front row began jeering at the proprietor. It was apparently a spontaneous and personal action, and very sudden. The outraged showman slouched past him several times, looking at him out of the corner of his eye in the most ludicrous fashion, and with his head thrust out as though he were going to crow. He rubbed his hands as before chastising the clown. This new event evidently perplexed him considerably. He went and complained to the clown in a whisper. This personage had just revealed himself as an athlete, and now looked with a most serious and pompous eye at the audience. Supposing that his master's complaint referred to some drunken countryman, he advanced quickly and threateningly in the direction of the offender, but finding a thoughtful looking little boy, returned to his preparations for the next event.

This boy had probably never thought comically before. Like corrosive lavas that illuminate before they destroy the object in their path, the torrent of his thoughts wrapt this dim and brutal figure. Revealed by his own genial eruption he beheld it, with all the character of a vision. His oracular vehemence suggested a sudden awakening, as though the comedy of existence had burst in upon his active young brain without warning, and, in the form and nature of this awkward showman, was now raging within him like a heady wine. He had of a sudden opened his lips among the people and begun covering this man with his mockery. I was extremely moved and even awed at this sight.

The showman prowled about the enclosure, grinning, and casting sidelong glances at his poet. His vanity was in some very profound and strange way tickled. But his face would suddenly darken and he would make a rush at the inexplicable boy. This latter, however, was strong in his inspiration. He would no doubt have met death with the exultation of a martyr, rather than renounce this transfigured image of an old and despondent mountebank—like some stubborn prophet that would not forego the splendour of his vision—always of the gloom of famine, of cracked and empty palaces, and the elements taking new and extremely destructive forms for the rapid extermination of man.

NOTES

[1] Adriaen Brouwer (1605-1638), a Flemish painter.

[2] Very probably Clohars six miles from Quimperlé. This circus is apparently the one described in "A Breton Journal."

OUR WILD BODY

This, Lewis's first critical essay, was published in The New Age of May 5, 1910. It must have been written shortly before, as it shows a greater concern with the English scene than the texts written sooner after his return from France. Like "Some Innkeepers," and other contemporary theoretical analyses, it was neither republished nor even made partially use of—probably because it was too impressionistic and smacked too much of the pre-war age.

The essay has certainly none of the effulgence of "Inferior Religions," and is less lively—being more based on generalisations—than "Some Innkeepers." Yet it is of capital importance for an understanding of Lewis's evolution, and it is surprising that even its very existence should have been ignored by the critics. It marks the first recognition, on Lewis's part, that a binding principle could unify his early production. Later in 1911 (see page 16) he thought of using "A Soldier of Humour" as a title for his collected stories, but he went back to "Our Wild Body" in 1914 when it was agreed that Max Goschen would publish the collection, and the title was still with him in 1916 when he drew up "Writings"—though later, and possibly before, he may have thought of using "Inferior Religions" as a title (see the unpublished "Vita of Wyndham Lewis" and Pound's editorial note to The Little Review publication of "Inferior Religions"). Finally the changing of "Our Wild Body" to "The Wild Body" seems a perfect illustration of what in Rude Assignment Lewis described as an evolution leading from a vitalist to a formalist vision.

More precisely, Lewis, who hud so far concentrated on the paradoxical rites of pensions, hotels and circuses, came to identify the body as the hub and temple of all the savage rituals of hospitality. His comments on sports as an opium of the people, on the exploitation of the body by publicity, on the degenerate relationship of modern "civilized" man to his own body, on the similarity between war and games—even if we are now used to such analyses—were then quite new, and part of the Modernist reaction against Victorianism and its inhibitions.

The body is sung about, ranted about, abused, cut about by doctors, but never talked about. If you will give me the license of a doctor and will not keep seizing my hand (not out of pain but modesty) as the patient seizes the dentist's, I will examine one or two points and prescribe treatment. It is not, however, the body that is ailing, but our idea of the body. This has become anæmic indeed.[1]

No one would be so indignant as the Englishman if you told him he ignored his body—outraged and amused, he would conduct you grimly to his bathroom. It has a room all to itself merely to be cleaned in! He would stride over to his bedroom, show you india-rubber implements dangling on the wall, Indian clubs, and a large coloured chart to direct his morning's exercises. But these things are only part of a vast Anglo-Saxon conspiracy against the body. The bath is, figuratively, to drown it in, the instruments on the wall to indebt it to science and tame it. With characteristic cunning, as in dealing with a native chief, the Anglo-Saxon pretends that he is working entirely in its interests. But he has reduced it at last to be the most practical symbol in the Anglo-Saxon world. Of all the triumphs of the English in substituting for imaginative vision a barren formula—something that does not hinder the course of civil life—this triumph is the greatest, the masterpiece of the modern Anglo-Saxon genius. This genius excels in interposing all sorts of ready-made and non-conducting ideas between us and this portion of ourselves. Englishmen and women, essentially of much the same stuff as other men and women, have become proverbial for their virtuosity in withstanding temptation or pretending it is not there.

But first of all I have decided to call two witnesses; one is the Continental gentleman, and the other the sanguine son of democratic France. Both these men, in opposite ways, will enrich my argument. I begin with the latter.

At the outset of my life in French hotels I listened with surprise, becoming more and more reflective, to the landlord's talk about his digestion and other gruesome functions of his organism. His customers were equally conflicting. But this is the French idea of hospitality—the hospitality of the body—making another at home in one's body, so to speak, courteously throwing open the fleshy doors that lead to apartments usually regarded as private. If a friend visit us for the first time in a new house, our first impulse is to show him over it, and we consider it by no means bad taste to speak of the drains.

The French bourgeois,[2] should he be at the same time a poet, if he admires your verses will take a far greater interest in your person than he otherwise would. You will become aware of an inclination on his part, without overstepping the limits of modesty, to establish a playful and more intimate relation between your respective persons—to glory in their warmth and fitness, to slap you on the shoulders, to take your arm in his hand, and once I was dreadfully tickled in the fat of the back by some sanguine and especially exuberant Gaul. This will not in the least detract from the severe and dignified attitude of your two minds, and their sentimental intercourses. The Frenchman regards our bodies as children, and when the minds, like two fathers, have become friendly, it seems natural to him that the bodies also should become better acquainted and have their little sport.

I am sure that physical contact of some description is essential to perfect sympathy between two people. The English rush from one extreme to the other, from their schooldays to their aloof manhood. I suppose that since handshaking has gone out of fashion, a couple of (unathletic) stockbrokers never touch at any point of their physique from year's end to year's end. The ills of a sedentary life, of the vitiated town atmosphere, is nothing compared to this ill, after the amount of rough but constant physical sympathy they have been accustomed to as boys. Often walking beside some man, nervous and exasperated, and silently imputing to him the whole gamut of stupidity and meanness, have you not felt that could you take him round the shoulders, or should you slip by chance on a piece of orange peel, catch at him instinctively, drag him down with you on the ground, and roll about a bit with him, that all would be well? A man driven, in one of these humours, to strike another, often feels, at the contact of his victim's nose or chin, his anger ebbing, and at the end of three minutes realises the futility of the pretext that had led to the struggle.

Dismissing the French bourgeois, he having served our preliminary purpose, before calling the second witness I will have a bout, to enliven the sitting, with a man who is constantly obtruding himself upon us, and who, in this connection, must be tackled sooner or later. He is a perplexing and rather terrifying figure. I nevertheless instantly close with him.

One of those who supersede with a sham and conventional outlook towards the body the original and eager vision here preferred, is the calisthenic quack. The body of the contemporary man is the prey of mercenary "strong men," he is lured with their muscle manufactories, or, to be more accurate, it is his body that they almost suck in, by the mere brute magnetism of size.[3] The contemporary man is hypnotized by the monotonous repetition of the same gigantic figure, seen with mesmeric regularity all along the road to and from his place of business. Its highly-coloured brawn is advertised wherever hoardings permit it standing room—there it lies in wait for the tired and small-muscled clerk every morning, and gradually dominates him. In the Tube—a fitting temple for it—he is shut up with this sinister idol. Its little empty-looking head is gazing also in fascination, at its own enormous and it would seem momentarily increasing bicep. After weeks of resistance he at last finds himself in the toils of this monster.

Probably if times were not so peaceful these men would not dare to be so strong. As it is they grow bigger and bigger. This new industry, the manufacture of muscles, attracts just those men most happily constituted for the championing of the real body, and dilutes and perverts their instinct for ever.

I think for this naked vision of the body's significance, naked in the sense of seeing the body stripped of Anglo-Saxon tweed-suit ideas,[4] of blazer or Norfolk jacket standpoints, we may take example in some things of the French.

A Frenchman considers a "beau gars"[1] in a much more primitive way than his English neighbour—not as an athlete, but as an animal. The idea of his strength is wedded to that of his nature, his humours, his lusts, his desires, and is a passionate thing and part of his mind and life. He regards it as that of an animal that might, pitted against the Judæan lion, overcome it, and put new truth into the fable; whose cares would be more burning, or who would bask in the sunshine more royally, than another.

Physical strength and prowess, being with the invention of modern weapons no longer a central and vital preoccupation, in other countries the body was left as an out-of-date tool or weapon, from one aspect of its utility in disuse, and gazed at as a magnificent relic. Once it was the only tool at all, and now has long been superseded in the art of war and other sovereign matters. But in England the body still continues to preoccupy us. We perpetuate in our games the primitive art of war—the triumph that, relying on mere skill, and physical strength and courage, one man or company of men may gain over another. But it is artificial and no longer a vital and fundamental part of life, this exercise of our strength. So we have wiped out the old sentiment for the body and its eternal significance that still exists in France, for instance, by renewing and perpetuating our interest in it, but in connection only with a travesty of life, a game instead of war. Even when two Englishmen fall out and fight they are bound by certain rules, as though they were playing a game. The Italian is called coward when he draws his knife. The choice of which epithet reveals the conviction in the Englishman's mind that the Italian is as great a moral coward as himself, and that at this opprobrious word he will put his knife away, and allow the Englishman to use his fists—his weapon—without extreme danger to himself. The hypocrisies of our civilisation in this, as in everything else, has robbed us of something of frankness and imagination. In any case, "the famous warlike spirit of the race" is diminished by these score of substitutes for war. It need not be, but it is. As Englishmen are fond of asserting, sport has made people less quarrelsome, and more orderly in their quarrels. We think of fighting as boxing, with the conditions varied a little, and we lose the wildness and

---

1 "Handsome fellow."

reality of the fact; and the heroic suggestions of the human form vanish with the various athletic uniforms.[5] And throughout the Anglo-Saxon world sport is studiously encouraged, and the particular spirit that has come to prevail in the conduct of all sports warmly lauded and fostered; for it is felt how useful sport, and this way of approaching it, is, in daunting and taming the body, and the spirit as well. And so games hem the Englishman in on all sides. There is not one, but a thousand. Every natural and heroic gesture and energetic impulse has been turned into a "game," has had the life taken out of it. There is cricket, hockey, football, tennis, rowing, fives games, all the contests of the gymnasium and innumerable other inventions. To those vivacious and thoughtful races for whom life is game enough, such a monstrous growth as this universal life of sport beside the real life would be impossible and above all unnecessary. This division weakens both life and play. But it is in our case meant as a blow at life, to divide life's forces. Art is only worth anything when the artist is as vulnerable in it as in his body.

Walking and talking are the two finest exercises in the world, and for the requirements of health no man needs any other. Conversation is the thing to be encouraged and cultivated for the proper chest development of the race; and beautiful boulevards, such as they make in Latin countries, should be arranged for, so that a population of philosophers have plenty of inducement to walk about and exercise the rest of their bodies, as well as their lungs.

In conclusion, who ever saw a woman who nursed her baby one half hour, and a wax-doll the next? When she gets old enough to have a baby she discards her doll. And yet one may see any day of the week men of all ages guilty of an absurdity of this nature. This only goes to prove—if proof were needed—that women live much more reasonably than men. If you reply that these men are taking exercise, and that war is the equivalent in man's life to marriage in woman's (I have already shown what connection games have in truth with war) I repeat, let them walk and talk, and when they cannot agree in their conversation, let them first blackguard each other and then have a fight, they need show no acquaintance with Queensberry rules: this programme, simple as it appears, will be found to answer every need.

In one sense, like some antique weapon, the last time the Frenchman's body was used as a supreme arbiter of war, was at Rinscevallas,[1] and the grit and sweat of those famous fields is still upon it, one might in many cases believe. But the Englishman's has been used so often on cricket fields, hockey fields, and at other inglorious contests for so many years, that it has lost its historic character; and it has been so often cleansed, that, always looking spick-and-span and brand new, it awakens no memories.

---

[1] I.e., "Roncesvalles" (or "Roncevaux" in French), where the battle celebrated in the *Chanson de Roland* took place in 778 A.D.

The French have a much greater sense of the expressiveness of the body. This is evident from their gestures, and in the style of their actors. But throughout the French people, the body is not neglected as a dull fellow, but shares with the face a man's consciousness. The Frenchman does not conceive as the Englishman, that it may be straggling, humped, dull and ridiculous, and not detract from the dignity of the face. One sees many an Englishman with an alert, masterful and intelligent face, and one is taken aback and extremely perplexed to find beneath it a grotesque, undignified, stupid, dawdling, "allure"[1], in the rest of his person. Or occasionally this isolating of the expression is taken even farther. Gazing at a body for which the owner obviously has the greatest contempt, and ostentatiously slights and disregards, and a face from which all expression has vanished, leaving an atrophied and cadaverous pall of flesh, one is positively startled on becoming aware in the midst of all this desolation, of an abnormally vivid and disarming eye. There is no doubt that in some respects England is a most uncanny country to live in.

So far, then, occasional good honest fighting—either "set-to's" or sword contests, according to the temper of the parties concerned, a peripatetic habit, and a general transferring of all the games back to life again, from which they have been stolen, is recommended. The animalism of the French bourgeois is neither attractive nor dignified. I have put him forward as a sort of easy first step for beginners wishing to arrive at the healthy state of mind here shadowed forth. For those of our contemporaries who have seen the need for such reform, this gross and grotesque figure has been the nearest they can get to the ideal condition—with a beer-swilling, conscious, northern barbarian, German colour given it. I will conclude my case by calling upon the European gentleman to step forward.

One of the things that perplexes him very much, especially if he be a German, is the accounts of ragging among officers of the English army. No doubt sport has something to do with the absence of delicacy in the English gentleman. The body loses some of its dignity in being tossed and kicked about, mauled and sprawled over in the course of compulsory games. A young man in England to retain any illusion of self-respect at all, is compelled to delineate very sharply—body from soul. For physical sympathy must always be discriminating, of course. There is a fine art in knowing just when to slip your arm under another man's, and just when to bump into him as you are walking along the street, conversing.

When an English family becomes positively drunken with the sensation of whizzing up in the social scale, and all sorts of arrogant fancies possess it, it never occurs to these people to allow the body to share in their increased dignity. It is still the same old body that was round by any camp follower of Cassivellaunus. It can still be punched at will, with the sole reservation and

[1] "Appearance."

understanding that it will punch back, as though it were its master's dog and not his person. In Europe a gentleman never feels the contact of a hand too rudely placed upon him or receives from another so much as a scratch, except at the end of a sword.

The principal signification of the body to a gentleman (however degenerate that mysterious person becomes), is connected with honour. Honour is that code in the upholding of which he must never be found wanting. This life must be thrown into the balance at every moment, that honour should prevail, and be the constant guardian of its principle in himself. And to him the great imaginative appeal of the body lies in the fact that it is the vessel of his life, the receptacle of his life vowed to honour, and the symbol of his recklessness. Although English gentlemen to-day are by no means lacking in courage, they no longer have this conception of honour. No more artificially than primitively has the body the same imaginative appeal as it has for our neighbours.

NOTES

[1] This is the first appearance of the doctor theme—a theme not prominent but certainly persistent and revealing in Lewis's works.

[2] The next two paragraphs echo the analysis of "Some Innkeepers" (see pp. 222-228).

[3] This recalls the description of Isoblitsky's friend (see pp. 214-215).

[4] See Augustus John's 1903 drawing of Lewis in tweeds (reproduced in *Rude Assignment,* opposite page 64), and this sentence in chapter 4 of the unpublished *Twentieth Century Palette:* "The next thing was that he found that his expensive tweeds were not proper to paint in. . ."

[5] Compare and contrast with the many boxers "blessed" in *Blast.*

A SPANISH HOUSEHOLD

Completely ignored by the critics, this charming collection of vignettes was Lewis's first contribution to The Tramp *(issue of June-July 1910) whose editor, Douglas Goldring, he had met through Ford Madox Hueffer, the editor of* The English Review. *It is an exaggeration to say with Geoffrey Wagner (in his bibliography) that it was "incorporated and expanded" in* The Wild Body, *but it is true that a number of details concerning Lewis's stay in Vigo in the Spring of 1908 mentioned here were used again in "A Soldier of Humour," and they prove beyond doubt that Ker-Orr's Pontaisandra is Lewis's Vigo. It would be tempting then to think that these vignettes are true to life, but the final episode of the arrested young man, when compared with its earlier version in "Crossing the Frontier," proves to have been melodramatically embellished, in addition to being transferred from San Sebastián to Vigo. As the portrait of the painter (the first of a long line in Lewis's works) further suggests, Lewis could invent the real in Defoe-esque fashion.*

If you intend to make a stay in such towns as Zaragoza, Vigo or León, to expect rest in the hotels would be *naïf.* There are sometimes as many as thirty commercial travellers in a hotel at a time, at the head of all their bales: it is as though there were a thousand emperors under the same roof together, each bearing magnificent presents, of silks and wines and handsome dresses, to some brother potentate. But for many reasons, the first thing a visitor to Spain must learn is to seek for furnished lodgings. This is how I learnt to do it, and incidentally came among a delightful household—a sort of human *olla podrida*[1] of the richest and most typically Spanish ingredients.

On my arrival in Vigo, in pursuance with a Valladolid friend's advice, having established myself in a hotel for the night, I set out to look for a furnished room.[1] Although this friend had told me that I should see cards in the windows advertising rooms to let, I saw none. I was informed eventually that the reason why there were no cards was because *every* house in the town was a lodging-house, and all I had to do, if I liked the look of a place, was to enter and tap at the different doors till I found what I required. And so, going from house to house and door to door like a water-rate official or postman, I wound up my investigations at the Doña Elvira's. She occupied a third floor in the Calle Real.[2] The next day I took up my quarters there.

The Doña Elvira was a small, stone woman with dark red arms and face, and, in some way, like one of Velasquez' dwarfs. With a sort of naked and direct glance, at once naïve and calculating, she possessed a frank, impetuous and imaginative spirit, with the shrewdness of a Sancho Panza and the fieriness of those who on divers occasions beat him. The husband, a retired officer of *gendarmerie,* now a printer, worked all night and slept all day in a darkened room; but he used to wander out among us sometimes, smoking a cigarette—I suppose walking in his sleep, and in any case very grave and silent. They occupied a bedroom and part of the kitchen. They let the rest of the floor to three families and myself. There was the *chef d'orchestre* of the principal *café* in Vigo, a Madrileño, his wife and child, and the 'cello-player and his daughter. We had our meals together in a large central room.[3]

A little glass door led out of this *salle à manger* into a small room, with a smaller glass-covered balcony attached. Here lived a Castilian painter and *his* family. Between them and the kitchen lay the den of an old curmudgeon—who had come back after twenty years spent in the Argentine, rich and friendless,[4] to his native land, and dwelt in a single room beside the kitchen. This was strategically very well placed, calculated to ensure him the maximum of discomfort and develop in him the maximum of anger. This was

---

1 A potpourri, a miscellany.

the nerve of the house, the sensitive part; and the children playing or the women talking never failed to set rumbling and knocking and snorting the furious old being within these three thin walls. An almost perpetual sound of discontent could be heard from the direction of his room, and when one least expected it there would be a tremendous eruption, he would be in one's midst—like a huge wave his anger would burst into the kitchen—and before any one had recovered from his astonishment it would be flowing back again, with a hollow roar and many minor gurglings; the door would close again, and it would be heard subsiding behind the plaster walls. The Doña Elvira would, in the meantime, be gradually kindling, would rush out, dash open his door again, and one could hear her within calling all the saints to witness that he was an old scoundrel, and that he must find another lodging. But he never went. Apart from the fact that it is not easy to uproot a volcano[5]—his anger must, by that time, have delved mystically into the very fibre and foundations of the house—she had another reason for her forbearance. She hoped he might die beneath her roof, and if so, although she had no other claim whatever, according to some Spanish law she would be entitled to all or part of his money, the supposed amount of which waxed in her fancy in proportion to the trouble he gave her. But he also was aware of this law, and knew why his whims and furies were suffered; and he gave her infinitely more trouble than his modest rental justified.

The painter, his wife and two children and his business man all slept in the little room off the *salle à manger.* Don Ramiro was a typical Spaniard; with a fat white skin and disordered black hair. He was rather knock-kneed, and very nervous in his movements. His face showed a solemn intentness on the little details of life, with great frankness and independence. He was away in Oporto during the first week of my residence there. He had gone down to Portugal with his business man to sell some pictures. An artist, Don Ramiro understood little about "negocios.'[1] He found it more satisfactory, and in the end more economical, to attach to his person a man thoroughly conversant with commerce in all its branches and supremely competent to cope with any man, from a dentist to a Lord Mayor, than to have dealings with an artistic agency that could never be relied on for pushing work. Don Ramiro's needed perpetual pushing, then it was all right. It was a modest sort of work, and perhaps would not be noticed in the crowd. But once a publican or little *bourgeois* with a sweet tooth, pictorially, had been compelled by the man of business to gaze on one of Don Ramiro's productions for some minutes, they proved that they had a gift to please, and usually found the way to the publican's or little *bourgeois'* purse. This is the explanation of the term I used, "business man," in enumerating Don Ramiro's household. Don Ram-

[1] Business. The Cornell typescript has "les affaires" crossed out.

iro and family passed the day as follows. His wife would get up about half-past eight, and, placing a little table just without the door of their room and in the *salle à manger,* would prepare a cup of coffee and place it there. Don Ramiro would then slip from the slowly heaving side of the oblivious man of business, put on his shirt, trousers and slippers, and sit down at the table. If I entered the room about this time, as I often did, he would offer me politely his breakfast, according to Spanish custom. "Lo quiere?" he would exclaim, indicating with his fat but expressive finger his coffee and bread. The meal over, he would retire to the glass-covered balcony and paint two or three pictures. When these were finished, about half-past ten, the most arduous part of his day's work was over. He chiefly painted on backs of plates, on cheap and unserviceable-looking palettes, on tambourines or, in short, on anything except canvas or paper. His repertoire consisted of three idyllic scenes. The façade of a Moorish palace reflected in a livid stream, with palms waving against a torrid sky—with this he was in the habit of beginning his morning. He painted it with relish, humming a *flamenco* or a *sevillaña,* smoking his cigarette in quick little gasps, jerking back with alarming suddenness from his chair to catch sight of it from another point of view, to change so suddenly his position and distance from his work as to startle himself into a freshness of vision. He would sometimes add a piece of flaunting colour to his palace, put some azure rag to float at one of its casements, and wave in the stream beneath—as a lover, in gay mood, will plant a rose in his sweetheart's hair. He knew every corner of the scene; it gained him his daily bread, and all the sincerest flattery that his artist's vanity had received was mixed up inextricably in memory, with it, for the last ten or twenty years. The morning's routine of painting this picture was not disagreeable to him. It was as though he had had to dress every day, garment by garment, some languid and fastidious woman, whose beauty and *belle parure* [1] reflected great credit on him, and to whose forms he never grew *blasé.* As to the other two items of his stock-in-trade, they were subject to considerable variation. Sometimes there were three boats on his sea, sometimes only one put forth. It was difficult to tell what this might signify, what mysterious law was responsible for the appearance or not of these craft. The third picture showed a water-mill in the mountains. His attitude towards these two landscapes was determined by the nature of their sale the week before. I once saw him painting the mill with deliberate lack of skill and labour, and humiliating economy of paint. I suppose that for days he had been changing it—putting a tree to shade it, throwing a rainbow behind it; he may even have ventured on a human being in the middle distance, but that the public had remained unmoved and received it with consistent chilliness.

[1] Beautiful attire.

Such unaccountable runs of ill luck will beset the best of mimes, plays or pictures. His way with it seemed to afflirm that it repaid not even the cheapest adornment. At half-past ten Don Ramiro's wife would go into the kitchen and heat a second cup of coffee. This was for the man of business, whose brain had just assumed its normal waking state and whose body was resuming its severe commercial outfit. His toilet was a much more important affair than the artist's. No coquetry, but the grim and engrossing labours of the day had already begun with the adjusting of his cravat, and the snipping off of little bits of hair above the ears, rendered rebellious in the disorder of sleep. He, unlike the artist, partook of his breakfast within their room, on the back of the trunk they all had in common, and only issued forth when, a little after eleven, all was ready for the daily expedition. I never saw him properly, thinking him merely a very assiduous visitor for some time. Don Ramiro often returned despondent, and sometimes only very late and drunk. But the man of business did not share his relapses: their relations were purely business relations. Every one agreed that Don Ramiro was *buen muchacho*,[1] a considerate husband and a sincere and admirable man, although unfortunate in his calling, whereas the chief violinist and head of the *café* orchestra was agreed to be a bad and ill-natured man. He spent his afternoons, his off time, in worrying his wife to get money out of her mother. After hours of passionate altercation she would come into the kitchen with the corners of her mouth nearly touching her chin-bone, and only the lower part of her eyes visible above the encroaching whites. I was told that her husband would kill her if she left him. He was a thin little man with a large dark moustache, keen eyes, long cuffs and a jaunty walk.

His colleague, Don Manuel, the 'cello-player, was tall, sallow, humped, and melancholy, his large knees never straightened out; I always supposed that his 'cello was too small for him. To marry too small a woman may influence adversely the gracefulness of one's person, but it must be a much graver matter, if one is a tall man, to get used to a fat little 'cello. He had rather a depressed and worn look, as though music did not suit him, and as though he had many things to put up with, many trials with his 'cello, many discords—in their domestic life too little harmony! He never spoke about these things, however. He looked resolute and resigned, as though accepting the choice he had made. I would occasionally hear his companion's grave voice of an afternoon, but never saw its ripe, matronly and polished form. Also I had a strange feeling of *pudeur* towards Don Manuel and this side of his life. I should have felt just as embarrassed to talk shop with him as to discuss with another man his most private feelings for his spouse.

His daughter Carmen was ten or twelve years old, her father the only

---

1 A good chap.

companion or parent she had ever known. She was naturally a gawky, clumsy girl, and she imitated her father with dog-like devotion; like him she stooped and stumbled—fell into reveries in which her eyes became heavy, like him. But when these latter occurred at meal-times, her arm, waving meditatively a spoon one moment, would the next subside listlessly into her soup, or she would sink hunched up over the table, as though falling asleep, with her eyes wide open. Don Manuel, gradually waking from his own reverie, would become aware, out of the corner of his eye, of his daughter's. The liveliest fury would therewith possess him. Stealthily he would move his arm backwards, and with a shout bring it down on Carmen's dreaming head. Her dusky skin would become the colour of the darkest red of the peach, she would squint in front of her, frowning, and then suddenly bury her face in the crook of her arm, her bony elbow up in the air. Also her walk, a faithful imitation of his own, and the ungracefulness of her gestures, he severely criticised.

La Carmencita's companions were Julio, Don Ramiro's son, and the *chef d'orchestre's* anæmic infant, a year older than Julio—about five I suppose. Julio was the nicest child I ever knew. Composed of his father's fat white flesh, but with a pearly tint added, he had a large frowning head and enormous black eyes, a long body and short corpulent legs—knock-kneed, another inherited trait—that carried him about the house at break-neck speed and often launched him against my chest like a catapult, where he would remain paralysed with excessive laughter. As though the room where his family lived and slept were not already sufficiently full, he was persuaded that certain supernatural beings also inhabited it—black-faced men. *"Hay cocones en mi habitación,"* [1] he would tell me, in a whisper. He would say it in that absent-minded, matter-of-fact tone of children, his eyes on the ceiling, as though repeating a lesson. They often merely imitate their mother's tone and look during these confidences, in repeating her inventions. Still these *cocones* were endowed with real existence for him. I suppose this tale of the black-faced men is a survival from those times when Catholic mothers took the Moor, their own readiest cause of terror, as the model for their child's bogey-man.

The gathering-place for the women and children was the kitchen, where they did all their cooking. Doña Elvira cooked for the old curmudgeon, for Don Manuel and myself. All day she was the most unpretentious and dirty of housewives. But the night arrived, and the supper finished, she would cover her dark red arms in silk sleeves and encircle her shining red face in a black mantilla with black lace gloves and a laced fan in her hand. After her husband had gone off to his work at the printing office, she would repair to the

---

1 "There are cocones in my dwelling."

balcony, call across to an opposite house where her sister dwelt, and a few minutes later, with two of her nieces, take her departure, bound for the theatre, the *cinematographo*, a concert, or whatever was on. Five nights out of the seven this occurred. A steady and dogged light of pleasure would settle on her face; one felt rather intimidated by her love of pleasure; it would be dangerous to stand in its way. It was imposing and rather grim. If one said, "So you're off to the theatre?" she would reply with a peculiar look of triumph in her face, as though she were doing something very clever.

La Flora, the servant, was a tall, lithe and handsome fisher-girl. Her eyebrows always raised in weary, affected fatalism, her mouth hanging in affected brutal listlessness, she was very fond of notice and had one of the best of hearts. A typical Gallega, as the natives of Galicia are called, when the Castilian boarders made fun of her speech she would let her mouth hang still more, and her eyes would become leaden with pretended stupidity to please them and as a form of coquetry. The natives of this country are treated by the Spaniards as the Bretons are by the French. Because of their strange dialect, a mixture of Portuguese and Spanish, their shrewdness and boorishness, they are the laughing-stock of their Castilian neighbours.[6]

I once, on entering the kitchen, found La Flora seated by the door and doing nothing, except that she was constantly beating her mouth with the palm of her hand, and tears had stained her cheeks. The other women were taking no notice of her whatever and discussing life in the Balearics, or something equally remote. But Doña Elvira did not tell her to get on with her work. She was simply left alone. She could hardly carry the dishes in that day, dragged her feet slowly along and behaved like a woman with a fever. I heard afterwards that, returning from market, she had seen the *carabineros* taking a young man of seventeen or eighteen years to the prison, his elbows tied behind his back[7] and his shirt blood-stained. A few hours before a discussion had sprung up between this young man and a comrade about nothing: "*una muchacha, una nada!*" La Flora herself said, in giving me details later on: "*Mi novia es mas bonita que la tuya!*"—"My sweetheart is more beautiful than yours!"—This simple statement, at the end of a few minutes argument, had cost one of them their lives.[8] The sight of this boy being led away "to be killed" as she constantly affirmed, had caused her so much affliction. Her songs were the wildest I have ever heard, and often her chanting, while she was washing the dishes or otherwise busy about her work, would have made the most barren gorge of the Urals seem a mild and smiling place in comparison with the spirit of her song.

A Spanish Household

NOTES

[1] The narrator does here exactly what Ker-Orr is to do in "A Soldier of Humour."
[2] Ker-Orr's pension is also located in the Calle Real in "A Soldier of Humour."
[3] Ker-Orr's short-lived friend was also a conductor and a native of Madrid. The plan of this flat is the same as that of the Pension in "A Soldier of Humour."
[4] A few analogies suggest that this character may have entered in the composition of Monsieur de Valmore in "A Soldier of Humour."
[5] This is the first—and rather brilliant—manifestation of the Lewisian volcano.
[6] The same comments on the Gallegos are to be found in "A Soldier of Humour."
[7] For a first—milder and more enigmatic—version of this incident, see "Crossing the Frontier."
[8] Should be "his life."

A BRETON INNKEEPER

This is another of Lewis's earlier texts to have been systematically ignored by the critics—with the exception, it is true, of Robert Chapman and C. J. Fox who reprinted it in Unlucky for Pringle *(1974). It was published in the August 1910 issue of* The Tramp, *and never reprinted or made use of in the author's lifetime. In his bibliography (p. 322) Geoffrey Wagner states that it was "incorporated and expanded" in* The Wild Body, *but not one significant echo can be detected there. Why Lewis did not re-use "A Breton Innkeeper" is easy to understand: in a collection of stories it would have appeared as an inferior rehash of "Bestre," as it does not even contain the ghost of a plot. In that sense it could be looked upon as the least memorable of the Ur-*Wild Body *texts, were it not that it was the first to make clear the notion of a system conditioned by the energy ("the heavy desperate geniality") of a vociferous hub. This notion was only latent in "The 'Pole'" and "Les Saltimbanques," but its elaboration surely appeared important to Lewis as, some time later, he referred to Roland insistently in the first version of "Inferior Religions."[1] A forerunner of Kreisler at the Bonnington Club dance, Roland was Lewis's first avowed Vorticist.*

---

[1] In "Inferior Religions," Roland, we suggest (see p. 319), is none other than Moran. Apparently Lewis paid little attention to his publications in *The Tramp*, for which he may have felt some contempt. For this see: (1) his letter to Ezra Pound, dated March 30, 1948 (*The Letters of Wyndham Lewis*, pp. 440-441): "A book has appeared . . . by a certain Douglas Goldring" etc., and (2) in "Writings," the conspicuous absence of "A Breton Innkeeper" and Lewis's uncertainty as to the destiny of "Grignolles."

He has been a gentleman's servant—though how this restless and vociferous mass can have been contained in any well-behaved diplomatic household is more than I can imagine. Before settling down here in Brittany as innkeeper he was five years in Vienna with a German *Chargé d'affaires*. I suppose, once he got there, they were so dismayed at his size and appearance generally that they lost their heads for the moment—hesitating to send him right about turn back again, after such a long journey. When some days after his engagement by letter, hailing from a distant registry office in France, Roland invaded, like the waters of a bursted reservoir, that consternated household, prompt action was needed if ever it were. They tried without doubt every *diplomatic* means of getting rid of him; but all their subtlety proved of no avail. I should have the gravest apprehensions for the peace of Europe if I heard that Roland was beneath the roof of a great and responsible official. Himself the very incarnation of method, he carries anarchy and chaos anywhere he goes outside his own walls.

By his stature and physique generally, although *not* by nature, a loud bullying person, he retains and even exaggerates a certain bullying tone and demeanour: cracks jokes in which he threatens "to get angry," and, in fact, puts in evidence the bully in himself, the brute strength, that his clients may have the exquisite sensation of the proximity of this bellowing, menacing force, but *their* heads he always spared.

And, indeed, this immunity he extends to everybody, down to the boy in buttons that he keeps in the bar—for I have never seen him forsake his farcical manner with any one. He rages often, cries *nom de Dieu*, stamps and fumes when the aforementioned youth does something that displeases him. And doubtless there is some *nuance* in this that touches the brass-buttoned boy—doubtless there is in that youth's exquisite instinct for Roland many a shade in this rough voice imperceptible to a stranger—some inflection that makes him scamper more hastily about his business. But outwardly it is the same heavy and desperate geniality.

So Roland, even with his staff, never departs from his *rôle* of buffoon. If the bull could suddenly be rendered avaricious, and were given a brutal cunning to direct him, he might not forsake his appearance of sullenness and fierceness, still reminding man that he retained his original and dangerous character, and so induce humanity to pay him to behave himself. Or, as Roland does, pretend to be angry, to butt people—Roland slaps people on the back and thumps them playfully sometimes—and people would quail deliciously beneath the impact of this murderous force, assured the while that (for his own ends) the bull would not desert his playful restraint. One of the most intense pleasures of childhood is being frightened, and made to quail physically, assured the while that no harm will ensue. Children's greatest favourites are those that procure them this pleasure: to be thrown up in the air, chased and roared at by a booby uncle—with real physical shrinkings, but reassured all the same by experience and custom. This makes them crow or giggle more feverishly than any other entertainment. What sends a boy out apple-stealing is the desire to taste this pleasure of fear. But this sensuality is universal, how universal will be best seen by drawing a simple picture of one of the most homely and familiar scenes in our national life. While the owner of the house is burying his head in the bed-clothes, transfixed with a delightful horror, and sweating as much with pleasure as with fear at the burglarious sounds arriving from below stairs, the burglar for his part is perhaps passing some of the most exquisite moments of his life, tingling with a delicious apprehension: while the policeman outside, gazing at the parlour window ajar and the many other signs of infraction, feels his flesh creeping all over with the familiar and cherished emotion of fear. Does a special aptitude for experienceing to the full this pleasure, and a natural though perhaps unconscious desire to multiply the occasions for doing so, induce so many stalwart fellows to adopt this profession? I do not say, however, that Roland's customers relish this form of amusement placed at their disposal. No doubt there are some who do. He is not a very popular *hôtelier,* although not at all unpopular.

Roland owns one of two hotels immediately in front of the station. It is extremely important and yet a thing demanding the utmost cunning to get past his hotel on arriving at St. Pol.[1] I have never succeeded in doing so, and am one of his best customers. It is not only strangers that are in jeopardy. The peasant on his way to market sees to his horse's condition, tightens the girth, and sets his own teeth with an oath on approaching Roland's.

A characteristic *geste*[1] of his on a market day this summer caused a good deal of talk. He had been drinking copiously. Drink stimulates inordinately Roland's commercial obsession, affecting him only in this way and inducing him to pursue more blindly and indefatigably than ever his methods and dreams. Two peasants were driving past, intending to put their cart up at his rivals, the neighbouring inn. Roland shouted to them, they slowed down, and he came up with a shower of pleasantries and greetings, grinning reprovingly, as though to say, "I know where you're going." He then, pursuing his customary tactics—applied to this especial case—began with gentle force to lead them, horse, cart, occupants and all, towards his stable door. Caressingly and with mirthful coaxing, he insinuated that they were going to stop with him this time, his momentarily trebled enthusiasm for his own methods lessening his capacities for nice observation. And indeed, after

---

[1] An epic action.

the first moment's acceptance of the joke, the two farmers showed signs of great unappreciativeness, and then began swearing. Or, rather, as they never speak without swearing, suddenly and with vehemence immensely increased their vocabulary, calling up that group of oaths, jealously preserved pure and undebased from common use, and reserved to lead the forlorn hope of Expression ere Action be resorted to. At this Roland, with the true impatience of the idealist, treating them as cyphers of his imagination and ruling passion, saying, "No! you *shall* come and stop!" ran them into the stable in their cart, and began unharnessing their horse. They sprang down and a noisy struggle ensued, Roland fighting with a somnambulic tenacity, and as a dog disturbed in the discussion of its bone—he prevented in the pursuance of his master idea, and they with the indignation and brutality of men that the dreamer has attempted to incorporate in his dream, or the enthusiast too importunately to win over to his theory. The police had to be sent for, and Roland, dazed, staggered back to his door, and his opponents went on to the adjoining inn.

Roland is like one of those "eccentric musicians," as they are called, that tear about in front of a row of different sized bottles, playing "Rule Britannia" with inconceivable agility. His perpetual verbosity and ubiquity are appalling. Rather than relapse into anything approaching calm, he will talk to his own wife, or to a little ragged boy that has stopped in the street to stare at the boy in buttons. He is capable of banging on the back of a saucepan or rattling the dishes to "keep things going."

This is his method. Economy of energy by a constant output of mere mechanical and empty force; and thereby disarming that bane of innkeepers, the customer requiring information and personal attention. Of course, in a hotel there are always people lying in wait for the Proprietor: they are often very difficult to detect, these customers. Often a man of an extremely shy and reserved appearance, taking advantage of a lull in the unwary innkeeper's activity—who thinks he at least may allow himself a rest in the presence of such a mild-looking man—will rise up and pin down his unfortunate host for three-quarters of an hour with swarms of unexpected questions. So innkeepers have to be constantly on their guard.

His wife is a fit mate for him in size. She is a shade more human, and a little more approachable. You are afraid with Roland to pose him any questions; there is a feeling that he is not to be approached with impunity, as with the wheels of a machine in motion. With Madame Roland you can speak as with a horseman or cyclist, who does not stop but will nevertheless listen to you—beside whom, as long as your breath holds out, you may run and converse, although obliged to quit him in the middle of a sentence, he shooting ahead.

Roland influences his staff in an uncanny way, and everything on his premises breathes *his* energy and no other, and takes colour from him. Chiefly remarkable are the two maids who wait in the restaurant, and the boy in green uniform who serves in the bar. This boy also goes over to the station at the arrival of each train, to attract customers into the hotel.[2] I say "to attract them" advisedly, for when the travellers arrive at the station, he seldom addresses them, but stands in their way, seeming to think that the Roland magnetism will be sufficient to draw them after him without any words or solicitations.

The large Roland's mechanical rolling gait becomes in one of these maid-servants a rhythmical, lurching trot, in the other a keen little stumbling roll. They seem drawn or impelled along, or suddenly left idle or listless, left stranded as though suddenly deprived of an exterior motive force. This ebb and flow of energy corresponds to Roland's approach or distant withdrawal, although they may not be aware of his movements. They generally go about in silence, and it is when addressed that they become suddenly and startlingly verbose. They each take somewhat of Roland's personal *cachet* and manner, adapting it unconsciously to their own physical characteristics. If you succeed in breaking through Roland's spell they become nonplussed and bewildered.

But as Roland is the sun of this system round which all revolve, they also are affected to each other. The lesser members of this household are doubly servient and satellite, circling in turn round that member that possesses most of the Roland fire, and most negative moral magnitude. One of the servants is a little round-shouldered girl with a fox-like face, insignificant chin, head thrust forward, and eyes shining with what would seem at first a continual roguish amusement. But this is a light left shining while he to whom it was entrusted is no longer there. I dare say she was, poor creature, a girl of "infinite jest"[3] before coming into Roland's service. I once, that she might discover her witty spirit, asked her what she was amused about. Grinning maliciously, and with a glance of wounding sarcasm—that she meant to be a smile of menial courtesy and a discreet glance of amiable respect—she completely rearranged everything on my table, salt-cellars, spoons, mustard-pots, eatables, so that I, who had got used to the first arrangement, could subsequently find nothing when I wanted it. My remark had evidently moved her, but she had not grasped its meaning. Roland was too strong in her. The other servant is a blonde, very fair; her expression is blank, astonished, with a shade of distress. She is heavier than her companion in body, and gyrates clumsily but swiftly round her, morally.

The boy is very curious. He is seventeen years old, and appears fourteen, both in manner, size, and expression. This retardation of his growth morally and physically is surely due to the fact of his having served in Roland's hotel for the last three or four years in this particular atmosphere. One thinks of him sometimes as being half-witted. He is rather like one of those dwarfs who have the appearance in middle-age of a dissipated boy in his teens. They arrived at the age, size, &c., of a boy of fifteen; why did not they, at least approximately, attain the growth and shape of a man of twenty-five? A question that, with no special scientific knowledge, it is difficult to answer, unless one should happen to know that at the age of fifteen they had met with Roland. This for me at least would be conclusive. In the case of the boy one knows his history, and that at thirteen he entered Roland's service. Any additional growth he may get will be nothing but Roland—has been nothing but Roland for the last four years. But always that charming nature of the boy of thirteen mixed into it, the freshness of his thirteenth year embalmed as it were beneath the beds of Rolandism. Roland descended on him like the cinders of a volcano,[4] and occasionally we are given glimpses of his nature as it was when this calamity overtook him. His small body rolls with Roland's steady, rolling, occasionally stumbling, gait. His forehead is seamed as his master's is with the constant elevation of his eyebrows: this wrinkled forehead being a characteristic of the whole household, by the way. These foreheads all seem puckered up in readiness for thought, whenever it may be the customer's good will to provoke it. Also there is an expression of wistful profundity over all their faces at times, largely contributed to by this. In conclusion, this youth speaks heavily, slowly, and somewhat nasally, as Roland does: and has the strangest little rough, bullying way imaginable—and a reassuring girl-like softness that is quite charming.

NOTES

[1] Apparently Saint-Pol-de-Léon, though this is Lewis's only reference to this part of Brittany.

[2] For a similar practice see "A Soldier of Humour," page 33.

[3] Hamlet's description of Yorick (V, 1, 170).

[4] This is the second appearance of the Lewisian volcano (see note page 265).

LE PÈRE FRANÇOIS
(A Full-length Portrait of a Tramp)

"Le Père François" was the third contribution by Lewis to The Tramp *and appeared in the issue of September 1910. Under the guise of a documentary investigation it presents a marginal world even more extreme than that of "The Death of the Ankou," the story it was to follow in* The Wild Body. *In spite of the abundant generalisations about the mentality and behaviour of tramps, this study in alcoholic vagaries aims—in avant-garde and pre-Beckettian fashion—at the telling of "Stories. . . for Nothing."*

I found him in front of a crowd of awe-struck children, the French vagabond, hoisting a box up under his arm, strapping it over his shoulder, and brandishing three ruined umbrellas. Music was his theme. In making use of certain expressions in the course of his rambling declamation, such as *andante* and *contralto,* he would add with sudden politeness "that is a term in music." Then towering over the children, with his arms stretched out, his head thrown back, he would call out menacingly his maxims, all on the subject of music. Afterwards, dropping his voice and turning his inflamed and meaningless eye on his audience again, he would add in a tone of confidence some further information or advice. Tall and loose-limbed, he wore a full grey beard and long hair falling over his shoulders, growing with an heroic and characterless sinuosity. His eyes were like a woman's—large, dark, and insinuating—his face handsome and theatrical. To look at him one would have said that the only emotion he had ever experienced was that provoked by the topical and sentimental songs of his country. He had become a very disreputable embodiment of them. His was the face of a man who had wedded, and been mastered by, the vague and neurasthenic heroine of the popular lyrical fancy; from constant intercourse with this shade he had grown as nearly as he could make himself her ideal. With his hat stuck over his eyes, his lips in a drunken and insolent pout, his nose red, and an ironical scowl on his countenance, as he appeared in passing me, I got a very unfavourable view of him. I ogled him, however. After looking at me uncertainly for a moment he turned in my direction, stretching out the hand with the umbrellas, and began singing a patriotic song in a lusty voice, his eyes fixed on mine. I offered him a cigarette. The singing stopped, but with difficulty, he evidently pulling hard at his vocal strings as a driver does at the reins, to arrest his impetuous song. His box and umbrellas were put down, and I found him installed at my side. His conversation was particularly interesting, but extremely obscure. My ignorance of music, the confusion caused in my mind by his prolonged explanation of difficult passages in his discourse, full of what I supposed to be musicians' slang, confounded with thieves' slang and Breton slang; the hiccups that engulfed so many of his phrases and often ruined a whole train of thought, nay, nipped in the bud entire philosophies, and the constant sense of insecurity consequent upon these repeated catastrophes, these were only a few of the disappoinments to be met with equanimity and becoming fatalism, and the obstacles to be overcome, if one were to establish profitable relations with this, at first seeming, inaccessible mind, between which and the outer world existed so many natural barriers.

After having been shown his throat, and having vainly attempted to seize between my thumb and forefinger an imaginary vessel that he insisted, with considerable violence, that I should find, our relations nearly came to an abrupt termination on my failing, and having, indeed, pursued song athwart his anatomy to its darkest and most lugubrious sources, I said irrelevantly that his hair was very long. He slowed down abruptly in his speech, but some sentences still followed. Then, after a silence, taking suddenly the most profoundly serious expression, he said, with a conviction of tone that admitted of no argument and paralysed all doubt, "I will tell you! It's too long! My hair is too long!" How vastly did this differ, although exactly what I had said myself, as far as the sense of the words went, from my own simple observation it is difficult even to hint. My words faded into nothingness, it was as though they had never been uttered, beside it. If he had crushingly contradicted my statement, with a thousand proofs confuted it, it could not have been more utterly submerged and obliterated than in this mere iteration of my thought —but how delivered. Another cause of obscurity in his conversation was that he spoke the major part of the time in a whisper. When I could not catch a single word, I yet often could judge, by the glances he shot at me, by the scornful half-closing of his eyes, screwing up of his mouth and nose, all the horrid cunning of his expression and nodding of his head, that he was enjoying his own penetration and wit to no small degree. At other times, by his angry and defiant looks, [he showed me] that my respect was being peremptorily claimed.

The remembrance of injuries constantly stirred within him, and he was for ever aggravating his sores. When, excited by his brave words, he had found some phrase happier than another to express his defiant independence, he felt keenly the chance he had lost. But his enemies had grown very vague in his mind, and considering the splendour of the opportunity, the difference between myself and one of them seemed negligible. So he turned on me to enjoy his victory, and triumphed over me with as much ruthless exultation as though I had been his hereditary foe.

He had sat down at my side without a single definite thought in his head about me. An inscrutable figure had beckoned to him for inscrutable reasons. He had sung to it. It was his invariable way of treating the many perplexing apparitions of this life. He had chosen a patriotic song without any consciousness of a reason for doing so. The musical sprite that presided over his existence had become aware, in a fine instinctive fashion, of the presence of a foreigner, and at once a stirring song, in which he thirsted for my blood, rose to his lips; the little musical sprite had deemed this appropriate. But I am sure that he himself was not privy to this untasteful choice. He was evidently destined to sojourn awhile with the figure on which his eyes were fixed, for a cigarette retained him like a vice. There was nothing east, west, north, or south in any of his perspectives that could dispute his allegiance with this minute but despotic object. I even assumed vaster proportions beside it, and became a comparatively momentous figure, although still strictly abstract. It was not that the cigarette was very much prized by him, or possessed any importance, except in being the only thing for the moment. Out of habit he gave himself up blindly, tranquilly, and fatalistically to anything definite of this nature. He had got used to the vague figures that retained him from time to time in the course of his wanderings, and whose mysterious bounties he had experienced before. So without any further investigations into my particular nature he took up his perpetual dissertation, and the development of his *rôle*, and his long self-conviction. His spirit craved delusion and entertainment, and to escape its shrewish persecutions and nagging he was forced to play to it and invent a hundred things from morning till night.

The Père François and his like spend their lives in a ceaseless dramatic effervescence. Their furious gestures, their dark sayings and invectives, are as harmless as the vacant menace of lonely and excited little boys, who occasionally take some notice of one in the streets. The only difference is that the children are conventional and romantic, whereas his impersonations are often of the most blood-curdling realism. You will find a beggar ranting in some Paris street, and with fiery exclamations he will be exciting an imaginary and sanguinary mob to revolution; or he will lash the watching people with his scorn like some misunderstood and outraged leader, and, rushing off, will constantly turn and shout his threats and reproaches at them from afar, as though he were leaving some doomed city. At the next street corner a fresh crowd will gather at his eccentric mutterings. He will treat them with incomprehensible amiability and indulgence, telling them of his wrongs, and covertly inciting them against the crowd he had just left, jerking his thumb darkly down the street and whispering huskily as though he were plotting with them the overthrow of the neighbouring boulevard. Or he will address some indignant old woman as though she were his wife, and pour out on her all the abuse that he has been ruminating for the last hour or so. When quite exhausted he will retire to the steps of some church, first, perhaps moved by the sight of this unhelpful edifice, hurling a few critical taunts at his Maker, with his eye fixed on the steeple as if God were inside, though keeping quiet and pretending not to hear. He will then, with a final oath, double himself up and go to sleep.

This type of man feels as much in another plane of existence as a child does. But instead of feeling not yet "grown up" his feeling is rather that of having in some mysterious way outgrown mankind, so that it is no longer very easy to understand them. He has become a giant, for his personal nature, its connection with the world dissevered in his pariah state, takes for him every day more formidable proportions. When in the scheme of life and an ordinary member of society, he lived largely in other people and through them; but now that he is isolated everything has come to inhabit him, and he feels constantly in his spirit the throbbing of multitudes. His fellow-mortals have lost all individuality for him; also he pursues his reflections heedless of them, as though they were children. Men would usually "think aloud" if there were no inconveniences attached to doing so, and their thoughts would perhaps become clearer. They would then certainly talk less to other people.

But as children impersonate men and women in the fantastic dramas that they are always playing to themselves, so he also draws from mankind the figures and situations of his phantasmagoric world—from another and opposite point of view, of course. The children are looking up, he looking down. And as children seldom try actually to draw grown-up folks into their comedies, so he, although letting some old woman or other stand for his wife and be passively addressed as such, would never caress or beat her. Again, sometimes he will stop in the street and address his thoughts to the passers-by, banteringly, bullyingly, comically, as an *homme d'esprit*[1] and intelligent fellow might do, finding himself in some negligible company, but experiencing an invincible inclination to open his mouth. He is like a big child, with all the experience and metaphors of life behind him instead of before him, and looking back at it from a state of illusion instead of forward to it from a similar state.

From being constantly laughed at while observed in their effervescent moments these men adopt a comic and quizzing air in turn, grinning sillily in imitation of the people, and cutting capers as a mocking and contemptuous concession to the public's stupid misapprehension. Or, instead of saying jibingly, "Ha, ha, now laugh again!" they do something extravagant that will provoke the further laugh, their very mute drollery being a form of mockery.

Some either prefer to be noticed, no matter on what conditions, rather than to wander about silent and unremarked, or else are men who enjoy particularly being the centre of a crowd of people.

Some prefer even to sleep in the midst of a gazing multitude, and will attract a large crowd by their antics, and then lie down on a bench in the middle of it and go to sleep. But this may be due to a mystical dread of sleep, when we seem to exist so little, and the belief that we exist most when the greatest number of people are aware of us; and a consequent desire on the part of the man in question, before surrendering himself up to this state of semi-annihilation, to gather a considerable number of beings, all wide awake, around him, for whom his person will be a living and extraordinary fact the while; in fact, a kind of leaving a mob of people to look after one's body while one's spirit is temporarily wrapped away.

---

1 A wit.

Some become vagabonds comparatively late in life, and exploit the ridiculous features of their former *bourgeois* life—primness or pompousness of manner, airs of respectability, and a thousand mesquin hypocrisies to gain an audience. They put such a zest into ridiculing their past selves that they provide a very moral performance for the bystanders. Also I have seen an old woman, the very essence of whose soul was mock modesty and prim pretence of chastity, and whom no change of life would change, using with the utmost exquisite humour this material of her nature and furnishing even one of the most indecent entertainments imaginable.

Or the part that they have played in life, now that they are out of life, so to speak, and all its real relations broken, they go on playing as though it were a theatrical *rôle*. Now that they are freest and least subject to restraint they dissemble more than ever, and their life is a constant characterisation. As [for] becoming *themselves*, stripped of all fanciful clothing, this would be the one thing that would make their unhappy life quite insupportable. This would be worse than the nakedness of the body. Becoming one's self would be the brand of the lowest degradation of which man is susceptible. The consistent dissimulation of our lives, apart from that due to motives of interest, has its origin in our *pudeur* [1] and the æsthetic sense—these two things so intimately connected. But the development of both becomes acute with many of these outcasts.

The Père François and I eventually moved into the *débit*, or bar-parlour, behind us. About this time his thoughts were running on a certain hotel keeper of the neighbourhood, whom he suspected of wishing to sell his present business. A few days before he had observed him looking up at a newly constructed building in a town not far away. In the course of his recital he complained of the proud spirit of this publican. On my catching the word "vermin," and showing renewed interest, he repeated what he was saying a little louder: "Anyone seeing me as I am, without profession, poor, might suppose that I had vermin in my beard. Yes," he added softly and meditatively. I forget whether at this point we fell, naturally and gracefully, into a conversation on cosmetics and the sacrifice of time that a man of leisure is obliged to make on his toilet. But after searching among the inner strata of his habiliment, he produced, with great dignity, the middle section of a comb, and made passes over his beard—without, however, touching it—which he shook scornfully. I was deeply impressed at this sight.

Then intervened a story in which he gave a glimpse of his physical efficiency and determination in moments of difficulty and doubt with hotel proprietors and the like. He stamped on the floor with his great sabots to render more vivid to himself this scene, and also to supply the indispensable element of noise which, owing to emotion, his voice was incapable of doing. He spoke with a dreadful intensity, in low chilly tones, glaring quizzingly in

1 Sense of modesty.

my face. Eventually he sprang up, struggling and stamping about the room, and made believe to fling an antagonist out of the door. He came back and sat down again, looking at me for a long time silently, with an air of most insolent triumph.

I could not blame him for this drastic measure, for he evidently experienced a great relief at the eviction of this imaginary landlord. He probably had thrown him out of every bar-parlour along the road. Ever since we had entered the bar he had been restless, and I was not sorry that he had rid us of this phantom, although I looked with a certain anxiety towards the door from time to time, half expecting a shadowy eruption. He now seemed enjoying the peace that he had so gallantly accomplished for himself with an almost sensual joy. His limbs were relaxed, his eyes softer. He assured me that he did not like turbulent people. "J'n'aime pas le monde turbulent!" And then he raised his voice, making the gesture of the teacher: "Socrates said, 'Listen, but do not strike!'" ("Socrate a dit: 'écoutez, mais ne frappez pas.'")

He abounded in a certain kind of proverb such as "Il ne faut pas confondre la vitesse avec la précipitation! Non! il ne faut pas confondre la vitesse avec la précipitation!" These sayings occurred to him quite fortuitously, and he would quote them *à propos* of something with which they had no connection. Instead of adroitly leading the conversation round in such a way that the *bon mot* might be introduced, as a less sincere or enthusiastic man would do, he boldly uttered it, taking it as a text for a new discourse, until another one turned up to bring what was often its most astounding career to an abrupt end.

He was called the Père François, and something had struck his fancy particularly. He told me how he had slept in the château of François I., at Chateaubriant.[1] It appeared that it was in giving information against his *bête noire*, some innkeeper or other, that he had come to sleep there; though what these two facts had to do with each other in bringing this about I could not by any means discover. He drew a picture in his brilliant and confused manner of a wintry night in the forest, of an inn arrived at, and of an "orgie" being held there. But here everything became blurred and phantasmagoric. He must have got drunk almost instantly in this sudden refuge. After having been exposed to great cold a man cannot stand very much drink. He grew extremely perplexed at this part of his story, and it staggered and came in flashes, and was wild to the last degree, until he most certainly reached the château. Arrived there, he became more composed again. I asked him where he had slept in the château, and he answered that he had slept on a mattress, and had had *two* blankets. On second thoughts he concluded that this would tax my credulity too much, and withdrew *one* of the blankets.

I told a man who had been drinking near us that the Père François was an original fellow. He that I had described in this way eagerly assented: "Oui, original, je suis original;" and suddenly turning to me, with the gravest of countenances, said, with a condescension that was too sincere to be wounding, "Je suis content de toi!"

However, the horizon became anew overclouded and tempestuous. He grew more and more violent, often getting up and whirling round without reason, like a dervish, with his ruined umbrellas shaken at arm's length. Afterwards he sat down and held his arm out stiffly towards me, looked at it, then at me, wildly, and contracting his muscles, as if searching for some thought that this suggested without finding it. Stretching his arm back suddenly as though about to strike, drawing his breath between his teeth, with the other hand he seized his forearm as though it were a living thing, and stared at it.

Night had fallen and he became noisier and noisier, singing and using the window as a drum, tapping with his arms on either side of it, and his head turned towards us. The landlord passed several times, grunting "Ouf, a pack of lies!" and other disobliging things about my friend's conversation. I discovered later the cause of the inn people's vexation. They were afraid they would have to give him a night's lodging in the barn. This would have cost them nothing, even in trouble, but they were very mean, and the idea revolted them. I eventually helped to turn him out. He did not notice in the least the traitorous nature of my action. Before he had reached the door, being propelled towards it by the innkeeper's stomach with great skill, I existed for him no longer.

Tramps always find a night's lodging in the "granges" at the various farms of the countryside. They make rendezvous, and often spend several nights together in this way. The farm people take their matches and pipes away from them, or else put them in the stable among the cattle. I saw him the next day for a moment through an inn window on the road to the next town. He was dancing in his heavy sabots, with his shoulders drawn up to his ears, and his arms akimbo, and assuring a group of sullen peasants, one laughing, that he had seen an Italian dance that way, that that was the way the Italians danced. On noticing me he began singing a love song, with as loud and strong a voice as ever, and without interrupting himself stretched his hand out for a cigarette. There was no recognition in his face while he sang, he seeming conventionally absorbed in the song, his lips protruding eloquently in keeping with the sentiment. That is the last I saw of him.

NOTE

[1] Rightly corrected as "Chambord" in 1927.

GRIGNOLLES
(Brittany)

"Grignolles," the only poem by Lewis to have been published during his lifetime apart from One-Way Song, *appeared in* The Tramp *of December 1910. Most of it was reprinted in C. H. Sisson's* English Poetry 1900-1950 *and it was included in* Wyndham Lewis: Collected Poems and Plays. *Alan Munton, the editor, used the holograph manuscript in the Cornell archive, the typography of which differs perceptibly from that of* The Tramp. *The latter was more orthodox, with its additional commas, conventional indentations and initial line capitals. It is clear that* The Tramp *sub-edited the poem, probably without consulting Lewis. "Writings" shows he was either unaware of its publication or had forgotten about it, which is less likely. So Alan Munton was correct in his choice and we have adopted his edition.*

The presence of this petrified shell amid the flamboyance of the Wild Body material may be surprising, but Lewis made the association clear in "Writings." Its absence from the final Wild Body *was obviously due to Lewis's desire to offer a coherent fictional world, but the degraded Unanimism of "Grignolles" constitutes surely an intuition of what was later expressed in "Inferior Religions."*

Grignolles[1] is a town grown bald
with[2] age; its blue naked crown
of houses is barer than any hill,
on its small hill;—it is a grey town.

It is like a cathedral, crowding and still,
all of a piece, like one sheer[3] house;
like a town built for worship, and called
Grignolles, from the land thereabout.

But it is like a cathedral from which have decayed
all after-thoughts, and generous things
added—the warm gradual weft—
all down-coverings from its naked wings.

It seems only first buildings are left,
the virgin soul of first architects;
only the first dream of a town as it leapt
in the brains of the lonely peasants—projects

which the dim granges shaped from their sides,
and a wilderness of gaunt fields that
needed a house as each holding does—
but a great warm house more human than that.

Now something of that first savageness,
and the keen sadness of first plains,
(although the country's grown bourgeois and green)
to the town has come as its soul wanes.

Within, Grignolles is listless and sweet;
its veiled life is not conscious how
its wandering cairn of walls can suggest
in one wild whole[4] things dead now:

just as a man forgets Time's waste,
and his soul's crumbling, and is blind
to a grandeur a little distance gives it—
lives a life veiled, moody and kind.

In the town people live an insect life,
there are three sorts of house in its streets,
and many gardens hid in its walls;
there are two sorts of people one meets.

Its gardens are odorous wells each house
hides with high walls—you never see
these—but you know each bleak[5] great house
has its harem—hid flowers and wind-scented tree.

Of the two sorts of people there met,
one are old—a fierce[5] shy race,
an old life revived as their soul dried;
the others are young, with bold[5] mild face.

Its bare houses are stuccoed and wide.
Grey like the stone-grey of the sky.
Blue like the dull shade of stone when wet:
and white, to tell its small inns[6] by,

as over the porch hangs mistletoe.
Its houses are bleak windy fronts
with stormy windows; or cabins low;
and wandering convents, and sheds chapels once.

NOTES

[1] Grignolles is an imaginary name and does not even sound Breton. In a letter to Augustus John (*The Letters of Wyndham Lewis,* page 45) Lewis described this name as "fabulous." It is quite possible that Lewis associated it with "guignol" (a puppet show), as is suggested by the misspelling in "Writings." This of course would add to its kinship with *The Wild Body.*

[2] The omission of initial line capitals is an original feature contributing to what C. H. Sisson calls "the invincible solidity" of the poem ("Introduction" to *Collected Poems and Plays*).

[3] *The Tramp* gave the "Elizabethan" spelling "shere."

[4] The Cornell typescript has a comma here.

[5] *The Tramp* has a comma here.

[6] Capitalized in *The Tramp.*

BROBDINGNAG

This—the early version of ''Brotcotnaz''—was published in The New Age *of January 5, 1911, and considerably revised in 1927. The subsequent giving up of the Swiftian title for a plain though picturesque Breton name is illustrative of the more realistic approach adopted later. The static full-length portraits found here were to be animated into a series of scenes—and the rather abstract conclusions made more explicit. Altogether the metaphysical parodic questioning of reality was toned down in* The Wild Body.

Should Frans Hals come to life again, and find himself in the doorway of the "débit" at Kermanec,[1] he would recognise Madame Brobdingnag at once as a figure in several of his masterpieces—this is allowing for slight inaccuracies of memory owing to the century or two that have elapsed since he last saw them, of course. The room would seem odd to him, no doubt; and how such a man as Brobdingnag came to be living conjugally with one of his masterpieces would baffle his understanding. He might even regard it as a suspicious and portentous circumstance, and consider his resurrection with uneasiness. But not to pursue the course of this sympathetic ghost's reflections, let it suffice that Madame B. would seem to him perfectly regular, and a genuine Frans Hals.[2] She has the mellow tones of old pictures—but it is not time but drink that has effected this happy result. The obstinate yellow of jaundice is not yet subdued by the dull claret colour that is becoming the official tint of her face, assuring its predominance in many tiny strongholds of eruptive red. Her eyebrows are forever raised. She could not lower them now, I suppose, if she wanted to. The wrinkles of the forehead must have become stiff, like springs, with the result that if she pulled her eyebrows down they would fly up again the moment the muscles were relaxed. She is very dark; her hair, parted in the middle, is tightly brushed down upon her head. She treads softly, and has generally the air of a conspirator, or such as have some secret they are hugging. Her secret is that underneath the counter on the left-hand side, hidden among tins and flagons, is an enormous bottle of "eau de vie," which, when everyone else has either gone to the river to wash or else are collected in the neighbouring inns, she approaches on tiptoe, and pouring herself out several glasses in succession, swallows them with little sighs. She will drop her voice to a whisper, and seems keeping her secret publicly, as it were, and with everybody, at all moments. Sometimes her consciousness of it becomes so intense, that, with strange perversion, she acts as if the bottle were listening—as if it were from her secret itself that she were keeping her secret. The emphasis of unreasonable sorrow and contrition with which pious old women always speak to the priest, the tone of "misericorde," is that in which Julie speaks. The sort of old women I mean are such as hail their priest's light-heartedest jokes with ghostly smiles, treating them as though they were some further and even more hideously ingenious form of rendering life sad and unbearable, of which only a priest was capable.

While approaching his house this year, I wondered if Brobdingnag, since last summer, had been drowned at sea, disappeared, or declined from his old self. A reassuring sight met my eyes on entering the "débit." Julie had her head bound up, and to judge from the bold and rugged outlines of the bandages, the face had lately undergone grave modifications. Brobdingnag's own person could not have made me more at home. The bandaged head welcomed me. The disfigurements seemed purposely bestowed, with a rare delicacy of intention, in case I should come in his absence. She told me that it was erysipelas; but she explained half-an-hour later that Brobdingnag had done it.

Once she told me that a few years previously they had had a jay; this bird knew when Brobdingnag was drunk; and when he came in from a wake or "Pardon," and sat down at the "débit" table, the jay would hop out of its box, cross the table, and peck at its hands and fly in his face.

Brobdingnag is a glorious and unique creature. This is not a merely florid introduction; it is the only sentence that seems to me at once adequate and exact. He is of very big and powerful frame, reddish hair, moustache and stubble. His eyes are blue and smiling, and always seem evenly suffused with a rich moisture. They are great, tender, wise, mocking eyes, and the sides of his massive forehead are often flushed, as it is with some people in moments of embarrassment. But with him, I think this affluence of blood is something to do with the extraordinary expression he puts into his gaze, and the tension this effort must cause in the surrounding vessels, etc. What we call a sickly smile, the mouth remaining lightly drawn across the gums—the set, painful grin of the "timide"—this seldom leaves Brobdingnag's face.

He walks softly, with a supple giving of the knees at each step. This probably comes from his excessive fondness for the dance—the Breton "gavotte"—in which he was so rapid, expert and resourceful in his youth.

"J'suis maître danseur; c'est mon plaisir," he will say. He also has composed many verses to the gavotte airs of his country. If you ask him, he will, with his set grin, intone and buzz them through his scarcely parted teeth, whose tawny rows look, on these occasions—he manipulating their stops with his tongue—like some exotic musical instrument.

He is a fisherman, but also a "débitant" or bar-keeper and "cultivateur."[1] Brobdingnag and his wife dissipated the last half of her fortune in building their present home; Brobdingnag's enthusiasm, as it rose brick by brick, being of the costliest description. When at length it stood complete, beneath the little red cliff hewn out for its reception, glaring white, with a bald slate roof and rows of steps leading up to the door, his inaugural fêtes left them with nothing but its four walls and the third share in a fishing boat.

His comrades will tell you that he is a "charmant garçon, mais jaloux," or that he is "traitre."[2] He has been married twice, and in the first ardour of youth beat Julie's predecessor to death. "And yet, despite this, that 'pauvre

---

[1] A farmer.

[2] "A charming fellow, but jealous . . . treacherous."

Julie' *would* have him: qu'est-ce qu'elles ont les femmes à aimer un tel homme?"[1] etc. He has "hérité" three times or more, and spent each heritage ere the relative who left it him was half-eaten by the worms.

But first, foremost and above all, Brobdingnag is *civilised*. He is often drunk and then loses the amenity and "sourire" of his nature. Some people get drunk to attain to this felicitous and cloudless state: he, on the contrary, does so that he may remain in this perfect mood of his sober hours. These are necessary retrogressions. He is thereby purged completely for the time of all the suggestions, all the excretions of violent thought, emotion, black anger, bilious dreams, deposed in small quantities each day, inevitably, beneath the suave surface of his existence. Brobdingnag smiles placidly, confidently. He has accepted the price of that humane, wise and tranquil life that is his habitually. Having made up his mind, he will allow it to occupy him no further. The morning after he has beaten his wife—she a mass of bruises, lying exhausted on the bed—he busies himself about her, gravely and thoughtfully, inquiring occasionally how she feels, applying remedies, as a doctor would do having successfully performed an operation, and having no anxiety for the consequences. He walks fifteen miles to Quimperlé and back to get the necessary medicines. As a man might tend a delicate wife, who suffers from some chronic complaint, so does he comport himself on the morning following one of those awful, unshunnable, and mysterious nocturnal disturbances.

He addresses his wife always with the greatest gentleness. Still there is a vague something in the bearing of both of them, as of two people who, resigned, have long shared a strong affliction; a constant intelligence and consciousness of something—of something soon to be borne, perhaps.

Once Julie, to make sure of some lodgers, had agreed to a very moderate charge, and also to do their cooking. Brobdingnag put down his foot. With inexorable tenderness he forbade her to take this burden upon her shoulders, already sorely over-taxed, reminding her of her "delicate health" and other responsibilities.

I rode over to Kermanec again just before I left Brittany. On entering the "débit de vin" I found several people gathered there, and Julie with her arm in a large sling, with glimpses of bandages, and four stiff, bloated fingers protruding from beneath stained cloths. As usual, I took no notice of her condition—were she dying I should not let her see that I observed the fact. I discussed the latest scandal about Bestre,[3] at great inconvenience to myself keeping my eyes away from her wounded arm. And yet a certain doubt existed in my mind. It is true that I had not far to look for a cause of all this mischief; a solution sound, traditional, satisfying to the reason, and exempt-

---

1 "What's wrong with women that they should love such a man?."

ing the mind at once from all further search or hesitation—in fact in place of which I could seek all day and find no theory that would stand for a moment against it, or compete in likelihood. In the reposeful figure of Brobdingnag, sitting in the dark corner of the "débit," and gazing into space, was a key more than adequate to the history implied in this maimed arm. But it was this very figure that had engendered the doubt in my mind. His expression puzzled me. He, whom I was accustomed to see always master of the situation, seemed overcome, stunned almost, like a man not yet recovered from a terrible experience. His usual expression on these occasions was one of resignation and acceptance of the ways of Providence—tinged with sadness. One could see that he was a participator in the dispensations of Fate that had visited his roof, even in some way a secret agent of Fate. But now he looked like a man hardly recovered from a prodigious surprise.

Had Fate acted without him? Such was the question that at length shaped itself in my mind.

But Madame Brobdingnag, too, pre-occupied me. When one entered her "débit" and found some part of her body bound up, she would ordinarily look disagreeable—her way of "behaving as though nothing had happened"—although she was never disagreeable at other times. But now she gazed into my eyes for several minutes with an expression of bitter amusement. Really, had I known a whit less well the habits of the house, and not assisted at so many "lendemains de pardon," I should have interpreted this gaze as an invitation to talk about her misfortune. All this quite apart from the fact that it was only two weeks since I had seen her in a similar condition, and from experience I judged this new visitation premature.

At last some one said, "See how her fingers are swollen!" and Julie looked at me carelessly; she then tossed her head, with a resignedly desperate snigger.

I at once made inquiries. The baker had asked her, on driving up the day before, to put a stone under the wheel of his cart, to prevent it from moving. Julie had bent down to do so, but the horse backed suddenly and the wheel went over her hand: she had been to the hospital at Quimperlé, and they had bandaged it. Her arm also was affected.

Brobdingnag now got on his feet, and approached me to give his account of the affair. He seemed to do this despite himself, rather as though impelled by the fact of a strange misunderstanding, or half understanding, on the part of his wife and all the others in this matter.

He had been at sea at the time. On landing he was met by a neighbour, who told him that his wife was injured. "Your wife is injured——."

"What, my wife injured? My wife injured!"

He repeated these words slowly, in a dazed way, in telling how he first heard of the accident. He really got something of the utter astonishment, dismay and shade of strange suspicion that his voice must have expressed when the neighbour first informed him of this happening. The intensity of his voice was startling. With my knowledge of him it gave me a lurid glimpse at once of his present condition of mind. In the first moment of hearing of his wife's injured state, the familiar image of her battered form as seen on the morrow of one of his relapses must have risen in his mind. He is assailed with a sudden incapacity to think of injuries in his wife's case except as caused by a human hand; he is astonished by the thought that he himself had not been there to be the sufficient cause of anything that might have happened. Then all his wild jealousy suddenly surges up, giving life to these twin ideas—only more exasperated than ever before. In a second of time a man is born—vague and phantom-like, but of prodigious strength—a rival! sickening his whole imagination, that has given it birth, as with a woman that has been delivered of some hero, already of heroic size. A moment of utter weakness and lassitude seizes him. This rival is such an astonishing being, that he remains powerless at the thought of him. Brobdingnag's mind is stunned and invaded by a torpor, at the sight of such overwhelming hate and daring, complicated with such unspeakable ingenuity as his rival has given proof of; an invention no less than this—not only to gain his wife's love; but, in an access of titantic arrogance, to conceive the idea of wrestling from Brobdingnag that most mystic, thunder-guarded, inmost and incommunicable of rights—to have hatched and carried out the outrageous scheme of giving her a beating. From sheer incapacity to grasp a genius of such scope; at the end of a burning and prodigious second, another form takes hold of his mind, that of Julie—electrifying him, charging him with the most infernal energy and fury. This form at least he can grasp! At this moment someone must have told him of the real cause of the injuries. He heard, took the sense of the words, without it penetrating his mind. The forms of his imagination remained distinct, unmodified and immobilized, the reality now having rushed in and filled up the vacuum, as it were, with a stoney characterless matter. I can imagine it was touch and go. This information given but an instant later, and it would have been too late. Brobdingnag would have rushed up the steps of his house, scattered the sympathising group of neighbours, fallen upon the maimed and prostrate Julie, and before the spectators could cross themselves or gulp down their spital, have rendered the injuries inflicted by the baker's cart unrecognizable—feeling that, in outdoing and obliterating all trace of his imaginary rival, he had in some way mitigated his own humiliation, and humiliated this monstrous personage in turn.

The reality, while paralysing the progress of his fancy and what would have been its terrible and catastrophic advance, had not dissipated it. There it hung, as it had flashed into life a moment after his hearing of the accident, suspended over Julie's head, with only a common fact, the restlessness of a baker's horse, between her and destruction.

So he repeated in a dazed way to me: "What, my wife injured? My wife injured!" And here also his narrative came to a sudden termination, the others completing it for him.

What effect this most unfortunate adventure may have on Brobdingnag it is difficult to say. I can imagine those nocturnal rites growing more savage and desperate, and afterwards his recovered wisdom becoming at first insecure, and then no longer confident, and more and more sombreness remaining with him, and finally the complete ruin of his ancient self. I felt, in quitting Kermanec, that the shadow of doom had fallen upon this roof.

NOTES

1 An invented place-name also present in "Bestre," "The Death of the Ankou" and "Franciscan Adventures."

2 Hals, whom Lewis was copying in Harlem as early as 1904, was one of the writer's essential masters, as can be seen in a chapter of his last unpublished novel, *Twentieth Century Palette* (chapter XII, "A Visit to Frantz").

3 This allusion to Bestre was dropped in 1927.

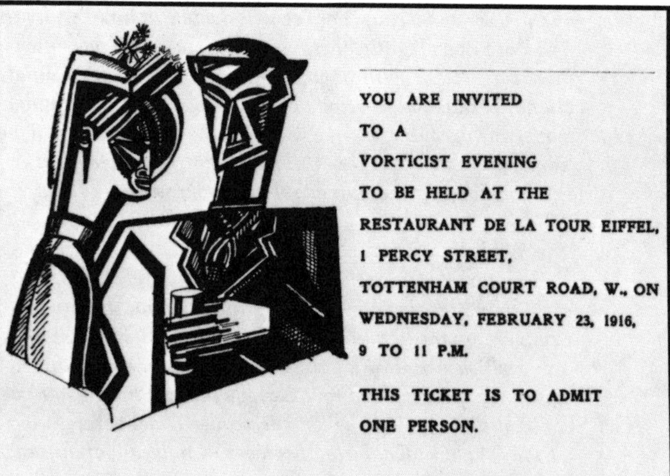

UNLUCKY FOR PRINGLE

This was the last work Lewis published in The Tramp *(February 1911). Not reprinted during the author's lifetime, it drew no comment from critics until 1973 when one perceptive page was devoted to it in* Wyndham Lewis: Satires and Fictions *by Robert Chapman. That same year, it was reprinted by Chapman and C. J. Fox in* Unlucky for Pringle: Unpublished and Other Stories. *Over sixty years had elapsed before the re-emergence of a remarkable story which may be held, with "Cantleman's Spring-Mate" and "Sigismund," as one of Lewis's major achievements in short fiction.*

Yet that it belongs to the Wild Body material is indisputably confirmed by its inclusion in "Writings," and—though its setting is London where Lewis had now been living for two years—it perpetuates the themes of the early works by presenting an intruder and a couple of French "restaurateurs." Why then was it not included in The Wild Body? *Quite obviously, Pringle—who has much in common with Ker-Orr (and by proxy, with Lewis)—could not be amalgamated with The Soldier of Humour. Both subject and object, he was too much dominated by his fantasies—by what, inspired by Lesage's* Le Diable Boiteux, *could be called an "Asmodeus Complex"—whereas Ker-Orr, not being subjected to the further attentions of an external observer, remained relatively immune. In short, the voyeuristic structure of "Unlucky for Pringle" was too complex to be compatible with the linear picaresque of* The Wild Body *encounters.*

Therefore it is clear that "Unlucky for Pringle" marks a radical departure from the early vignettes, even if the obsessions remain the same. With it, for the first time, Lewis enters the house of fiction—and this story must be seen as an elder brother of Tarr, *which actually borrowed one of its most picturesque paragraphs. The ambiguity of gestures and motivations (as met in "Bestre" or "Brobdingnag") is now consciously exploited, when the reader is deliberately left in doubt as to whom or what—Madame Chalaran, Monsieur Chalaran, or his saucepans—Pringle could not keep his hands off. In this sense "Unlucky for Pringle" can be seen as a perceptive example of pre-Freudian literature (with the exception of D. H. Lawrence, the Freudian message reached the literary spheres only after World War I), and even, in its parodic "huis-clos" as quasi-Sartrian in its approach to the world of intimacy.*

"Apartments to let." That sign never lost its magic for James Pringle. For others a purely business announcement, for him it appeared a soft and almost sensual invitation. It was the pleasant and mysterious voice of innumerable houses. A street with many of these signs almost agitated him. To instal himself in the midst of somebody else's life, like a worm in a wall, was a luxury and delight, a little vice fostered by migratory circumstances. Perhaps the ideal vocation for Pringle would have been that of a broker or sheriff's officer—an affable, rather melancholy one. As it was, he was a landscape painter,[1] whose circumstances confined his occupation of houses to rooms at ten or fourteen shillings a week, with north lights. If not certain about the length of his stay, it would be furnished apartments; otherwise he would move in his own furniture. "Rooms to let" meant that a warm, obscure, and typical life—that of the letter of the rooms and her possible daughters, husband, family, and friends—was free to be entered into and peacefully invested.

There for ten shillings a week he might inhabit that area, thickened, as it were, by their special personality into a wide, sluggish, and warm wall of Self. On the very frequently recurring occasions on which he set out to look for rooms he would savour the particular domestic taste of each new household he entered in the course of his search with the interest of a gourmet. Smiling strangely, as she thought, at the landlady who answered the door, he would at once go to her parlour—come for a debauch that she would never suspect.

On July 2nd of a recent year, at one o'clock in the afternoon, James Pringle walked down Beaufort Street, Chelsea,[2] scanning the houses with characteristic interest, and in the course of a characteristic occupation. He was looking for a room. But he was depressed. He knew Beaufort Street very well, and that he would find nothing there. It was true there still remained in the West End many streets in which he had so far culled no room. But then he was wearily reminded that Beaufort Street, Smith Street, Margaretta Terrace, had all been once upon a time, avenues charged with fanciful hopefulness for him. He had long learned to look on Beaufort Street as an interesting street, but of no practical interest to him; in Margaretta Terrace he had gathered two grimy and dubious flowers of lodging, which he had been compelled to throw away almost at once; he had not been happy in his dealings with Smith Street. Many will not understand how difficult it was for Pringle to find a room. But he understood. He said to himself that he had practically exhausted the resources of London. Vast as it was, he had taxed it to the uttermost in the matter of lodgings; it had given him all it had to give. (Any other city would have broken down long before.) In a year or so a new supply would no doubt have come into existence. The gradual decay of a generation of landladies was an almost imperceptible process. Still, the sleepy and musty mass would, in a year or two, have some way shifted—a chink the size of a pin's head have appeared where Pringle could creep. But, as it was, he would probably wander about all day and all the next and find nothing. Then hope set in again. There *were* tracts. It was one o'clock, and lunch time. He gave way to a suggestion that had presented itself to him many times already, and that he had experienced certain difficulty in resisting. "I'll go there; I suppose I must. I'll get it over at once."[3]

Pringle had just arrived in London after a year or so spent in Paris. He felt, in its new strangeness, as if he had returned to his London of five years previously, and not that he had left only a year before. When that morning he had set out to look for rooms the various places he knew of were marshalled in his mind. Every time that he was at a loss where to turn, and had rejected one idea after another, Marchant's house—in which he had sworn never to live again—presented itself in its inviting probable emptiness, low rents, and accommodating landlord. He seemed fated to go there, and unable to escape it. Had there been nothing else against it, the fact of its facility and the wearying solicitation of its emptiness was enough to repel him.

He felt that going there was a stale compromise, and that it had something insufferably ready-made, lax, and roomy about it. But now at one o'clock he gave way; but somewhat in exasperation, determined, as he said to himself, to "get it over."

Then this would be *something* to begin with. He would have seen *something*, anyhow; and then, perhaps, the thing he wanted would turn up more easily.

All he had to do was to cross the King's Road, pass through a few short streets, and there was Deisart Grove. The grove was gruesomely bowery—presumably its hirsute appearance had kept at a respectful distance those bent on "improvements"; it would, in fact, be a messy job to pull up and rebuild Deisart Grove.

No. 2, where Marchant lived, an old house resolutely decaying behind its allotment of shabby trees, looked as though it had stepped aside there to die. There was a strange air of wilfulness and menace about it, as though, disgusted with existence, it had determined to take its fate into its own hands, and if its owner refused to pull it down and went on demanding service of it, to tumble to pieces of its own accord; an air, in fact, of natural suicide about the whole place, a sullen revolt of inanimate things against the importunities of man, who would not leave them alone.

Here lived T. A. Marchant. His business in life was to exploit poor old ramshackle houses that could be obtained cheap. He would instal himself in them, let every available cranny, and live there till they fell to pieces. One felt that this one might at any moment take a terrible revenge. He was standing in his doorway as Pringle approached, as though undecided as to whether to go out or go in—his front door was an almost insuperable barrier for Marchant. He would get as far as that, and there remain, becalmed in his porch for considerable periods, until some exterior motive force, a lodger or errand boy, moved him in one direction or the other. Pringle acted as a blast driving him in—eventually, indeed, driving him up the stairs into several of his rooms, vacant and eligible.

"Well," he sniggered, "you back again? Where've you bin? Bin to France?" He had an educated cockney accent. He was very familiar, but chiefly through timidity, as though not only not daring to be distant, but not daring to be anything but familiar, or to withhold a single scrap of himself for fear it should be snatched from him. To avert the stringency of more heroic manners, the *timide* will sometimes affect this *sans gêne*,[1] invoking "our common humanity." Humour is called in to help in these systematic belittlements. Marchant was a very humorous dog. He was always sniggering and joking.

"Yes," said Pringle to his inquiries. "Have you got any rooms to let? But I'm not sure whether I'll take unfurnished rooms this time. Do you know anybody who has a furnished room to let, and who'd do my cooking?"

"Yes," Marchant replied truthfully; but he did not say *where*, or any more about it, and continued:

"I've got the rooms under yours—*yew* know—to let. 'Ave a look at them?"

And then they went upstairs, both of them, without any enthusiasm, and looked at several rooms. Marchant did nothing to induce his former lodger to take them, and when they had both depressed themselves with the sight of the empty rooms for some minutes, Marchant said:

"The people next door—well, it's the same house, but separate, they're French—*they* 'ave a furnished room to let, and would do anything you wanted, I expect."

On hearing they were French, Pringle at once determined to go round. He liked the French, although as a nation "furnished apartments" are unknown to them—and wanted practice in the language. The great question now was whether it were *really* next door or not. It had a different number—2B—whereas Marchant's was 2. Pringle had always regarded 2 as a particularly unlucky number. "What about 2B?" he reflected. "Does the addition of a 'B' really neutralise the horrible effects of 2?"

Two years ago, in helping the men to carry in his furniture, he had let a looking-glass fall. It had broken to pieces, and the man he had been helping with the lighter articles gazed for some minutes at him in pitying silence, and

[1] Offhandedness.

then said:

"Seven years, mister!"

Seven years' ill-luck seemed so ample a spell that there was no immediate anxiety. But that night, sitting in the midst of his furniture, this ill-omened accident on the threshold had its effect. His furniture was arranged more or less as it always was, a restricted and symmetrical scene he had sat in the midst of for several years in different districts of the city. This furniture moved with him like a gloomy cloud, in the heart of which he dwelt, with periodic returns to its garage, or the store-room, as mentioned. Only its contours changed slightly in the course of its slow progress. This last contour it had taken, that of Marchant's rooms, he had looked at dubiously. He looked out of his window, out of his cloud, and surveying the Cockneyfied trees. Moving into new rooms was invariably accompanied by a period of depression and restlessness with him, and doubt as to their suitability. This was strengthened and perpetuated in the present case by the breaking of the mirror. At the end of a month he had left, going to Paris. And so Marchant's French tenants had against them their connection with Marchant, and the fact that they lived under the same roof.

"Do you mean that little place round there at the side?" he asked.

"Yes, round there. I'll show you."

So he went round a narrow slabbed walk, and knocked at the adjoining door, Marchant retiring with a guilty nod and a snigger to his own threshold, as though he had put Pringle up to something naughty. A bearded and languid little man, the colour of a Chinaman, answered the door.

"Yes?" he asked, staring at the ground; then, as an afterthought: "You want see rooms?"

He seemed to have been expecting Pringle, or, to be quite exact, somebody rather like Pringle. He stepped aside and ushered him into a back room. Once there he lost all interest in his visitor, and wandered restlessly about, as though seeking to take up a listless life at the exact point where he had dropped it to answer the door. Pringle had hardly time to notice his new host's relapse, for he was superseded by an elegant, youngish woman, who advanced towards Pringle as if she had been waiting her "cue" in this back room, and now approached as though from the wings of a theatre into the gaslight.

"Good morning. You want rooms? I suppose Mr. Marchant recommended you? I'll show you what we have. Will you come upstairs?" said in very careful and respectable English.

There were two rooms adjoining each other at the back of the house, suitable in the subtlest sense. Pringle was elated. He looked at his guide. A constant, plaintive break in the high-pitched voice, which was precise, resigned, and distinguished, an obtrusive, plaintively challenging sincerity, and hint of pathos, but, above all, sincerity in the eyes, which were quiet black, and the elegance of the lady's *mise*[1] were the dominant points for Pringle. That plaintive break or quaver he had heard before. Had his experience been wider he would have connected it inevitably with the particular *âme*[2] developed in Geneva.

He took the rooms, and it was half an hour afterwards that he met me, I finishing, he beginning, lunch at the "Copper Gate" public-house, just off the King's Road.

The foregoing narrative is, no doubt, in every essential detail exact, as it is compiled from facts and impressions then directly noted and received, and from my exhaustive intuitive knowledge of Pringle.

Pringle has always remained the strangest of my friends. His is like the passion of the book collector or amateur of furniture and practical arts. Only his taste is for the accidental—just whatever life brings. One might almost say that the chief value of anything for Pringle is its accidental quality, its inevitability in the succession of the accidents of life—the fact that just *that* thing turned up (whatever it be) and no other. He is as much elated, in his way, by the shabby furniture in the rooms of some London lodging-house as another would be over a room full of Louis Quinze. In the case of a man of genius the mediocrity of his daily life—his lodging, however mean, with the rest—takes a warmth and vitality from him. No doubt Goethe felt somewhat the same glamour in living in his own house in Francfort-on-Maine[3] as any educated man would feel if he suddenly became the tenant of Goethe's house. An exhilaration, almost excitement, is reflected back to the artist from anything. Pringle, not possessed of exceptional gifts, had been strangely endowed with this gusto for the common circumstances of his life; or, rather than definitely "endowed with," I should suppose it to have developed in the following way. Originally seeking merely for suitable conditions for his work, etc., but conceiving of these conditions too fastidiously and morbidly, gradually this got the upper hand, as it were, so that it seemed almost—as I have described my friend—that his sole preoccupation consisted in sampling those conditions.

There, beneath the somnolent chimney of the "Copper Gate," with a laconic eloquence, he told me about his "find," and discoursed generally of the difficulty of discovering rooms. The existence of any eccentricity in Pringle was not so much as hinted at between us, or, for that matter, often realised by him. Everything was translated into commonplace psychical formulas. For instance, his delight in the landlord or landlady would appear as a gleeful or humourous "interest in character." As to the details of the

---

1 Appearance.

2 Soul, mood.

3 I.e., German "Frankfurt am Main"; English "Frankfort on the Main"; or French "Francfort-sur-le-Main."

rooms, they would be referred, in his description, either to his requirements as a painter or comforts as a man. But I, having the key to my friend's strangeness, had no difficulty in casting this back into its original and veritable idiom.

I left Pringle in Sloane Square, he being bound for Charing Cross, where he had left his boxes. I did not see him again for six weeks. Then one day I found him drifting along in front of me. I followed him the length of Oakley Street. His eyes were cast up at the ground floor windows and the glassy spaces above the front doors. Being more or less in the neighbourhood of the "Copper Gate," we repaired there, and I learnt of the following extravagant conclusion of Pringle's second tenancy in Deisart Grove.

"I hate looking for rooms," said Pringle.

But I could not transcribe his words on this, or any other occasion, because frankly I have not the vaguest recollection of them; and although his bulging eyes and easy gestures are very familiar to me, lacking invention, I could not reconstruct our interview, memory having deserted me.

On the other hand, I have a quite distinct picture of the Pringle of the six weeks in Deisart Grove. That is why I always consider him the strangest of my friends. I always forget the Pringle before me to see the Pringle he is telling me about, or who appears in his words. I seem to see the intimate Pringle, the soul of Pringle, in its favourite pursuits and experiences. When I think of him I never think of the man I have sat with in the "Copper Gate," but of the man he has given me glimpses of in his talk. So it would be simpler for me at once to describe how, having got his boxes at Charing Cross, he hurried back to No. 2B Deisart Grove, his conversation with his landlord, and even his most secret reflections, than what passed between us in the bar of the public-house.

Pringle sent for some of his furniture the same afternoon, to supplement his new room's exiguous contents. On driving up with his boxes, he felt the customary rank depression[4]—the indigestion of Reality. The reality always overwhelmed him at first; then came an Homeric struggle with it, usually ending in its assimilation. He was very fond of reality; but he was like a man very fond of what did not at all agree with him. When he at last found himself—the things deposited on the floor, the door finally closed upon him—alone with his new room, nothing short of horror descended on him. To undo and let loose upon the rooms his portmanteaus' squashed and wrinkled contents, like a flock of birds and pack of dogs, the brushes dashing to the dressing-table, the photographs crowding to the chimneypiece, the portmanteaus, boxes, and parcels creeping under the bed and into corners, was a martyrdom for him. The unwearied optimism of these inanimate objects, how they occupied stolidly and quickly room after room was appalling. Then they still had the staleness of the former room about them, and the souvenir of a depressing hour of tearing up and packing.

On this particular occasion he at once descended into the back-parlour on the ground floor, and thence into the kitchen beyond, to seek consolation in his French host.

The parlour, windowless, and lighted from the kitchen, found the bedroom preferred to it on the one hand, and the kitchen on the other. The kitchen in a certain sense took advantage of its position, abused it, for it was extremely dirty, and did not attempt to make amends for its smallness by being tidy. It lay in the full glare of day, with its glass door and large window; a slut of a room, dribbling at the sink, full of unsavoury pails, garishly dirty. A dresser occupied one side—an Alps of a dresser, with gloomy glaciers of unused plates, rifts of mouldering tarts, and a crowding landscape at its base; the outer side was the glass door and window and the ribs of the dresser; the opposite side the gas-stove and shelves.

Pringle, not quite used to his new quarters, entered and tentatively remained in the parlour, opening a conversation with his host. It did not take him long to discover the position this room held in the house, however, and he moved into the kitchen, with an obsequious leer at the sink. Monsieur Chalaran continued to take Pringle quite as a matter of course. It was only later, indeed, that he appeared to become less used to Pringle, and to regard him as it is natural for human beings to regard each other at the first. The result of this inverted order of things was that Pringle became an "inmate" in the full sense of the word, remarkably quickly. In fact, when I met him, he appeared rather dazed with the suddenness that had marked all the stages of his stay with the Chalarans. For it is the *becoming* in things that bulks out, so to speak, and leaves behind it a substantial impression of a lapse of time. And I, in telling his story, now I come to think of it, only have a few almost abrupt "states" to record, and not a series of "becomings," as should be the case.

Here, anyhow, we find him seated in front of Monsieur Chalaran, and at once engrossed in a first and superficial examination of the latter's health. Monsieur Chalaran's familiarity was of another order to that of Marchant. "One's sure to be at ease and comradelike with this person in a couple of days—why not at once? One pays a man too great a compliment in being distant," he would seem to have said. Then it was pathologic; the listlessness and indifference caused by his disease had its share in it; also democratic sentiments.

He had been a chef.

"I tried to go back to work," he told Pringle; "in fact, I had no idea I was finished, first of all. I got four or five places; in each I had to leave after a day or two. I've been here four years;" he said in answer to Pringle, who was surprised on reflecting that only four years ago his host had been an active worker. Monsieur Chalaran sat with his eyes affectedly staring, his bearded lips thrust out, and desperate amusement painted on his yellow face.

As to the nature of the disease, Monsieur Chalaran said *he* knew very well what it was. Madame Chalaran also would say sometimes that *she* knew very well what it was. But they neither of them liked to hear the other say this.

"If I've seen specialists!" he said on this occasion to Pringle. "But they don't know what it is. One said it was probably something or other, but he didn't know. For me, it's rheumatism!"

He always called it rheumatism in his brighter moments, but when he had his headaches he was willing to call it anything he could lay his tongue to—even paralysis. What it exactly was Pringle never knew, except that the poor man suffered a great deal, and took morphine all the time.

His wife "earned good money" as a milliner near Sloane Street. Meantime, left alone in this little house, he was converting everything within his reach into something else—the flower-beds into a lawn, one of the outhouses into an aviary, an old trunk into a sort of ping-pong game, etc. These activities corresponded to bursts of energy, he seeming more or less to gauge the probable extent and duration of each of them at its advent, and to undertake something that would occupy him for just so long as it would last.

Pringle left Monsieur Chalaran, recovered from his depression, and the terms of his stay arranged. He should have his meals in the kitchen with the Chalarans—at least, one meal a day. In the end he had all his meals there. Everything turned out *à souhait.*[1] In a week Pringle was savouring the delights of "lodging" as he had never done before, having lost less by actual inhabiting than usual. On the next stage of his stay in this house I got a unique picture of Pringle. It was a scene of almost patriarchal peace, Pringle being the patriarch. There in the small, garish kitchen he spent the greater part of his days, sheltered from the world by the encompassing personalities of Monsieur and Madame Chalaran, occasionally also Marchant, and all the other objects and details of his new life in this household. His meals were cooked by a first-class chef, whose operations he could watch and discuss. He would sit smoking in the kitchen, gazing at M. Chalaran tossing up potato cakes, arguing with him about the respective hanging of French and English meat, obtaining an insight into the life of a large, populous kitchen, hearing of the chef's perquisites and tradesmen's canvassing, etc. Then he would enjoy the luncheon *à trois* with the Chalarans, contending with madame that the hats she made were unbeautiful, as was all modern dress, with the threadbare arguments of "the classic nude."

"C'est un jeune homme fort intelligent, je trouve,"[2] Madame Chalaran said to her husband. He said nothing, not being by nature addicted to praise.

---

[1] To perfection.

[2] "He's a very intelligent young man, I think."

Pringle's cup of content, in short, was full. And this, in my opinion, was the trouble. Perhaps he showed his satisfaction too much. This mystic contentment of his may have been registered by the acute nerves of the invalid, and in some way resented. Perhaps the latter realised that he was being enjoyed, without understanding how. Pringle, in his delight, could not apparently keep his hands off things—with difficulty even off persons. Monsieur Chalaran's saucepans, among other things, were touched.

The ex-chef's professional pride suddenly awoke. And Pringle's account of the first slight friction was Monsieur Chalaran finding him peering into one of his pots—coming up brusquely—whisking the saucepans about, clashing them down and saying, his eyes averted,

"Je n'aime pas qu'on touche à mes outils![1] Je n'aime pas ça, Monsieur James. I don't like that!"

Then, after a pause:

"I don't like that!"

But this was certainly not the first of it. Pringle, too, felt that. Monsieur Chalaran's animal-like selfishness and self-absorption hardly revealed any new element in his inner life until it was ripe. The realisation of a peculiarity in Pringle, and of its nature—a "contentment," a gloating, even—must have taken a considerable time in sinking through his torpor, and then, having done its work, in emerging again.

Pringle, still absorbed in his sensations of an almost enervating peace and well-being, was oblivious to this little cloud the size of a man's hand.

The natural pathos of Madame Chalaran's manner, the restrained nobility she preferred, fitted in with her present unfortunate situation. Still, it was possibly more of a chance than she would have asked for; her husband's illness was like a malicious and mocking gift of Fate. But Pringle was not fastidious in matters of this sort, and Madame Chalaran's "heroism" pleased him along with everything else. Monsieur was a "brave garçon,"[2] and liked by Pringle.

On coming down to breakfast one morning, Pringle found Madame alone, her face rather drawn, and thrown back as it always was when something unusual had occurred.

"My husband has had a very bad night. I've not closed my eyes once. His groaning keeps me awake."

Pringle, concerned, asked for further news.

"Oh, I expect he'll be up in an hour or two. He'll cook your lunch for you. He was very bad last night; he has not been so bad for a long time."

A certain curtness in madame's speech struck Pringle, as though she hardly trusted herself or hardly had the patience to say any more in this

1 "I don't like anyone to handle my tools!"

2 "A good chap."

restrained and conventional way, and that indignation and the truth were very near her lips. What Pringle noticed was something *sullen* about her. "Something has gone wrong," he thought.

Pringle himself did eventually see through all this, and, retrospectively, grasp how things had stood. He would never have arrived at this point of clairvoyance had it not been for his personal sufferings. The pain it caused him to leave the Chalaran's roof at the last moment threw a vivid light on the whole situation.

So Pringle, in his later and enlightened state, thought he could detect the germ of this first additional indisposition of monsieur's. This germ was a conversation over the supper table two days earlier. This, he had no doubt, had caused Monsieur Chalaran's relapse. But (characteristically) it had taken two days to grip and finally become manifest in his organism. For two days Monsieur Chalaran had been visibly ailing. He did not even know what was the matter himself. No specialist could have helped him. But he, and Pringle, too, became, shortly, wiser than a specialist.

The conversation had been sustained by madame and Pringle alone, monsieur being compelled to remain silent for some time. It had dealt with a sex question. Pringle had enjoyed the frankness permitted by the calm and scientific nature of the discussion, especially as it was with French people. Had it been *légère,* or even *grivoise,*[1] Charlaran would probably have seen no particular objection. But there was something almost uncanny to him in this way of handling nakedly such a delicate question. Pringle, for his part, seemed to think he was giving these French people, noted for their ribald and indecent frankness, a specimen of English *sans gêne.*

Monsieur Chalaran had shown his displeasure and discomfort by eating up hastily everything within reach; as a man might stop his ears, Monsieur Chalaran stopped his mouth.

Madame held her own wonderfully. She kept her head raised, her eyes became almost heavy with sincerity and intelligence. She "understood," of course. Her husband was twice reproached with a hushed and weary dignity for gobbling up his food.

"Emile, don't bolt your food like that! We're not going to take it away from you," she drawled.

In any case, what his indisposition succeeded in doing was definitely to enlighten him as to his feeling for Pringle. He rose from his bed implacable. He had had enough of James Pringle.

When that evening—Chalaran's indisposition passed—they were all three at table again, a change had evidently come in the relations of husband and wife. Madame was dangerously considerate.

---

[1] Improper, or even ribald.

"I shouldn't drink so much coffee, Emile. You know it's not good for you."

"Oh, je m'en fous pas mal.[1] If it kills me."

"Yes, but it doesn't kill you: it's apt, though, to make you pass bad nights."

Further, she told Pringle of her husband's sufferings in the past, discussed his illness, etc. Monsieur Chalaran quite naturally looked moved and sorry for himself at this talk. He took it all to himself. His careless and matter-of-course invalid's greediness was evidently a source of intense irritation to his wife. She was manufacturing this pathos for her own consumption, but half anticipating her husband's attitude; and now she remained ironically and venomously starving. Pringle, by this time somewhat shaken out of his beatific state, noticed so much, puzzled.

Chalaran felt the steady, invisible sirocco of his wife's indignation. He sullenly bowed his head. His usually bent head aided in this mental picture. Pringle and his strange passion was now appearing a stirrer up of strife, and divider of wife and husband. He vaguely realised his new *rôle*. On the fourth day, however, Chalaran completely recovered from his relapse, and in a burst of energy that lasted two afternoons built a summer-house at the bottom of the garden. The summer-house, no doubt, saved Pringle. But had Pringle grasped then the at once compact and elemental character of these bursts of activity, and his own position as regards Chalaran, he would have shaken in his shoes. For who could say whether the next time a storm of such violence as to build a summer-house might not seize on some more substantial and apposite object?

During these days of doubtful relationship Chalaran resorted often to a violin, to give voice in a sort of abstract and peculiarly exasperating way to his dissatisfaction. He would not look at Pringle once during lunch time. But the moment he had gone upstairs to work Monsieur Chalaran would take his fiddle out and begin playing at him underneath in the kitchen. The violin appeared afflicted with exactly Monsieur Chalaran's disease, and its "rheumatism" found expression in the same way. He could not be ill himself the *whole* time. It was the complement of his own malicious relapses. Pringle felt the intention; and it was possibly noticing this connection that first put him on the road to the truth of the situation.

One evening madame took on a very good-natured expression, and began bantering Chalaran on his sluggishness and silence. Pringle, not understanding, joined in a little. His host looked so near breaking forth into some unusual and quite *inédit*[2] passionate state that he desisted, and retired soon

---

1 "I don't give a damn."

2 Unprecedented.

after. Then the final stage was reached. No two days to take effect this time! A half an hour later it happened. With a howl Monsieur Chalaran flung himself on the bed, come to the end of his patience or torpor. No more Pringle! He meant it this time. He cast himself down with a howl. A doctor had to be sent for, and by the next day he had succeeded in dragging himself to the edge of the grave.

There is nothing more to be told, for there was only one course for Pringle—once more to quit Deisart Grove.

He had passed like a ghost, in one sense, through a hundred unruffled households. Scores of peaceful landladies, like beautiful women caressed in their sleep by a spirit, had been enjoyed by him. Their drab apartments had served better than any boudoir. But at last one of the objects of his passion had turned in its sleep, as it were, its sleep being the restless slumber of the sick—had done more than that, had cried out and chased Pringle away. His late landlord no doubt gave the sleepwalker or spirit in Pringle a considerable shock. I found him very much shaken.

He could only judge of the intensity of madame's indignation and the treatment that awaited monsieur on his recovery by the way in which *he*, Pringle, even, had been implicated. When she came upstairs to speak to him about her husband's condition she was not uncivil, but she *looked less sincere*. The significance of this could not be exaggerated. She had come with the intention of uprooting Pringle there and then, as she felt, no doubt, how firmly he was fixed, and the need there would be of loosening the roots.

"I have written to my young sister at Bexhill to come and stay here and look after my husband during the day."

This was the first wedge. There would be nowhere to put the sister unless Pringle vacated his room. Then the wedge was worked about and Pringle's roots disturbed, prodded, and tugged at.

"I can't ask her to come if I don't provide some accommodation for her," etc.

Pringle stood quite still—too still—under the operation, and watched the face of the operator.

"I'm afraid you'll find it very uncomfortable here, Mr. Pringle," etc.

Pringle did not wince; but when he felt that finally the ground had been taken away from under his feet, and, in fact, that there was not a square inch which had not been accounted for in Madame Chalaran's cutting and clearing operations, he pulled himself together. He said that in the circumstances perhaps he had better look for another room.

"You know, Mr. Pringle, I wouldn't turn you out," she said. But he saw with surprise how he had suffered even in her estimation. Perhaps his defeat by her husband may in some unseizable way have contributed to this. Just at the last she may even have realised that there was something strange in

Pringle. Anyhow, this house *would* vomit him forth; it could not assimilate him. Glasses crashed down at its doors as he was entering; its inhabitants became filled with mysterious hatred for him.

Pringle found a room remarkably soon. But this was not a good sign. Also he inhabited it alarmingly long. I felt for many months after this that Pringle was living *anywhere*. But now he has quite recovered, become a great believer in Pimlico, and is changing his rooms with perfect regularity. His hygiene, in short, leaves nothing to be desired.

NOTES

[1] Because of his idiosyncrasies (his nomadism, digestive approach to reality and obsessive attention to objects), Pringle could be interpreted as a projection of the author—but his being "a landscape painter" certainly signals an ironic distance, which is reinforced by the presence of the anonymous perceptive author-narrator.

[2] This is the part of London Lewis adopted on his return from France, when he settled in Whiteheads Grove, Chelsea.

[3] Compare with "The "Pole,'" page 212.

[4] The end of this paragraph was incorporated with some modifications in *Tarr*, IV, 11 (12 in 1928).

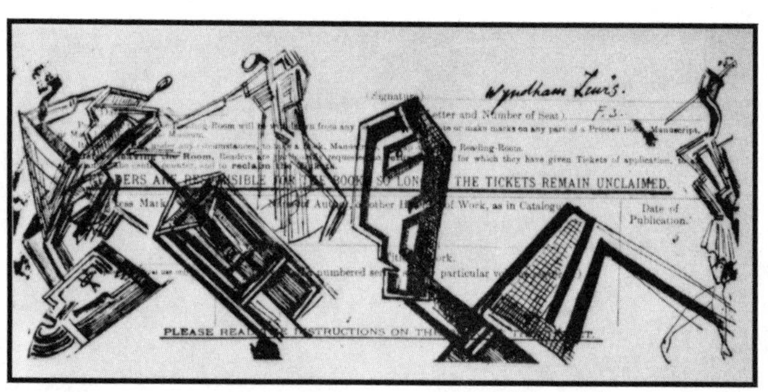

INFERIOR RELIGIONS (1917)

This essay was first published in September 1917 in The Little Review *thanks to Ezra Pound who, during the war, acted as Lewis's impresario. In an "Editor's note" Pound said:*

> *This essay was written as the introduction to a volume of short stories containing "Inn-Keepers and Bestre," "Unlucky for Pringle" and some others. . . The book was in process of publication (the author had even been paid an advance on it) when war broke out. The last member of the publishing firm has been killed in France, and the firm disbanded. The essay is complete in itself and need not stand as an "introduction." It is perhaps the most important single document that Wyndham Lewis has written. . .*

The absence of "Inferior Religions" from "Writings" suggests that it must have been written early in 1917, when Lewis was still training as a bombardier—which certainly accounts for its explosive style, though the influence of Vorticism, which in its manifestoes had been Dadaist two years before Dada, is just as considerable.

I

To introduce my puppets, and the Wild Body, the generic puppet of all, I must look back to a time when the antics and solemn gambols of these wild children filled me with triumph.

The fascinating imbecility of the creaking men-machines some little restaurant or fishing-boat works, is the subject of these studies. The boat's tackle and dirty little shell keep their limbs in a monotonous rhythm of activity. A man gets drunk with his boat as he would with a merry-go-round. Only it is the staid, everyday drunkeness of the normal real. We can all see the ascendance a "carrousel" has on men, driving them into a set narrow intoxication. The wheel at Carisbrooke imposes a set of movements on the donkey inside it, in drawing water from the well, that it is easy to grasp. But in the case of a fishing-boat the variety is so great, the scheme so complex, that it passes as open and untrammeled life. This subtle and wider mechanism merges, for the spectator, in the general variety of Nature. Yet we have in most lives a spectacle as complete as a problem of Euclid.

Moran, Bestre and Brobdingnag[1] are essays in a new human mathematic. But they are each simple shapes, little monuments of logic. I should like to compile a book of forty of these propositions, one deriving from and depending on the other.

These intricately moving bobbins are all subject to a set of objects or one in particular. Brobdingnag is fascinated by one object for instance; one at once another vitality. He bangs up against it wildly at regular intervals, blackens it, contemplates it, moves round it and dreams. All such fascination is religious. Moran's damp napkins are the altar cloths of his rough illusion, Julie's bruises are the markings on an idol.

These studies of rather primitive people are studies in a savage worship and attraction. Moran rolls between his tables ten million times in a realistic rhythm that is as intense and superstitious as the figures of a war-dance. He worships his soup, his damp napkins, the lump of flesh that rolls everywhere with him called Madame Moran.

All religion has the mechanism of the celestial bodies, has a dance. When we wish to renew our idols, or break up the rhythm of our naïvety, the effort postulates a respect which is the summit of devoutness.

II

I would present these puppets, then, as carefully selected specimens of religious fanaticism. With their attendant objects or fetishes they live and have a regular food for vitality. They are not creations but puppets. You can be as exterior to them, and live their life as little, as the showman grasping from beneath and working about a Polichinelle. They are only shadows of energy, and not living beings. Their mechanism is a logical structure and they are nothing but that.

Sam Weller, Jingle, Malvolio, Bouvard and Pécuchet, the "commissaire" in *Crime and Punishment*, do not live; they are congealed and frozen into logic, and an exuberant, hysterical truth. They transcend life and are complete cyphers, but they are monuments of dead imperfection. Their only reference is to themselves, and their only significance their egoism.[2]

The great intuitive figures of creation live with the universal egoism of the Poet. They are not picturesque and over palpable. They are supple with this rare impersonality; not stiff with a common egotism. The "realists" of the Flaubert, Maupassant, and Tchekoff school are all satirists. "Realism", understood as applied to them, implies either photography or satire.

Satire, the great Heaven of Ideas, where you meet the Titans of red laughter, is just below Intuition, and Life charged with black Illusion.

III

When we say "types of humanity," we mean violent individualities, and nothing stereotyped. But Othello, Falstaff and Pecksniff attract, in our memory, a vivid following. All difference is energy, and a category of humanity a relatively small group, and not the myriads suggested by a generalisation.

A comic type is a failure of considerable energy, an imitation and standardising of self, suggesting the existence of a uniform humanity,—creating, that is, a little host as like as ninepins; instead of one synthetic and various Ego. It is the laziness of a successful personality. It is often part of our own organism become a fetish.

Sarah Gamp and Falstaff are minute and rich religions. They are illusions hugged and lived in. They are like little dead Totems. Just as all Gods are a repose for humanity, the big religions an important refuge and rest, so these little grotesque idols are. One reason for this is that, for the spectator or participator, it is a world in a corner of the world, full of rest and security.

Moran, even, advances in life with his rows of bottles and napkins; Julie is Brobdingnag's Goddess, and figures for intercessions, if the occasion arises.

All these are forms of static and traditional art, then. There is a great deal of divine Olympian sleep in English Humour. The most gigantic spasm of laughter is sculptural, isolated and essentially simple.

IV

1 Laughter is the Wild Body's song of triumph.
2 Laughter is the climax in the tragedy of seeing, hearing and smelling self-consciously.
3 Laughter is the bark of delight of a gregarious animal at the proximity of its kind.
4 Laughter is an independent, tremendously important, and lurid emotion.
5 Laughter is the representative of Tragedy, when Tragedy is away.
6 Laughter is the emotion of tragic delight.
7 Laughter is the female of Tragedy.
8 Laughter is the strong elastic fish, caught in Styx, springing and flapping about until it dies.
9 Laughter is the sudden handshake of mystic violence and the anarchist.
10 Laughter is the mind sneezing.
11 Laughter is the one obvious commotion that is not complex, or in expression dynamic.
12 Laughter does not progress. It is primitive, hard and unchangeable.

V[3]

The chemistry of personality (subterranean in a sort of cemetery whose decompositions are our lives) puffs in frigid balls, soapy Snow-men, arctic Carnival-Masks, which we can photograph and fix.

Upwards from the surface of Existence a lurid and dramatic scum oozes and accumulates into the characters we see. The real and tenacious poisons, and sharp forces of vital vitality, do not socially transpire. Within five yards of another man's eyes, we are on a little crater, which, if it erupted, would split up as a cocoa-tin of nitrogen would. Some of these bombs are ill-made, or some erratic in their timing. But they are all potential little bombs.

Capriciously, however, the froth-forms of these darkly-contrived machines, twist and puff in the air, in our legitimate and liveried masquerade.

Were you the female of Moran (the first Innkeeper) and beneath the counterpane with him, you would be just below the surface of life, in touch with a nasty and tragic organism. The first indications of the proximity of the real soul would be apparent. You would be for hours beside a filmy crocodile, conscious of it like a bone in an Ex-Ray, and for minutes in the midst of a tragic wallowing. The soul lives in a cadaverous activity; its dramatic corruption thumps us like a racing engine in the body of a car. The finest humour is the great Play-Shapes blown up or given off by the tragic corpse of Life underneath the world of the Camera. This futile, grotesque and sometimes pretty spawn, is what in this book is Kodacked by the Imagination.

Any great humourist is an artist; Dickens as an example. It is just this character of uselessness and impersonality in Laughter, the fibre of anarchy in the comic habit of mind, that makes a man an artist in spite of himself when he begins living on his laughter. Laughter is the arch-luxury that is as simple as bread.

VI

In this objective Play-World, corresponding to our social consciousness as opposed to our solitude, no final issue is decided. You may blow away a Man-of-bubbles with a Burgundian gust of laughter, but that is not a personality, it is an apparition of no importance. Its awkwardness, or prettiness is accidental. But so much correspondence it has with its original that if the cadaveric travail beneath is vigorous and bitter, the mask and figurehead will be of a more original and intense grotesqueness. The opposing armies in Flanders stick up dummy men on poles for their enemies to pot at, in a spirit of fierce friendliness. It is only a dummy of this sort that is engaged in the sphere of laughter. But the real men are in the trenches underneath all the time, and are there on a more "decisive" affair. In our rather drab Revel there is certain category of spirit that is not quite anaemic, and yet not very funny. It consists of those who take, at the Clarkson's[4] situated at the opening of their lives, some conventional Pierrot costume, with a minimum of inverted vigour and the assurance of superior insignificance.

The King of Play is not a phantom corresponding to the Sovereign force beneath the surface. The latter must always be accepted as the skeleton of the Feast. That soul or dominant corruption is so real that he cannot rise up and take part in man's festival as a Falstaff of unwieldy spume; if he comes at all it must be as he is, the skeleton or bogey of True Life, stuck over corruptions and vices. He may a certain "succès d' hystérie."

VII

A scornful optimism, with its confident onslaughts on our snobbism, will not make material existence a peer for our energy. The gladiator is not a perpetual monument of triumphant health. Napoleon was harried with Elbas. Moments of vision are blurred rapidly and the poet sinks into the rhetoric of the will.

But life is invisible and perfection is not in the waves or houses that the poet sees. Beauty is an icy douche of ease and happiness at something suggesting perfect conditions for an organism. A stormy landscape, and a Pigment consisting of a lake of hard, yet florid waves; delight in each brilliant scoop or ragged burst, was John Constable's beauty. Leonardo's consisted in a red rain on the shadowed side of heads, and heads of massive female aesthetes. Uccello accumulated pale parallels, and delighted in cold architectures of distinct colour. Korin found in the symmetrical gushing of water, in waves like huge vegetable insects, traced and worked faintly, on a golden pâte, his business. Cézanne liked cumbrous, democratic slabs of life, slightly leaning, transfixed in vegetable intensity.

Beauty is an immense predilection, a perfect conviction of the desirability of a certain thing. To a man with long and consumptive fingers a sturdy hand may be heaven. Equilibrium and "perfection" may be a bore to the perfect. The most *universally* pleasing man is something probably a good way from "perfection." Henri Fabre was in every way a superior being to Bernard,[5] and he knew of elegant grubs which he would prefer to the painter's nymphs.

It is obvious, though, that we should live a little more in small communities.

NOTES

[1] Brobdingnag is of course the future Brotcotnaz, but Moran poses a problem, for there is no extant text with a character bearing this name. As is made clear further, he is an innkeeper, and it is very likely that Lewis—who probably wrote this essay in a Dorset camp far from London and his books—mixed up Moran with the Roland of "A Breton Innkeeper." And it is hard to believe that after "Bestre" and "A Breton Innkeeper" Lewis would have devoted one more sketch to an hôtelier.

[2] Lewis's analysis may be seen as anticipating E. M. Forster's definition of "flat characters" in *Aspects of the Novel* (1927), with this difference that Lewis's "flats" are fascinating whereas Forster's cannot surprise the reader.

[3] *The Little Review* numbered this section as "VI," the next ones being given as "VII" and "VIII." See note 2 page 154.

[4] An "Editor's note" by Ezra Pound gave: "Clarkson, a London theatrical costumer."

[5] Emile Bernard (1868-1941), a French artist and friend of the Post-Impressionists who later turned back to academicism.

A SOLDIER OF HUMOUR (1917)

There are numerous differences between the 1917 and 1927 texts, but these do not in the least affect the plot, since the early version was already a full-fledged story. Even the names of places and characters (with the exception, it is true, of Ker-Orr, first named Mr. Pine) are respected, which is rare with Lewis who, in Tarr, *for instance, went on modifying names till the final edition of 1951. First there are essential additions affecting the showman, Ker-Orr, who in 1927 is given an ironical family background of great significance for an understanding of The Wild Body and Lewis's development. Deletions affect the secondary characters of the American trio described at greater length in 1917. Secondly, Part I was split into two parts in 1927, and practically rewritten, though this only affected the style, with greater expressiveness, better arrangement of words and greater flexibility of dialogue—not to speak of the mere compulsion, so typical of Lewis, to alter for alteration's sake ("Cherokee" instead of "Mohican," for instance). On the contrary Part II (Part III in 1927) was only subjected to minor stylistic alterations. Did Lewis get bored with his rewriting? More probably, it is simply that the second half of the story, being much more dramatic and episodic, did not require the modifications which the static descriptions and analyses of the first half called for.*

PART I

Spain is an overflow of sombreness. "Africa commences at the Pyrenees." Spain is a check-board of Black and Goth, on which Primitive Gallic chivalry played its most brilliant games. At the gates of Spain the landscape gradually becomes historic with Roland. His fame dies as difficultly as the flourish of the cor de chasse. It lives like a superfine antelope in the gorges of the Pyrenees, becoming more and more ethereal and gentle, Charlemagne moves Knights and Queens beneath that tree; there is something eternal and Rembrantesque about his proceedings. A stormy and threatening tide of history meets you at the frontier.[1]

Several summers ago I was cast by Fate for a fierce and prolonged little comedy,—an essentially Spanish comedy. It appropriately began at Bayonne, where Spain not Africa begins.

I am a large blonde Clown, ever so vaguely reminiscent (in person) of William Blake, George Alexander, and some great American Boxer[2] whose name I forget. I have large strong teeth which I gnash and flash when I laugh, as though I were chewing the humorous morsel. But usually a look of settled and aggressive naïvety rests on my face. I know I am a barbarian, who, when Imperial Rome was rather like Berlin to-day, would have been paddling about in a coracle. My body is large, white and savage. But all the fierceness has become transformed into laughter. It still looks like [a] Visi-Gothic fighting machine, but is really a laughing machine. As I have remarked, when I laugh I gnash my teeth, which is another brutal survival and thing Laughter has taken over from War. Everywhere where formerly I would fly at throats, I howl with laughter!

A German remains in a foreign country for thirty years, speaks its language as well as his own, and assimilates its ideas. But he is the ideal spy of Press-Melodrama, because he remains faithful in thought to his Fatherland, and in his moments of greatest expansiveness with his adopted countrymen, is cold, more or less:—enough to remain a German. So I have never forgotten that I am really a neo-Teuton barbarian, I have clung coldly to this consciousness with an almost Latin good sense.[3]

I realise, similarly, the uncivilized nature of my laughter. It does not easily climb into the neat Japanese box, which is the "cosa salada" of the Spaniard, or French "esprit." It sprawls into everything. It has become my life.

All this said, I have often passed quite easily for a Frenchman, in spite of my Swedish fairness of complexion.

There is some Local genius or god of adventure haunting the soil of Spain, of an especially active and resourceful type. I have seen people that have personified him; for the people of a country, in their most successful products, always imitate their gods. You feel in Spain that it is safer to seek adventures than to avoid them. You have the feeling that should you refrain from charging the windmills, they are quite capable of charging you; in short, you come to wonder less at Don Quijote's eccentric behaviour. But the deity of this volcanic soil has become more or less civilized.—My analysis of myself would serve equally for him in this respect.—Your life is no longer one of the materials he asks for to supply you with constant amusement, as the conjuror asks for the gentleman's silk hat. Not your life,—but a rib or two, your comfort or a five pound note are all he needs. With these things he juggles and conjures from morning till night, keeping you perpetually amused and on the qui vive.

It might have been a friend: but as it happened it was the most implacable enemy I have ever had that Providence provided me with as her agent representative for this journey.

The comedy I took part in was a Spanish one, then, at once piquant and elemental. But a Frenchman filled the principle rôle. When I add that this Frenchman was convinced the greater part of the time that he was taking part in a tragedy, and was perpetually on the point of transplanting my adventure bodily into that other category: and that although his actions drew their vehemence from the virgin source of a racial hatred, yet it was not as a Frenchman or a Spaniard that he acted,—then you will conceive what extremely complex and unmanageable forces were about to be set in motion for my edification.

What I have said about my barbarism and my laughter is a key to a certain figure. By these antecedents and modifications of a modern life such another extravagant warrior as Don Quijote is produced, existing in a vortex of strenuous and burlesque encounters. Mystical and humourous, astonished at everything at bottom (the settled naïvety I have described) he is entitled to worship and deride, to pursue like a riotous moth the comic and unconscious luminary he discovers; to make war on it, and cherish it, like a lover.

It was about ten o'clock at night when I reached Bayonne. I had started from Paris the evening before.

In the market square near the station I was confronted with several caravansaries shamelessly painted in crude intimate colours; brilliantly shining electric lights of peculiar hard, livid disreputable tint illumined each floor of each frail structure; eyes of brightly frigid invitation. Art of Vice, cheap ice-cream, cheaply ornamented ice wafers on a fête night, were things they suggested. "Fonda del Universo," "Fonda del Mundo": Universal Inn, and the Inn of the World, two of them were called. I had not sufficient energy left to resist these buildings. They all looked the same, but to keep up a show of will and discrimination I chose the second, not the first. I advanced along a narrow passage-way and found myself suddenly in the heart of the Fonda del Mundo. On my left lay the dining-room, in which sat two travellers. I was standing in the kitchen,—a large courtyard round which the rest of the hotel and a house or two at the back were built. But it had a glass roof on a level with the house proper.

About half a dozen stoves with sinks, each managed by a separate crew of grimy workers, formed a semicircle. One had the impression of hands being as cheap, and every bit as dirty as dirt. You felt that the lowest scullery maid could afford a servant to do the roughest of her work, and this girl in turn another. The abundance of the South seemed manifesting in this way, as well, in a richness and prodigality of beings, of a kind with its profusion of fruits and wine. Instead of buying a wheelbarrow would not one attach a man to one's business?—instead of hiring a removing van engage a gang of carriers? In every way that man could replace the implement he would here replace it. An air of leisurely but continual activity pervaded this precinct, extensive cooking going on. I discovered later that this was a preparation for the morrow, a market day. But to enter at ten in the evening this large and apparently empty building, as far as customers went, and find a methodically busy population in its midst, cooking a nameless Feast, was naturally impressive. A broad staircase was the only avenue in this house to the sleeping apartments; a shining cut glass door beneath it seemed the direction I ought to take when I should have made up my mind to advance. This door, the stairs, the bread given you at the table d'hôte all had the same new, unsubstantial appearance.

I stood waiting, my rug on my arm, before penetrating further into this enigmatical world of the "Fonda del Mundo." Then the hostess appeared through the glass door—a very stout woman in a dress like a dressing gown. She had the air of sinking into herself as if into a hot enervating bath, and the sleepy leaden intensity of expression belonging to many Spaniards. Her face was so still and impassible that the ready and apt answers coming to one's questions were startling. The air of dull resentment meant nothing except that I was indifferent to her. Had I not been so this habitual expression would not have been allowed to remain, a cold expressionlessness would have replaced it.

She turned to the busy scene at our right and called out with guttural incisiveness several orders in Spanish, all having some bearing on my fate; some connected with my supper, the others with further phases of my sojourn in her house. They fell in the crowd of leisurely workers without causing a ripple. But they gradually reached their destination.

First I noticed a significant stir and a dull flare rose in the murky atmosphere, as though one of the lids of a stove had been slid back preparatory to some act of increased culinary activity. Then elsewhere a slim, handsome young witch left her cauldron and passed me, going into the dining-room. I followed her and the hostess went back through the cut glass door.

Supper began. The wine may have been Condy's Fluid. It resembled it, but in that case it had been many years in stock. I made short work of the bacalao (cod,—that nightmare to Spaniards of the Atlantic seabord). The stew that followed had no terrors for me, a spectator would have thought. But the enthusiastic onlooker at this juncture would have seen me suddenly become inert and brooding, would have seen my knife fall from my nerveless right hand, my fork be no longer grasped in my left. I was vanquished. My brilliant start had been a vain flourish. The insolent display of sweets and dessert lay unchallenged before me. Noticing my sudden desistance, my idle and defenceless air, the only other ocupant, now, of the salle à manger, and my neighbor, addressed me. He evidently took me for a Frenchman. I could maintain that rôle, if need be.

"Il fait beau ce soir!" he said dogmatically and loudly, staring blankly at me.

"Mais non, voyons! It's by no means a fine night! It's cold and damp, and, what's more, it's going to rain."

I cannot say why I contradicted him in this fashion. Perhaps the insolent and mystical gaze of drollery his appearance generally flung down was the cause.

My neighbor took my response quite stolidly however, and probably this initial rudeness of mine would have had no effect whatever on him, had not a revelation made shortly afterwards at once changed our relative positions, and caused him to look on me with different eyes. He then went back, remembered this first incivility of mine, and took it, retrospectively, in a different spirit to that shown contemporaneously. For he now merely inquired,

"You have come far?"

"From Paris," I answered, gazing in consternation at a large piece of cheese, which was about to advance upon me at every moment, and finish what the cod, its sauce and the dreadful stew had begun.

The third occupant of the salle à manger had just retired to rest a few moments before this dialogue began after a prolonged and apparently drawn battle with the menu, for he looked by no means unscathed. He had been hard pressed by the sweets, that was evident. You felt that had not the coffee been the last item of the bill of fare, he would inevitably have succumbed. Honour was saved, however, and he hurried to bed head erect, but legs,—that part of his person farthest removed from the seat of his indomitable will,—in palpable disarray. As to the individual who had addressed me, he showed every sign of the extremest hardiness. He lay back in his chair, his hat on the back of his head, finishing a bottle of wine with bravado. His waistcoat was open, and this was the only thing about him that did not denote the most facile of victories. I considered this as equivalent to a rolling up of the sleeves: it was businesslike, it showed that he respected his enemy. Had his waistcoat remained buttoned down to the bottom, it would have been more in keeping with the rest of his fanfaronading manner. But after all, it may have been because of the hat.

His straw hat served rather as a heavy coffee-coloured nimbus,—such a nimbus as some Browningesque Florentine painter, the worst for drink, might have placed, rather rakishly and tilting forward, behind the head of a saint. Above this veined and redly sunburnt forhead gushed a lot of dry black hair. His face had the vexed, wolfish look often seen in the Midi. It was full of character, but had no breadth of touch: it had been niggled at and worked all over, at once minutely and loosely, by a hundred little blows and chisselling of fretful passion. His beard did not sprout with any shape or symmetry. Yet in an odd and baffling way there was a breadth, a look of possible largeness somewhere. You were forced at length to attribute it to just that *blankness* of expression I have just mentioned. This sort of blank intensity spoke of a real possibility of real passion, of the sublime. (It was this sublime quality that I was about to waken, and was going to have an excellent opportunity of studying).

He was dressed with a sombre floridity. In his dark grey-purple suit with thin crimson lines, in his dark red hat band, in his rich blue tie, in his stormily flowered waistcoat, one had a feeling that his taste for the most florid of colouring had everywhere struggled to assert itself, and everywhere been overcome. But by what? That was one of this man's secrets, and one of the things that made him a puzzling person. Again, the cut of his clothes, in a kind of awkward amplitude, seemed out of place.

He was not a commercial traveller. I was sure of this. For me, he issued from a void. I rejected in turn his claim, on the strength of his appearance, to be a small vineyard owner, a man in the automobile business and a "rentier." He was part of the mystery of this extraordinary hotel; his solitude, his ungregarious appearance, his aplomb before that menu!

In the meantime his little sunken eyes were fixed on me imperturbably, blankly.

"I was in Paris last week:" he suddenly announced. "I don't like Paris. Why should I?" I thought he was becoming rather aggressive, taking me for a Parisian. "They think they are up-to-date. Go and get a parcel sent you from abroad, and go and try and get it at the Station Depôt. See how many hours you will pass there trotting from one little bureau clerk to another before they give it to you. Then go to a café and ask for a drink! The waiter will upset half of it over your legs! Are you Parisian?" He asked this in the same tone, the blankness slightly deepening.

"No, I'm English," I answered.

He looked at me steadfastly. This evidently at first seemed to him untrue; then he suddenly appeared to accept it implicitly.

After a few minutes of silence, he addressed me, to my surprise, in my own language, but with every evidence that it had crossed the Atlantic at least once since it had been in his possession, and that he had not inherited it but acquired it with the sweat of his brow.

"Oh! you're English? It's fine day!"

Now, we are going to begin all over again. And we are going to start, as before, with the weather. But I did not contradict him this time. My opinion of the weather had in no way changed. I disliked that particular sort as much as ever. But for some reason I withdrew from my former attitude of uncompromising truth, and agreed.

"Yes," I said.

Our eyes met, doubtfully. He had not forgotten my late incivility, and I remembered it at the same time. He was silent again, evidently turning over dully in his mind the signification of this change on my part; and, before my present weak withdrawal, feeling a still stronger resentment in remembering my wounding obstinacy of five minutes before. Yes, this was now taking effect.

And then, almost threateningly, he continued,—heavily, pointedly, steadily, as though to see if there were a spark of resistance anywhere left in me, that would spit up under his trampling words.

"I guess eets darn fi' weather, and goin' to laast. A friend of mine, who ees skeeper, sailing for Bilbao this afternoon, said that mighty little sea was out zere, and all fine weather for his run. A skipper ought'know, I guess, ought'n he? Zey know sight more about zee weader than most. I guess zat's deir trade,—a'nt I right?"

A personal emotion was rapidly gaining him. And it seemed that speaking the tongue of New York helped its increase considerably. All his strange blankness and impersonality had gone, or rather it had *woken up,* if one may so describe this strange phenomenon. He now looked at me with awakened eyes, coldly, judicially, fixedly. But he considered he had crushed me enough, and began talking about Paris,—as he had done before in French.

He spoke English incorrectly, but, like many foreigners, the one thing linguistically he had brought away from the United States intact was an American accent of the most startling and uncompromising perfection. Whatever word or phrase he knew, in however mutilated a form, had this stamp of colloquialism and air of being the real thing. He spoke English with a careless impudence at which I was not surprised; but I had the sensation besides that the vague but powerful consciousness of the authentic nature of his accent, made him still more insolently heedless of the faults of his speech. His was evidently to the full the American, or Anglo-Saxon American, state of mind: a colossal disdain for everything that does not possess in one way or another an American accent. It seemed almost that my English, grammatically regular though it was, lacking the American accent was but a poor vehicle for thought compared with his most blundering sentence.

Before going further I must make quite clear that I have no more prejudice against the American way of accenting English than I have against the Irish or English. The Irish brogue is prettier than English (despite Irishmen's alternate disparagement and exploiting of it); and American possesses an indolent vigour and dryness which is a most cunning arm when it snarls out ironies. The American accent is the language of Mark Twain, and is the tongue, at once naive and cynical, of a thousand inimitable humourists.

I remember at the three or four schools I succesively went to, that at all a curious and significant belief prevailed. I always understood, up to my seventeenth year, that an Englishman could reckon, without undue vanity and as a matter of scientific fact, on overcoming in battle seven Frenchman. That he need feel by no means uneasy if threatened by twenty, or fifty, for that matter; but that the sort of official and universally acknowledged standard was one Englishman corresponding to seven Frenchmen. I remember also a conversation I had in Paris with a young Englishman. We were both nineteen, and very tall and lanky. He was a slow, awkward and rather timid youth. We were discussing nocturnal aggressions, and he said quietly that these Paris roughs "wouldn't ever tackle an Englishman." "They knew better."—This same young man also was very conscious of the difference of his walk from that of Frenchmen. He referred to it quite seriously as "the walk of the conquering race." I could never see any difference myself, except that his legs were disproportionately long, and he seemed a rather incompetent pedestrian.

Now I have met nowhere else in Europe with this excellent illusion of national superiority. A Frenchman knows he will have to use his utmost cunning to circumvent and eventually exterminate or maim one single German. The German reflects he will have to eat a great deal of Leberwurst and Sauerkraut to be able to crush with his superior weight the nimble Frenchman. "The God's Own Country" attitude of some Americans is more Anglo-Saxon than their blood. I can now proceed without fear of misinterpretation on the part of my American friends.

I had before this met Americans from Odessa, Buda Pest and Pekin. Almost always the air of the United States, which they breathed for a month or two, had proved too much for them. They were never any good for anything afterwards, became wastrels in their own countries,—poets and dreamers.

This man at once resembled and was different from them. The cause of this difference became apparent when he informed me that he was a United States citizen. I believed him unreservedly and on the spot. Some air of security in him that only such a ratification can give, convinced me.

He did not tell me at once. Between his commencing to speak in English and his announcing his citizenship came an indetermined neutral phase in our relations. In the same order as in our conversation in French, we progressed from the weather topic,—a delicate subject with us,—to Paris.

Our acquaintance had matured wonderfully quickly. I already felt instinctively that certain subjects of conversation were to be avoided; that certain shades of facial expression would cause suspicion, hatred or perplexity in his soul.—He, for his part, evidently with the intention of eschewing a subject fraught with dangers, did not once speak of England. It was as though England were a subject that no one could expect him to keep his temper about, and that if a man *did* indeed come from England he would naturally resent being reminded of it,—as though he might feel that the other was seeking to take an undue advantage of him. He was in fact indulgently pretending for the moment that I was an American.

"Guess you' goin' to Spain?" he said. "Waal, Americans are not like' very much in that country. That country, sir, is barb'rous; you *kant* believe how behind in everything that country's is! All you have to do is to *look* smart there to make money. No need to worry there. No, by gosh! Just sit round and ye'll do bett' dan zee durn dagos!"

The American citizenship wiped out the repulsive fact of his southern birth, otherwise he would have been almost a dago himself, being a Gascon.

"In Guadalquiver,—waal—kind of State-cap'tle, some manzanas or kind of shanties, see?—waal"—

I make these sentences of my neighbour's much more lucid than they were in reality. But he now plunged into this obscure swirl of words with a story to tell. The story was drowned in them, but I gathered it told of how, travelling in a motor car he could find no petrol anywhere in a town of some importance.

He was so interested in the telling of the story, that I became rather off my guard, and once or twice showed that I did not quite follow him, did not quite understand his English. He finished his story rather abruptly and there was a silence. It was after this silence that he divulged the fact of his American citizenship.

And now things took on a very gloomy aspect.

With the revelation of this mighty fact he seemed to consider it incumbent upon him to adopt an air of increased arrogance. He was now the representative of the United States. There was no more question of my being an American. All compromise, all courteous resolve to ignore painful facts, was past. Things must stand out in their true colours, and men too.

As a result of this heightened attitude, he appeared to doubt the sincerity or exactitude of everything I said. His beard bristled round his drawling mouth, his thumbs sought his arm-pits, his feet stood up erect and aggressive on his heels, at the delicate angle of a drawing by Pascin. An insidious attempt on my part to induct the conversation back into French, unhappily detected, caused in him a sombre indignation. I was curious to see the change that would occur in my companion on feeling on his lips once more and in his throat, the humbler tongue. The treachery of my intention gradually dawned upon him. He seemed taken aback, was silent and very quiet for a few minutes, as though stunned. The subtleties, the Ironies, to which he was exposed!

"Oui, c'est vrai", I went on, with frowning, serious air, over palpably absorbed in the subject we were discussing, and overlooking the fact that I had changed to French: "les Espagnols ont du chic à se chausser. D'ailleurs, c'est tout ce qu'ils savent, en fait de toilette. C'est les Américains surtout qui savent s'habiller!"

His eyes at this became terrible. He saw through it all. And now I was *flattering*, was flattering Americans, and above all, praising their way of dressing. The guile of this was too much for him. He burst out vehemently, almost wildly, in the language of his adopted land:—

"Yes, *sirr* and that's more'n see durn English do!"

He was a typical product of the French midi. But, no doubt, in his perfect Americanism—and at this ticklish moment, his impeccable accent threatened by an unscrupulous foe, who was attempting to stifle it temporarily—a definite analogy arose in his mind. The red-skin and his wiles, the heriditary and cunning foe of the American citizen, no doubt came vividly to his mind and he recognized, in its evoking this image, the dastardliness of my attack. Yes, wiles of that familiar sort were being used against him, Sioux-like, Blackfeet-like manœuvres. He must meet them as the American citizen had always met them. He had at length overcome the Sioux and Mohican. He turned on me a look as though I had been unmasked, and his accent became more accentuated, rasping and arrogant. I might say that his accent became venomous. All the elemental movements of his soul were always acutely manifest in his American accent, the principal vessel, as it were, of his vitality.

After another significant pause he brusquely chose a subject of conversation that he was convinced we could not agree upon. He took a long draught of the powerful fluid served to each diner. I disagreed with him at first out of politeness. But as he seemed resolved to work himself up slowly into a national passion, I changed round and agreed with him. He glared at me for a moment. He felt at bay before this dreadful subtlety of mine. Then he warily changed his position in the argument, taking up the point of view he had begun by attacking.

We changed about alternately for a little. At one time, in taking my new stand, and asserting something, either I had changed too quickly, or he had not quite quickly enough. At all events, when he began speaking, he found himself *agreeing* with me. This was a terrible moment. It was very close quarters. I felt as one does at a show, standing on the same chair with some uncertain tempered person. I was compelled rapidly to disagree with him and just saved the situation. A moment more, and we should have fallen on each other, or rather, he on me.

He buried his face once more in the sinister potion in front of him, and consumed the last vestiges of the fearful aliment at his elbow. I felt the situation had become perfectly blood-curdling.

We had not been once interrupted during these happenings. A dark man, a Spaniard, I thought, had passed into the kitchen along the passage. The sound of bustle came to us uninterruptedly from within.

He now with a snarling drawl engaged in a new discussion on another and still more delicate subject. I renewed my tactics, he his.

Subject after subject was chosen, and his volte-face, his change of attitude in the argument, became less and less leisurely and more and more precipitate, until at length whatever I said he said the opposite brutally and at once. But still my cunning was too great for him. At last, pushing his chair back with a frightful grating sound, and thrusting both his hands in his pockets—at this supreme moment the sort of large blank look came back to his face again—he said slowly:—

"Waal, zat may be so—you say so—waal! But what say you to England, ha! England!—England! England!"

At last it had come! He repeated "England" as though that word in itself were a question—unanswerable question. "England" was a question that a man could only ask when very, very exasperated. But it was a thing hanging over every Englishman, the possibility of having this question put to him. He might at any moment be silenced with it.

"England! ha! England! England!" he repeated as though hypnotised by this word; as though pressing me harder and harder and finally "chawing me up" with the mere utterance of it.

"Why, mon vieux!" I said suddenly, getting up, "how about the South of France, for that matter—the South of France, the South of France!"

If I had said "America" he would have responded at once, no doubt. But "the south of France"! A look of unutterable vagueness came into his face. The south of France! This was at once without meaning, dispiriting, humiliating, paralysing, a cold douche, a stab in the back, an unfair blow. I seemed to have drawn a chilly pall suddenly over the whole of his mind.

I had fully expected to be forced to fight my way out of the salle-à-manger, and was wondering whether his pugilistic methods would be those of

Alabama or Toulouse—whether he would skip round me with his fists working like piston rods; or whether he would plunge his head in the pit of my stomach, kick me on the chin and follow up with the "coup de la fourchette", which consists in doubling up one's fist, but allowing the index and little finger to protrude, so that they may enter the eyes on either side of the bridge of the nose.

But he was quite incapable of dealing adequately with this new situation. As I made for the door, he sat first quite still. Then, slowly, slightly writhing on his chair, his face half turned after me. The fact of my leaving the room seemed to find him still more unprepared, to dumfound him even more, than my answer to his final apostrophe. It never had occurred to him apparently, that I should perhaps get up and leave the room!—Sounds came from him, words too—hybrid syllables lost on the borderland between French and English, which appeared to signify protest, pure astonishment, alarmed question. I got safely out of the kitchen.

In the act of lighting my candle I heard a nasal roar behind me. I mounted the stairs three steps at a time, with the hotel boy at my heels, and, ushered into my room, hastily locked and bolted the door.

I knew perfectly well that I had not treated the little Frenchman at all well. To drag in France in that way—"the south of France",—was brutalising to this tender flower of the Prairies of the West. But to leave the room at that point of our conversation, at that point in our relationship, was still more unpardonable.

My room was at the back. The window looked on to the kitchen; it was just over the stairs leading to the bedrooms. From that naturally unfresh and depressing port-hole above the cauldrons, I could observe my opponent in the murky half court, half kitchen, beneath. He looked very different, inspected from this height and distance. I had not till then seen him on his feet. His Yankee clothes, evidently cut beneath his direction by a Gascon tailor, made him look as broad as he was long.

His violently animated leanness imparted a precarious and toppling appearance to his architecture. He was performing a war-dance in this soft national armour just at present beneath the sodden eyes of the Proprietress. It had shuffling cake-walk elements, and cacophonic gesticulations of the Gaul. It did not seem the same man I had been talking to before. He evidently, in this enchanted hotel, possessed a variety of incarnations. Or it was as though somebody else had leapt into his clothes, which hardly fitted the newcomer, and was carrying on his quarrel. The original and more imposing man had disappeared, and this little fellow had taken up his disorganised and overwrought life at that precise moment and place, at exactly the same pitch of passion, only with fresher nerves, and identically the same racial sentiments as the man he had succeeded.

He was talking to the proprietress in Spanish—much more correct than his English. She listened with her leaden eyes crawling swiftly over his person, with an air of angrily and lazily making an inventory. In his fiery attack on the adamantine depths of langour behind which her spirit lived, he would occasionally turn and appeal to one of the nearest of the servants, as though seeking corroboration of something. What was he accusing me of? I muttered rapid prayers to the effect that that mock-tropical reserve might prove unassailable. For I might otherwise be cast bodily out of the Fonda del Mundo, and in my present worn-out state, and with a dyspeptic storm brewing in this first contact with primitive food, have to seek another and distant roof. I knew that I was the object of his discourse. What effectively could be said about me on so short an acquaintance? He would, though, certainly affirm that I was an extremely suspicious character, unscrupulous, resourceful, slippery, diabolically cool; such a person as no respectable hotel would consent to harbour, or if it did, would do so at its peril. Then he might have special influence with the Proprietress, be a regular customer and old friend. He might only be saying, "I object to that person; I cannot explain to you how I object to that person! I have never objected to anybody to the same fearful degree. All my organs boil. My kidneys are almost cooked. I cannot explain to you how that Island organism tears my members this way and that. Out with this abomination. Oh! out with it before I die at your feet from over-heating and phlegm!!!"

This way of putting it, the personal way, might be more effective. I went to bed with a feeling of extreme insecurity. I thought that, if nothing else happened, he might set fire to the hotel. I slept quite soundly in spite of the dangers obviously infesting this establishment for me.

In the morning breakfast passed off without incident. I concluded that the complete American was part of the night-time aspect of the Fonda del Mundo and had no part in its more normal day-life.

The square was full of peasants, the men wearing dark blouse and beret connected with Pelota. Several groups were sitting near me in the salle à manger. A complicated arrangement of chairs and tables, like man traps in their intricate convolutions, lay outside the hotel, extending a little distance into the square. From time to time one or more peasants would appear to become stuck, get somehow caught, in these iron contrivances. They would then, with becoming fatalism, seeing they could not escape, sit down and call for a drink. Such was the impression at least that their gauche and embarrassed movements in choosing a seat gave one.

A train would shortly leave for the frontier. I bade farewell to the Patrona, and asked her if she could recommend me a hotel in Burgos or in Pontaisandra. When I mentioned Pontaisandra, she said at once—"You are going to Pontaisandra?" She turned with a sluggish ghost of a smile to a loitering servant and then said, "Yes, you can go to the Burgalésa at Pontaisandra. That is a good hotel."

I had told her the night before that my destination was Pontaisandra, and she had looked at me steadfastly and resentfully, as though I had said that my destination was Heaven, and that I intended to occupy the seat reserved for her.

I regarded the episode of the supper room, the night before, as an emanation of that place. The Fonda del Mundo was a very mysterious hotel, despite its more usual aspect in the day time. I imagined it inhabited by solitary and hallucinated beings, like my friend of the night before— or such as I myself might have become. The large kitchen staff was occupied far into the night in preparing a strange and excessive table d'hôte. For the explanation of this afforded me in the morning by the sight of the crowding peasants did not efface my impression of midnight. The dreams caused by its lunches, the visions conjured up by its suppers, haunted the place.

This is the spirit in which I remember my over-night affair.

When I eventually started for the frontier, hoping by the inhalation of a Picadura to dispose my tongue to the coining of fair Spanish, I did not realise that the American adventure was the progenitor of other adventures; nor that the dreams of the Fonda del Mundo were to go with me into the heart of Spain.

PART II

Burgos was to break my journey. But San Sebastián and León seemed eventually better halting places.

This four days journeying was an interlude—an entr'acte filled with appropriate music; the lugubrious and splendid landscapes of Castile, the extremely selfconscious pedantic and independent spirit of its inhabitants, met with en route. Fate was marking time, merely. On with the second day's journey I changed trains and dined at Venta de Baños, the junction for the line that branches off in the direction of Palencia, León and the Gallician country.

The Spanish people, while travelling, have a marked preference for the next compartment to that that they have chosen. No sooner has the train started than one after another, heads, arms and shoulders appear above the wooden partition, and you occasionally have the entire human contents of the neighbouring compartment gazing gloomily into your own. In the case of some theatrical savage of the Sierras, who rears a dishevelled head before you in a pose of fierce abandon and hangs there smoking, you know that it may be some instinctive pride that prevents him from remaining in an undignified position huddled in a narrow carriage. In other cases it is probably a naive conviction that the occupants of other compartments are likely to be more interesting.

The whole way from Venta de Baños to Palencia the carriage was dense with people. Crowds of peasants poured into the train, loaded with their heavy vivid horse-rugs, gaudy bundles and baskets; which profusion of mere matter, combined with their exuberance, made the carriage appear positively to swarm with human life. They would crowd in at one little station and out at another a short way long the line, where they were met by hordes of their relations awaiting them. They would rush or swing out of the door, charged with their goods and accoutrements and catch the nearest man or woman of their blood in their arms with a turbulence that outdid Northerners' most vehement occasions. The waiting group became at least twice as vital as ordinary human beings, on the arrival of the train, as though so much more blood had poured into their veins. Gradually we got beyond the sphere of this Fiesta and in the small hours of the morning arrived at León.

Next day came the final stage of the journey to the Atlantic seaboard. We arrived within sight of the town that evening just as the sun was setting. With its houses of green, rose and white, in general effect rather subdued and faded, it was like some Oriental town in the nerveless tempera tints of a fresco. Its bay, thirty miles long reached out to the sea.

On the train drawing up in the Central station, furious contingents furnished by every little raggamuffin café as well as every stately hotel in the town were hurled against us. I had mislaid the address given me at Bayonne. I wished to find a hotel of medium luxury half-way between the ghastly bouge[1] and the princely hostelry. This was a method with me. The different hotel attendants called hotly out their prices at me. I selected one who named a sum for board and lodging that only the frenzy of competition could have fathered, I thought. Also the name of this hotel was, it seemed to me, the one the Patrona at Bayonne had mentioned. I had not then learnt to connect Burgalésa with Burgos. With this man I took a cab and was left seated in it at the door of the station while he went after the heavy luggage. Now one by one the hotel emissaries came up; queer contrast between their fury of a few minutes before and their present listless calm. Putting themselves civilly at my disposition, they thrust forward matter-of-factly the card of their establishment, adding that they were sure that I would find out my mistake.

I now felt in a vague manner a tightening of the machinery of Fate—a certain uneasiness and strangeness in the march and succession of facts and impressions, like the trembling of a motor bus about to start again. The interlude was over.

---

1 Slum, hovel.

After a long delay the hotel man returned and we started. The method I have spoken of consisted in a realization of the following facts:—when your means are very restricted, it is best to go to a cheap hotel and pay a few pesetas more a day for "extras". This is more satisfactory than affecting second class "houses." You can never be sure in any hotel especially in Spain, of the menu not containing every dish you most loathe. But there is something private, almost home-made, about Extras. You always feel that a single individual has bent over the extra and carefully cooked it and that it has not been bought in too wholesale a manner. I wished to live on Extras—a privileged existence.

The cabman and hotel man were discussing some local event. But we penetrated farther and farther into a dismal and shabby quarter of the town. I began to have misgivings. I asked the representative of the Burgalésa if he were sure that his house was a clean handsome and comfortable house. He dismissed my doubtful glance with a gesture full of assurance. "It's a splendid place! You wait and see: we shall be there directly," he added.

We suddenly emerged in a broad and imposing street, on one side of which was a public garden: "El Paseo", I found out afterwards, the Town-Promenade. Gazing idly at a vast palatial white building with an hotel omnibus drawn up before it, to my astonishment I found our driver also stopping at its door. A few minutes later, in a state of stupefaction, I got out and entered this palace, noticing "Burgalésa" on the board of the omnibus. I followed dumbly, having glimpses in passing of a superbly arrayed table with serviettes that were each a work of art that a diner would soon haughtily pull to pieces to wipe his moustache on—tables groaning beneath salvers full of fruit and other delicacies. Then came a long hall, darkly panelled at the end of which I could see several white-capped men shouting fiercely and clashing knives, women answering shrilly and rattling dishes—a kitchen; the most diabolically noisy and nauseous I had ever approached. We went straight on towards it. Were we going through it? At the very threshold we stopped, and opening a panel-like door in the wall, the porter disappeared with my portmanteau, appeared again without my portmanteau, and hurried away. At this moment my eye caught something else, a door ajar on the other side of the passage, and a heavy wooden, clothless table, with several squares of bread on it, and a fork or two. In Spain there is a sort of bread for the rich, and a horrible looking juiceless papery bread for the humble. The bread on that table was of the latter category.

Suddenly the truth flashed upon me. With a theatrical gesture I dashed open again the panel and passed into the pitchy gloom within. I struck a match. It was a cupboard, quite windowless, with just enough room for a little bed; I was standing on my luggage. No doubt in the room across the passage I should be given some cod soup, permanganate of potash and artificial bread. Then, extremely tired after my journey, I should crawl into my kennel, the pandemonium of the kitchen at my ear for several hours.

In the central hall I found the smiling proprietor. He seemed to regard his boarders generally as a mild joke, and those who slept in the cupboard near the kitchen a particularly good but rather low one. I informed him that I would pay the regular sum for a day's board and lodging and said I must have another room. A valet accepted the responsibility of seeing I was given a bedroom, and the landlord walked slowly away, his iron-grey side whiskers, with their traditional air of respectability, giving a disguised look to his rascally face. I was transferred from one cupboard to another. Or rather, I had exchanged a cupboard for a wardrobe—reduced to just half its size by a thick layer of skirts and cloaks, twenty deep, that protruded from all four walls. But still the little open space left in the centre would ensure me a square foot to wash and dress in, with a quite distinct square foot or two for sleep. And it was upstairs.

A quarter of an hour later, wandering along a dark passage on my way back to the central hall, a door opened in a very violent and living way and a short rectangular figure, the size of a big square trunk, issued forth, just in front of me. I recognized this figure fragmentarily—first, with a cold shudder, I recognized an excrescence of hair: then with a jump I recognized a hat held in its hand; then, with a shrinking, I realized that I had seen those flat pseudo-American shoulders before. With a tidal wave of surging emotion, I then recognized the whole man.

It was the implaccable figure of the Fonda del Mundo.

He moved along with wary rigidity ahead, showing no reciprocal sign of recognition. He turned corners with difficulty, with a sort of rapid lurch and seemed to get stuck on the stairs just as a large American trunk would, borne by a sweating porter. At last he safely reached the hall. I was a yard or two behind him. He stopped to light a cigar, still taking up an unconscionable amount of space. I manœuvred round him, and gained one of the doors of the salle à manger. But as I came within his range of vision, I also became aware that my presence in the house was not a surprise to this sandwich-man of Western citizenship.[4] His eye fastened on me, with ruthless bloodshot indignation, a crystallised eye blast of the Bayonne episode. I had distinctly the impression of being face to face with a ghost, he was so dead and inactive. And in all my subsequent dealings with him, this feeling of having to deal with a ghost, although a particulary mischievous one, persisted. If before, my anger at the trick that had been played on me had dictated a speedy change of lodging, now my anxiety to quit this roof had, naturally, a tremendous incentive. After dinner, I went forth boldly in search of the wonderful American enemy. Surely I had been condemned, in some indirect way, by him, to the cupboard beside the kitchen. No dungeon could have been worse. Had I then known, as I learnt later, that he was the owner of this hotel, the mediaeval analogy would have been still more complete. He now had me in his castle.

I found him, in sinister conjunction with the Proprietor or Manager as I suppose he was, in the lobby of the hotel. He turned slightly away as I came up to him, with a sulky indifference due to self-restraint. Evidently the time for action was not ripe. There was no pretence of not recognising me. As though our conversation in the Fonda del Mundo had taken place a half an hour before, we acknowledged in no way a consciousness of the lapse of time, only of the shifted scene.

"Well, colonel," I said, adopting an allocution of the United States, "taking the air?"

He went on smoking.

"This is a nice little town."

"I'm glad you like it," he replied in French, as though I was not worthy even to *hear* his American accent, and that, if any communication was to be held with me, French must serve.

"I shall make a stay of some weeks here", I said with indulgent defiance.

"Oui?"

"But not in this Hotel."

He got up with something of his Bayonne look about him.

"No, I shouldn't. You might not find it a very comfortable hotel."

He walked away hurriedly, as a powder magazine might walk away from a fuse, if it did not, for some reason, want to blow up for the moment.

The upstairs and less dreadful dungeon with its layers of clothes, would have been an admirable place for a murder.

Not a sound would have penetrated its woolen masses and thick Spanish walls. But the next morning I was still alive when I woke up. I set out after breakfast to look for new quarters. My practised eye had soon measured the inconsistencies of most of the pensions of the town. But a place in the Calle Real suited me all right and I decided to stop there for the time.

This room again was a cupboard. But it was a human cupboard and not a clothes cupboard. It was one of four tributaries of the dining-room. My bedroom door was just beside my place at table—the entire animal life being conducted over an area not exceeding fifteen compact square feet.

The extracting of my baggage from the Burgalésa was easy enough, except that the rogue of a proprietor charged a heavy toll, sunk somewhere in the complications of the bill. As at Bayonne, there was no sign of the enemy in the morning. But I was not so sure this time that I had seen the last of him.

That evening I came amongst my new fellow-pensionnaires for the first time. This place had recommended itself to me partly because the boarders would probably speak good Spanish. They were mostly Castilians. My presence caused no stir whatever. Just as a stone dropped in a small pond which has long been untouched and has a good thick coat of mildew, slips dully to the bottom, cutting a clean little hole on the surface slime, so I took my place at the bottom of the table. But as the pond will send up its personal odour at this intrusion, so these people revealed something of themselves in the first few minutes, in an illusive and immobile way. They must all have lived in that pension together for an inconceivable length of time. My neighbour however promised to be a little El Dorado of Spanish; a small mine of gossip, grammatical rules and willingness to impart his native riches. I struck a deep shaft of friendship into him at once and began work without delay. He yielded in the first three days a considerable quantity of pure ore—coming from Madrid, this ore was at least 30 carat thoroughly thetaed and Castilian. What I gave him in exchange was insignificant. I taught him nothing. He knew several phrases in French and English, such as, "if you please" and "fine day"; I merely confirmed him in these. Every day he would hesitatingly say them over and I would assent "quite right" and "very well pronounced", and then turn to extracting his natural riches from him for the next hour or two. He was a tall bearded man, head of the orchestra of the principal café in the town. Two large cuffs lay on either side of his plate during meals, the size of serviettes, and out of them his hands emerged without in any way disturbing them and served him with his food as far as they could. But he had to remain with his mouth quite near his plate, for the cuffs would not move a hair's breadth. This somewhat annoyed me, as it muffled a little the steady flow of Spanish, and even was a cause of considerable waste. I tried to move the cuffs once or twice without success. Their ascendancy over him and their indolence were phenomenal.

But I was not content merely to extract Spanish from him. I wished to see it in use: to watch this stream of Spanish working the mill of general conversation, for instance. But, although willing enough himself, he had no chance in this Pension.

On the third day he invited me to come round to the café after dinner and hear him play. Our dinners overlapped, he leaving early. So, dinner over, I strolled round, alone.

The café Pelayo was the only really Parisian establishment in the town. It was the only one where the Madrileños and other Spaniards proper, resident in Pontaisandra, went regularly. I entered, peering round in a business-like way at its monotonously mirrored walls and gilded ceiling. This was a building that must contain prodigious quantities of Spanish every evening. Here I should virtually pass my examination.

In a lull of the music, my chef d'orchestre came over to me, and presented me to a large group of "consommateurs", friends of his. It was an easy matter, from that moment, to become acquainted with everybody in the café.

I did not approach Spaniards in general with any very romantic notion. Each man I met possessed equally an ancient and admirable tongue, however degenerate himself. He often appeared like some rotten tree, in which a swarm of words had nested. I, like a bee-cultivator, found it my business to transplant this vagrant swarm to a hive prepared—in which already two kindred swarms were billeted, as I have said. A language has its habits and idiosyncrasies just like a species of insect, as my first professor comfortably explained; its thousands of little words and parts of speech have to be carefully studied and manipulated. So I had my hands full.

When the café closed, I went home with Don Pedro, chef d'orchestre, to the Pension. Every evening, after dinner—and at lunch time as well—I repaired there. This lasted for three or four days. I now had plenty of opportunity of talking Spanish. I had momentarily forgotten my American enemy.

On the fifth evening, I entered the Café as usual, making towards my most useful and intelligent group. But then, with a sinking of the heart, I saw the rectangular form of my ubiquitous enemy, quartered with an air of demoniac permanence in their midst. A mechanic who finds a big lump of alien metal stuck in the very heart of his machinery—what simile shall I find for my dismay? To proceed somewhat with this image, as this unhappy engineer might dash to the cranks or organ stops of his machine, so I dashed to several of my formerly most willing listeners and talkers. I gave one a wrench and another a screw but I found that already the machine had become recalcitrant.

I need not enumerate the various stages of my defeat on that evening. It was more or less a passive and moral battle, rather than one with any evident show of the secretly bitter and desperate nature of the passions engaged. Of course, the inclusion of so many people unavoidably caused certain "brusqueries" here and there. The gradual cooling down of the whole room towards me, the dreadful icy currents of dislike that swept over the chain of little drinking groups—little eddies, or tiny whirlpools of conversation—from that mystical centre of hostility, that soul that recognised in me something icily antipodean too, no doubt; the immobile figure of America's newest and most mysterious child, apparently emitting these strong waves without effort, as naturally as a fountain: all this, with great vexation, I felt happening almost in the first moment. It almost seemed as though he had stayed away from this haunt of his foreseeing what would happen. He had waited until I was settled and there was something palpable to attack. His absence may have had some more natural cause.

What exactly he said about me I never discovered. As at Bayonne I saw the mouth working and I felt the effects only. No doubt it was the subtlest and most electric thing that could be found: brief, searching and annihilating.

Perhaps something seemingly crude—that I was a spy—may have recommended itself to his ingenuity. But I expect it was a meaningless or rather indefinite, blast of disapprobation that he blew upon me, an eerie and stinging wind of personal unexplained scorn and hatred. He evidently exercised a queer ascendancy in the café Pelayo, explained superficially by his commercial prestige, but due really to his extraordinary character—moulded by the sublime force of his illusion.

His inscrutable immobility, his unaccountable self-control (for such a person, and feeling as he did towards me) were of course the American or Anglo-Saxon coolness and coldness as reflected, or portrayed, in this violent human mirror.

I left the Café earlier than usual, before the chef d'orchestre. It was the following morning at lunch when I next saw him. He was embarrassed. His eyes wavered in my direction fascinated and inquisitive. He found it difficult to realise that his respect for me had to end and give place to another feeling.

"You know Monsieur de Valmore?" he asked.

"That little cur of a Frenchman, do you mean?"

I knew this description of my wonderful enemy was vulgar and inexact. But often with an ordinary intercourse it is necessary to be vulgar and inexact.

But this way of describing Monsieur de Valmore appeared to the chef d'orchestre so eccentric, apart from its profanity, that I lost at once in Don Pedro's sympathy.

He told me, however, all about him; vulgar details that did not touch on the real conditions of this life.

"He owns the Burgalésa and many houses in Pontaisandra. Ships, too. Es Americano" he added.

The American War[5] was still fresh in the memory of all Spaniards. But being obviously a Frenchman, they could allow themselves to admire in him all the commercial cunning and other qualities that their disgusted souls admired in the Yankee.

Vexations and hindrances of all sorts now made my stay in Pontaisandra useless and depressing. Don Pedro had generally almost finished when we came to dinner and I was forced to shut up the mine, so to speak. Nothing more was to be extracted, except uncomfortable monosyllables. The rest of the boarders remained morose and inaccessible. I went once more to the Café Palayo, but the waiters even seemed affected. The new café I chose yielded nothing but Gallego chatter, and the garçon was not gregarious.

There was little encouragement to try another pension and stay on in Pontaisandra. I made up my mind to go to Coruña. This would waste a bit of time. But there is more Gallego than Spanish spoken in Galicia, even in the cities. Too easily automatic a conquest as it may seem, Monsieur de Valmore had left me nothing but the Gallegos. I was not getting anything like the practice in Spanish necessary, and this necessity infected the whole air of the place. I began to get neurasthenic about the necessity of learning this tiresome language. I would go to Coruña in any case. On the following day, some hours before the time for the train, I paraded the line of streets towards the station, with the feeling that I was no longer there. The place seemed cooling down and growing strange already prematurely and looked very cheerless. But the miracle happened, coming with a gradual flowering of beauty. A more beautiful checkmate never occurred in any record of exquisite war-fare.

The terrible ethnological difference that existed between Monsieur de Valmore and myself up till that moment showed every sign of ending in a weird and revolting defeat for me. The "moment" I refer to was that in which I turned out of the High Street, into the short hilly avenue where the Post Office lay. I had some letters to post, communications adorned with every variety of expletives about Spanish, Pontaisandra and other opposite things.

On turning the corner I at once became aware of three anomalous figures walking just in front of me. They were all three of the proportion known in certain climes as "husky". When I say they were walking, I should describe their movements more accurately as *wading*—wading through the air, evidently towards the Post Office. Their carriage was slightly rolling like a ship under weigh. They occasionally bumped into each other, but did not seem to mind this. Yet no one would have mistaken these three young men—for such they were—for drunkards. But I daresay you will have already guessed. It would under other circumstances, have had no difficulty in entering my head. As it was, there seemed a certain impediment of consciousness when any phenomena of that sort was concerned. These three figures were three Americans!—This seems very simple, I know, very simple. This was abstract fact, however. This very simple and unabstruse fact trembled and lingered before completely entering into my consciousness. The extreme rapidity of my mind in another sense—in seeing all this fact, if verified, might signify to me—may have been responsible for that. Then one of them, on turning his head, displays the familiar features of Taffany, a Mississippi friend of mine. I simultaneously recognized Blauenfeld and Morton, the other two members of a trio. A real trio, like real twins, is rarer than one thinks. It is one of the strangest and closest of human relationships. This one was the remnant of a quartet. I had met it first in Paris.

In becoming, from any three Americans, three of my friends, they precipitated in a most startling way the vivid and full-blooded hope, optimism, reinstatement of vitality, contained in the possibilities wonderfully hidden in this meeting.

Two steps brought me up with them and my cordiality almost exceeded theirs.

"Why, if that doesn't *beat* everything! How did you get here?" shouted Taffany.

"Been here long? How do you like it? What do you think of the town?" pressed Blauenfeld.

"Where are you staying? Hve you struck a good Hotel?" demanded Morton.

Optimism, consciousness of power (no wonder, I thought) surged out of them. Ah, the kindness! the *overwhelming* kindness. I bathed voluptuously in this American greeting—this real American greeting. Nothing naturalised about *that*. At the same time I felt almost an awe at the thought of my friends' dangerous nationality. These good fellows I knew and liked so well seemed for the moment to have some intermixture of the strangeness of Monsieur de Valmore.

However, I measured with enthusiasm their egregious breadth of shoulder, the exorbitance of their "pants." They could not be *too* American, or American enough, for me. Had they appeared in a star and stripe swallow tail suit, like the cartoons of Uncle Sam, I should not have been satisfied.

I felt rather like some Eastern potentate who, having been continually defeated in battle by a neighbour because of the presence in the latter's army of half a dozen elephants, suddenly becomes possessed of a couple of dozen himself. The amount of Americanism at my disposal now was overwhelming. Talk of super-Dreadnoughts! But there is no such thing as a super-American. It can't be done. It is one thing that can't be supered.

Or I felt like some chemist who gets a temporary monopoly of a rare and potent chemical substance. The amount of pure unadulterated American stuff in my possession at present would neutralize the Americanism in Monsieur de Valmore in a brace of shakes, and leave nothing but a scraggy little Gascon.

I must have behaved rather oddly to my friends. As a starving man, unexpectedly presented with a shilling, might squeeze it tightly in his fist and run along, for fear of its melting or escaping in some way, till he gets to the nearest cook shop, so I cherished my three Americans. I was inclined to shelter them as though they were fragile, to see they didn't get run over, or expose themselves to the sun. Each transatlantic quaintness of speech or gesture I received with a positive ovation.

All thoughts of Coruña disappeared. The letters remained unposted.

First of all I took my trio into a little café near the Post Office, and told them at once what was expected of them.

"There's one of the 'boys' here," I said.

"Oh? An American?" Morton asked seriously.

"Well, he deserves to be. But he began too late in life, I think. He hails from the South of France and Americanism came to him as a revelation when youth had already passed. He repented tardily but sincerely of his misguided early nationality. But his years spent as a Frenchman have left their mark. In the meantime, he won't leave Englishmen alone. He persecutes them, apparently, wherever he finds them."

"He mustn't do that!" Taffany said with resolution.

"Why, no, I guess he mustn't," said Blauenfeld.

"I knew you'd say that," I continued. "It's a rank abuse of authority and I was sure would be regretted at headquarters. Now if you could only be present, unseen, and witness how I, for instance, am oppressed by this fanatic fellow citizen of yours; and if you could then issue forth, and reprove him, and tell him not to do it again, I should be much obliged."

"I'm very sorry you should have to complain, Mr. Pine, of treatment of that sort—but what sort is it, anyway?"

I gave a lurid picture of my tribulations, to the scandal and indignation of my friends. They at once placed themselves, and laughingly, their Americanism—any quantity of that mixture in their organisms—at my disposal.

I considered it of the first importance that Monsieur de Valmore should not get wind of what had happened. I took my three Americans cautiously out of the café, and as their hotel was near the station and not near the enemy's haunts, I encouraged their going back to it. I also supposed that they would wish to make some toilet for the evening, and relied on their good sense to put on their baggiest trousers—I dreamed of even baggier ones than they had on—I knew that, unlike other nations, the smarter an American's clothes, the more American they are.

My army was in excellent form. A rollicking good humour prevailed. I kept them out of the way till nightfall and then after an early dinner, by a circuitous route, approached the café Pelayo.

I have not yet described my forces. I will adopt the unusual method of describing what was in their pockets. What is in a man's pockets is generally the outposts of his soul; and being only a tenth of an inch below the surface and infinitely more accessible than the soul, I wonder that this compromise has never been hit upon in the history of exuberant and creative fiction. I feel it would have suited the clothes of Dickens' characters. The contents of a man's pockets is like a spiritual deposit just beneath the surface, or like bubbles from the deep well beneath.

Of course it will be only guesswork. But had I pretended to deeper insight it would be more so still. The soil of Taffany, if I may so describe his clothing, was of a rich uniform, brown earthen appearance, with little veins, like the trace of some attenuated mineral running down it. His trouser pockets contained a couple of knives, a revolver, a reckless mass of coin and some string. The form of these knives denoted at once a fierce and inventive nature. One of them was not unlike a "bowie" knife, although it had, I think, never been used for slaughter. No doubt in "whittling" a stick or paring his nails its appearance in his hand helped to the sensation of some blood-thirsty act. The other knife when opened was a little hedgehog of stumpy blades, skewers, poking and prodding implements and corkscrews. With this Taffany went through life prying open obstinate fruit tins, pulling out corks, manufacturing pipes, etc. The mass of money, silver and copper, accounted somewhat for the richness of the soil in which it lay (as I have mentioned)—although this may not tally with any known geology—also, along with the notes in the pockets above, acted as fuel to impel Taffany over wide lapses of land and sea. By its disposition and neighborhood it should belong to a man who regarded it rather as water to draw, and in large quantities, often, according to the needs of life—a sober life—and for whom it had none of the attributes of wine or drugs—not even of beer! Just homely water, of which there must be much. The revolver was the only voice one would hear of the thoroughly roused Taffany.

This was the practical area. As one mounted higher in this mountainous soil one came to the sentimental and intellectual tracts about the breast, letters from his family, paper cuttings and so on.

Blauenfeld had in his coat pocket the "Digit of the Moon". So had Morton in his. This book had been recommended to them by an American girl in a Paris studio. They had very seriously and gratefully made a note of it, after several weeks had procured it and were now reading it assidiously. Blauenfeld's money was in strata—copper, silver, etc. He had more than Taffany, but paid more attention to it. A rich black enveloped him.

Morton possessed a little seraglio of photographs of ladies that his undecided and catholic fancy had made him indulge in. They all had great sexual charm, tactfully displayed. He had his favorite photograph, of course. It was the least tactful, merely, I am afraid.

Then there was a card-case, a dictionary, a map, with much other matter. In fact, what was found in Morton's pockets was of such a complicated nature that it would be difficult to classify it. His soul, as it happened, was momentarily nearer the surface than in the case of his companions.

That these three men were my willing instruments needs no explanation, as we were excellent comrades. A sense of humour is the chief and most inalienable right of the American citizen. It goes always hand in hand with Liberty. These three good fellows went campaigning with me, even put themselves under my orders, with enthusiasm. They were in sympathy with my cause, which was that of humour. We were all four Soldiers of Humour. But, as it was my magnificent discovery and patent quarrel, it was my battle, and they willingly marched at my heels, as I should have done at theirs had it been the other way about. The natural enemy of the Soldier of Humour, and against whom he carries on uproarious, endless and delighted warfare, is the man or the multitude bereft of that astonishing sense. This wonderful warrior, to make the battle more exquisite will even feign a dullness, and falling away from the keenness, of that sense. In my historic struggle with Monsieur de Valmore, sometimes I pretended to go down into the headlong cockpit of his unconsciousness, and grappled with him on equal terms.

But no doubt such encounters nowadays are mostly bloodless. I am sure that many of the soldiers and adventurers of the Middle Ages were really Soldiers of Humour, unrecognised and unclassified. I know that many a duel has been fought in this solemn cause. A man of this temper and category will, perhaps carefully "entretenir" or cherish a wide circle of accessible enemies that his sword may not rust. Any other quarrel may be patched up. But what can be described as a quarrel of humour divides men for ever.

It is usually conceded that Humour is the discovery of the Anglo-Saxon race. I felt this racial solidarity as I was marching on the Café Pelayo.

I revised my plan of action. Taffany and his two friends were to enter the café, establish themselves autocratically there, become acquainted with Monsieur de Valmore—almost certainly the latter would at once approach his fellow-citizens,—and then I was to put in an appearance.

The Café was entered to the strains of

"There is a tavern in the town, in the town"

sung by my three allies.

I imagined the glow of national pride and delighted recognition that would invade Monsieur de Valmore on hearing this air. Apart from the sentimental reason—its use as a kind of battle-song—was the practical one that this noisy entrance, would at once attract my enemy's attention.

I awaited events at a neighbouring café.

Ten minutes passed, and I knew that my friends had "located" Monsieur de Valmore, even if they had not begun operations. Else they would have returned to my place of waiting. I wallowed naively in a superb coolness and indifference; as a man who has set some machinery going, which can now run by itself, turns nonchalantly away, paying no more attention to it. I felt strongly the stage analogy. I became rather conscious of my appearance. I must await "my cue" but was sure of my reception. From time to time I glanced idly down the road, and at last saw Blauenfeld making towards me, his usual American swing of the body complicated by rhythmical upheavals of mirth into trampling and stumblings and slappings of his thigh somewhere in the folds of his clothes. I paid for my coffee while he was coming up, and then turned to him.

"All ready?"

"Yep! we've got him fine. Come and have a look at him."

"Did he carry out his part of the programme according to my arrangements?"

"Why, yes. We went right in, and all three spotted him at the same time. Taffany manœuvred in the vicinity, and Morty and me coquetted round in his pro-pinquity. We could see his eyes beginning to stick out of his head, and his mouth watering. At last he could hold himself in no longer; we came together with a hiss and splutter of joy. He called up a tray full of drinks, to take the rawness off our meeting. He can't have seen an American for months. He just gobbled us up. There ain't nothing left of Taffany. He's made us promise to go to his Ho-tel tonight."

I approached the lurid stronghold of citizenship, with its pretentious palmy terrace, my mouth a little drawn and pinched, eyebrows raised, like a fastidious expert called in somewhere to decide a debatable point. This figure dictated my manner now. I entered the swing doors and looked round in a cold and business-like way as a doctor would in saying loftily, "Where is the patient?"

The patient was there right enough, surrounded by the nurses I had sent. There sat Monsieur de Valmore in as defenceless a state of beatitude as possible. He stared at me with an incredulous grin at first. I believe that in this moment of exquisite plenitude of life he would have been willing to extend to me a temporary pardon—a passe-partout to his café for the evening.

I approached him with impassive professional rapidity, my eye fixed on him (the physician analogy) already making my diagnosis. I was so carried away by this that I almost began things by asking him to put out his tongue. Instead I sat down carefully in front of him and examined him in silence.

In the midst of an enervating debauch, or barely convalescent from a bad illness, confronted by his mortalest enemy, no man could have looked more blank. But as such a man might turn to his boon companions or to his nurse or attendants for help, so Monsieur de Valmore turned with a characteristic blank childish appeal to Taffany. Perhaps he was shy or diffident of taking up actively his great role, when more truly great actors were present. Would not divine America speak, or thunder, through them, at this intruder?

"I guess you don't know each other," said Taffany, "Say, Mr. de Valmore, here's a friend of mine, Mr. Arthur Pine."

My enemy pulled himself together as though the different parts of his body all wanted to leap away in different directions, and he, with a huge effort, were preventing such disintegration. An attempt at a bow appeared as a chaotic movement of various limbs and organs. The bow had met other movements on the way, and never became a bow at all. An extraordinary confusion beset his body. The beginning of a score of actions ran over it blindly and disappeared.

"Guess Mr. de Valmore ain't quite comfortable in that chair, Morty. Give him yours."

And in this chaotic and unusual state he was hustled from one chair to the other, like a sack of mildly expostulating potatoes.[6]

His racial instinct was undergoing the severest revolution it has yet known. It was somewhat in the state of a South American Republic which has had three Presidents and an Emperor in a fortnight and is just electing a provisional Dictator. It was as though an incarnation of sacred America herself had commanded him to take me to his bosom. And, as the scope of my victory dawned upon him, his personal mortification assumed the proportions of a national calamity. For the first time since the sealing of his citizenship he felt that he was only a Frenchman from the Midi—hardly as near an American in point of fact, as even an Englishman is.

The soldier of Humour is chivalrous, though implacable. I merely drank a bottle of champagne at his expense; made Don Pedro and his orchestra perform three extras, all made up of the most intensely national English light comedy music, such as *San Toy* and *Our Miss Gibbs*. Taffany, for whom Monsieur de Valmore entertained the maximum of respect—held him solemnly for some time with a detailed and fabulous enumeration of my virtues. Before long I withdrew with my forces to riot in barbarous triumph elsewhere for the rest of the evening.

During the next two days I on several occasions visited the battlefield, but Monsieur de Valmore had vanished. His disappearance alone would have been sufficient to tell me that my visit to Spain was terminated. And in fact two days later I left Pontaisandra with the Americans, parting with them at Tuy and myself continuing on the León, San Sebastián route back to France and eventually to Paris.

I was taking away with me a good deal of Spanish, but in a rather battered or at least fragmentary condition. I interpret Spanish now, among other things, but with a hesitating lack of finish that shows traces of the stress of this time I have just described.

Arrived at Bayonne, I left the railway station with a momentarily increasing premonition. It was already night time. Stepping rapidly across the square, I hurried down the hall-way of the Fonda del Mundo, and turning brusquely and directly into the dining room of the Inn gazed round me almost shocked not to find what I had half expected. I sat down, piloting myself alertly and safely through the menu. Although Monsieur de Valmore had not been there to greet me, as good or better than his presence seemed to be attending me on my withdrawal from Spain. I still heard in this naked little room, as the wash of the sea in a shell, the echo of the first whisperings of his weird displeasure. Next day I arrived in Paris, my Spanish nightmare shuffled off long before I reached that hum-drum spot.

NOTES

[1] Typical of Lewis's fascination with the Spanish frontier (see "Crossing the Frontier," *The Revenge for Love* and the unpublished *Twentieth Century Palette*).

[2] Lewis's constant interest in boxers and boxing (see *The Revenge for Love*, "The Bishop's Fool," "The Man Who Was Unlucky With Women," *Self Condemned* and the unpublished "Creativity") was already apparent in the "Blesses" of *Blast*.

[3] This paragraph was deleted in 1927, probably because of these remarks on "Teutons." For the same reason the first preface of *Tarr* was suppressed in 1928.

[4] There is some implausibility—though a car drive or a night train, and phone calls from Bayonne to Pontaisandra might be put forward—in Monsieur de Valmore's lead over Ker-Orr, but this may be seen as part of the uncanny atmosphere proper to this encounter.

[5] The 1898 war.

[6] Compare this to the "sack of potatoes" at the end of "The Meaning of the Wild Body."

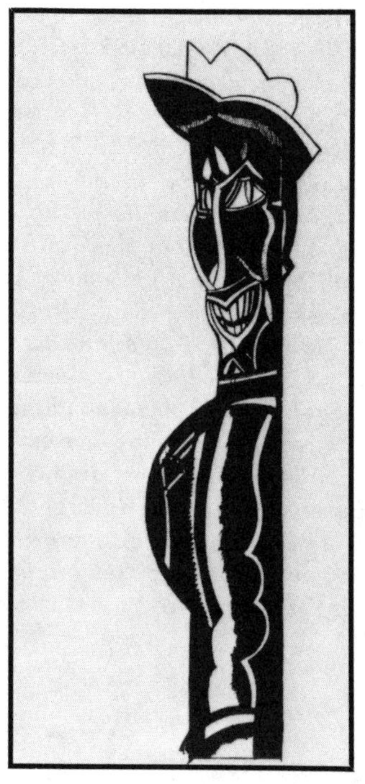

TYROS AND PORTRAITS

This is the "Foreword" to the catalogue of the exhibition "Tyros and Portraits" held at the Leicester Galleries in April 1921. To coincide with its opening Lewis published the first issue of The Tyro, *which reproduced, as an editorial, the section "Notes on Tyros." This manifesto of sorts was echoed in the interview "Dean Swift with a Brush" (see next item), and later republished in the Frank Case reprint of* The Tyro *(1970), in* Wyndham Lewis on Art *and in* Wyndham Lewis. Paintings and Drawings.

The Tyro phase was more than a late development of the initial Breton intuitions. For one thing, it was essentially a pictorial moment. However, it seems to have been caused by the revision of "Bestre" (published in The Tyro no. 2). *That the impulse behind the ludicrous totemic pictorial Tyros was literary is confirmed by the numerous echoes of "Inferior Religions" to be found in the present piece. This may explain why the pictorial impulse was short lived. Only five Tyros were exhibited in April 1921, and none of the ten promised for the second issue of* The Tyro *ever appeared. Ultimately we are left with less than ten extant Tyros. The Tyro impulse, as witnessed by the contents of* The Tyro *no. 2, revealed itself as more philosophical than artistic (a confirmation of this can be found in "Dean Swift with a Brush").*

But the importance of this abortive phase should not be underestimated. Though few, the designs produced were particularly impressive and remain among Lewis's most memorable ones. Lewis, we know, felt it necessary to rewrite all his early works from the "The 'Pole'" to "Enemy of the Stars." Clearly the Tyro phase acted as a relay, both reactivating the old urge and permitting a clearer perception of the underlying absurdity which determined it from the start, and which was only to be identified and named when the corpus coalesced in 1927 with "The Meaning of the Wild Body."

I have narrowed this exhibition to two phases of work. One is of work done directly in contact with nature, or with full information of the natural accidental form. The other phase is one which I have just entered, that of a series of pictures coming under the head of satire; grotesque scenes of a selected family or race of beings that serve to synthetise the main comic ideas that attack me at the moment. What I mean by the term Tyro is explained in a further note.[1]

Unnecessary as it would appear to point out that these Tyros are not meant to be beautiful, that they are, of course, forbidding and harsh, there will, no doubt, be found people who will make this discovery with an exclamation of reproach. Swift did not develop in his satires the comeliness of Keats, nor did Hogarth aim at grace. But people, especially in this country, where satire is a little foreign, never fail to impeach the artist when he is supposed to be betraying his supreme mistress, Beauty, and running after what must appear the strangest gods.

Most of the drawings are drawings from nature. It is important for an experimental artist and for experimental artists generally, to demonstrate that these activities are not the consequence of incompetence, as the enemies of those experiments so frequently assure the public. I do not know if all these drawings will be productive of that conviction, but some of them may.

There are no abstract designs in this exhibition, and I have included no compositions or purely inventive work except my new vintage of Tyros, wishing to concentrate attention on this phase of work.

I will add one general indication of direction. There are several hostile camps within the ranks of the great modern movement which has succeeded the Impressionist movement. The best organized camp in this country looks on several matters of moment to a painter today very differently from myself. The principal point of dispute is, I think, the question of subject-matter in a picture; the legitimacy of consciously conveying information to the onlooker other than that of the direct plastic message. Is the human aloofness and various other qualities, of which even the very tissue and shape of the plastic organization is composed, in say, a Chinese temple carving, to be regarded as compromising?

My standpoint is that it is only a graceful dilettantism that desires to convert painting into a parlour game, a very intellectual dressmaker's hobby, or a wayward and slightly hysterical chess. Again, abstraction, or plastic

---

[1] Tyro—An elementary person; an elemental, in short. Usually known in journalism as the Veriest Tyro. [All the Tyros we introduce to you are the Veriest Tyros.] [Author's note. In *The Tyro* this footnote was attached to "Note on Tyros."]

music, is justified and at its best when its divorce from natural form or environment is complete, as in Kandinsky's expressionism, or in the experiments of the 1914 Vorticists, rather than when its basis is still the French Impressionist dogma of the intimate scene. Prototypes of the people who affirm and flourish this new taboo of 'pure art', which is not even *pure*, will in twenty years' time be reacting obediently against it. Twenty years ago, 'art for art's sake' was the slogan of the ancestor of this type of individual. Our present great general movement must be an emancipation towards complete human expression; but it is always liable in England to degenerate into a cultivated and snobbish game.

My Tyros may help to frighten away this local bogey.

NOTE ON TYROS

This exhibition contains the pictures of[1] several very powerful Tyros.

These immense novices brandish their appetites in their faces, lay bare their teeth in a valedictory, inviting, or merely substantial laugh. A laugh, like a sneeze,[2] exposes the nature of the individual with an unexpectedness that is perhaps a little unreal. This sunny commotion in the face, at the gate of the organism, brings to the surface all the burrowing and interior broods which the individual may harbour. Understanding this so well, people hatch all their villainies in this seductive glow. Some of these Tyros are trying to furnish you with a moment of almost Mediterranean sultriness, in order, in this region of engaging warmth, to obtain some advantage over you.

But most of them are, by the skill of the artist, seen basking,[3] themselves, in the sunshine of their own abominable nature.

These partly religious explosions of laughing Elementals are at once satires, pictures and stories. The action of a Tyro is necessarily very restricted; about that of a puppet worked with deft fingers, with a screaming voice underneath. There is none of the pathos of Pagliacci in the story of the Tyro. It is the child in him that has risen in his laugh, and you get a perspective of his history.

Every child has its figures of a constantly renewed mythology. The intelligent, hardened and fertile crust of mankind produces a maturer fruit of the same kind. It has been rather barren of late. Here are a few large seeds.[4]

NOTES

[1] The *Tyro* editorial begins with: "We present to you in this number several. . ."

[2] See "Inferior Religions," page 151 (IV, 10).

[3] See "How One Begins" and *Rude Assignment* ("saurianly-basking sloth").
[4] *The Tyro* added the following concluding paragraph: "Ten especially potent Tyros will be seen in our next number. Also a clash between the Cept and the Megaloplinth." The Cept figured on the cover of *The Tyro*, no. 1, but the Megaloplinth apparently remained still-born.

DEAN SWIFT WITH A BRUSH. THE TYROIST EXPLAINS HIS ART.

This is the text of an interview on the occasion of the Leicester Galleries exhibition published in The Daily Express *of April 11, 1921. It was thus introduced:*

> *"What is a Tyro? Everyone who has seen and heard of Mr. Wyndham Lewis's fantastic exhibition of paintings at the Leicester Galleries is asking this question.*
>
> *The fact is Mr. Wyndham Lewis has created a new race."*

The interview was accompanied by a sketch of a Tyro "specially drawn for the 'Daily Express' yesterday by Mr. Wyndham Lewis," somewhat similar to the painting reproduced on the preceding page. The interview was reprinted in Walter Michel's Wyndham Lewis. Paintings and Drawings *(pp. 99-100).*

Though it reads like a simplified and flatter version of "Notes on Tyros," it isolates for the first time–with such words as "purposeless" and "vacuity"—the essential sense of absurdity which will be proclaimed in "The Meaning of the Wild Body."

A Tyro is a new type of human animal like Harlequin or Punchinello—a new and sufficiently elastic form or "mould" into which one can translate the satirical observations that are from time to time awakened by one's race.

Satire is dead to-day. There has been no great satirist since Swift. The reason is that the sense of moral discrimination in this age has been so blurred that it simply wouldn't understand written satire if it saw it.

People are, in fact, impervious to logic, so I have determined to get at them by the medium of paint.

Hence the Tyro.

Teeth and laughter, as you see, are the Tyro's two prominent features, and I will explain why. Do you remember the remark of a celebrated Frenchman on all Englishwomen? They have such handsome teeth, he said, that they are all like death-masks.

Well, there you have it! The Tyro, too, is raw and undeveloped; his vitality is immense, but purposeless, and hence sometimes malignant. His keynote, however, is vacuity; he is an animated, but artificial puppet, a "novice" to real life.

At present my Tyros are philosophic generalisations, and so impersonal.

Is this a new departure in art? No, not quite. You must remember that Hogarth didn't die so long ago.

Art to-day needs waking up. I am sick of these so-called modern artists amiably browsing about and playing at art for art's sake.

What I want is to bring back art into touch with life—but it won't be the way of the academician.

TYRONIC DIALOGUES —X. AND F.

MEETING BETWEEN THE TYRO, MR. SEGANDO, AND THE TYRO, PHILLIP.

MR. SEGANDO:[1] The mood of nostalgia, our fancies, Phillip, is soon frightened off by the bombastic shadow of my hair!

PHILLIP: But I wonder why it ever comes.

MR. S.: Come it must, Phillip, like other moods. Three-quarters of my moods move about me like well-trained servants, and when they have gone I find a delicate polish on what was previously dull.

PH.: I have one mood that frightens me.

MR. S.: Indeed?

PH.: Yes. It is one that has one word, like Poe's RAVEN. It says, over and over again, CREATE! Create! Create! On one of its visits it threw me into such a state that I designed a hat for Phillipine. She wears it to this day.

MR. S.: Ah, yes, a charming contrivance. I have often remarked it.

NOTE.—Mr. S. at your left hand. Phillip with pipe.

[1] The name "Segando" echoes "Mr. Segando in the Fifth Cataclysm," a mock S.-F. piece by John Rodker published on the following page of *The Tyro* no. 1. The above title for this short piece appears in the "Contents" of *The Tyro* no. 1 and the dialogue was used as a caption for the drawing reproduced on the preceding page.

"Tyronic Dialogues—X. and F." was published in the second issue of The Tyro *(1922), and with numerous alterations—all of a very minor nature—later reprinted in* Wyndham Lewis the Artist, From 'Blast' to Burlington House *(1939), which significantly presented it as a coda to "Essay on the Objective of Art in Our Time," a long survey which had also appeared in* The Tyro *no. 2. The 1922 version of "Tyronic Dialogues" is reproduced here, as it is nearer in time to* The Wild Body.

This dialogue—together with the much shorter one used as a caption for "Meeting Between the Tyro, Mr. Segando, and the Tyro, Phillip," published in The Tyro *no. 1 and reproduced on the opposite page—represents the entire meagre contribution of the Tyro period to imaginative literature.*

The inclusion here of "Tyronic Dialogues," which is quite removed from the world of the Wild Body, is justified by the "Editorial" of The Tyro *no. 2 in which Lewis states that "The only Tyros this number contains are Bestre, and X and F. . ." The Tyro literary output was more critical and intellectual than creative, and this certainly corresponds to the now conscious vision and manipulation of the absurd. "Tyronic Dialogues" just like "Sigismund" presents a systematic demonstration. As the graphic Tyros also show, the artist has moved from the primitive "saurians" evoked in "Tyros and Portraits" to more sophisticated nonentities directly heralding* The Apes of God. *For the Wild Body with its magnetic opaqueness Lewis is substituting the satirical pedagogue, The Enemy, whose first literary manifestation is discovered with X. This relationship was made clear in* Rude Assignment *(page 197): "The particular note of solitary defiance. . . I find. . . in 'The Tyro,' as much as in 'The Enemy'. . ." As far as imaginative exploration goes, this dialogue may be seen as the termination point of the Wild Body saga.*

Scene: A Studio.

[*Two forms in dark tweed coats are seen gesticulating against a large blank canvas on which the sun's breakfast light is glowing. As the dialogues advance the canvas is noticed to be gradually darkening and to be becoming a picture.*]

X.—Remember, my dear F., that you are for every man a little picture of himself: a badly drawn and irritating picture of himself. Therefore, never show that you notice, if a painter, writer or musician, the existence of another artist's work. Above all, never be so uncircumspect as to praise it. For the man so treated will say: "F., I was told, has said something nice about my work. The dirty dog! I suppose he means people to think that my work is so contemptible that he can afford to praise it. Or is his game to suggest that I am a follower of his? Or does he intend to sell that drawing of mine that he gave me five pounds for, and is he stimulating the market? Or does he just wish to strut down the street with a nice feeling of being generous and grand? In any case, he wishes to belittle me either by giving himself a cheap extra two inches, or by chipping an inch or two off me by making me appear inoffensive. Any way, the *dirty* dog, I'll pay him, I will!"

F.—But what are you to say if a man shows you a painting that you consider good?

X.—My dear F.—Fool![1] *And* that so rarely happens!

F.—But should it happen, what is to be done?

X.—To remain on good terms with your fellow artists you must explode with derisive invective: sneer a little or whatever is expected of you. That will be reported to them and they will feel that all is well: that you appreciate them.

F.—But what is then left for you to do when you are shown *bad* paintings?

X.—Oh, you always say that *they* are good! Charming, jolly, or good.

F.—But does that apply to your dealings with the really good artist?

X.—If you cling to your pathetic belief in the existence of such a thing, yes: for he would never believe that you understood the world so little as not to see the damaging effect your geniality as regards him would have.

Scene: Same.

F.—I am having some trouble with B. He lies freely about me. He intrigues. He ——

X.—Hush!

F.—What do you mean, dear X.?

X.—That you must never allow such things to pass your lips. With me, of course, you may. But even with me it might produce in you the habit of such naivetés. That is, of course, the great danger, for you, of intercourse with me. You might get the habit of naivetés.

F.—But what I have said of B. is true, and further I can substantiate it.

X.—I can see that I shall have to instruct you once more on a very simple matter. Suppose, then, for instance, you utter to anyone else (a member of your circle of acquaintanceship, your little world), what you have just said to me. What will happen? They will be embarrassed, vexed and shocked if they are well-disposed. They will say: "What a *suspicious* cuss you are, aren't you?" rather as they would speak to a dog.

F.—Suspicious! I have good reason to be.

X.—Hush, hush! "Suspicious," you understand, is the word the world has found to apply to those liable, through lack of self-control, to make a scandal. It is a word that bears with it an element of reproach. It is contrived by society as a punishment. It is not so severe as the label "bore" (which is administered for the crime of discussing things that people are too lazy or stupid to be attracted by), but still one that carries with it a social stigma.

F.—How true that is.

X.—Yes, I thought you would think that true.—I expect you are often a bore!—But to return to your "suspiciousness." You are supposed to take it for granted, you see, that everyone does you any slight damage they can. If they are competing with you in a closer sense than the general social one, they will, of course, damage you to the full extent of their ability. You are supposed, naturally, to be engaged in similar activities on your side. There are a multitude of more or less intense cross-currents as well: others battering subterraneously at you, and at each other. Your blow may arrive at the same moment in the bosom of some opponent as another blow posted from a source quite unknown to you, weeks before your own missive. He may stagger in consequence more than you expected. Under these circumstances, to suddenly announce, as you have to me, that someone is paying you undesirable attentions of the usual malignant type is equivalent to hitting a man in the eye in a drawing room, or assaulting a lady in public who would be delighted to accommodate you in the usual way and less publicly.

You see now more or less what you are doing? Every civilized milieu is, and always has been, engaged perpetually in a sort of subconscious, subvisible lawyer's brawl. It is the devouring jungle driven underground, the instinct of bloody combat restricted to forensic weapons.

It is a nightmare, staged in a menagerie. The psycho-analysts with their jungle of the unconscious, and monsters tipsy with libido, have made a kind of Barnum and Bailey for the educated. But people do not apply this sensational picture as they could do with advantage.

Our social life is so automatic that the actors are often totally unaware of their participation in the activities about which we are talking. The world is in the strictest sense asleep, with rare intervals and spots of awareness. It is almost the sleep of the insect or animal world. No one would in the least mind, of course, being a *tiger* like Clemenceau. But what makes him or her highly indignant is to be unmasked as a *rat* or a *cat!* It is as though you burst in upon a fashionable Beauty too early in the day.

Everyone is outwardly and for the world a charming fellow or woman, incapable of anything but the most generous and kind (always KIND, this is a key-word) behaviour. Everyone knows that in reality everybody is a shit, as much as he or she *dare* to be. (And this "courage" involved again endears the thoroughly dirty dog to his fellows. It supplies the tincture of romance.) The reticence and powers of hypocrisy of our English race enhance this situation.

So, if you find yourself injured all of a sudden—find, that is, an unexpected pin sticking into your hide obtruded from the eminently respectable obscurity; or a particularly vicious pinch administered; examine the finger-print or abrasion: retaliate at the earliest opportunity. Twenty years hence, if you cannot before. But *never* declare yourself as you have declared yourself to me. Such candour smacks of impotence. And, above all, it implies with a boring directness, the Truth that you need be no sage to know. Every kitchenmaid knows that all the people by whom she is surrounded are shits, and if it is to their interest or if they can, they will let her down, injure or rob her.

F.—You exaggerate the viciousness——

X.—And am *suspicious!* But I only exaggerate with *you*. I am never guilty of exaggeration at any other time. You must not give me away!

Scene: The same.

X.—Ha, ha! my dear F., I am "having some trouble" with Q.

F.—Hush!

X.—I know, but observe the way in which I deal with this matter. It will be a nice little object lesson for you!

F.—I am glad to find, all the same, that you are sufficiently human to have trouble with our fellow-animals at all.

X. (*sighing*).—It is as an animal that I resent "trouble." However, here is the letter I have written to the cadaverous Q.:—

Dear Q.—Would you, as a proof of the friendship you profess, share a secret of yours with me?

(I may be asking the impossible, for you may not know your own secret).

O puzzling Q., you have made great speeches; you entertain with a benevolent haste all those approaches by societies and particulars, the entertaining of which would tend to make, as you see it, your importance grow. When the X^2 society's support, even, is in question, for Yorkshire, Cambridge, or the South Pole, with an unblushing speed you interpose yourself, and replying for others, speak as though, instead of being Q., as you really are, you all the while were X.

Now what I have asked myself is (you will forgive me) if you are *really* so young as to believe that such procedures are worth while? Or if you only pretend to be (compelled in some sense to throw out ballast by the shallowness of the milieu), and if in reality you know that they are not. That you are affecting to be living, in short, at a point of development that you have some time past?

Having asked my question, I will give you *my* answer first. I do not believe that the above is the answer. I believe in reality that you are only half conscious of what you do; just as the forger or murderer in most cases forges or murders as it were in his sleep. I believe in these little matters you are an automaton; and that the acts of the automaton have not the full consent of your mind. That is why, my dear Q., I continue to frequent you (only keeping an eye open, the while, for the slim, but rather harmlessly Dickens-like, rascality that is in hiding: for you are really a Dickens figure, are you not? a Boz?), and why I remain (has it ever occurred to you how this epistolary form implies "still am, in spite of everything"),

Your humble servant,

X.

F.—But, my dear X., you must be mistaken about Q. He is a most sympathetic, charming fellow.

X—You have taken our last conversation to heart!

F.—Of course I have; but I mean what I say about Q.

X.—So do I.

Scene: The same.

X.—What, you, here again so soon? My dear old boy, you must be in love with your silhouette against that canvas, or you must be trying to form a habit, or break yourself of one about which you haven't told me.

F.—Our conversations, excellent X., attack all my habits: but since these do not disintegrate quickly enough, I return repeatedly to quicken the process.

X.—Well, what habit is it requires poisoning this morning?

F.—I find that the habits you have scared away, have merely passed into their opposites, availing themselves of your reasoning, and stereotyping it. I am now going about seeing black where I formerly saw white, or *vice-versa,* and it is really much the same thing. Perhaps a satisfactory migration of your thought cannot be effected into me?

X.—Ah, the reason for what you tell me may lie in the fact that I have been a little too brutal. Have I stamped things in too much, and buried them? Let us see if we can disinter them.

I wish you had been with me yesterday. I saw many of our friends: and I can truly say that I found them all asleep, just as I had been describing them to you at our former meeting. I met P. and P.R. in the street. They literally seem to have grown into each other. P., the smaller, sharper one, seems to do the *carrying*. P.R. has the appearance of hanging, rather unreally, like a Signorelli figure in the picture of the damned, on his life's partner, with the superannuated languish of an old maid. I went to see Z. and C. They discharged a lot of putrid gossip into my ear; or, since you have to grin while this is going on, into my mouth. For my contribution, I handed them a few of their own yarns back, which will be dished up at once as mine. In the evening I met Z.D.G. and D.T. in the restaurant. D.T. was already blind. So *he* was an unmixed automaton. The others were eating, making a few remarks they had made many times before, and preparing to go to a party they had been to many times before. But I need not enumerate my experiences: they are in a measure also yours. By the hard times, no doubt, everyone has been driven into any automatic unconscious life they can find; for their vitality announces peremptorily that no more adventures, risks or efforts can be allowed. People, also, for this programme, are thrown outwards on each other more and more—driven out of themselves; for in themselves imagination or effort awaits them.

That this has always characterised people, and especially civilized people, that it is, in fact, life, is indisputable. But I should be inclined to assert that our time could provide the student of such phenomena with as good a specimen as he could wish.

F.—You make me uncomfortable, X. I feel that my words, as I utter them, are issuing from a machine. I appear to myself a machine, whose destiny it is to ask questions.

X.—The only difference is that I am a machine that is constructed to provide you with answers.

I am alive, however. But I am beholden for life to machines that are asleep.

NOTES

[1] So apparently "F." stands for "Fool"—and "X.," the Ur-Enemy, may echo the neo-Vorticist "Group X."

[2] An ambiguity eliminated in 1939: "the *K* society's . . ."

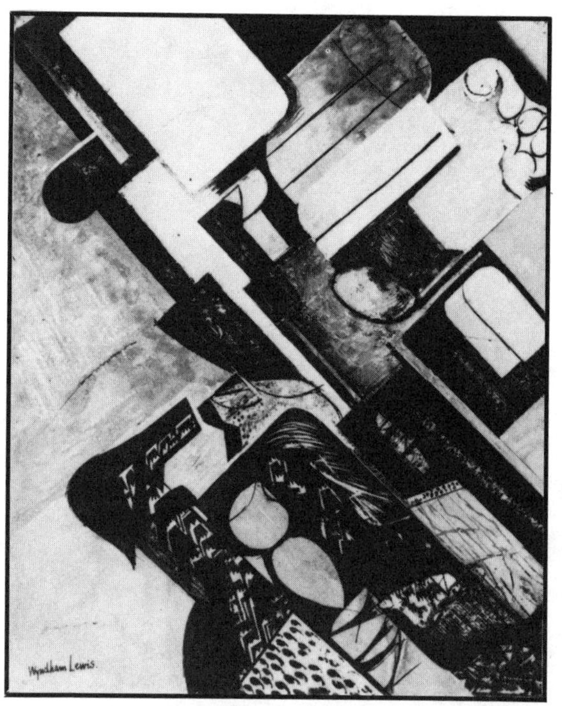

BEGINNINGS

This is an extract from Lewis's untitled contribution to Beginnings, *a collection of essays by various hands, published in 1935 by Thomas Nelson and Sons. Lewis's essay was reprinted in* Wyndham Lewis on Art. *It was Lewis's first evocation of his early years.* Blasting and Bombardiering, *his first autobiography, covered only the period from Vorticism to 1926.*

From all this it will emerge, I hope, that most such questions as: 'Which art do you prefer—painting or writing?' addressed to a writer who is at the same time a painter, or contrariwise; or all such remarks as 'So-and-so is a *better* this than he is a that' (advanced in connection with a dual personality in the arts) are[1] somewhat superficial. The only question that is sensible and not entirely beside the point is: *Which have you done the most of?* or *To which have you devoted most time and energy?* But this is usually obvious, anyway: so those questions, too, are unnecessary.

If you have regarded this preamble as needlessly dilatory, where I am supposed to have set out to inform you 'How I began to write', you have, I can assure you, not allow sufficiently for the especial difficulties in which a writer who never had had a half-finished canvas far away from the desk at which he wrote—who possesses a twin brother in another art—must find himself if interrogated as to 'how he began'.

For he began, at least that was the case with me, in a painting academy. He wrote his first short story (if the writer in question is the author of *The Apes of God*) while he was painting the subject of it with hog-hair brushes, in petrol quick-drying medium, if I remember rightly; and the short story was shorter than the painting, I believe I should be correct in saying, in the matter of the time that it took to write. The short story referred to here is one of those to be found in *The Wild Body*.

Technically, then, the short story, as we call it, was the first literary form with which I became familiar; and I think I may say that the dramatic necessities of this form of art were immediately apparent to me—namely, that *action* is of its essence. And acquainted as I was with both French peasants and English villagers, I chose the former deliberately, because I have always considered that my turn of mind is better suited by the spectacle of people to whom the fundamentals of life are still accessible. Also, I like a wild and simple country, with a somewhat inhospitable skeleton of rock. And if I have not gone to seek these conditions in such parts of these islands as may be found to provide them, it is largely on account of the incessant deluges of water that fall from the Britannic firmament, or because of the detestable Scotch mists that continually conceal everything, and which cause one to become a walking sponge. This is partly owing to an innate dislike for rain, and partly it is, beyond any question, due to the professional reactions of the painter to a climate where he is continually checkmated by poor visibility or by a downright night-by-day. But I very much enjoy the sun as such—apart from any complex reasons for avoiding as far as possible the rain. When I go to a film like *The Man of Aran*,[2] I shudder at what I see: I recognize that the dry intervals in which it was possible to shoot the film must have been very few and far between; and this pall of rain (into which I have passed many times, on board incoming liners, both from Africa and from America) which stands over England fills me with a hideous melancholy. Rain and no snow! The absence of snow is, if anything, worse than the presence of the rain! Coronation Gulf or the Bay of Whales can be contemplated with pleasure, at least by me. But Aran or the Hebrides! However, I will expatiate upon this no longer. Why my short stories must occur in other parts of Europe, then, or perhaps in the sub-tropical belts, is climatic mainly. I would rather have written *On an African Farm* than *Wuthering Heights,* because in order to write the latter one would have to exist for many years in a perpetual drizzle. To write the former one would at least have to live in uninterrupted sunshine for a considerable length of time.

It was the sun, a Breton instead of a British, that brought forth my first short story—*The Ankou* I believe it was: the Death-god of Plouilliou.[3] I was painting a blind Armorican beggar. The 'short story' was the crystallization *of what I had to keep out of my consciousness while painting.* Otherwise the painting would have been a bad painting. That is how I began to write in earnest. A lot of discarded matter collected there, as I was painting or drawing, in the back of my mind—in the back of my consciousness. As I squeezed out *everything* that smacked of literature from my vision of the beggar, it collected at the back of my mind. It imposed itself upon me as a complementary creation. That is what I meant by saying, to start with, that I was so *naturally* a painter that the two arts, with me, have co-existed in peculiar harmony. There has been no mixing of the *genres.* The waste product of every painting, when it is a painter's painting, makes the most highly selective and ideal material for the pure writer.

NOTES

1 Corrected from the ungrammatical "is" of the first printings.

2 Robert Flaherty's documentary *Man of Aran,* 1934.

3 See page 115, note 2.

HOW ONE BEGINS

"How One Begins" presents two excerpts from Lewis's second autobiography, Rude Assignment *(1950): the conclusion of chapter 21 ("How One Begins," pp. 113-114) and a passage from chapter 22 ("Early Life and Shakespeare," pp. 116-118).*

This revisiting is of considerable interest as it shows the accuracy of Lewis's vision of his own development and the lasting fundamental importance of The Wild Body in all its manifestations.

Gradually the bad effects of English education wore off, or were deliberately discarded. Being with 'foreigners' all the time who never 'played the game', I rapidly came to see that there was, in fact, no game there at all. It was a British delusion that there was always a game—to whose rules, good or bad, you must conform. However, I need not detail the phases of this metamorphosis: I became a European, which years in Paris and elsewhere (Spain, Germany, Holland) entailed; hastening the process however, with a picturesque zeal. There are in England many invisible assets, to do mostly with character; they are not tangible and make no show of a kind to appeal to the barbaric eye of youth. All that was apparent to me, at that time, was the complacent and unimaginative snob of the system I had escaped from, the spoiled countryside, sacrificed in order to manufacture Brummagem, long ago when it was discovered that England was really a coal mine; and I noted with distaste the drab effects of Victorian mediocrity. I may add that the defects of the French were as hidden from me as those invisible assets I have spoken of belonging to the English.

My literary career began in France, in the sense that my first published writings originated in notes made in Brittany. Indeed, this period in retrospect, responsible for much, is a blank with regard to painting. There was for instance the beginning of my interest in philosophy (attendance at Bergson's lectures at the Collège de France one evidence of that). But what I started to do in Brittany I have been developing ever since. Out of Bestre and Brotcotnaz grew, in that sense—if in no other—the aged 'Gossip Star' at her toilet, and Percy Hardcaster. Classifiable I suppose as 'satire', fruits of much visceral and intellectual travail and indolent brooding, a number of pieces were eventually collected under the title of 'The Wild Body'. To those primordial literary backgrounds, among the meadows and rocks and stone hamlets of Finistère thundered at by the Atlantic, in a life punctuated with Pardons, I will now make my way back, and try and remember how my first rational writings came to assume the shape they did.

. . . .

It was therefore an innovation for me to take to prose, when I began preparing material for stories in Brittany—at the time I felt a little of a come-down, or at least a condescension. My first attempts naturally were far less successful than the verse.[1] The coastal villages of Finistère in which I spent long summers (one of them with the artist, Henry Lamb) introduced one to a more primitive society. These fishermen went up to Iceland in quite small boats, they were as much at home in the huge and heaving Atlantic as the torero in the bull-ring: their speech was still Celtic and they were highly distrustful of the stranger. They brawled about money over their fierce apple-juice: when somebody was stabbed, which was a not infrequent occurrence, they would not call in a doctor, but come to the small inn where I stayed, for a piece of ice.[2] A great part of their time was spent, when not at sea, jogging up and down between 'Pardons', all the women provided with large umbrellas. Their miniature bagpipe is a fine screaming little object, to the music of which star dancers would leap up into the air, as if playing in a feudal ballet.[3] On the whole, however, the dancing was sedate and mournful, compared with Rubens' peasants.

Long vague periods of an indolence now charged with some creative purpose were spent in digesting what I saw, smelt and heard. For indolent I remained. The Atlantic air, the raw rich visual food of the barbaric environment, the squealing of the pipes, the crashing of the ocean, induced a creative torpor. Mine was now a drowsy sun-baked ferment, watching with delight the great comic effigies which erupted beneath my rather saturnine but astonished gaze: Brotcotnaz, Bestre, and the rest.

During those days, I began to get a philosophy: but not a very good one, I am afraid. Like all philosophies, it was built up around the will—as primitive houses are built against a hill, or propped up upon a bog. As a timely expression of personal impulses it took the form of a reaction against civilised values. It was militantly vitalist. Only much later was I attracted to J.-J. Rousseau, or it might have had something to do with his anti-social dreaming.

The snobbishness (religion of the domestic) of the English middleclass, their cold philistinism, perpetual silly sports,[4] all violently repudiated by me were the constant object of comparison with anything that stimulated and amused, as did these scenes. I overlooked the fact that I was observing them as a privileged spectator, having as it were purchased my front-row stall with money which I derived from that other life I despised. In spite of this flaw the contrast involved was a valid one: of the two types of life I was comparing, the one was essentially contemptible, the other at least rich in surface quality: in the clubhouse on an English golf-links I should not have found such exciting animals as I encountered here—undeniably the golfers' values are wanting in a noble animal zest. This is, however, a quandary that cannot be resolved so simply as I proposed—namely, the having-the-cake-and-eating-it way.

The epigraph at the beginning of my first novel, 'Tarr', is an expression of the same mood, which took a long time to evaporate altogether. It is a quotation from Montaigne. 'Que c'est un mol chevet que l'ignorance et l'incuriosité?'[5] Even books, theoretically, were a bad thing, one was much better without them. Every time men borrowed something from outside they gave away something of themselves, for these acquisitions were artificial aggrandisement of the self, but soon there would be no core left. And it was the core that mattered. Books only muddied the mind: men's minds were much stronger when they only read the Bible.

The human personality, I thought, should be left alone, just as it is, in its pristine freshness: something like a wild garden—full, naturally, of starlight and nightingales, of sunflowers and the sun. The 'Wild Body' I envisaged as a piece of the wilderness. The characters I chose to celebrate—Bestre, the Cornac and his wife, Brotcotnaz, le père François—were all primitive creatures, immersed in life, as much as birds, or big, obsessed sun-drunk insects.

The body was wild: one was attached to something wild, like a big cat that sunned itself and purred. The bums, alcoholic fishermen, penniless students (generally Russians) who might have come out of the pages of 'The Possessed', for long my favourite company, were an anarchist material. And as ringmaster of this circus I appointed my 'Soldier of Humour', who stalked imbecility with a militancy and appetite worthy of a much more light-hearted and younger Flaubert, who had somehow got into the universe of Gorky.

There is a psychological factor which may have contributed to what I have been describing.—I remained, beyond the usual period, congealed in a kind of cryptic immaturity. In my social relations the contacts remained, for long, primitive. I recognised dimly this obstruction: was conscious of gaucherie, of wooden responses—all fairly common symptoms of course. It resulted in experience with no natural outlet in conversation collecting in a molten column within. This *trop-plein* would erupt: that was my way of expressing myself—with intensity, and with the density of what had been undiluted by ordinary intercourse: a thinning-out which is, of course, essential for protection.

Observing introspectively this paradoxical flowering, this surface obtuseness, on the one hand, and unexpected fruit which it miraculously bore: observing this masterly inactivity, almost saurianly-basking sloth,[6] and what that condition produced, something within me may quite reasonably have argued that this inspired *Dummheit*[1] was an excellent idea. *Let us leave well alone!* may have been the mental verdict. I know everything already: why add irrelevant material to this miraculous source? Why acquire spectacles for an eye that sees so well without them? So there was superstition, and, I suspect, arrogance.

But I am gazing back into what is a very dark cavern indeed. An ungregarious childhood may have counted for something. A feature of perhaps greater importance was that after my schooldays, even with my intimates, I was

---

[1] Stupidity.

much younger than those with whom I associated, since I had left school so early. And, finally, at school itself, developing habits as I did which appeared odd to the young empire-builders by whom I was surrounded, may have stiffened the defence natural to that age.

The rough set of principles arrived at was not, I have said, a very good philosophy. Deliberately to spend so much time in contact with the crudest life is, I believe, wasteful of life. It seems to involve the error that raw material is alone authentic life. I mistook for 'the civilised' the tweed-draped barbaric clown of the golf-links. But, as a philosophy of life, it principally failed in limiting life in a sensational sense. After two or three intermediate stages I reached ultimately an outlook that might be described as almost as formal as this earliest one was the reverse.

NOTES

1 Refers to the early "Shakespearian" sonnets.

2 See "Beau Séjour," page 60.

3 See "Brotcotnaz," page 138.

4 See "Our Wild Body," pp. 253-254.

5 *Les Essais*, III, 13 ("De l'expérience"). The sentence in full reads: "O que c'est un doux et mol chevet, et sain, que l'ignorance et l'incuriosité, à reposer une teste bien faicte!" Florio's translation: "Oh how soft, how gentle, and how sound a pillow is ignorance and incuriosity to rest a well composed head upon."

6 See "Tyros and Portraits," page 354.

APPENDICES

WRITINGS[1]

Possible books: names for them in italics and underlined
for purposes of these notes only. No other
titles to be used.)

1. "TARR"

———

———

2. "OUR WILD BODY"

———

——— (1. Essays and stories from
English Review first numbers : &
New Age of same, dates approximately:
including May, "Our Wild Body"
2. "Pringle" from Tramp.
3. Story called "Soldier of
Humour" (in possession of Pound.)
Essays are 1. *Pere Francois*
2. *Some Inn Keepers*
And Bertie .
3. *Brobdingnag.*
4. *Poles*
5.Etc. Etc. ?
Poem called "Guignolles" if it
can be found intact.

[1] This is an excerpt from an important document in the Lewis archive at Cornell. Drawn up in view of his imminent departure for the Front in France probably late in 1916, this listing provides vital information about the dates of composition of all the early writings, and is often referred to in the notes to this edition. The opening sections are reproduced here with the original typography and often telling misprints or irregularities. The whole document was first published in *Enemy News*, no. 10.

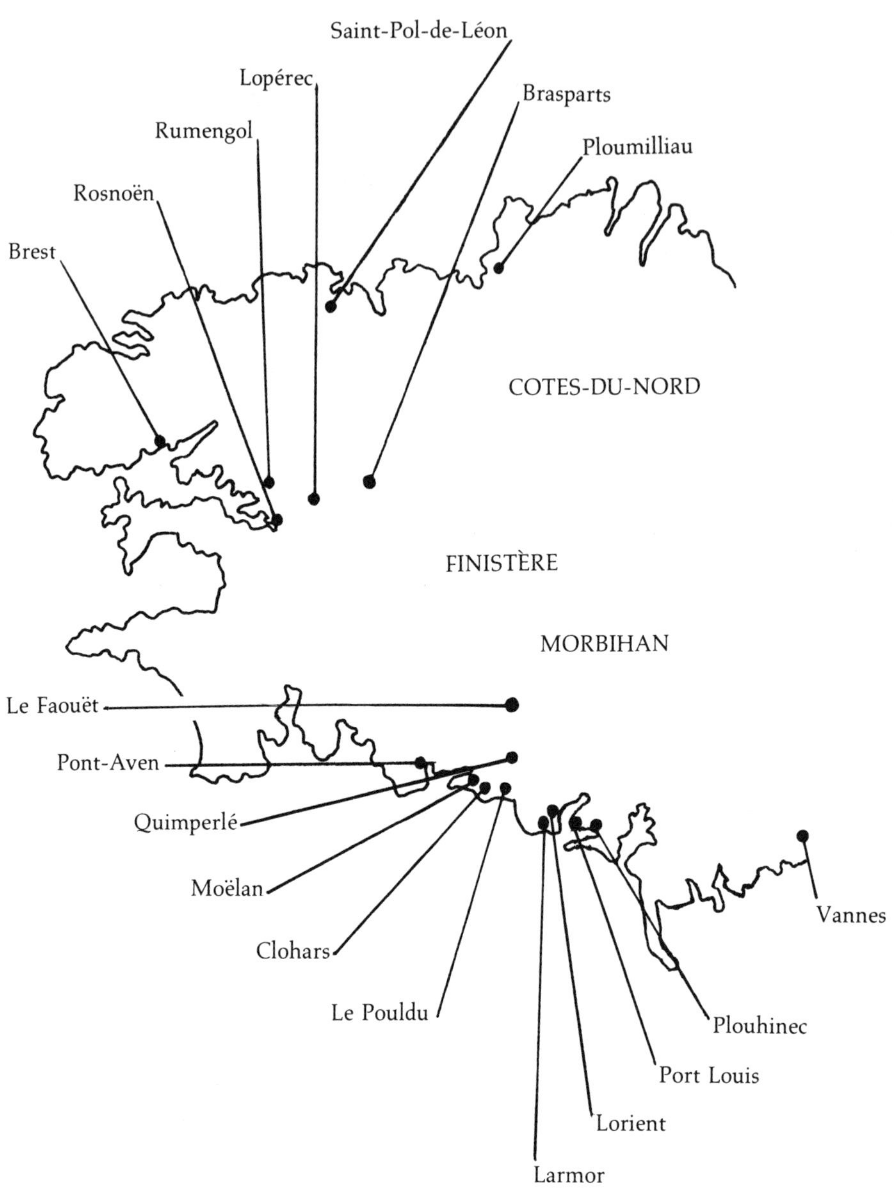

WYNDHAM LEWIS'S BRITTANY.

(Wyndham Lewis's Brittany—unlike his Spain—is largely imaginary, though not systematically—and the location of the stories often varies in a disconcerting way from one version to the next. Here is a map of the "real" cities and villages mentioned in the stories and documents.)

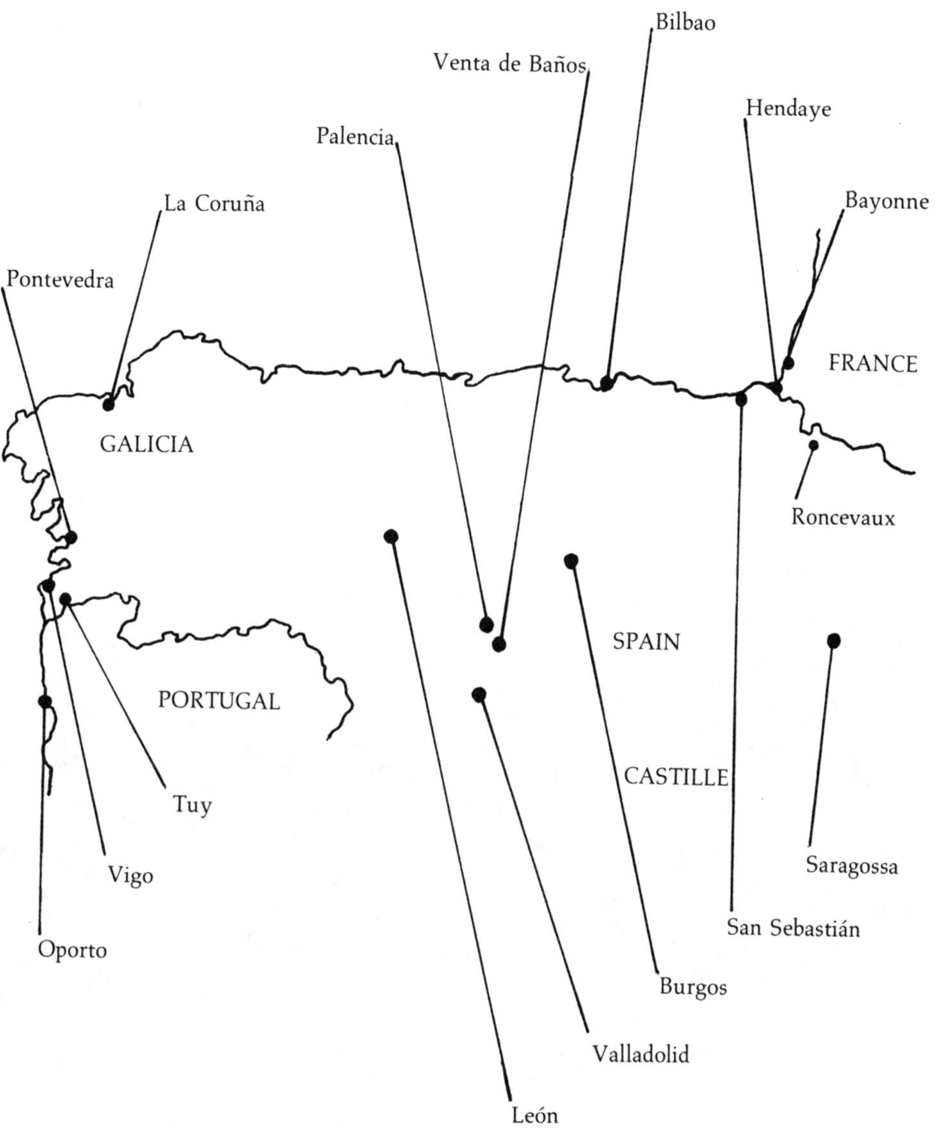

WYNDHAM LEWIS'S SPAIN.

(With the exception of Pontaisandra, an imaginary name, Lewis's Spain is more in keeping with official geography than his Brittany.)

A BIBLIOGRAPHY OF THE WILD BODY
(arranged chronologically)

I—*WORKS BY WYNDHAM LEWIS:*

"The 'Pole.'" *The English Review,* II (May 1909) 255-265 (Revised as "Beau Séjour").

"Some Innkeepers and Bestre." *The English Review,* II (June 1909) 471-484 (Revised as "Bestre").

"Les Saltimbanques." *The English Review,* III (August 1909), 76-87 (Revised as "The Cornac and His Wife").

"Our Wild Body." *The New Age,* II, no 1 (May 5, 1910), 8-10.

"A Spanish Household." *The Tramp: an Open Air Magazine,* I (June-July 1910) 356-360.

"A Breton Innkeeper." *The Tramp: an Open Air Magazine,* I (August 1910) 411-414 (Reprinted in *Unlucky for Pringle: Unpublished and Other Stories*).

"Le Père François (A Full-Length Portrait of a Tramp)." *The Tramp: an Open Air Magazine,* I (September 1910) 517-521 (Revised as "Franciscan Adventures").

"Grignolles (*Brittany*)." *The Tramp: an Open Air Magazine,* II (December 1910) 246 (Reprinted in *Collected Poems and Plays*).

"Brobdingnag." *The New Age,* VIII (Literary Supplement), no. 10 (January 5, 1911) 2-3 (Revised as "Brotcotnaz").

"Unlucky for Pringle." *The Tramp: an Open Air Magazine,* II (February 1911) 404-414 (Reprinted in *Unlucky for Pringle: Unpublished and Other Stories*).

"Inferior Religions." *The Little Review,* IV, no. 5 (September 1917) 3-8 (Revised as "Inferior Religions").

"A Soldier of Humour. Part I." *The Little Review*, IV, no. 8 (December 1917) 32-46 (Revised as "A Soldier of Humour," parts I and II).

"A Soldier of Humour. Part II." *The Little Review*, IV, no. 9 (January 1918) 35-51 (Revised as "A Soldier of Humour," part III).

"Sigismund." *Art and Letters*, III, no. 1 (Winter 1920) 14-31 (Revised as "Sigismund").

Tyros and Portraits. Leicester Galleries (April 1921) 5-8 (Partly reprinted in *The Tyro* no. 1; reprinted in *Wyndham Lewis on Art* and *Wyndham Lewis. Paintings and Drawings*).

"Note on Tyros." *The Tyro*, I (April 1921) 2 (Reprints part of "Tyros and Portraits").

"Will Eccles." *The Tyro*, I (April 1921) 6 (Revised and expanded as "You Broke My Dream").

"Meeting Between the Tyro, Mr. Segando, and the Tyro, Phillip." *The Tyro*, I (April 1921) 7.

"Dean Swift with a Brush. The Tyroist Explains His Art." *The Daily Express*, no. 6548 (April 11, 1921) 5 (reprinted in *Wyndham Lewis. Paintings and Drawings*).

"Tyronic Dialogues—X. and F." *The Tyro*, 2 (March 1922) 46-49 (Revised in *Wyndham Lewis the Artist, From 'Blast' to Burlington House*).

"Bestre." *The Tyro*, 2 (March 1922) 53-63 (Revises "Bestre"; revised as "Bestre"; the two issues of *The Tyro* were reprinted in facsimile by Frank Cass, 1970).

The Wild Body. A Soldier of Humour and Other Stories. London, Chatto and Windus, 1927 (Revises "The 'Pole,'" "Some Innkeepers and Bestre," "Les Saltimbanques," "Le Père François," "Brobdingnag," "Inferior Religions," "A Soldier of Humour," "Sigismund," and "Will Eccles"; adds "Foreword," "The Death of the Ankou" and "The Meaning of the Wild Body"; reprinted in 1932 in the Centaur Library series; facsimile reprint by Haskell House, 1970).

The Wild Body. A Soldier of Humour and Other Stories. New York Harcourt, Brace and Company, 1928 (similar to the English edition except that it corrects a dozen mistakes affecting the French dialogue. Lewis was mos probably not responsible for these corrections; see note 2, page 87).

"Wyndham Lewis," *Beginnings* (by various hands, edited by L. A. G. Strong), London, Thomas Nelson, 1935, 91-103 (Evokes the writing of "The Death of the Ankou"; reprinted in *Wyndham Lewis on Art.*

"Der Tod des Ankou." *Europäische Revue*, XIV, no. 3 (March 1938) 215-224 (Translation of "The Death of the Ankou" by Joachim Moras).

Wyndham Lewis the Artist, From 'Blast' to Burlington House. London, Laidlaw and Laidlaw, 1939 (Includes "Tyronic Dialogue—X and F," which revises "Tyronic Dialogues—X. and F.," pp. 361-370; facsimile reprint by Haskell House, 1971).

A Soldier of Humor and Selected Writings (Edited by Raymond Rosenthal). New York, Toronto, London, A Signet Classic, The New American Library, 1966 (Reprints "A Soldier of Humor," "The Death of the Ankou" and "Inferior Religions," pp. 22-73).

Wyndham Lewis on Art (Edited by Walter Michel and C. J. Fox). London, Thames and Hudson, 1969 (Reprints "Tyros and Portraits," pp. 187-190 and "Beginnings," pp. 291-296).

Michel, Walter. *Wyndham Lewis. Paintings and Drawings.* London, Thames and Hudson, 1971 (Reprints "Dean Swift with a Brush," pp. 99-100, and "Tyros and Portraits," pp. 437-438).

[A Breton Journal]. In *Wyndham Lewis: A Descriptive Catalogue* (compiled by Mary F. Daniels). Ithaca, Cornell University Press, 1972, p. 3 (contains a facsimile reproduction of the first page of "A Breton Journal").

Unlucky for Pringle: Unpublished and Other Stories (Edited by C. J. Fox and Robert T. Chapman). London, Vision, 1973 (Reprints "A Breton Innkeeper" and "Unlucky for Pringle," pp. 23-44).

Crossing the Frontier (Edited by Bernard Lafourcade and Bradford Morrow). Santa Barbara, Black Sparrow Press, 1978.

Collected Poems and Plays (Edited by Alan Munton). Manchester, Carcanet, 1979, 1981 (Edits "Grignolles," pp. 15-16; paperback edition, 1981).

"Writings" (edited and discussed by Bernard Lafourcade). In "A Key List of the Early Works," *Enemy News*, no. 10 (May 1979), 11-13.

Le Corps Sauvage (Wyndham Lewis et la France—tome I). Textes présentés par Bernard Lafourcade et traduits par Odette Bornand, Pierrette et Bernard Lafourcade. Lausanne, L'Age d'Homme, 1982 (Edits "A Breton Journal"; translates *The Wild Body* minus "Sigismund" and "You Broke My Dream"; translates "A Breton Journal," "Some Innkeepers," "A Breton Innkeeper," "Grignolles," "Unlucky for Pringle," "Our Wild Body," and "How One Begins").

II—*REVIEWS AND STUDIES OF* THE WILD BODY *AND ITS CONSTELLATION:*

P., E. (i. e. Ezra Pound). "Editor's Note," *The Little Review*, IV, no. 5 (September 1917) 3, 7 (An introduction and footnote to "Inferior Religions").

Eliot, T. S. "Tarr," *The Egoist*, V, no. 8 (September 1918) 105-106 ("'Inferior Religions' as the most indubitable evidence of genius, the most powerful piece of imaginative thought, of anything Mr. Lewis has written").

Drey, O. R. "Exhibitions of the Week," *The Nation and Athenæum*," XIX, no. 3 (April 16, 1921) 106-108 (Stresses "the immense zest" of "Tyros and Portraits").

S., H. "Art," *The Spectator*, CXXVI, no. 4844 (April 30, 1921) 555 (Analysis of the Tyros).

Parker, Kineton. "Tyronics," *Drawing and Design*, no. 14 (June 1921) 464.

Hannay, Howard. "Tyros and Portraits by Wyndham Lewis," *The London Mercury*, IV, no. 20 (June 1921) 204-205.

Sickert, Walter Richard. *The Burlington Magazine*, XLI, no. 135 (October 1922) 200 (A review of *The Tyro*).

Empson, William. "Where the Body Is. . . ," *Granta*, XXXVII, 821 (October 2, 1927) 193 (A favourable review of *The Wild Body*).

Taylor, Rachel Annand. "Some Modern Pessimists," *The Spectator*, CXXXIX, no. 5,188 (December 3, 1927) 1016-1019 (Stresses *The Wild Body*'s "French romantic" taste for monsters).

"The Wild Body," *The Times Literary Supplement*, XXVI, no. 1349 (December 8, 1927) 930 (A favourable review of *The Wild Body*).

C., A. E. (i.e., A. E. Coppard). *The Manchester Guardian* (December 9, 1927) 9 (An unfavourable review of *The Wild Body* stressing its unpleasantness and lack of imaginative treatment).

Hartley, L. P. "New Fiction," *The Saturday Review*, CXLVI, no. 3764 (December 17, 1927) 862-863 (A favourable review of *The Wild Body*, finding the author tormented and confused).

"Myth and Sentiment," *Glasgow Herald* (December 22, 1927) 4 (A favourable review of *The Wild Body* objecting to the essays accompanying the stories).

Brittain, Vera. "New Fiction," *Time and Tide*, VIII, no. 51 (December 23, 1927) 1159-1160 (An unfavourable review of *The Wild Body* which claims Lewis "never succeeds in getting anywhere").

Muir, Edwin. "Fiction" *The Nation and Athenæum*, XLII, no. 12 (December 24, 1927) 488-489 (Finds *The Wild Body* "both brilliant and disappointing").

Connolly, Cyril. "New Novels," *The New Statesman*, XXX, no. 765 (December 24, 1927) 358-359 (A favourable review of *The Wild Body:* its only fault is that it does not apply "the religion of the grotesque" to "a beautiful creature").

Robinson, M. "Sex and Sanity," *The Adelphi*, I, no. 3 (March 1928) 266-269 (A favourable analysis of *The Wild Body*).

Gorman, Herbert. "Mr. Lewis Laughs," *New York Herald Tribune Weekly Book Review*, (April 1, 1928) 3-4 (A favourable review of *The Wild Body*).

Cowley, Malcolm. *The New Republic*, LIV, no. 697 (April 11, 1928) 253 (A favourable review of *The Wild Body* suggesting readers "will demand that character should result in action").

Aiken, Conrad. *The New York Evening Post* (April 14, 1928) 14 (A review of *The Wild Body* which calls Lewis "a first rate narrator" who is also "less fortunately a theorist"; contradicts Eliot's praise of "Inferior Religions").

The Bookman, LXVII, no. 4 (June 1928) 463 (A review of *The Wild Body*).

"Tales by Wyndham Lewis," *The New York Times Book Review* (July 1, 1928) 13 (A critical review of *The Wild Body* concluding that "a multiplication of Wyndham Lewises would mean a sterilization of fiction").

Hull, Robert R. "The Comic Cosmos," *The Commonweal*, VIII, no. 13 (August 1, 1928) 335-336 (A favourable review of *The Wild Body*).

Bates, Ernest Sutherland. "A Cathedral of Gargoyles," *The Saturday Review of Literature*, V, no. 11 (October 6, 1928) 181-182 (A critical review of *The Wild Body*).

Baker, A. Ernest and James Packman. *A Guide to the Best Fiction.* London, Routledge, 1932 (Discusses "the harsh brutal and aggressively vulgar style" of *The Wild Body*).

Gawsworth, John (i.e., Terence Ian Armstrong). *Apes, Japes and Hitlerism. A Study and Bibliography of Wyndham Lewis.* London, Unicorn Press, 1932 (Chapter 4 discusses *The Wild Body*).

Porteus, Hugh Gordon. *Wyndham Lewis: a Discursive Exposition.* London, Desmond Harmsworth, 1932, pp. 43, 86, 178, 188, 204, 230.

Dobrée, Bonamy. *Modern Prose Style*, Oxford, Clarendon Press, 1934, pp. 48-51 (Discusses the style of "Bestre").

Bates, Ralph. "Wyndham Lewis," *Time and Tide*, XVI, no. 2 (January 12, 1935) 35-37 (Discusses the "visuality" of *The Wild Body*).

Armitage, Gilbert. "A Note on 'The Wild Body,'" *Twentieth Century Verse*, nos. 6-7 (November-December 1937) 24-26.

Kenner, Hugh. "The War With Time," *Shenandoah*, IV, nos. 2-3 (Summer-Autumn 1953) 18-49.

Wagner, Geoffrey. "*The Wild Body:* a Sanguine of the Enemy," *Nine*, IV, no. 1 (Winter 1953) 18-27 (reprinted in *Wyndham Lewis: A Portrait of the Artist as the Enemy*).

Kenner, Hugh. *Wyndham Lewis.* Norfolk, New Directions, 1954.

Tomlin, E. W. F. *Wyndham Lewis.* Writers and Their Work, no. 64, London, Longmans, Green and Co., 1955, pp. 21-26.

Wagner, Geoffrey. *Wyndham Lewis: A Portrait of the Artist as the Enemy*, New Haven, Yale University (London, Routledge and Kegan Paul) 1957 (reprints "The Wild Body: a Sanguine of the Enemy").

Pritchard, William H. *Wyndham Lewis.* New York, Twayne Publishers, 1968.

Materer, Timothy. "The Short Stories of Wyndham Lewis," *Studies in Short Fiction*, VII, no. 3 (Fall 1970) 615-624 (reprinted in *Wyndham Lewis the Novelist*, 1976).

Michel, Walter. *Wyndham Lewis. Paintings and Drawings.* London, Thames and Hudson (Berkeley, University of California Press) 1971, pp. 48-52, 98-102.

Sisson, C. H. *English Poetry, 1900-1950.* London, Rupert Hart-Davis, 1971, pp. 224-226 (an analysis of "Grignolles").

Pritchard, William. *Wyndham Lewis.* Profiles in Literature. London, Routledge and Kegan Paul, 1972, pp. 12-15 (A study of the style of "Bestre").

Chapman, Robert T. *Wyndham Lewis: Fictions and Satires.* London, Vision Press, 1973, pp. 47-58.

Fox, C. J. and Robert T. Chapman. "Introduction," *Unlucky for Pringle: Unpublished and Other Stories*. London, Vision, 1973, pp. 7-17.

Parker, David. "The Vorticist, 1914. The Artist as a Predatory Savage," *Southern Review*, VII, no. 1 (March 1975) 3-21 (contains an analysis of Ker-Orr).

Materer, Timothy. *Wyndham Lewis the Novelist*. Detroit, Wayne University Press, 1976, pp. 30-45 (reprints "The Short Stories of Wyndham Lewis").

Cook, Richard. *Vorticism and Abstract Art in the First Machine Age. Volume I: Origins and Developments*. London, Gordon Fraser (Berkeley, University of California Press), 1976 (Contains a few references to the Wild Body stories).

Fox, C. J. "Lewisnews," *Lewisletter*, no. 6 (June 1977) 3 (Description of a proof copy of *The Wild Body*).

Cassidy, Victor M. (ed.) "The Sturge Moore Letters," *Lewisletter*, no. 7 (October 1977) 8-23.

Beatty, Michael. "The Earliest Fiction of Wyndham Lewis and *The Wild Body*," *Theoria*, 48, 1 (1977) 37-45.

Lafourcade, Bernard and Bradford Morrow. "A Note on the Text and Composition of 'Crossing the Frontier,'" *Crossing the Frontier*. Santa Barbara, Black Sparrow Press, 1978.

Jameson, Fredric. *Fables of Aggression: Wyndham Lewis, the Modernist as Fascist*. Berkeley, Los Angeles, London, University of California Press, 1979, pp. 106-108.

Lafourcade, Bernard. "A Key List of the Early Works," *Enemy News*, no. 10 (May 1979) 11-13 (Discusses "Writings").

Lafourcade, Bernard. "The Taming of the Wild Body," *Wyndham Lewis: A Revaluation. New Essays* (edited by Jeffrey Meyers). London, The Athlone Press, 1980, pp. 68-84.

Meyers, Jeffrey. *The Enemy. A Biography of Wyndham Lewis*. London and Henley, Routledge and Kegan Paul, 1980.

Farrington, Jane. *Wyndham Lewis*. London, Lund Humphries (in association with the Manchester City Art Gallery), 1980 (Catalogue of the exhibition with a number of references to *The Wild Body*).

Murray, Robert. "'Our Wild Body': Lewis's Forgotten Essay?" *Enemy News*, no. 14 (Summer 1981) 15-17.

Lafourcade, Bernard. "Off to Budapest—With Freud. A Note on 'A Soldier of Humour'," *Enemy News*, no. 15 (Winter 1982) 6-10.

Lafourcade, Bernard. "The Wild Body, Bergson and the Absurd," *Enemy News*, no. 15 (Winter 1982) 23-25. (An answer to Robert Murray).

Lafourcade, Bernard. "Introduction," *Le Corps Sauvage (Wyndham Lewis et la France—tome I)*. Lausanne, L'Age d'Homme, 1982, pp. 7-12.

Cianci, Giovanni. "Il Lewis prebellico e vorticista" in *Wyndham Lewis. Letteratura/Pittura* (a cura di Giovanni Cianci). Palermo: Sellerio, 1982, pp. 25-66.

Duncan, Ian. "Towards a Modernistic Poetic: Wyndham Lewis's Early Fiction," *ibid.*, pp. 67-85.

Munton, Alan. "Wyndham Lewis: The Transformations of Carnival," *ibid.*, pp. 141-157 (centrally concerned with *The Wild Body*).

Carapezza, Attilio. "Il comico e il satirico nell'opera di Wyndham Lewis," *ibid.*, pp. 158-164.

NOTES ON THE ILLUSTRATIONS

Since Lewis, keeping apart the two media at his disposal, never directly illustrated the characters of his stories and their adventures, the graphic works selected here to accompany each of the texts had to be chosen subjectively—on grounds of echoes in themes, situations or moods. Otherwise the only guiding principle was that of chronological homogeneity—*The Wild Body* being illustrated by post-war designs, and its "Archaeology" by pre-war ones (with one exception). Where known, the medium of each illustration is given.

p. 1: "Gesticulating Figure," 1929. Reproduced on the title-page of "The Diabolical Principle" in *The Enemy* no. 3 (*Wyndham Lewis. Paintings and Drawings,* plate 93, no. 652).

p. 2: "Self-portrait," 1911. Pencil. Inscribed "W. Lewis" and on the reverse, "'Self-portrait' about 1912. W.L." (*Wyndham Lewis. Paintings and Drawings,* plate 4, no. 24).

p. 11: "Couple," 1921. Pen and ink. Signed, with on reverse a dedication to Kate Lechmere, dated 1921 (*Wyndham Lewis. Paintings and Drawings,* plate 79, no. 454). The ambiguous complexity of the two figures may well reflect the parental tensions characteristic of *The Wild Body.*

p. 15: "The Brombroosh," 1921. Black ink. Reproduced in *The Tyro* no. 1 (*Wyndham Lewis. Paintings and Drawings,* plate 75, no. 449). This drawing could pass as a convincing portrait of Monsieur de Valmore in "A Soldier of Humour."

p. 47: "The Dancers," 1925. Pen and ink. Inscribed "Wyndham Lewis, 1925" (*Wyndham Lewis. Paintings and Drawings,* plate 83, no. 610).

p. 75: "Cover Design for 'The Tyro' no. 2," 1922. Reproduced on the cover of *The Tyro* no. 2 (*Wyndham Lewis. Paintings and Drawings,* plate 75, no. 494). This may have been inspired by "Bestre" included in this issue of *The Tyro.*

p. 89: "Study," 1919. Pen and ink, watercolour. (*Wyndham Lewis. Paintings and Drawings*, plate 38, no. 358).

p. 105: "A Panel," 1929. One of four panels, oil on plywood. (*Wyndham Lewis. Paintings and Drawings*, plate 87, no. P 39).

p. 117: "Figure," 1930. Pen and ink. (*Wyndham Lewis. Paintings and Drawings*, plate 95, no. 697).

p. 131: "The Cliffs," 1920. Pen and ink. Inscribed "W. Lewis, 1920. The Cliffs." (*Wyndham Lewis. Paintings and Drawings*, plate 73, no. 388).

p. 147: "Abstract Figure Study," 1921. Pen and ink. Inscribed "W. L., 1921." (*Wyndham Lewis. Paintings and Drawings*, plate 78, no. 446).

p. 155: "Studies of Performers," 1923. Pen and ink. Inscribed "W. L., 1923." (*Wyndham Lewis. Paintings and Drawings*, plate 83, no. 593).

p. 161: "Sensibility," 1921. Pen and ink, wash. Inscribed "Wyndham Lewis. 1921." Reproduced in *The Tyro* no. 2. Known also as "The Contemplator." (*Wyndham Lewis. Paintings and Drawings*, plate 80, no. 483). The small red heart ironically justifies the title.

p. 179: "Abstract Composition: Two Figures," 1921. Pen and ink, wash, gouache. (*Wyndham Lewis. Paintings and Drawings*, plate 78, no. 443).

p. 189: "The Enemy of the Stars," 1913. Pen and ink, ink wash. Inscribed "Wyndham Lewis. 1913." (*Wyndham Lewis. Paintings and Drawings*, plate 24, no. 143). May have been influenced by Epstein's "Female Figure in Flenite."

p. 191: "Dieppe Fishermen," 1910. Pen and ink. Inscribed "Wyndham Lewis 1910." (*Wyndham Lewis. Paintings and Drawings*, plate 2, no. 19). With "Café" (see p. 282), the only drawing of the period depicting a French scene associated with the experiences of *The Wild Body*. Jane Farrington sees in it the influences of Matisse (*Wyndham Lewis*, Manchester City Art Galleries, p. 50).

p. 201: "Figure (Spanish Woman)," 1912. Pen and ink, gouache. Inscribed "Wyndham Lewis. 1912." (*Wyndham Lewis. Paintings and Drawings*, plate 11, no. 65).

p. 207: "Courtship," 1912. Pen and ink, chalk. Inscribed "W. L. 1912." (*Wyndham Lewis. Paintings and Drawings*, plate 9, no. 45). The correspondence with the early stories has often been noted; this series of primitives is also reminiscent of Tarr's production (see *Tarr*, 1918, part IV, chapter 11; chapter 12 in *Tarr*, 1928).

p. 219: "Chickens," 1912. Pen and ink, ink, wash. Inscribed "W. L. 1912." (*Wyndham Lewis. Paintings and Drawings*, plate 9, no. 43).

p. 235: "The Theatre Manager," 1909." Pen and ink, watercolour. Inscribed "W. Lewis, 1909." (*Wyndham Lewis. Paintings and Drawings*, plate 1, no. 15). This important piece which shows the influence of Picasso has often been discussed (see Jane Farrington, *Wyndham Lewis*, Manchester City Art Galleries, pp. 49-50).

p. 249: "Two Muscular Figures," 1912-1913. Pen and ink, ink wash. (*Wyndham Lewis. Paintings and Drawings*, plate 8, no. 122).

p. 257: "Spanish Dance," 1914. Pen and ink, ink wash, wash, gouache. Inscribed "Wyndham Lewis, 1914. Spanish Dance." (*Wyndham Lewis. Paintings and Drawings*, plate 25, no. 172).

p. 267: "The Green Tie," 1909. Pen and ink, wash. Inscribed "Wyndham Lewis, 1909." (*Wyndham Lewis. Paintings and Drawings*, plate 2, no. 12).

p. 275: "Anthony," 1909. Pen and ink, gouache. (*Wyndham Lewis. Paintings and Drawings*, plate 2, no. 11). Shows Lewis's interest in the sculptures of the Easter Island (see Jane Farrington, *Wyndham Lewis*, Manchester City Art Galleries, p. 41).

p. 285: "A Berber Stronghold in the Valley of the Sous," 1931. Pen and ink, watercolour, pencil. Inscribed "Wyndham Lewis. 1931." (*Wyndham Lewis. Paintings and Drawings*, plate 97, no. 707). This is the only departure from the principle of illustrating these texts with contemporary drawings. Lewis disdained landscape painting (see his ironical comments in "A Spanish Household" and

"Unlucky for Pringle") and used natural or architectural motifs only in his backgrounds, or in semi-abstract design such as "Bagdad," save for this one major exception. His discovery of the Kasbahs of the Atlas during his 1931 visit to Morocco impressed Lewis by the sort of massiveness he had long before met in Brittany. This was more than a coincidence: in "Grignolles" each house had "its harem," and in 1933 Lewis discussed the possible Celtic origin of the Berbers ("What are the Berbers," *The Bookman*, December). See also the descriptions in *The Revenge for Love*, part I.

p. 289: "Café," 1910. Pen and ink, ink wash, black chalk, watercolour, wash, gouache. Inscribed "Wyndham Lewis 1910," and "Wyndham Lewis 1911." (*Wyndham Lewis. Paintings and Drawings*, plate 2, no. 18).

p. 297: "Invitation to a Vorticist Evening," 1916. Printed invitation for February 22, 1916. (*Wyndham Lewis. Paintings and Drawings*, plate 31, no. 213).

p. 313: "Reading Room," 1915. Pen and ink. Inscribed "Wyndham Lewis." (Reproduced in *Wyndham Lewis: Fifteen Drawings; Wyndham Lewis. Paintings and Drawings*, plate 38, no. 209).

p. 321: "The Vorticist," 1912. Pen and ink, chalk, watercolour. Inscribed "Wyndham Lewis. 1912." (*Wyndham Lewis. Paintings and Drawings*, plate 10, no. 118). The influence of Japanese prints presenting warriors has been noted: the Vorticist is a soldier (see Jane Farrington, *Wyndham Lewis*, Manchester City Art Galleries, p. 55).

p. 351: "The Cept," 1921. Illustrates the cover of *The Tyro* no. 1. (*Wyndham Lewis. Paintings and Drawings*, plate 75, no. 451).

p. 357: "Mr. Wyndham Lewis as a Tyro," 1920-1921. Oil on canvas. (*Wyndham Lewis. Paintings and Drawings*, plate 74, no. P 27).

p. 361: "Meeting Between the Tyro, Mr. Segando, and the Tyro, Phillip," 1921. Black ink. Reproduced in *The Tyro* no. 1 (with the caption). (*Wyndham Lewis. Paintings and Drawings*, plate 75, no. 470). In *The Tyro* this illustration precedes a utopian skit entitled "Mr. Segando and the Fifth Cataclysm" by John Rodker, but this text and Lewis's drawing (and short dialogue) have little or nothing in common.

p. 371: "Creation Myth," 1920s. Collage, pen and ink, watercolour. Inscribed "Wyndham Lewis." (*Wyndham Lewis. Paintings and Drawings*, plate 86, no. 658).

p. 375: "Drawing for Timon," 1912. Pen and ink, watercolour. Inscribed "Wyndham Lewis. Drawing for Timon." (*Wyndham Lewis. Paintings and Drawings*, plate 21, no. 109). Bears a great resemblance to the early self-portraits.

p. 381: "A Reading of Ovid (Tyros),"1920-1921. Oil on canvas. (*Wyndham Lewis. Paintings and Drawings*, plate 74, no. P 31).

AFTERWORD

by Bernard Lafourcade

To get some idea of the present status and sweeping magnitude of this remarkable collection of stories—Wyndham Lewis's great initial outburst and constant source of reference for what was to prove most actively vital in his vision—imagine a population of Easter Island monoliths lying face down, half buried in the dust. This spectral host must sooner or later be recovered from oblivion as one of the great exhumations of Modernism, and the object of this book is to promote a long overdue recognition by presenting the procession of these stories complete for the first time.

Pondered and elaborated by Lewis over a period of nearly twenty years, the early intuitions of 1909 eventually yielded a collection of stories, *The Wild Body* of 1927—a landmark in the history of English short fiction as significant as *Dubliners*, but which, for a variety of reasons, has remained largely ignored. The final product, with the exception of a second meagre impression in 1932, was not reissued during the author's lifetime, though Methuen planned a reprint in the early fifties—and since Lewis's death, only one facsimile reprint has been made available. Moreover none of the constitutive monoliths of *The Wild Body* was ever included in any of the numerous anthologies of the modern short story—which in the course of half a century is surprising, to say the least, unless it is realized that these objects must have been perceived from the start as disturbingly alien, not to say incomprehensible, thus confirming Hugh Kenner's diagnosis of Lewis as "a one-man alternative avant-garde."[1] Surely, as was so often the case with Lewis, and still is, the pundits felt that, rather than grappling with complex nonconformity, it would be simpler to ignore the whole thing altogether. Thus "the alternative" remained in the cupboard.

So, these sketches, essays and stories sank into oblivion outside the narrow circle of Lewis's critics. But even the latter bear some responsibility for this neglect. Though the early reviewers of 1927-1928 had often proved enthusiastic and sometimes highly perceptive, the recent commentators have not approached Lewis's uncouth tribe systematically. Unanimous in asserting the importance of "The Wild Body" in the shaping of the author's *Weltanschauung*, but often at variance about the value of the stories, they usually contented themselves with a few random samples before moving on to the study of the more accessible and homogeneous novels, which means that a number of the "bodies" have hardly been anatomized, and some of them not at all. The most obvious idiosyncrasies of these "little dead totems" have been discussed, but the organization of their clan, its genesis and growth, its changing philosophy, its collective unconscious and structural obsessions must still be ascertained. An overall vista is needed—the cliché of Lewis the man springing from nowhere being still too often used as a smoke screen. True enough, there are signs that a more attentive attitude is appearing, but this comprehensive spectrum of the work of Lewis *jeune* is still likely to come as a revelation to many.

A saga no doubt, but no mere Ur-Lewis for the delight of experts alone. The evolution from the earlier texts to the final *Wild Body*—or, to cut a long story short, from groping vitalism to rigid formalism—was considerable. But from the start the central Lewisian gap between creator and creation was there. The earlier, almost Lawrentian, observation of reality was already undermined by phantasmic parody. The documentary accidentalness of the travelogue was in fact selective of aspects of reality which were both haunted and haunting. As to the more polished and fictional final products, they were to perpetuate this initial tension by "a verbal impasto" thanks to which, according to Hugh Kenner, Lewis "exalted his vices into a style,"[2] downgrading reality to present it as an artificial mechanism. A diagnosis confirmed by Jean-Jacques Mayoux who, when analysing the rationale behind Lewis's style and vision, remarks that "no sooner has subjectivity been kicked out than it bursts in through the window."[3] However brief the expulsion, it leaves its mark, turning interiority into a sort of collage. This may well constitute the essence of the Lewisian "alternative," and suggests a "post-modernism" before the hour.[4]

The prolonged distillation of such paradoxes is probably responsible for the most salient feature of *The Wild Body*. It stands as one of these rare collections of stories which, though elusive, are felt to be intensely controlled by "a logical pattern," "an inherent design," or "a strong sense of form," as John Gawsworth[5] recognized fifty years ago. In the final version of "Inferior Religions," Lewis saw his characters as a colony of "theorems," and one is tempted to evoke here—though they have with them little in common apart from some pivotal concern with the body—such collections as Roussel's or Kafka's "machines célibataires"[6], Joyce's *Dubliners*, Hemingway's "Nick" sketches and Sartre's *Le Mur*. There must be a few more, but not many, of these systematic "Diaboliques," and on all counts *The Wild Body* and its characters belong to that party of sublime extremists.

Such comparisons may at least shed some light on the practice of the Lewisian "alternative." Lewis's "bodies" are not submitted to a crucial test—epiphany, fracture or execution. Half-document, half-fiction, these "stories" generally present a gang of active paralytics prone to mock aggressions, by means of which they project a primitive tottering shadow for the benefit of an ambiguous observer or *agent provocateur*. A world of degraded myths inviting the reader to recognize some ancestral grimace filtering through our existential routine. Not characters facing a liberating crisis, but "shells," congealed in rituals, whose very human, though degenerate, gestures told Beckettian "Stories and Texts for Nothing," long before the hour. Lewis did with Descartes, Goethe, Dostoevsky and Bergson what Beckett was to do with Dante, Geulincx, Proust and Joyce.

A late but characteristic postscript to this manipulation of the real is offered in the opening pages of *Snooty Baronet* (1932), when Kell-Imrie (first named Carr-Orr, which suggests that this novel was initially conceived as a sort of sequel to *The Wild Body*) defines himself in these terms:

> I am not a narrative writer. As to being a "fiction" writer, I could not bring myself to write down that I am not *that*. I may never I hope be called upon to repudiate an imputation of that order. But the art of narrative, that is a different matter to "fiction." To Defoe I take off my hat. Then there was Goldsmith. I should prefer to make it clear at once at all events that I occupy myself only with scientific research. Such claim as I may have to be a man-of-letters reposes only upon the fact that my investigations into the nature of the human being have led me to employ the arts of the myth-maker, in order the better to present (for the purposes of popular study) my human specimens. Henri Fabre dramatized his insects in that way. . .

Lewis's reverence for Defoe is suggestive: the forefather of the English novel only began his literary career (shuffling reporting and forgery) when he found himself hopelessly entangled in the "fictions" of a treble *agent double*. Such contamination is typical of *The Wild Body*. It explains why these stories are only animated by the ghost of an action—the "narrative" vector becoming a "fictional" vortex, with no compensatory introspection being allowed in. These are severe limitations, and one may wonder what is left to fill up the stories. An answer may be sketched by doing what Lewis did for "Laughter" in "Inferior Religions," when he decided to "catalogue (its) attributes." We can name six basic "attributes" of The Wild Body: 1) a real presence, 2) fascination, 3) and 4) comedy and tragedy, 5) the grotesque, and 6) the absurd. At least implicitly, all these elements were present from the start, but it is only progressively that they came to be recognized as such—and this in the above order, just as in a monogram the intertwined letters are to be read in a given succession. Elucidating these took Lewis twenty years—a highly significant process paralleled by the similar rewriting or repeating of the rest of his early creative production (the two *Tarrs* and the two *Enemy of the Stars*, "The War Baby" duplicating "Cantleman's Spring-Mate").

1) A REAL PRESENCE. The prerequisite for any of these stories is a casual meeting with a "body" or group of "bodies" perceived as foreign, strange, and alien. Such presence is "given"—apparently imposed from the outside

on the anonymous witness. It is not invented and organized by an author as will be the case later with sophisticated productions like "Sigismund." Often presented as an illustration of some sociological or cultural observation, the documentary vignettes exploit the picturesque and the picaresque, as if Baedeker and Dickens were joining hands to caricature national types—provocative, yet essentially flat. Some of Ker-Orr's poses smack of a typically English superiority complex towards foreigners. Yet, ascribing strange physical aspects or behaviours to a national mould was not the original object, as Lewis's elimination of capital letters for adjectives of nationality will soon prove. The nation—like games and sports (see "Our Wild Body")—was recognized as one more "opium du peuple"—an inferior religion. In fact the characters of the early stories all tend to overdo their foreignness by their being so marginal, eccentic or primitive—a multi-storeyed alienation culminating in Monsieur de Valmore, this French pseudo-American operating in Spain. What it must have meant for young Lewis was that French mechanical Cartesianism, the Slav soul feeding on Dostoevskian contradictions, and the baroque austerity of the Spaniards combined to infect the dreamy imagination of a slow-developing Briton. There "the alternative" found its first expression—in a reality, which, being selected by an obscure emotion, could not be properly focused, could not yield a clear message.

2) FASCINATION. A coherence, which is compulsive and disquieting, gives the travelogue another dimension—magnetic, ontological, and problematic—and herein lie the difficulty and significance of The Wild Body. Irreducible yet split, it acquires an existence less touristic than Berkeleyan, being inseparable from that other presence, the beholder's. The only mode of perception allowed by its gesticulating opaqueness is fascination. Bestre, the "eye-man," became Lewis's "enfant chéri," because he was the arch-fascinator of the tribe; le Père François exists only in so far as his disjointed utterances turn reality into a mesmerizing patchwork full of holes; whereas Ludo shut in an opaque body by his blindness is killed by a reflected otherness he embodies. According to Maurice-Jean Lefevre[7], "the awareness of a fissure in reality," making it appear "super-real," constitutes the essence of fascination. This applies very well to what is constantly happening in The Wild Body. An author may handle his material so as to make it appear fascinating, but fascination here is rooted in an uncertainty involving both subject and object. The puzzled observer is as paralyzed as the object of his perception—and perception always seems to imply a dangerous frontier and cruel no-man's-land. This was not obvious at first because the author-narrator remained impersonal, but "A Breton Journal," which embodied the first apprehensions of The Wild Body, was animated by such "fissures"

suggested by static characters exuding a "super-reality" of sorts (a "sub-reality" might be a better word in view of the future "*Inferior* Religions"). Postures suspend time, and the body becomes "a tableau vivant."

The Wild Body and its "fissures" offer an approach to an understanding of Lewis's dual genius. In "Beginnings" we learn how, when he started writing in Brittany, Lewis kept drawing and story-telling in tight compartments—the story feeding on what was left over after the drawing had been completed. Yet the literary Lewis remained manifestly visual. A prisoner of his fascination? This suggests an unresolved tension, the enduring effects of which probably determined—to name only two significant developments contemporary with the long story of The Wild Body—the adoption of the Vortex (an archetype of fascination with its centripetal immobility), and the defence of space and fixity as expressed in *Time and Western Man*. That the prolonged rumination of The Wild Body was not accidentally due to World War I but was more fundamentally personal, solipsistic and Berkeleyan seems confirmed by the way its saga came to its conclusion. Lewis redoubled the duplication by endowing his "eye" with a distinct personality and body—that of a showman with a full name and a family background secretly and ironically modelled on his own (see "A Soldier of Humour"). Ker-Orr, acting as a screen, reduced the effect of fascination and enabled the paralyzed observer to complete his saga and eventually emerge as The Enemy[8].

Then, retrospectively, fascination could be seen as corresponding with the repressed recognition of an intimate trauma. But here the *Zeitgeist* should not be ignored. Lewis belonged to a generation of exiles repelled by the debilitating respectability of the Victorian scene and attracted by the artistic ebullience of the Continent. The two most conspicuous "anti-Lewises," Joyce and Lawrence, are obvious names here, but also the more transitional Forster with such contemporary novels as *Where Angels Fear to Tread*. All these writers specialized in "fascinating fissures" of one sort or another—and all suffered from a parental deficit, on the father's side. Let us concentrate on a so far unexplored comparison with J. M. Synge, whose formative years—not long before Lewis's—greatly resemble those which saw the incubation of The Wild Body. Like Lewis, who, by his own admission, was "congealed in a kind of cryptic immaturity" (see "How One Begins," a diagnosis confirmed by Augustus John in his memoirs), Synge squandered years of his life in that Mecca of the arts, Paris, gripped by an inertia redolent of "fin de siècle" *ennui*, before, suddenly, on his homecoming, erupting into creativity with the discovery of a liberating primitivism. Synge's Connemara played a part strikingly similar to Lewis's Brittany and the Playboy is a wild body par excellence. Synge's Parisian exile and subsequent primitivist explosion can be reasonably linked to a parental "fissure" (his father died when he was very young) which the Oedipal explosions of *The Playboy of the*

Western World can be seen to perpetuate by an extraordinary jargon akin to that of the final "Bestre" for instance—this in an atmosphere of comedy both exacerbating and bridging the abysmal paralyzing absence.

Bridging impossible existential gaps is precisely what—for structural anthropology—seems to be the *raison d'être* of mythic thought. Lewis's "saurian" immersion in the Breton summer and his somnambulic approach to his "bodies" may well have reflected the circumstances of his early life—his family romance—and an "indigestion of reality" which later Pringle obscurely recognized. Let us recall that Lewis's parents separated when their son was eleven, and that the "fissure" was spatially intensified by his father being American and his mother British.[9] As time passed his mother asserted herself as protectress, confidante and money-lender while the father (who had eloped with the maid) receded into the role of an absentee. Much could be made out of this to explain aspects of Lewis's future behaviour, but such approaches are irritating in that they seem amateurishly to oversimplify things, yet it may also be that such an easy geometry recaptures something of the original fascination—and it must be recognized, at least, that this is the sort of explanation Lewis himself succumbed to later when he wrote:

> My mother's and father's principal way of spending their time at the period of my birth was the same as mine now: my mother painting pictures of the farmhouse where we lived, my father writing books inside it. . . For a person like myself to both write and paint is being bi-lingual.[10]

This is a reconstruction on the author's part, but nonetheless telling. This idyllic vignette, rather reminiscent of Lewis's Breton scenes, constitutes an attempt at bridging the gap and going back to the Golden Age home—and Lewis's dual genius, as defined here, appears as an indirect effort to reunify the separated (and now dead) parents. That this sketch should not have been included in *Rude Assignment* is all the more revealing—it was probably thought too intimately limpid.

Seen in this light the basic fictional ingredients of The Wild Body take on "a family likeness" confirming the secret coherence of these stories, and the lasting effects of the fascination.

Settings: foreign inns and hotels, cafés and boarding houses—rooms, opposing their ambiguous privacy to the bleak openness of public places, mostly streets and squares. Clearly a frontier world of doors and windows for this decadent version of the Romantic Wanderer, the then fashionable Tramp (see Augustus John, W. H. Davies and Douglas Goldring). One telling exception, the only "private house" is the Ankou's—and it is a cave, a troglodytic tomb to which the narrator is refused admission.

Actions: no plot, but all the grotesqueries of hotel life—the violent enticing of customers, invasion and trespass, parasitism and voyeurism, escape and expulsion.

Characters: vagrants and guardians, all specialists in hospitality or inhospitality—with even the Saltimbanques offering the brief shelter of their tent and benches.

Couples: young lovers are rare and aggressive—"amours ancillaires" exclusively (again, Charles Lewis had eloped with the maid). Married couples are bitter, destructive and generally childless—the Saltimbanques exhibiting their "gytes" only to make the world more fundamentally gloomy. The only happily united family (that of the painter in "A Spanish Household") is comically mechanical.

Children: unexpectedly, from what has just been said, a very active group, with the true children, such as the laughing apocalyptist of "Les Saltimbanques," the Picasso-esque shadows of "A Breton Journal," and the Soutine-esque dull groom stunned by Roland in "A Breton Innkeeper," but above all the permanently infantile characters who contaminate the adult world, such as the child-man persecuted by brats in the final snapshot of "The 'Pole.'" Ultimately all the inmates of The Wild Body will be defined as "wild children" in "Inferior Religions."

Showmanship: the author-narrator may be suspected of being the arch-child of the whole system—and to pass from the impersonal narrator of 1909, through Pringle (the devouring "child" and uncertain lover), to the aggressive showman of 1927, is to pass from the foundling to the bastard of the Freudian family romance,[11] an evolution confirmed by that of the rather meek Isoblitsky of "The 'Pole'" into the enigmatic Zoborov who, like a hermit crab, usurps the erotic shell of "Beau Séjour."

Parental figures: if the conquest of a home can be seen as the mainspring of these stories, then the childless fascinating "bodies" animating them should be susceptible to interpretation as father and mother images. Madame Brotcotnaz (curiously associated through heavy drinking with Ker-Orr's absent mother), or Madame Chalaran, or the Cornac's wife seem to present various facets of the mother seen from the son's point of view (a victim of male brutality, a money guardian, a charming companion, etc.). Treated in sympathetic half-tones, they are definitely less prominent than the father images. The isolation of these may stand for the father's absence—and they are brutally dealt with. Wrecks and invalids (Monsieur Jules Montort, Ludo, le Père François, Monsieur Chalaran), or else unstable giants (Monsieur Brobdingnag, Monsieur de Valmore), all are manipulated, humiliated or killed by fate, or the "son's" aggressiveness. To this, two exceptions: "Beau Séjour," in which various "sons" compete in the absence of any parent—and Bestre, first taken as a model reconciling life and art, but eventually discarded, though dearly loved (a typical ambivalence), as a degenerate impotent exhibitionist.

The body: why is it a "body" and why is it "wild"? Here is the central question. An answer should now be less tentative. The body prevailed over the person, because full identity had been denied it by the parental split—the home disappearing and leaving it as the only remaining "shell." Its wildness is therefore inseparable from the absence of a hospitable family nucleus. It is condemned to an exile during which layer upon layer of externality is built up to make up for the lost identity and protect the inner void—see the image of the Russian doll in *Tarr* or Turgenev's "Six Unknown" in "The Code of a Herdsman." This process of aggressive reappropriation is nowhere so obvious as in Ker-Orr's triumphant big gnashing teeth which, in his victory over Monsieur de Valmore, confirm him both as an American and as an Enemy.

Recrossing these tempestuous thresholds after the war, and the death of his parents, Lewis—in all likelihood thanks to his recent acquaintance with Freud[12]—probably came to an understanding of what had animated the Breton fascination. This did not lead him to exorcism but allowed him to use laughter as a smoke-screen for sex. The Wild Body had acted as a sort of rite of passage for this slow-developer. A rite of passage—is this not a primitive equivalent of the *Bildüngsroman?*

3) and 4) COMEDY and TRAGEDY. The other basic constituents of The Wild Body are easier to assess because they translate a subliminally perceived existential anguish into clear formal patterns. The obscure fascination exerted by the actors of The Wild Body—which Lewis was unable or reluctant to understand—had to be tamed, given a reassuring vestment making the story communicable and lively while preserving its secret message. Comedy provided this great cloak—all the more easily as its eruptive gaiety harmonized with Lewis's release from his long Continental inertia. Like Synge, Lewis, quite naturally, opted for forms of comedy closely associated with the body—farce, horseplay, practical jokes and the burlesque—wrongly considered as "low" forms, whereas they are in fact more profound than intellectual wit through being—as with Jonson or Swift—near to sheer physical reality, or the unconscious. Just as in *The Playboy of the Western World* the parricidal mood arouses a collective explosion of joyful physical liberation, the Lewisian vortex of fascination is strategically counterbalanced by the bumping acceleration of the fête surrounding it.

Alan Munton, who shrewdly investigated this aspect, rightly relates it to the celebrations of Carnival and the *commedia dell'arte* deriving from it—and surely from Paris to Munich, from balls to travelling circuses, Lewis explored a festive Europe. This leads Munton to draw a convincing contrast between the vitalistic celebrations of the early stories and the sour intellectual satires of Lewis's post-World War I period. It is true that the feast is no longer to be found in "Sigismund" or "You Broke my Dream." But this does not mean that the early Wild Body was just "good fun," and Munton makes it clear that not only comedy but satire originates in the Carnival impulse, which is intensely concerned with the body, its dark contradictory functions and revitalizing dismemberment. As R. C. Elliott's studies of satire and utopia[13] confirm, the topsy-turvidom of The Feast of Fools allows the mixing of *genres* so typical of The Wild Body. Degenerate rites, inferior myths, apocalyptism (so very close to utopia), sordidness, decay and death are just as active in these stories as the enjoyment of the ludicrous, or the cultivation of black humour (see Timothy Materer's analysis), or the pursuit of an "idée fixe" (see Robert Chapman's study).[14] Laughter has its shadow—and in tragi-comedy even the killing of Death reasserts the "fissure" over which "it is impossible for logic to throw any bridge."[15]

Such dualism marks the limits of Lewis's primitivism when compared with D. H. Lawrence's "polarity." Lawrence, when he perceives the "fissure" (in "Snake" or "Medlars and Sorb-Apples") makes a rush for it to merge the conflicting poles of his fascination down there in the darkness. Lewis, on the contrary, explodes out of it—volcanically. Just compare—for the final confrontation of the body and its impending fate—the Orphic torches of Lawrence's "Bavarian Gentians" with the high voltage bulb Lewis lights in "The Sea Mists of the Winter" as a defence against blindness. Jean-Jacques Mayoux is certainly right when he defines Lawrence as "the last of the great anti-absurdists."[16] With Lewis—inseparable from an intense lucidity—the paradox went on asserting itself, as can be seen in the neo-Nietzschean aphoristic definitions of "Inferior Religions" where comedy systematically collides with tragedy, thus belittling the mythopoeic vision. By 1917, sure enough, the Carnival had become "arctic"—frozen.

5) THE GROTESQUE. The effort to dominate the still obscure fascination by associating its "fissure" with the clash of comedy and tragedy in the mixing of *genres* led to the growth of a strained, bombastic, out of the way style. In the early sketches, the behaviour of the characters was definitely grotesque, but not the style and viewpoint communicating them—and their fascination remained encapsulated in the objectiveness of the travelogue. With "Unlucky for Pringle," fiction and reality begin to overlap in exploding combinations—the plea for a healthy physical communication advocated in "Our Wild Body" being systematically flouted. On the one hand Lewis pays lip service to fictional verisimilitude by introducing dialogues and an apparently realistic two-storeyed narration. But the commentary corrupts this to exalt voyeurism and the tortuous paradoxes of body and home, digestion and excretion. We find such sentences as "the unwearied optimism of these inanimate objects, how they occupied stolidly room after room, was appalling," or "Monsieur Chalaran had shown his displeasure and discomfort by

eating everything within reach," or towards the end of the story "the house *would* vomit him; it could not assimilate him." Formal sophistication and stylistic amplification marked the first "Soldier of Humour," and, under the influence of the Vortex and the War, blew up in the exuberant imagery of "Inferior Religions." Thereafter it was caught up in the extreme "impasto" of the 1922 "Bestre" which paved the way for the final systematic exploitation of the grotesque in the general rewriting of 1927. It was then only that Ker-Orr spoke of "stylistic anomaly" and "grotesque realism."

The grotesque shows a remarkable structural similarity to fascination, in that it stylistically expresses an "unresolved clash of incompatibles."[17] Here is the "fissure" again, with this difference perhaps that the grotesque seems to be essentially a gesticulation whereas fascination paralyzes the beholder. Besides, grotesque exaggeration turns reality into a collage, and this is why grotesque characters are necessarily "flat," to use E. M. Forster's distinction. It is appropriate here to note that this grotesque flatness has been linked with "Oedipal arrest."[18] The obsessions of The Wild Body, as well as the cryptic disclosure of Ker-Orr's family backdrop, do not contradict such ascription. The "fissure" of laughter was superimposed onto that of sex, and the resulting wildness—which may well be a tongue-in-cheek sublimation—nonetheless perpetuates the rich initial incomprehensibility by a perverse gibberish. It is not surprising therefore that such a pioneer in non-communication and mind-"massaging" nonsense should have turned out to be one of Marshall McLuhan's mentors.

6) THE ABSURD. The aphorisms of the 1917 "Inferior Religions" made it clear that Lewis was in search of a philosophy to replace the superficial vitalism of "Our Wild Body," and fit his new turbulent style in which each word made grimaces at its neighbours. Philip Thomson comes to the conclusion that the "consistent perception of the grotesque, or the perception of grotesqueness on a grand scale, can lead to the notion of universal absurdity."[19] This was the road followed by Lewis, and it led to the apparently illuminating discovery of the concept of the absurd in the final act of The Wild Body—"The Meaning of the Wild Body"—in which the word "absurd" occurs no less than seven times in seven pages. Lewis seems to have been the first to use this word systematically as a formal critical concept. The Lewisian "alternative"—this intuition of post-modernism—is closely associated with this exaltation of the absurd, which in many ways prefigured not only existentialism (see *Self Condemned* and *The Writer and the Absolute*) but the formalist distortions of The Theatre of the Absurd and the Dark Humourists, as well as the geometric expressionism of the "Nouveau Roman."

The part played by the absurd in The Wild Body has been sufficiently analysed by Robert Chapman and myself to make all but attention to a few essential points unnecessary here. The final exaltation of the absurd does not mean that it was absent from the earliest work (see the antics of the Farceur in "The 'Pole'"), but it is only later that Lewis came to perceive its universality. For surely there is not one literary work which, at one stage or another, does not make use of absurdity, but this universalizing—a complete reduction—is compulsory for a work to be "a work of the absurd." In the case of Lewis, this discovery coincided with the 1914-1918 war, and also probably with the death of his parents—the old personal fascination of the Breton summer was superseded by a general theoretical vision of the absurd, whose structure is in fact similar to that of both fascination and the grotesque ("the chasm lying between being and non-being"). It operates however on the level of logic, for it takes a logical man to perceive the absurd—a situation congenial to the mechanical paradoxes of Lewis's dualism. The elimination of personal involvement and the use of a systematic reduction separate the two post-war stories ("Sigismund" and "You Broke my Dream") from the main stream of The Wild Body; yet they were included in the final *Wild Body* because reduction and irreducibility are twins after all.

The final organization of *The Wild Body*, with its core of seven stories, its accompanying essays, and its comet tail—and all its talk about "theorems" and "propositions"—constitutes the stringent demonstration of "a system of feeling." This suggests what is the specific, and indeed unique and paradoxical, nature of the Lewisian absurd—its energy. Vitalism expelled, there remained the sheer energy of the Vortex—the Eye.

The Wild Body has an origin, but no message, outside the turbulence which surrounds its fixity.

NOTES

[1] Preface to the Black Sparrow Press bibliography of Lewis, page 11.

[2] *Wyndham Lewis*, page 92.

[3] "Wyndham Lewis ou la puissance du sensible," *La Quinzaine Littéraire*, XVI, no. 347 (1-15 May 1981), page 24.

[4] See Fredric Jameson's important study, *Fables of Aggression: Wyndham Lewis, the Modernist as Fascist*, 1979.

[5] *Apes, Japes and Hitlerism: A Study and Bibliography of Wyndham Lewis*, 1932.

[6] To use Michel Carrouges' seminal metaphor. See *Les Machines Célibataires*, Paris, Arcanes, 1954—and the ensuing recent exhibition of the same title at the Centre Pompidou.

[7] *L'image fascinante et le surréel*, Paris, Plon, 1965, page 267.

[8] A liberation comparable, perhaps, to Conrad's who, when "blocked" in the writing

of the intensely autobiographical *Lord Jim*, hit on the idea of Marlow, the mediator.

[9] His having been born on a yacht—his father's yacht—may also contribute to explain Lewis's "quartered" vision of space.

[10] "The Vita of Wyndham Lewis," an unpublished biographical sketch written in 1949, Cornell University.

[11] See Marthe Robert's *Roman des Origines, Origines du Roman*, Paris, Grasset, 1972.

[12] See the introduction of the word "libido" in the 1922 "Bestre," Ker-Orr's family background in the 1927 "Soldier of Humour," the deletion of "succès d' hystérie" in the final "Inferior Religions," Zoborov's "inferiority complex," and what Lewis said on Freud in *Time and Western Man.* See also my "Off to Budapest with Freud."

[13] *The Power of Satire*, Princeton University Press, 1960. *The Shape of Utopia*, The University of Chicago Press, 1970.

[14] *Wyndham Lewis the Novelist*, 1976. *Wyndham Lewis: Fictions and Satires*, 1973.

[15] "The Meaning of the Wild Body."

[16] *D. H. Lawrence. Poèmes*, Paris, Aubier, 1977 page 64.

[17] Philip Thomson. *The Grotesque*, 1972, page 27.

[18] See Mark Spilka's *Dickens and Kafka*, 1963.

[19] *The Grotesque*, page 32.

Printed August 1982 in Santa Barbara & Ann Arbor for the Black Sparrow Press by Graham Mackintosh & Edwards Brothers Inc. Design by Barbara Martin. This edition is published in paper wrappers; there are 750 cloth trade copies; & 276 deluxe hardcover copies numbered & signed by the editor have been handbound in boards by Earle Gray.

WYNDHAM LEWIS (1882-1957) was a novelist, painter, essayist, poet, critic, polemicist and one of the truly dynamic forces in literature and art in the twentieth century. He was the founder of Vorticism, the only original movement in twentieth century English painting. The author of *Tarr* (1918), *The Lion and the Fox* (1927), *Time and Western Man* (1927), *The Apes of God* (1930), *The Revenge for Love* (1937), and *Self Condemned* (1954), Lewis was ranked highly by his important contemporaries: "the most fascinating personality of our time . . . the most distinguished living novelist" (T. S. Eliot), "the only English writer who can be compared to Dostoievsky" (Ezra Pound).

BERNARD LAFOURCADE was born in 1934 in Grenoble and attended the universities of Grenoble, Oxford (Worcester College) and the Sorbonne. He is a lecturer in English literature at the University of Savoy in Chambéry. Co-author of *A Bibliography of the Writings of Wyndham Lewis* (Black Sparrow, 1978), he has written a number of articles on Lewis and translated "Cantleman's Spring-Mate" (Paris, 1968), *Tarr* (Paris, 1970), *The Revenge for Love* (Lausanne, 1980) and *The Wild Body* (in collaboration, Lausanne, 1980). He is the European editor of BLAST to be published by Black Sparrow Press.